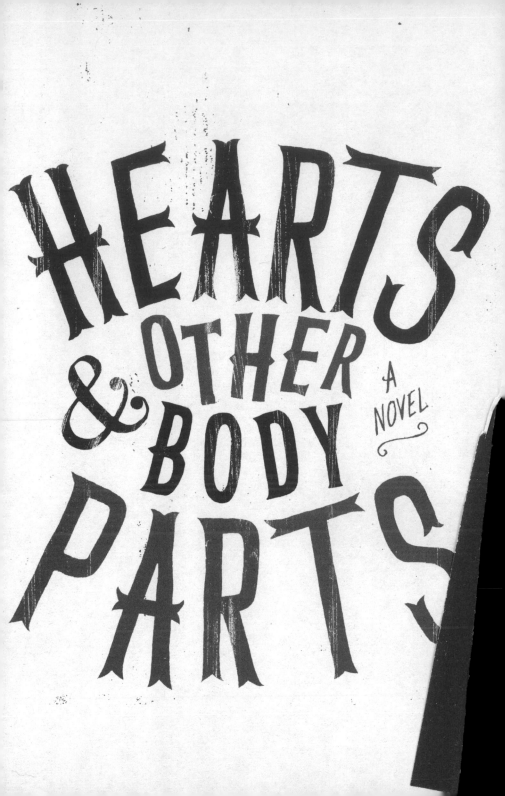

Scholastic Press / New York

IRA BLOOM

HEARTS

OTHER

& BODY

PARTS

A NOVEL

Library of Congress Cataloging-in-Publication Data

Names: Bloom, Ira (Ira Mitchell), 1959– author.
Title: Hearts & other body parts / Ira Bloom.
Other titles: Hearts and other body parts
Description: New York, NY : Scholastic Press, [2017] | Summary: There are two new boys at Middleton High: Norman, who is eight-feet-tall and looks like he was put together after an accident, and Zack, the impossibly handsome transfer from Europe, and soon the three witch sisters, Esme, Katy, and Ronnie, are in an all out competition for Zack's attention—but Esme is also drawn to Norman, and he is the only one who seems to notice that students who go off alone with Zack seem to suffer from amnesia, or disappear entirely.
Identifiers: LCCN 2016037798 | ISBN 978-1-338-03073-0 (hardcover)
Subjects: LCSH: Vampires—Juvenile fiction. | Monsters—Juvenile fiction. | Witches—Juvenile fiction. | Dating (Social customs)—Juvenile fiction. | Magic—Juvenile fiction. | High schools—Juvenile fiction. | Detective and mystery stories. | CYAC: Mystery and detective stories. | Vampires—Fiction. | Monsters—Fiction. | Witches—Fiction. | Dating (Social customs)—Fiction. | Magic—Fiction. | High schools —Fiction. | Schools—Fiction. | GSAFD: Mystery fiction. | LCGFT: Detective and mystery fiction.
Classification: LCC PZ7.1.B636 He 2017 | DDC 813.6 [Fic] —dc23 LC record available at https://lccn.loc.gov/2016037798

10 9 8 7 6 5 4 3 2 1   17 18 19 20 21

Printed in the U.S.A. 23

First edition, April 2017

Book design by Nina Goffi

For Isabella, a limitless source of material

1

THREE SISTERS AND NORM

"Oh. My. Goddess," said Katy as all the noise in the cafeteria suddenly died.

Veronica, her younger sister, looked up from her compact, in which she'd been studying her reflection with a great deal of fascination. "Wow," she affirmed. "That's just . . . wow. Did you see him, Esme?"

Esmeralda, the oldest, did not look up from her book. "His name is Norman. He's in two of my classes so far," she said. "Don't gape, Ronnie, you're being rude."

Veronica attempted to avert her gaze, but it was like looking away from a wall: He took up most of her line of sight. "That's the most horrible . . . I mean, what happened to him? It looks like he got all mangled up in some farm machinery or something." She tried to appear interested in her salad but her fork shook noticeably as she raised it to her lips.

The three sisters made every effort not to gawk. The other students in the cafeteria weren't as polite. What started as a hushed, shocked silence at the boy's appearance and almost comical attempts to look away soon became a low murmur with clandestine glances in his direction, and finally escalated into overt

1

ogling and chatter. Unkind words were heard over the cafeteria cacophony. Some students even brandished cell phones, taking pictures and posting them.

The new boy waded through the tide of ridicule and hostility with remarkable dignity, Esme observed. He was carrying a lunch tray and looking for a place to sit. Students were hunching their shoulders and spreading out, circling the wagons around their tables. Esme tried not to look but was as guilty as anyone else of stealing glances.

It wasn't the boy's face that drew so much attention. He had dysmorphic features within a frame of ghastly scars, a bulging brow, and a large, square jaw. But that wasn't why people were staring. He had one green eye mismatched to a walleyed brown one, and the odd pallor of his skin made him look like a walking corpse, but that was hardly even worth mentioning. He walked with a pained, shuffling gait, a complex contraption of a brace on his left leg, and his left shoe was orthopedic, two inches thicker than the other, his legs entirely asymmetrical. But even that wasn't his most freakish attribute.

It was the sheer immensity of the boy, the impossible scale of him, which would have earned him top billing at any carnival sideshow in the land. He was easily seven and a half feet tall and probably closer to eight, Esme estimated, because he hunched himself over and drew in his elbows, like he was trying to make himself appear somehow smaller, somehow less visible. As if he could. His hands were enormous, his legs like trees. Esme did a quick calculation and decided there was easily over four hundred pounds to him.

The giant shuffled toward three sophomore girls occupying a table for eight, knapsacks scattered over the empty seats. There was fear in their eyes, that he would ask to sit there, of social ostracism by association, humiliation, cooties, and possible dismemberment by a monster in their own school. He bent low and made a quiet request of one of the girls. She gathered up her knapsack to give him space. He placed his lunch tray down and hoisted one enormous leg over the bench. The table looked like doll furniture under him. Before he could sit down, all three girls had bolted, taking their trays and bags and books with them, as if they'd all suddenly remembered somewhere else they urgently needed to be.

"Disgusting," Esme declared. "Absolutely revolting."

"Esmeralda Silver!" Katy said. "You don't know a thing about him."

"Not him, Katy. Us. Everyone. But especially us—we should know better. We're all so judgmental and intolerant. Somebody has to do something."

The sisters observed the new student in quick glances. He was picking at the food on his tray, a ludicrously small serving for a boy his size. Esme discerned the mortification in his expression despite the false bravado.

"Don't look at me," Veronica said. "This is my first week of high school, I can't be seen . . . I mean, maybe if we all went . . ."

"We'd overwhelm the poor thing," Katy supposed. "I guess . . . it should be me, right? I mean, weird is my department."

Esme stood. "No, I'll go," she said. She gathered her book bag. "He's in my grade."

⁓ ⁓

"Do you mind if I sit here?" the girl asked.

An attractive girl with horn-rimmed glasses slid onto the bench opposite Norman Stein and proceeded to unpack her lunch.

Which was rather unanticipated. Norman hadn't exactly come into a new school in a new town expecting to be welcomed with open arms. He knew what he looked like.

"Not at all," he replied. He was self-conscious about the fact that his legs took up the entire space beneath the table and pressed up against the opposite bench, so she was forced to sit kitty-corner from him. He drew his elbows in closer to his sides. "Did you draw the short straw?" he asked, regretting it almost before the words were out of his mouth.

The girl's lips tightened, then a faint blush of embarrassment came to her cheeks, followed closely by an eyebrow raised in acknowledgment. "Fair enough," she said. "You saw me with my sisters. You knew we were talking about you. You don't know me. But the fact is, we all wanted to come and sit with you. We just didn't want to overwhelm you."

"I'm sorry. I shouldn't be so cynical about people's motivations."

The girl smiled at him. "I'm Esme Silver. We have AP calculus and biology together. Welcome to Middleton High. Go Timberwolves."

"Norm," he replied. He smiled back at her. "Short for 'normal brain.'"

~⌒つ ⌒⌒⌒

Esme thought he looked a bit less freakish when he smiled, the teeth good, the asymmetry wry but earnest. "On behalf of the rest of humanity, I'd like to apologize for my fellow students. They're all jerks, obviously."

Norman shrugged his immense shoulders in a rolling motion like tectonic plates shifting. "I'm not fussy. As long as they aren't coming after me with pitchforks and torches." His scarf slipped a bit as he shrugged, and he was quick to readjust it, but not fast enough.

"Oh," said Esme, embarrassed for him. "Are those . . . ?"

"Yeah," he confessed, a bit bitterly. "As if the rest of this weren't bad enough, I have bolts in my neck. I'm getting them out in November, though."

"I-I know, right?" she stammered. "I just got my braces off last summer, and I swear I didn't smile for two years."

He nodded. "You must have felt hideous."

Esme surveyed the remains of her sandwich, alternating between self-loathing and indignation. Was he mocking her? Was that sarcasm? Around them, other students were still discussing him, and she picked up words like "monster," "Halloween mask," and "Frankenstein." Except, now, she heard her own name added to the mix.

"You know," she said, when she became so self-conscious about her silence she felt awkward, "you're actually not half bad-looking."

"Really? Which half?" he asked.

It was somehow reassuring, that he could joke about his condition. "It's not all in one place. A little bit here, a little bit there, but all put together . . . not half bad-looking."

"Good thing you didn't see me before it was all put together," he said.

WEIRDNESS BEGINS AT HOME

Barry Silver was fishing a ham hock out of a pot of sixteen-bean soup when daughters one and two entered the kitchen and started opening cupboards. "You'd like him, Katy, I promise," Esme said. "He has this dark, self-deprecating sense of humor, like yours."

"I don't know," Katy hedged. "Everyone's hating on him. I mean, I'm a big fan of weird, but seriously? Bolts in the neck? Who has bolts in their neck?"

"Think of it as cutting-edge body modification," Esme said. "By next year, everybody could be wearing them. Just sit with us at lunch tomorrow."

Barry looked up from the cutting board. "You two are talking about Franklin, aren't you. Did you meet him? He's supposed to start at your school this semester."

"No, Dad," Katy replied, with a tone of exasperation she'd honed from constantly having to explain stuff to the most clueless father in the universe. "It's this kid named Norman. You'd know him if you saw him, he's, like, eight feet tall."

"Right, Franklin Norman Stein. I guess he goes by 'Norman.' His father is Doctor Frederick Stein—he teaches neuroscience at the university in the city. Brilliant man. He hired me on retainer. Heck of a nice boy, Franklin. And very smart." Barry scooped up the chopped meat and returned it to the pot to boil. He discarded the fat and saved the bones for Katy's dogs.

"Wait a minute," Katy said. "Franklin Stein?"

"Frank N. Stein, if you want to be technical," Esme noted. "Is there anything else we need to know about him, Dad? Like, did his father build him in a lab?"

"That's not very nice," Barry said. "I can see why he prefers to use his middle name. He's just a regular kid who's had some pretty severe health problems. Be nice to him, okay?"

"Of course, Dad. We don't care about appearances." Esme went to the stove and lifted the lid off the pot of bean soup. "This smells good, I think I'll have some. You didn't put too much salt in it, did you? With your blood pressure?"

"What kind of health problems?" asked Katy. "How come he looks like that?"

"I can't tell you much," Barry said. "Confidentiality."

"Can you tell us why Dr. Stein hired you?" Esme asked.

"Just as a preemptive measure. He's afraid his son's civil rights will be violated. Norman has had to change schools several times in the last two years. Apparently, he's a magnet for bullying. And he ends up getting suspended or kicked out of school because the administration always stereotypes him as the aggressor because of his appearance and size."

Katy dropped an armload of salad vegetables onto the center island of the kitchen. "Who in the world would be stupid enough to bully somebody that big?"

"I believe him," Esme said. "He isn't the type to instigate stuff. You saw the reaction he got today in the cafeteria."

"He could totally crush anyone," Katy insisted. "All he has to do is fall on them."

Barry shook his head. "He told me he's a bleeding-heart pacifist. He hates violence. And he has so many ongoing health issues, he's actually very vulnerable. I hope you girls will go to the principal if you see anyone bullying him."

"Don't worry, Dad," Esme promised. "Nobody's going to mess with Norman this time. I've got his back."

"No hexing now," Barry warned.

"Dad. Please. *Cogitationis poenam nemo patitur.* Thinking about doing it doesn't make me guilty."

"Ad avizandum," he replied.

Esme found her father much easier to deal with, since she'd gone to the trouble of studying some of his old law books and memorizing a few Latin terms.

⌒つ⌒⌒

Esme's room in the cellar was homey and always ten degrees cooler than the rest of the house, but in late August it was pleasant. There was a cat door at ground level, two feet below the ceiling. There was a monstrous carpet-covered cat structure with hideouts and clawing posts that topped out to a platform just below the cat door, so Esme's cats could come and go at will, and there was no need for litter boxes and all the associated odors.

Esme put out some dry food for the cats and went to her computer for a half hour, browsing Amazon for new releases. It was the first week of school and there was no homework. She retrieved a volume from the huge freestanding bookshelf, packed with books that seemed to gravitate from every corner of the house to Esme's room, then relaxed into the comfy chair to read. Murasaki was first on her lap, the prize spot, which annoyed Mandela, who sulked on a platform of the cat structure, glaring at Esme accusingly as if to say *You let that lowlife sit on your lap? You're dead to me.* Mandela and Murasaki had territorial issues. Kali sat on the arm of the chair; Charlie took the comfortable spot on the ottoman, curved against her feet; and Esme, in her element, settled in to read a book about the life of Rikyu, the sixteenth-century Japanese tea master.

All was peaceful for an hour until Kasha returned, strutting through the cat door like he owned the place. Kasha jumped onto the ottoman and walked straight onto Esme's lap, chasing Murasaki away with an angry hiss. Charlie gave up his spot immediately.

"Where have you been all night?" Esme asked Kasha, scratching him behind the ears. He kneaded her lap, digging claws, and purred in response.

"Out by the barn," he said, his voice raspy. "There's a female out there, I can smell her."

"I'll bet that big earless Tom is keeping her to himself. You better stay away from him, his neck is huge."

"I'm not afraid of him. I'd eat him, but I don't care for cat." Kasha dug his claws in deeper.

"Hey!" Esme protested. "I said no more clawing!" She reached behind her back and pulled out the pillow, which she placed on her lap for protection.

"I love the feel of my claws sinking into your flesh. It's so soft, like gopher bellies." Kasha climbed up onto the pillow, advancing up Esme's chest and putting his front paws on her clavicles, so he could sniff her breath. "You're eating pig corpses, and you're feeding us dry food," he accused.

"Do you want some tuna?" she offered. It was a bit extravagant, but hey . . . a talking cat. Even in a house full of witches, it wasn't something you came across every day. Or ever, even. If Katy only knew, she'd shut up about her stupid dogs.

Kasha jumped down off the chair and made toward the cat structure, and outside. "I ate already," he said dismissively, as if he were insulted by the notion of eating perfectly good tuna out of a can. Kasha stopped and tensed, as if to poop. He started heaving, throwing his entire body into it as he hacked up something huge onto the kilim rug.

"Not on the rug!" Esme yelled, standing quickly to try to push Kasha onto a bit of bare floor, too late. Something large slid out in mid-heave, mummified in hair and accompanied by some visceral liquid, like a stillborn baby being ejected in a rush of amniotic fluid.

"Gophers," Kasha said, taking a tentative step away from the mess on the rug. "Can't lay off 'em, can't keep 'em down. Clean that up for me, will ya, baby? I'm gonna cut out." And then he was up the cat structure and out the cat door and into the night.

3

RESTRAINT

Esme hadn't known quite what to expect, though she was not so naïve as to think she could sit with an untouchable at lunch with no repercussions. She never wasted a minute of her time or intellect on social media, so she'd missed all the late-night insinuation and character assassination on Facebook and Instagram. The only warning she had, before her arrival at school that day, had been a cryptic comment from Veronica in the car:

"Watch out," Ronnie had warned. "The natives are restless."

First period was AP calculus, the most stimulating course on her schedule, which Esme thought was a bracing way to get her brain charged up for the day.

"Here comes Esme's boyfriend," said Lisa Vaughn, when the bulk that was Norman Stein filled the doorway. The students laughed, in the snickering, superior way that smart kids laugh.

Lisa Vaughn: the second-smartest girl in every class she had with Esme, always simmering in resentment. But Esme never took anything off of anyone. It set a bad precedent.

The Silvers adhered to the Rede of the Z Budapest lineage, a handy moral compass and code of conduct for Wiccans, which meant Esme rarely engaged in actual spellwork. The sisters had tried a little hexing in middle school, when Katy had run afoul of a clique of mean-spirited girls over the way she dressed and acted. Whether the spells had worked was the subject of some debate, but one eighth grader who'd gotten scraped up in a bicycle accident went into hysterics and refused to attend school, convinced Esme had put a spell on her. Another girl had, coincidentally, come down with a severe case of meningitis, which she feverishly blamed on Katy. This had caused a ruckus among a loosely organized group of evangelical and fundamentalist parents, who wanted the "Satanists" out of their kids' school. Barry Silver had to sue the school district to defend his daughters' civil rights to attend public school regardless of their religion.

As a result, the sisters had promised that they wouldn't call themselves "witches" anymore in public, or work spells. They could call themselves "Wiccans," which had a measure of social acceptance, though they did not like the designation. Their family had been witches for hundreds of years, passing down the matrilineal traditions and lore, and Wicca was a relatively recent mishmosh of a religion. Esme did not cast spells, though she was comfortable with a little ambiguous cursing now and then: small utterances made in a whisper, little intentions sent out into the eldritch cosmos.

Esme directed a few choice Latin words under her breath at Lisa: *"te tua fata determinat,"* while twisting a clandestine thumb into a *feig* to nail the curse home.

Lisa was someone who remembered all the accusations from middle school. She glared at Esme, angry but with some caution, before turning back toward her desk. She stepped on a pencil, which rolled out from under her shoe, causing her to fall on her butt. Grasping for her desk, she brought it down on top of herself. A roar of laughter went up from the class. Esme opened her textbook and flipped through pages to find today's lesson. Nonchalance was all part of the staging.

Before second period, AP biology, the taunts became nasty. Stephan Reese and Brandon North were discussing whether Norman was anatomically proportionate, and whether Esme, as his girlfriend, was up to certain tasks. Again, Lisa was in the thick of the hazing:

"Why else do you think she likes him?" she suggested.

Esme flushed scarlet, mortified. She was angry enough, at that moment, to do something that she'd promised her mother she wouldn't.

But the indecency of the comments was enough to rouse Norman to action. His desk was a lab table in the back of the room with a very sturdy chair the school had provided. He rose from his seat slowly and lumbered deliberately toward the two boys. Stephan and Brandon sat at desks next to each other, about half-way to the back of the room, with an aisle between them. When Norman stood in that space, the immensity of him blocked out the fluorescent lights behind him, and he cast a shadow. On both their desks.

"Guys," he said gently. Stephan paled beneath the giant. Norman's hand was larger than his head. Brandon shook nervously. They were not large boys: more to the geek end of the spectrum. "Guys, have a little decency, would you?" was all he asked.

But it was more than enough. When he passed Lisa's desk, on the way back to his table, he looked at her and shook his head slowly back and forth in disapproval, with a sad expression. She hung her head and didn't look up for the rest of the period.

The third incident of the day occurred in the hallway after third period, on the way to lunch. When Danny Long, a senior who until the day before had been the largest boy at Middleton High, passed Norman in the hallway, he knocked the books out of Norm's hands.

"Sorry," Danny joked. "I didn't see you."

All the students in the vicinity halted to watch. Danny was the toughest kid at Middleton High, and with him was Jackson Gartner, the meanest, and their leader, Logan Rehnquist, the most antagonistic. Danny was on the football team. Jackson was academically ineligible this year. Logan got his workouts off-campus, in a mixed-martial-arts dojo. All three were very large boys, but standing in a semicircle harassing Norman Stein, they didn't seem so big.

"Accidents happen," Norman replied amiably.

"How come your face is all messed up like that?" Jackson asked. People in the crowd snickered.

"It's a long story," Norman replied, relatively calm. "If you'd like to come sit with me at lunch, I'll fill you in on the details."

"Nah," Jackson said. "Ain't nobody gonna sit with you."

"How'd you get so huge?" Logan accused. "That isn't natural. You're some kind of freak, aren't you?"

"Actually, that one's easier to explain. I have acromegaly. It's a rare glandular disease that causes the anterior pituitary gland to overproduce growth hormone. All the best giants have it."

"Do you know who you look like?" Danny asked, edging into Norman's personal space.

"I get Zac Efron a lot," Norman suggested.

"He looks like Frankenstein!" Danny announced, in a very loud voice, turning to the crowd for affirmation. "But uglier!"

The laughter of the crowd didn't shake Norman's calm demeanor. "Actually, Frankenstein was the name of the doctor. He was perfectly normal-looking," Norman said. "I think what you wanted to say was I look like Frankenstein's monster. Listen, Danny, isn't it? You're in my computer lab. Do me a favor and pick up those books for me, would you? I've got this thing on my leg, it's a little difficult to bend down."

"Are you telling me what to do?" Danny returned, with that mock anger bullies get, when they're trying to pick a fight. Norman was quite familiar with it. Whatever he said from that point on, Danny was going to take as a personal affront. Danny shoved Norman hard, with both hands. With his size, Danny was one of the most effective high school defensive linemen in the state. When Danny Long shoved somebody with both hands like that, they went flying across the hallway and into a wall. In Norman's case, Danny would have had better luck with the wall.

"And so it begins," Norman said.

And so it might have, if Coach Ashcroft, pushing his way through the crowd, hadn't witnessed the attempted shove. Students scattered or drifted away, and Danny and Logan slunk off, Jackson bringing up the rear with a halfhearted "Hey, Coach," as he headed toward the student parking lot. Esme knelt to help pick up Norm's books.

The coach stopped in front of Norman, looking him up and

down like a judge at the county fair eyeing a prize heifer. "Son," he said. "Football is a game of inches."

Norman was puzzled. "Uh . . . if you say so."

"Inches, son. You've got more of them than I've ever seen," the coach clarified. "You ever want to play for the Middleton Timberwolves, you come and see me, y'hear? Coach Ashcroft. You just made the team."

"Uh . . . thanks, uh . . . Coach? But I've got this thing on my leg," Norman explained, waving a mammoth hand at the appendage. "Maybe next year, if it's still open?"

Coach Ashcroft looked Norman up and down one last time before turning in the direction of the teachers' lounge. "Oh, it'll still be open," he promised. "Norman, isn't it? Norman, just remember this: football. That's your sport. Forget about basketball. I want you on my defensive line, rushing Jefferson High's quarterback."

"I was very impressed with you back there," Esme told Norman at lunch.

Norman had brought a bag lunch, and the rations looked more appropriate for his size. Norman was a sandwich guy: He had six of them, of various cold cuts with the works. Also, a full bag of chips and a half-gallon carton of milk. In his hand, it seemed about right.

"I try not to let them frame the terms of the conflict," he explained. "I'm a pacifist."

"And you sure put Stephan and Brandon and Lisa in their place, in biology."

"That was different," Norm explained. "I'll take action to

protect innocent bystanders from collateral damage. Just because I'm a giant ugly freak and a beautiful girl is nice enough to sit with me at lunch, doesn't mean they have to go after you."

Esme wanted to say something reassuring, but there was nothing in her repertoire of trite aphorisms to counter "giant ugly freak," so she just looked down at her food. Yogurt and fruit. Norman's sandwiches sure looked good.

"Hey, slide over," Katy said, dropping her sack lunch on the table. "Ronnie's sitting with some pretty girls in short skirts, so I need to pretend I'm not the most pathetic, friendless person in the world."

"She's not," Esme assured, sliding over. "Norm, this is my very weird but talented sister, Katy. Katy, this is my very intelligent and sweet friend, Norman."

Katy offered a hand to shake. "Pleasure to meet you."

Norm took the hand between his thumb and forefinger, so as not to entirely engulf it in his palm, and shook gently. "The pleasure is all mine."

"Well it should be," Katy claimed. "You don't meet someone as weird as me every day."

"Norman was telling me he thought I was beautiful," Esme mentioned. She didn't know what else to do about such an awkward thing for Norm to have said, so she brushed it off as a joke.

"I stand corrected," Katy announced with a raised eyebrow. "He's obviously much weirder than me." She removed some fruit from her bag, and a Tupperware container full of quinoa with tempeh and steamed broccoli.

Norman picked up the nearest sandwich and took a good bite, about half. "Uh . . ." he said, a little self-conscious, after swallowing, "does anyone want a sandwich? I've brought too many."

Katy wrinkled her nose. "Is that meat?" she asked.

"I'd like a half of one of those turkey sandwiches, if you really have enough," Esme said.

"You don't eat meat?" Norman asked Katy.

"She calls herself a 'compassionate vegetarian,'" Esme explained.

Norman opened his bag of chips and offered them around. Esme took one; Katy wrinkled her nose. "I don't get the whole vegetarian thing," he said. "I mean, where do you draw the line?"

Katy pealed a banana and took a bite. "I don't eat anything that's capable of affection."

"No," Norman argued. "Take that banana, for instance. Did you know that the banana shares fifty percent of its DNA with humans? And who's to say that bananas don't experience pain?"

Katy set her banana down and looked at it with disgust. "Thanks a lot. Now I feel guilty."

"Don't," Norman reassured her. "If the situation were reversed, the banana wouldn't hesitate."

"Man-eating bananas," Esme said, approving Norm's quick wit. "*That's* a disturbing image."

"Now I've got it stuck in my mind," Katy declared. "It's congealed, like jellied eels."

"Talk about a disturbing image . . ." Norman said. "Listen, two words of advice—"

"I hope they aren't 'get therapy,' because I hear that a lot."

"That's the voices in your head again," Esme said. "Try stabbing them with an ice pick."

"I was going to say 'complex proteins,'" Norm said, "but I think I agree with your voices."

Katy brightened. "Hey!" she told Esme. "I like this guy. He totally gets me."

A very attractive girl approached the table, opposite Norman. She was a curvy strawberry blond with a genuine smile and dimples. "Hey, Esme. Hi, Katy." She extended a hand across the table to Norman. "Hi, my name is Sandy Hardesty. I'm in your English class?"

Norman took the hand gently. "Nice to meet you, I'm Norman Stein."

"Yeah, I know," she said. She never stopped smiling the whole time, and her eyes never left Norman's face. "Norman, I just . . . I'd like to welcome you to Middleton High. I hope you didn't get a bad impression of us already, mostly the people here are really nice once you get to know them. Once they get used to you."

"That's very nice of you to say, Sandy," Norman returned. "I'm sure I'd get along fine, if everyone were as nice as you."

"That's a pretty high standard," Esme said. "Sandy here is about as nice as they come."

"Pathological, practically," Katy added.

Sandy let out a little laugh. She put her hand on Katy's shoulder and gave her a squeeze. "You're the expert," she said. "I've gotta go, Norman, I just wanted to say, uh . . . you know. Hang in there?" She left with a charming little wave.

"She seemed nice," Norman said.

"She really is," Esme agreed. "She can see the good in everyone."

"Yeah, even Logan Rehnquist," added Katy.

4

SOMEWHERE IN EASTERN EUROPE

"We must flee immediately," said the Ancient. "As we've practiced. Leave no trace."

"The police?" asked the younger.

"Interpol," came the reply.

The Ancient did not appear ancient. In human terms, he could pass for middle-aged. He was of medium height and medium build, Mediterranean in complexion, and he wore expensive Italian suits and custom-made shoes, to accommodate his extremely high arches. He looked pleasant enough, to the casual observer. His looks were a deception.

The younger one appeared to be a teenager of sixteen or seventeen, and strikingly handsome. He'd been chosen primarily for his looks because he served a specific function, and the Ancient had infinite time and patience to make his selections.

"Are your things packed?" asked the elder.

"I can be ready in ten minutes, Master," the younger promised.

"Do not call me that," the Ancient reprimanded. "Call me 'Father.' Practice it. A mistake may be fatal, while we are traveling. And you are 'Zack.' Never forget."

"Yes, Father."

"Move in haste," the Ancient commanded. "We must finish our affairs."

"What of the brides, Father?" asked Zack. "Some of them are too weak to travel."

The Master took the boy by the shoulders, and held his gaze. "We must finish our affairs."

The youth did not have the force of personality to defy the compelling power of his master's will, but somewhere within his youthful eyes there still lurked a thread of humanity, which he could not mask.

"Not Madeleine," Zack ventured. It was not an objection. He knew better than to even hint at defiance. It was more a request for clarification, tinged by the suggestion of hope.

"Kill them all."

Zack lowered his eyes. "She's near turned already; she'll make us a good companion, I promise. She only wants to serve you."

The Master snarled, showing fangs. "I do not negotiate. She cannot travel with us, and she cannot live. She must be destroyed, like the others. I command it."

The boy was bound in his master's thrall. He did not cry. Once, he might have, but that was when he was a different kind of creature altogether. "As you command."

The mansion was all that remained of an estate once owned by the descendants of a long-dead lord. It was many kilometers from anything resembling civilization, the location ideally suited to the Ancient's needs. There was only one road in, across a small bridge over a quick stream. To the rear, there were woods on jagged landscape, impossible to traverse in any kind of vehicle. There was running water and electricity, but few luxuries. The furnishings were high-quality Victorian antiques in shoddy condition. The infrastructure was grandiose. There were sweeping staircases with hand-carved rococo banisters, and marble floors, and a very fine crystal chandelier in the dining room, covered in cobwebs.

In the library, the living room, and the great hall were immense, ornate fireplaces. The library was well stocked with books in various languages, especially English. There was no television or Internet, so Zack read voraciously, whatever he could get his hands on, which was mostly great literature from the library shelves and best sellers that he bought in the used bookstore in the nearest village, on the rare occasions he was permitted to leave the mansion.

In the cellar, there were nine brides.

The mansion suited the Ancient's purposes. He had little use for warmth and light and cozy beds. He needed only brides, privacy, and an escape route. Nothing could catch them in those woods. Nothing could move as fast as they could, in the dark.

"I'll take care of the five in the seraglio," declared the Ancient at the foot of the stairs to the cellar. "You will finish the other four. Drink deep of them all. It may be some time before we can refresh ourselves again."

The Master went left, down the hallway. Zack removed a ring of keys from his jeans pocket and sorted them in the very dim light. Zack had excellent night vision. He found the key to the padlock on the door and unlatched it. The room was slightly musty, but the furnishings were clean and fresh. Three brides resided. They were all very happy to see Zack. Though none would ever give voice to such a sentiment, they all much preferred the boy to the Master.

Zack went first to Helena. She rose up on one elbow to greet him. Helena had left her homeland and family to seek a career as an international fashion model. Her contract had been sold to a nefarious human trafficking organization in Berlin that the Master had an interest in. She was nineteen, and had always been thin. Zack sat by her side and kissed her eyes.

"Helena, Helena me love," he whispered in her ear. He had a nascent gift for enthrallment, an attribute of his ilk. With the brides, he reverted to his easy Manchester slang. The Master considered colloquial speech coarse, and demanded proper English in his presence.

She smiled up at him weakly. She'd been ill with the fever from the very first, one whose immune system would fight the infection to the death. Her death. Many could never go through the change.

"Helena, I spot a bit o' color, in your cheek. You're looking much healthier today," he cooed.

This made Helena smile in earnest. Nothing would please the boy more than for her to regain her health, and pleasing him was all she desired. "I had broth, my love," she said in a breathy whisper, all she could manage.

When she smiled, it reminded Zack of how beautiful she'd been, before he'd had his part in destroying her. "Give us a snog then," he said, and she shivered in anticipation. It had been so long since the beautiful boy had kissed her. She turned her neck to him. When his teeth nipped at her, just below the left ear, she moaned in pleasure. Zack's kisses were her opium.

Helena's blood tasted anemic and herbaceous. The Master would no longer touch her at all. He said she was like a Cru Bourgeois in a bad vintage, twenty years past her prime. Zack removed his pearl-handled folding straight razor, a gift from the Ancient, from his back pocket. In one stroke, he cut Helena's throat across and very deep, so that she could die with the pleasure still in her smile. She had remarkably little blood. She'd been dry for weeks.

Zack rose and inspected himself for blood. It wouldn't do to travel covered in the evidence of his crimes. He wiped his blade on the bedding, and arranged Helena in a position for eternal repose, before returning his attention to the other two brides. Neither Natasha nor Nadia seemed alarmed in the slightest to have witnessed him murdering Helena so casually.

"She was ill, me beauties," Zack explained, moving toward Natasha.

Natasha, the mail-order bride with the pale Moldovan complexion and the dark, silky hair. The Ancient had ordered her from an online catalog, though he'd made the observation that Moldovan mail-order brides were rarely as beautiful as their pictures. They had Photoshop in Moldova—they were not entirely primitive. He'd been pleasantly surprised by Natasha, though he judged her closer to thirty-five than her advertised age of twenty-seven.

"The boss said Helena wouldn't survive, it was a mercy to her," Zack explained, kneeling beside Natasha's chair to bring his face to a level with hers. "I'm gutted over it." He gazed into her black, shining eyes. Natasha set her knitting aside in anticipation.

"The Master is taking the others and leaving," Zack told her. "He told me to pick just two, me own two true loves, and so I chose you and Nadia. We're getting out of here, and we'll all be together, and I'll love you both forever. Are you as chuffed as I am?"

"I'm very happy," Natasha replied in her thick accent, moistening her lips. "I share you only with one, not with eight others."

He caressed her face. She leaned into the cup of his hand. "So it's just us three then, innit? Unless, uh . . . do you think we have time for a little snog first?"

"I always make time for kiss from you," Natasha purred. Her skin was flushed and moist and hot where he stroked her hair back from her face and tucked it behind her ear. His fingernails grazed the tender spot beneath her ear, and she tilted her head, her eyes glazed with intoxication.

Natasha's blood always tasted a little metallic to Zack. The Ancient said it reminded him of Chilean Malbec. For wine, the Master preached, choose age and terroir and structure; for blood, choose youth and purity and health. Zack was in an awkward position to slit Natasha's throat, but he managed with minimal mess.

Nadia watched the scene from her position on the bed. If she was the least bit shocked to see Natasha so summarily butchered, she didn't show it. She never stopped painting her toenails. Helena and Natasha had been Nadia's friends, and her sisters in matrimony, but still, they were her rivals. She knew she was Zack's favorite. He'd always told her so.

"It was you, always you, only you," Zack promised as he approached her bed.

Nadia returned the brush to the vial of nail polish and screwed the cap shut. She set the vial on the nightstand and unbuttoned the top two buttons of her nightgown.

Zack lay down beside Nadia. She squirmed into his arms.

Despite the fever she was still densely muscled. She'd been a gymnast until she'd failed to qualify for the Belarus Olympic team. Though in her early twenties, she had the body of a muscular, undeveloped child, from her severe training. She was strong—she would survive the change—and showing the first signs of the transition: the redness to the eyes and the calm, stony facial expression.

Zack kissed Nadia on the lips, but she turned her face away from him and offered her throat, rubbing it against his mouth to snag it on a fang, like a cat brushing against a pant leg. They did so love the venom. It made Zack's work too easy.

"Not like this, love," he whispered in her ear. "From behind. You have wet polish on your toenails, and these are new pants."

Nadia tucked herself around and wriggled backward into his arms. She twisted a very strong leg around his, hooking his calf with her foot, heedless of the polish on her toes. She pulled her hair back, exposing her nape. She rubbed her neck against his lips until the skin scraped on his fangs, so he bit her hard. She wanted it so much.

Nadia's blood was always hot and lush. She was the Master's favorite: He said she tasted like a big, juicy Australian Shiraz. Zack drank deep, and soon, sated, held her in his arms for a few moments. "You and me, Nadia," he promised. "Just as we always dreamed."

Nadia moaned in ecstasy, luxuriating in his embrace. But then a thought crossed her mind: "What of Madeleine?" she asked.

"She can't hold a candle to you," he swore as he slipped the blade from his pocket. She died with that reassurance in her ear.

Zack disentangled himself from Nadia's limbs and arose from the bed. He surveyed the room. The three brides looked to have died in peaceful recline, except for all the gore. The smell of blood was pervasive, but Zack was well filled. He made his way toward the padlocked door to the rear of the room—the bridal suite—and Madeleine.

From behind, the door to the hallway burst open, and there stood the Ancient, his eyes fiery with bloodlust. He held a gasoline can in one hand. The other dripped blood. Zack's master did not kill with a blade, or with kindness. "You're taking too long," he reprimanded. "I need to take a quick shower and change. Maria was a bit feisty. Interpol is coming soon. I've blown the bridge; that should buy us a half hour, but we need to leave in ten minutes."

"I'll be ready," Zack promised. "I have to say good-bye to Madeleine."

"Do so, quickly," the Master commanded. "Here is gasoline and matches. The brides in the other room are prepared for their pyre. Douse these four as well, and set everything ablaze before you ascend."

"As you command, Father," Zack replied, sorting one last key in his hand.

❧ ❧

There was a king-sized bed in the bridal suite, with luxurious bedding. Madeleine had a vanity, and makeup to replace the fading bloom of her cheeks and lips. She was too close to turning to be trusted in the same room with the other girls, so she was separated. When Zack entered, she was at her vanity, brushing her hair. There was an alertness to the vivid red eyes that the other brides had not possessed.

Madeleine was the only bride Zack had acquired for the collection. He'd stolen her from some kind of family trip, in Paris. It was her accent that had attracted him. She was not beautiful; pretty at best. She'd been wearing horn-rimmed glasses when he'd met her, though she didn't need them anymore. Everything about Madeleine reminded Zack of home. Zack's memories—not his ability to remember, but the ghostly draw of those things that he still cherished recalling—were fading steadily, with his humanity.

Madeleine was a big girl, just Zack's height. She was English, from Middleton. Zack was from Cheetham Hill, practically next door, near Manchester but not close enough to be a fan of City. They often talked of places they'd both visited, of sights they'd both seen. Maddy was intelligent, and the change hadn't diminished her sense of humor. She liked Manchester United. That was her team, and no other. And this was a quality that couldn't be replaced.

"Have you killed the others?" she asked softly. She rose and stood before him in her nightgown. All the brides wore nightgowns. Maddy's eyes were very red, the sockets rimmed in shadow. Her fangs were protracted, and her skin radiated the heat of the final fever. She would survive the transition.

"I did," he confessed. "We have to leave. The Master made me. It was for their own good."

"I smell Nadia's blood," she remarked. "I think I'd fancy her, over the others. Are you going to kill me, too? I may have a different opinion about what's for my own good."

"The Ancient commanded me to," he confessed. "I gotta leave with him. He'll know if I defy him. Bloody awful, innit?"

"Go ahead and kill me," she declared. "I'd rather die, if I can't be with you." She unbuttoned the top buttons of her gown. She had tears in her blazing eyes. They sizzled and evaporated as steam against her hot cheeks.

Instead, Zack crossed the room to the dresser. He shoved it away from the wall, revealing a low, padlocked door. He removed his keychain again, sorting for the right one. "Through here there's a crawl space that leads to a root cellar," he told her urgently, tossing the lock on the bed. "It was our emergency escape route. I have to set the funeral pyre. Stay in the crawl space for as long as you dare. Don't track us. We're going north. You need to go west."

"But what of the Master?" she pled. "He'll know if you lie. He always knows."

"A bit dicey, but I'll chance it," Zack insisted. He kissed her, but on the lips. He did not drink of her, though he wanted to, one last time.

The Ancient and Zack stood and watched the mansion blaze from the vantage of the woods to the north. There were no sirens, but the Master knew they were near. He paid well for his intelligence, but it was a trifling to one who'd accumulated a fortune over the centuries. It's easy for the ruthless to amass wealth, in certain trades.

"We must go," said the Ancient, turning. "Carry my bag."

Zack picked up his master's steamer trunk by an end handle and hefted it onto his back with one hand, then picked up his valise with the other. They made a rapid pace, but Zack was very strong and nearly tireless.

They walked on through the darkness, through the countryside. The Master had told Zack there could never be any survivors, and yet he'd again allowed himself to hope. He could never again allow himself to think of brides as people. He could never again allow himself to get attached.

"Europe is a little precarious these days," the Ancient lectured. "A number of my colleagues are feeling the heat from the authorities. It would be prudent to go somewhere else for a few decades, until things settle down here."

"Where shall we go, Father?" asked the youth.

"America. Land of the free-range, milk-fattened, organic maiden. I've always wanted to go. A middle-sized town in the middle of nowhere, where we can operate without the interference of meddlesome authorities."

They walked briskly until nearly dawn, when they reached the outskirts of a rustic, hilly village. They'd be out of the country within a few hours, and then on to their new life, with their new identities. They stopped in the village square, near the train station, and sat on a bench in the little park to wait for the day to begin. When the first rays of the sun peeked over the horizon, Zack and the Ancient put on their dark sunglasses.

"How was Madeleine?" the Master asked casually. He rarely engaged in idle chitchat.

"I did not drink of her, Father. I sated myself on Nadia. She was so delicious."

"That she was," the Ancient agreed. "But you killed Madeleine, didn't you?"

"She is dead," Zack replied.

The Master raised his dark glasses up for a moment and

focused on his protégé. Zack did not give himself away. It was a mere detail of ambiguity, but enough of one that the Master did not suspect the lie to it. Zack could not directly lie to him, but Madeleine *was* dead, technically. As was the Ancient. As was Zack.

DA HEAD BONE CONNECTED TO DA
NECK BONE

A relatively uneventful week passed, and it seemed like people at Middleton High were getting used to Norman. Esme and Norm were in three classes together, all Advanced Placement, so she saw a lot of him. She soon realized that if she wanted to stay the top student in every class, as had been her compulsion since grade school, she was going to have to work harder, because she finally had some serious competition. Especially in biology. Norm was miles ahead of the rest of the class in biology.

On Friday, Esme sat at lunch with Norman again. She'd been up late the previous evening memorizing the bones and muscles of the hand, and wanted to work them into the conversation somehow, to let Norm know she was not going to lie down and accept second best, in any subject. Particularly biology.

"Your hands are so huge," she mentioned eventually, when the topic of conversation had not casually turned to bones of the hand. "I'll bet you have sesamoid bones as large as some people's phalanges."

Norman raised an eyebrow. "You know, sesamoid bones are just ossified nodes. So I'd think, no matter how large my hands were, the sesamoids wouldn't be as large as even the distal phalanges of a pinkie finger."

"Well, I'll bet your distal phalanges are bigger than my meta-carpals, anyway."

Norman examined his hand. "I believe you may be correct, Esme." His mouth twisted into a smile. "Have you been reading ahead in the textbook? Because I don't think we've covered that material yet."

Esme was demure. "I like to stay ahead of the game. You seem to know a lot about anatomy."

"Call it a morbid obsession, from someone who's been under the scalpel six dozen times."

"You're ahead of me now," Esme admitted, opening a sand-wich bag full of vegetable sticks. "But give me a few months." She chomped down on a carrot stick defiantly.

Norman grinned back at her. "I'll watch my back."

Is he mocking me? she wondered. There was something smug going on with the eyes, hidden in the shadows under the heavy brow ridge. Norman always seemed grateful for her company when she sat with him at lunch, but there was an underlying thing, an overconfident intelligence humbled by the indignity of his appearance. Norm was the gentlest person she'd ever met, but Esme also sensed a trace of superiority and condescension, which irritated the crap out of her. She frowned and munched vegetable sticks, looking down so he could not see her agitation, feigning fascination with the open calculus textbook on the table in front of her. *Why do I always do this to myself? Why can't I just admit that somebody else could be smart?*

A lunch tray clattered noisily to the table directly opposite

Esme. A boy was sliding onto the bench across from her, beside Norman.

"Hey," he said. Esme knew him, from junior high. Wilson Armond. On the large side, and muscular, with close-cropped brown hair and acne. Wilson wore jeans and a T-shirt with a checked flannel shirt over top, unbuttoned like a cardigan, just like half the other boys at Middleton High.

"Hey," Norm replied.

"Yeah," Wilson said. "I'm Wilson."

"Nice to meet you," Norm said. "I'm Norman Stein. Do you know Esme?"

"Yeah," he returned.

"Hey," said Esme.

"Yeah," Wilson reiterated. "Hey, I heard Coach asked you to play football next year."

"He said I should try out," Norman said. "Are you on the team?"

"Barely," Wilson said. "But I got field time in the Jefferson game last year."

"I heard you guys got creamed," Esme mentioned.

"Totally. Most of the starters are graduating in the spring. I'm trying to make varsity next year, so I'm bulking up." Wilson curled an arm into a muscleman pose and slapped his biceps. "I saw Danny shove you, you didn't budge an inch. You gotta be pretty strong, huh?"

"I *am* pretty strong," Norman admitted.

Esme watched Wilson reach way up and pat Norm's shoulder. The gesture was casual, but Esme had observed this uniquely male behavior before. Always sizing each other up. She supposed if they'd been dogs, they'd have just sniffed each other's butts and been done with it.

"Damn, Norm, you're solid as a rock," Wilson appraised. "Listen, some of us work out in the weight room after school. Why don't you come hang out today and show us what you've got?"

"I don't know . . ." Norman hedged. He looked to Esme for an opinion. She just shrugged.

"Dude," Wilson said, raising his arms in open-handed supplication. "I'm asking you. Don't leave me hangin'. If you wanna fit in around here, you should be more open to . . . you know, doing activities and stuff."

"When you put it like that, how can I say no?"

"Cool." Wilson stood and picked up his lunch tray. "I'll see you in front of McKinley Hall at three fifteen," he said over his shoulder.

Norman turned to Esme for a second opinion. "You know that guy?" he asked.

"I knew him in junior high."

"Is he okay?" Norm asked. "Is he someone who starts a lot of trouble?"

"Couldn't tell you. I haven't heard anything about him, good or bad. Why?"

"Oh, I don't know." Norm paused. "Smells a little off."

"Maybe you shouldn't go," she said. "It did seem a little staged."

"No, I'd better do it anyway. Best to let them satisfy their curiosity."

6

CONFLICT RESOLUTION

Esme waited in front of McKinley Hall after school for her posse. Veronica arrived first. "What happened to your leggings, Ronnie?" Esme asked, in a tone of disapproval.

"I only wore those to get past Dad this morning," Ronnie explained. "I hate when he tells me my skirt is too short."

"Your skirt is too short."

"See, when *you* say it, it doesn't bother me."

"If you bend over, your underwear will be showing," Esme critiqued.

"So? It's cute underwear."

Katy arrived, one arm in her cardigan, backpack slung over the shoulder, the other side of the sweater hanging. "You know Mrs. Finkle, the English teacher? She's got the most adorable litter of miniature pinschers you've ever seen. You guys have to help me figure out how to get one."

"No way, Katy, you already have five dogs," Esme said.

"Not one I can carry around with me!"

"Dad said you can't bring anything else into the house that poops," Esme reminded her.

"You better back off, Esme, she's got that look," Veronica warned.

Katy was flat-out slobbering crazy for dogs, and dogs for Katy. Dogs can always tell when a person loves them unconditionally with her heart on her sleeve. "We'll talk about this later," Esme said, motioning with her chin. Norman had just appeared in front of McKinley Hall.

They watched Norm hobble down the stairs, his descent hampered by his unwieldy, unbendable left leg. At the bottom, Wilson was waiting with Nick, a boy Esme recognized from grade school. Nick was short but heavyset, with the weightlifter's hulking tightness to his upper body. Norm high-fived Wilson, and the three headed off toward the gym.

"Come on," Esme said. "Don't let them know we're following." The boys arrived at the gym, but instead of going in, they kept walking. "Are they going in the back way, do you think?"

"No," Katy said. "The weight room's on the other side. They're going out by the Dumpsters."

"Hurry up!" Esme said.

The sisters rounded the far corner of the gym just in time to see Norman limp past the corner to the back. Esme and Katy quickened their pace, turning the final corner at a near run, Veronica trailing behind in her heels. Behind the building a small crowd waited, perhaps thirty. In the middle of the group were Danny Long, Jackson Gartner, and Logan Rehnquist.

The space behind the gym was perfectly suited to clandestine activities, such as a romantic tryst or a beat-down. Stoners frequented the spot during school hours. There was a service road to accommodate the trash trucks. There was an eight-foot-high chain-link fence, overgrown with weeds and potato vines, which entirely obscured the clearing between the two huge Dumpsters and the gymnasium's industrial air-conditioning unit.

"Hey, Norman," Logan called in a vocalized sneer.

"Gentlemen," Norm acknowledged.

Esme walked around in front of Norman and stood with her back to him, facing the crowd, her eyes blazing in fury. "What the hell is this?" she sputtered. "Wilson, you know my father is your mother's attorney, right? How is she going to feel when he calls her up tonight and tells her what you did here?"

"Logan just wanted to talk to him," Wilson mumbled, eyes downcast, the excuse as porous as a sieve, the lie dripping through to puddle on the ground at his feet.

Katy stood beside her sister and faced the crowd as well. "You should all be ashamed of yourselves. Come on, Norman, we're getting out of here."

"Good thing you have your girlfriend and her crazy sister to fight your battles for you, freak," Danny taunted.

"Does Sandy know what you're doing here, Logan?" Esme asked.

"You bitches better stay out of stuff that don't concern you."

The word was enough to bring Veronica around to the forefront, to stand in solidarity with Esme and Katy. "What did you just call my sisters?" she yelled, throwing her head back in an impressive manner. Another perk of striking beauty is stage presence.

Norman didn't like how things were spiraling out of control. He felt his self-restraint slipping, his ire rising in his craw like bilious mercury in a thermometer. "Esme," he said, in a very quiet voice. "Let me deal with this."

Esme unclenched her fist and breathed. Boys. He'd said he would react to protect her, and here she was, forcing his hand.

"What do you want?" Norman asked the three main instigators. "I'm not going to fight. I'm a pacifist, so I'm morally opposed to any kind of violence."

"That's too bad," Logan replied. He spun around and landed a leaping roundhouse kick squarely on Norman's shoulder.

If Norman felt anything from the kick, he didn't give Logan the satisfaction. It didn't budge him an inch. "Do you mind if I ask you why you just did that?" he asked.

"We don't like you," Logan explained, bouncing back and forth on the balls of his feet, planning his next strike.

"Is it because I'm Jewish?"

"You're some kind of monster or freak or something, I don't know what, but something ain't right about you," Logan accused.

"We don't want you in our school," Danny added. He put his head down and rushed Norman, as if he were trying to break through an offensive line, and shoved him with both hands for all he was worth. Danny's momentum was enough to rock Norman back a few inches. He had to take a step back to keep his balance.

Jackson attacked next, punching Norman in the gut, pushing off with his legs and firing from the shoulders like a boxer working a heavy bag, emphasizing every word of his grievance with a punch: "We. Don't. Want. To. Look. At. Your. Ugly. Face. In. Our. School."

"If we all talked this through like civilized people I'm sure we could reach a consensus that would be acceptable to all parties." Norman's tone of voice was perfectly reasonable, as if Jackson had not just punched him with all his might twelve times.

This infuriated the three even more. They redoubled their efforts and attacked again rapidly, in pairs or in turns, Logan kicking, Jackson punching, and Danny charging in between rounds, trying to topple the giant. Norman was forced to take a few steps back, but otherwise appeared to be impervious to injury—until Logan landed a low kick to the brace on Norman's knee. The giant winced noticeably. The reaction was not lost on Logan, who sensed a vulnerability. He shuffled to the right. Norman shifted his leg to the rear, to protect it.

"That's enough, Logan," Esme shouted, moving into the conflict.

"You better control your girlfriend," Logan warned, circling, "or she's gonna get hurt."

Esme saw it then, that thing in Norman's eyes, the glint under the shadow of his brow, the flash of anger under the Herculean self-restraint. Norman had had enough. With surprising speed, the giant's hand shot out and grabbed Logan by the head.

Logan's head looked like a large grapefruit in the hand of a shopper in the produce aisle. Logan struggled to get away, punching out ineffectively at Norman's forearm, to no avail. And then, Logan was lifted off the ground, his toes sweeping desperately to find purchase, his body thrashing like a fish hauled out of the water on a line. Norman lifted Logan a foot off the ground. "Okay, Logan," the giant advised. "You're starting to piss me off."

For a fleeting moment, something in the reptilian part of her brain made Esme's heart flutter. It was so odd; Norm was decisively unattractive, but the raw, masculine power was a turn-on.

"Let go of me, you ugly freak!" Logan shouted, struggling. He grabbed Norman's wrist with both hands to steady himself, then tried to kick him, to no effect. Danny and Jackson stood back, startled by Norman's sheer strength. Logan weighed over two hundred pounds.

"Logan," Norman said sharply. "You need to calm down. We have to talk this through."

"What?" Logan shouted back, an edge of panic in his voice. He was nearly sobbing.

"Okay," Norm said. "First of all, I want you to stop saying that Esme is my girlfriend. It's very insulting to her. She's a beautiful girl, and she could have a normal-looking boyfriend if she wanted one. She would never date a huge ugly freak like me."

"Okay!" Logan yelled, sobbing. "I'm sorry, okay? Put me down!"

"That's excellent, Logan. We're making progress. Now there's just one more thing, and I said this already, but I don't think you were listening."

"Just put me down!" Logan sobbed.

"In a second. What I want to say is, I'm a pacifist, and it's against my principles to fight. But if I have to defend myself, I will. You should stop thrashing around like that, Logan, and settle down. Your neck is only strong enough to support your head, not your entire body. Now me"—here he removed his scarf with the other hand, revealing the bolts in his neck for the first time—"I have surgical-grade titanium rebar in my neck, that's why I have these bolts here. But all you have are regular cervical vertebrae, which are pretty fragile. Are you following me?"

Logan was blubbering by now, so it was a little difficult to hear his response, but Norman was soon satisfied enough to continue. "Okay, that's good, Logan. I'm really embarrassed to be in this situation right now. But if I snapped you like a whip, you would definitely be a quadriplegic for the rest of your life. I'd rather not injure you, on account of being a pacifist and all, so if

I had to do something like that, I would feel just terrible for compromising my principles. You, on the other hand, would have to get one of those motorized wheelchairs that you steer with your tongue. So, like . . . there would be consequences for you, too. It would totally be a lose-lose situation. Anyway, we don't have to be friends or anything, but in the future, if you have any problems with me, I'd really prefer that you didn't resort to violence. I'm going to put you down now, okay?"

Logan was, by this time, incapable of communicating. When Norman set him down, he collapsed to the ground, then scampered away like a crab on his back.

"He's a monster!" Jackson screamed. "That wasn't human, people!" He looked from face to face in the crowd, searching for consensus. But nobody appeared to be the least bit interested in furthering an assault on Norman Stein. Danny was edging back, ready to make a run for it. "We should . . ." Jackson pled to the crowd, trying in vain to raise a mob. "Somebody has to do something about him!"

"Naw, man," Wilson said. "He beat Logan. He could take all three of you. At least. You started it; he finished it. It's over."

"He attacked Logan!" Jackson yelled. "He could have killed him!"

"Could have," said Wilson's friend Nick. "But he didn't."

"Self-defense," Wilson chimed in. With a chorus of murmurs, the crowd agreed.

"I recorded the whole thing," Veronica added, displaying her iPhone. "Self-defense."

"Dude," said Wilson. "You should totally post that to YouTube."

A small pack of cheerleaders suddenly burst onto the scene

from around the corner of the gym, led by a curvaceous strawberry blond. Sandy Hardesty crouched down by Logan, where he lay in the dirt. "I heard about the fight; I had practice," she told her boyfriend. "Are you all right?"

"Yeah," he replied, a bit dazed. "That guy's a monster."

"No, *you're* the monster," Sandy accused, slapping Logan hard across the cheek. "We're done."

7

INVITATION AND INVOCATION

The dinner party was all Katy's idea, so Veronica suggested it, and Esme quickly agreed, so they only had to convince Katy to go along with it, which was rather easy, as it had been Katy's idea. Katy had a gift for getting people to do what she wanted them to do and making them take responsibility for the fallout, in case everything didn't work out as planned. Norman arrived at 6:58 and waited on the doorstep for two minutes before ringing the bell. This produced a cacophony of barking from Katy's dogs.

"It's Norm—Dad, can you get that?" Esme said. All three sisters were busy putting the finishing touches on their dishes. Veronica had made a mixed greens salad; Katy had made boiled tofu with veggies. Esme had gone all out with lasagna and a full loaf of garlic bread. The smell was all over the house.

After pulling the lasagna out of the oven, Esme went looking for Norman. She found him with her dad in the living room, deep in a discussion about human rights and the ACLU, for which Barry did pro bono work occasionally. "Dad, I left you some garlic bread and lasagna, and Ronnie made you a salad. Hi, Norm, we're eating in the basement."

"I thought we were all eating in the dining room," Barry teased. "You never said anything about having boys in your room."

"He's just a friend," Esme said flatly. "Come on, Norman, you can help us carry stuff down."

For a makeshift dining table, Esme had found an old door and two sawhorses in the barn, which she'd set up in her room. There was a yellow floral tablecloth and an arrangement of speckled toad lilies for a centerpiece. There was not much conversation during dinner, besides a few complimentary observations about the food. Norman, always self-conscious about his size, was loath to gorge himself in front of three beautiful girls, though he was quite impressed by Esme's culinary skills. After dinner, Katy ran the dishes up to the kitchen and came back with a homemade pie, which she served out. Esme's work again. Hand-pitted cherry and blueberry combination. Homemade crust. *Best pie ever*, Norm thought.

By 9:00, the table was cleared and a pot of tea was steeping. Lights were dimmed, music turned off, and candles in assorted holders were distributed about the room, a few on the table. Katy rose and rang a large Tibetan singing bowl that was on a shelf of the bookcase. She returned to the table as the first, second, and third harmonics resonated through the room.

"The circle has come to order," Esme intoned.

"Merry meet," chanted Veronica and Katy, as one.

Norman grinned. "Seriously?" he asked.

"Do you mock us?" Veronica challenged.

"No, of course not," he said. "I'm just . . . well, this is a surprising turn of events."

"We're Wiccans," Esme said. "We're inviting you into our inner circle."

"I don't have a problem with that," he replied. "But I'm an atheist, you know. I uh . . . don't really believe in that stuff. I like science."

"A scientist should have an open mind," Esme said.

"No, of course," Norman said. "Totally. No judgment here. Proceed."

A cat jumped up on the table and circled, sniffing. He lay down on his side in the middle, and proceeded to groom himself.

"Is that a feral cat?" Katy asked. "He looks familiar."

"His name is Kasha." Esme half hoped he'd start talking, just to freak everyone out.

"Beautiful markings," Veronica said, reaching forward to scratch the cat behind his ears. Kasha rolled on his back, purring, and wormed his way toward her.

"He looks like a little striped lynx, with those ears," Norman observed. The cat took a position under the toad lilies like a sphinx, watching Norman. "So, uh . . . sorry, what was this circle thing again?"

"We invoke the circle so that we can speak freely," Esme said, "and ask and answer questions without anyone judging us or telling anyone outside the circle our secrets. We're inviting you, Norman, because we think you're really interesting and we want to know more about you. It's a huge thing, we've never invited any outsiders before."

Norman was pretty sure he knew what they wanted to know

about him. "Or, you could just ask me. Do I get to ask you girls questions, too?"

"Of course," Katy replied. "We're all friends here, in the circle."

Norm opened his huge hands. "Ask away."

Veronica pounced. "I have a question for you, Norm," she said. "Okay. Like, what's with your face? I mean, all the scars and all? And the thing on your leg? I heard you had operations, but why? Were you in an accident?"

Three sets of eyes were focused on the giant. Four, counting the cat's. Norm was a little miffed that they felt the ruse was necessary. Still, he was sitting at a table with three beautiful girls. That was progress for his social life, anyway. "Did anyone else have a related question?" He glanced back and forth from Katy to Esme, eyebrows raised.

"Uh, yeah," Katy said. "Your height, I guess. I know you're a giant and all, but I don't understand why. The science and all."

"Okay, the scars, the height. Got it. Esme?"

Esme poured Norm some tea. She raised the pot and met eyes around the table. Katy proffered a cup. "You mentioned titanium rebar once . . . And how come you're so strong? That's not normal, regardless of how big you are."

"Actually, it's a really interesting story. I guess the place to start is with the acromegaly," he said. "You probably know it better as gigantism. I have a pituitary adenoma, which is a kind of tumor that causes the overproduction of growth hormone. I've always been large. I was over six feet tall in fifth grade, and by eighth grade I was seven feet tall and two hundred and fifty pounds."

"How tall are you now?" Katy asked.

"Seven feet, eight and a half inches," he said. "I'm the ninth-tallest man in the world. Anyway, when I was thirteen, I started to get sick. Really sick. Every kind of cancer you can imagine: leukemia, bone cancer, lungs, you name it. Entirely malignant. All the growth hormone in my system was feeding the cancers, and they were growing so rapidly there wasn't anything the doctors could do about it. I had years of chemotherapy and dozens of operations to remove tumors and three bone marrow transplants, but whenever they cleared the cancer out, it just came back somewhere else. The oncologist at the cancer center gave me a week to live once, but I recovered. Then I got the lung cancer."

"I'm so sorry, Norman," Esme said, putting her hand on his hand across the table. "It must have been horrible for you."

"Yeah, it was pretty bad. I was in a lot of pain for a long time. But my father never gave up on me. He was there for me the whole time, trying to figure out how to save my life."

"How about your mom?" Veronica asked.

"Oh, she died when I was little. Leukemia. It runs in the family."

"I'm so sorry," Katy said.

There was an awkward silence. A moment of respect, for Norm's mom. Esme finally spoke, when she felt it was right: "But you survived after all, Norman. That's the important thing."

"Well, this is the sort of creepy part," Norman said. "I didn't, actually. I mean, I went into a coma, and I flatlined. I was uh . . . sort of, technically . . . uh . . . dead. For about five years."

8

HOW TO BUILD A MONSTER

Norman had never discussed his story with anyone before, mostly because he had no friends to discuss it with. It was not a secret in the medical community. His father was presently publishing his findings on the advancements he'd made in the fields of cryogenics and neurosurgery to keep his son alive. Dr. Frederick Stein's name, though tainted to a degree by the circumstances of his son's illness and a few somewhat sketchy liberties he'd taken along the way, was being considered for a Nobel Prize nomination. Still, it was with some trepidation that Norman confessed that he had a history of illness and death. Considering his freakish appearance, he was hesitant to admit that he'd done a stint on the slab. But the expressions on the faces of the girls made it all worthwhile.

The Silver sisters sat rapt for the next half hour while Norm described how his father had frozen him cryogenically at the moment of death in a procedure that maintained his cells at just below zero while supplying his brain with enough oxygen and nutrients to avoid damage from deterioration. In the meantime, his body was disassembled, the individual parts and organs scoured for any traces of cancerous growth and treated with radiation or microsurgery. A lot of the body parts were too cancerous and had to be discarded, including some major organs, left arm but not hand, entire left leg, parts of his pelvis, the right eye . . . Norman did not iterate the entire list. The sisters all had queasy looks on their faces. The next step was replacing the missing parts with organs and limbs of a like scale, no easy task given Norman's size. The leg and arm were harvested from another giant, who'd died at age twenty-six from massive coronary failure. Norm's skeleton was reinforced with titanium at this point, as he'd always had a tendency to bone breakage due to his superhuman musculature.

"If a body builder or athlete wanted to inject himself with as much growth hormone as I produce on a daily basis, it would cost him a fortune," Norman explained.

"Are all giants as strong as you?" Katy asked.

"We tend to be pretty strong, just because of our size," Norm replied. "But I've always worked at it. Physical therapy, working through the pain. I get in a zone and just keep pushing myself. And again, while I was in cryogenics and somewhat disassembled, my bones knit, so since I woke up, none of the growth hormone is going to growth. It's all going to muscle. Well, we are lengthening my left leg, to get it the same length as my right."

"Is that why you have the brace?" Esme asked.

"Yeah. They break the bone and create a gap. The brace holds everything in place. Then bone cells fill the gap. They keep adjusting the gap, stretching it, until they get the length they want. In my case, the whole process is accelerated, because of the growth hormone. They never were able to fix that. I mean, you can't exactly go in and remove someone's pituitary gland. Anyway, the brace should be off in another month. I can't wait."

Veronica rose. She rounded the table and stood in front of

Norman. She wrapped her arms around his neck and gave him a hug. "You are definitely the most interesting person I've met at Middleton High School," she told him.

"Hear, hear," said Esme, and Katy chimed in her agreement.

"So does that answer your questions?" Norman asked.

"I think so," Esme said.

"One quick follow-up," Katy requested. "How old are you, on your driver's license?"

"Twenty-one. They use your birth certificate for ID. Why?"

"Nothing," she mused. "You could have bought us wine, is all."

Esme swirled her tea reflectively. Norman's story made him even more fascinating, and she was already a fan. She resolved to meet his father—what could be more interesting than a conversation with a man with such a mind? She had a thousand follow-up questions.

"I have one more question," Veronica said. "Do you have a girlfriend?"

"Why, are you interested?" Norman returned. His face was as red as a matador's cape. He'd just been describing most of his vital organs in detail to the three sisters, but suddenly the conversation had grown all too intrusive.

"No, but I might know somebody," she said, glancing conspicuously at Esme.

If Esme's eyes had been lasers, Veronica would have been a pile of ash.

"I, uh . . . I-I-I mean . . ." Norm stammered.

"Don't pay attention to Ronnie," Katy cut in. "She's a wicked witch."

"But you like girls, don't you?" Veronica pressed.

"Cut it out, Ronnie," Esme said.

"No, it's okay," Norm said. "I do like girls. In fact, my dad and I are building one in his lab, so I'll have a prom date."

Veronica's jaw dropped. But Norman couldn't keep a straight face, and Katy gave Norm a hand to high-five. "Good one!"

Esme, though, could only laugh self-consciously. She would give Veronica a piece of her mind later for putting Norm on the spot like that. "Norman, you're a great guy," she said. She had to say *something*. "A girl would have to be stupid not to see all your qualities. And anyone who can't, doesn't deserve you. There's a girl out there for you somewhere."

"Maybe right under your nose," Veronica proposed, again with a glance at Esme.

"Everyone is under his nose," Katy mentioned. "His nose is seven feet off the ground."

"It's getting late," Esme mentioned, stifling a fake yawn.

Norman glanced at his watch. "Ten o'clock," he noted. "Guess I should go get my beauty sleep. Uh . . . let me just ask one question, then, okay? To Esme?"

"I have a test tomorrow," Esme hedged.

"It's okay," Norman said. "It's an easy one. I was just wondering, what's that book?"

"What book?"

"The one you have hidden on top of your bookcase, pushed up against the wall."

"I . . . don't . . . uh . . . what are you talking about? What book?" Esme stalled, all the while thinking *Idiot! I'm an idiot! The perfect hiding place, on top of a seven-foot bookcase, pushed all the way back, entirely invisible from anyplace in the room. Except to a seven-foot-nine-inch boy.*

Norman rose and strode quickly to the bookcase. "You should

dust up here," he mentioned, retrieving the book. He brought it back to the makeshift table.

"You're not supposed to have this!" Veronica accused.

"You stole it from Mom's cedar chest," Katy charged. "She'll kill you when she finds out."

"Why?" Norman asked. "What is it?"

The tome on the table was bound in leather. Obviously, it was quite old, and the condition was not excellent. There was a raised pentangle on the cover. A strap was sewn around the spine, so that the book could be closed with a lock. There was no lock on the book, however. There was a musty smell to it. Norman opened the book and fanned slowly through the pages.

"Don't open that!" Katy snapped, slamming the book shut and pulling it to her side of the table. "It's for family only!"

Norman had only taken a quick glance, but the pages were hand-written on parchment, with hand-drawn illustrations. "But what is it?" Norman insisted again.

Esme rescued the book back from Katy, and hugged it to her chest. "It's a family . . . like a family Bible," she improvised. "It has our history, going back more than three hundred years."

"I'll bet I can guess," Norman said. "It looked like an old recipe book, with pictures of herbs and lists of ingredients in Latin. But from the way you're all acting, I'd say it has something to do with Wicca. Except, I think Wicca only goes back a hundred years or so, and this looks much older. A spell book? Or potions?"

"Yeah," Esme admitted. "Something like that. Before our family adopted Wicca, we were witches, going back to colonial times. But there are too many negative connotations to the word, so we don't use it in public. If it was just my thing, I'd tell you, but this concerns family secrets. We can trace our direct lineage through at least sixteen generations. There's some apothecary stuff, holistic remedies for treating warts and injuries, and herbal liniments, stuff like that. That's about all I can tell you. You see how upset my sisters are that I even have the book in my room."

"Okay," Norm agreed. "I can respect that."

"It's getting late," Katy noted. She rose and went to the door and flipped on a light switch, illuminating the room.

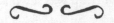

After Norman left, Katy and Veronica confronted Esme. "I don't know what you think you're doing with that book," Katy accused, "but you'd better put it back where you found it."

"Mom never said we couldn't use it," Esme argued weakly.

"That's because she thought we had enough sense not to mess with it, after all those warnings she drilled into our heads since . . . since forever," Veronica said. "Especially you, Esme. You're supposed to be the responsible one."

Alone with her thoughts and her guilt, Esme slumped into her comfy chair with a sigh. The wick smoke of a dozen extinguished candles thickened the air. Maybe if she sat for a while, she'd gather the energy to clean up.

Kasha appraised Esme from the ottoman. "What a specimen," he said. "You gonna tap that?"

"Excuse me?"

"That boy. You should lock that in, before your sisters cut you out of the action. Though it looks like there's enough of him to go around."

"Norman?"

"Try to keep up."

"We're just friends," Esme disclaimed. *What the hell did a cat know about boys?*

"He's into you, I can tell," Kasha argued. "The biggest, strongest human I've ever seen, and you could get him."

"Kasha, size isn't important for humans. There are other factors."

Kasha stepped onto the chair and walked up the arm, so his eyes were level with hers. "So what's more important than size?"

"I don't know, brains maybe? Personality? Sense of humor?"

"How's he rank for brains?" the cat challenged.

"He's brilliant," she admitted. "Great personality, good sense of humor . . . really kind, too."

"Ah," Kasha said. "I can see why you're not interested."

"You wouldn't understand. I'm not saying looks are important, but he's . . . kind of hideous, to be honest. All the scarring, and the asymmetry . . ."

"Are you kidding me? The battle scars are the best part. Females go crazy for that stuff, it's sexy as hell. You know that earless Tom out by the neighbors' barn? One eye scarred over, face mauled, neck as big around as your leg? Thick with ticks and fleas? Believe me, he does very well for himself with the ladies."

Esme rose and started cleaning up the teacups. Kasha jumped up on the table and sniffed at the ancient book. "So how long have you been keeper of the grimoire?" he asked.

"What do you mean?"

"The grimoire. Your great-aunt Becky was the keeper, when I knew her. Then it passed to your mother. It should probably go to Katy, you know. She has the most talent."

"Wait . . . you knew my great-aunt Becky? But she died, like, twenty years ago."

Kasha pawed open the cover. "I was her familiar. Look, here's one that makes your boobs bigger. I bet Norman would like that. Where it says Solomon's seal, don't just use the leaf. That's an amateur mistake."

9

NOVEMBER

Veronica saw him first. It was a Monday before school, in front of the main hall. A large black Mercedes with dark tinting pulled up to the curb and sat for a few minutes, motor idling. Veronica had been talking to Carly and Michaela and Karina, but they'd all been standing in a circle facing each other, and she'd been facing the street, so she'd seen him first, before anybody else in the entire school. So everybody else could just back off.

The car door opened a crack, and an umbrella jutted out and opened up over the passenger door, so when he stepped out of the car, he was entirely covered. Odd, as it wasn't raining. He wore white gloves and a bowler hat and goggles with very dark lenses. He wore a fitted tailcoat over a ruffled shirt. His pants were slim and tucked into boots.

Veronica knew a thing or three about fashion. Steampunk was a joke, a sad little cosplay cry for help, but on him it was pure genius. She knew it was good by the quality, by the detail. The little buttons on the kid gloves. The pearl cufflinks in the ruffled cuffs, peeking out from under the jacket sleeves. The fit of the jacket over the black, studded leather vest, accentuating his perfect physique: slim waisted, broad shouldered, tight in the butt, lanky in the leg, just how she liked them. Boots with big, industrial-looking buckles. Bangs over one eye. Handsome, even at a distance, with his face partly covered by goggles. *Extremely* handsome.

There was only one girl at Middleton High who was good enough for this boy, Veronica decided. She was very certain of this, as she spent a lot of time every day with that girl's face in her mirror. The boy walked toward her, and Veronica tried to play it cool, but Michaela had caught wind of him, which drew Carly's and Karina's stupid, gawking stares. There was no way Veronica could play it cool and pretend to ignore him while laughing at something funny Carly had just told her, because Carly was presently a goo-goo-eyed fool.

Veronica looked at her iPhone as he passed, not the coolest pose, but not bad for a quick improvisation. She caught a glimpse of him out of the corner of her eye, and she was sure he smiled at her. She looked up, intending to appear uninterested, but got caught up in his smile and ended up ogling him like an idiot. He smelled amazing.

⌀⌀

Katy was the first to talk to him, and it was all from her easy non-chalance and a fluke of dumb luck. Because Katy had chosen that particular Monday, of all days, to go to school dressed in full Gothic Lolita, which went with steampunk like a cherry on a sundae.

Katy was wearing her brown hair straight with newly shorn bangs and a mid-thigh-length frilly black princess dress over stockings with a pentangle design. She had black lace-up boots to the knees, and elbow-length black gloves, and a punkish black leather choker with spikes. They met in the hallway, between second and third periods, and stopped to regard each other.

Katy had natural aplomb in situations like this. She was no stranger to coincidences working out in her favor, the result of an unconscious vibe she put out into the eldritch cosmos. She offered an arm. "Shall we?" she invited.

They strode down the hallway like a Victorian couple strolling through a park, and people parted before them. Katy had been taking crap all day off her classmates for dressing like an undead baby doll. By the next day, half the girls in the school would be dressing the same way. The boutiques in downtown Middleton that afternoon would sell out of black lace and leather.

"I'm Katy," she said, walking slowly with the handsomest boy she'd ever seen. She didn't know what she was feeling, but she was giddy. Love, she supposed. What a kick.

"Zack," he replied. "It's me first day. Dead brill, your outfit."

He was English. Katy had never thought about it before, but an English boy was definitely what she'd been waiting for her whole life. "You too," she replied. "I love the goggles, the boots, the little details. And the English accent." She was usually cleverer than this, but Zack had her addled. "So what brings you to our little hick town, Zack? You strike me as a city boy."

"Oh, me dad. Business. I was raised in England, but I'm actually an American. Not that I ever admitted that to me mates."

Katy laughed. He was so funny. So interesting. So perfect, in every way.

"Well, this is me, here," he said, halting in front of a classroom door. "Room 142, Algebra 2."

Katy didn't want to relinquish Zack's arm, but could think

of no excuse to keep it. Could she audit algebra, just this one period? "I suppose I'll see you around," she suggested wistfully.

He bowed and kissed her gloved hand. "Thank you, for making me feel welcome at your school," he said. "Until our paths cross again?"

"Don't be a stranger," she said, but by then he was in the classroom, hunting for a desk.

⌒ᴑ ᴄ⌒

"Look at those whores," Veronica said at lunch to Esme. Carly, her soon-to-be-ex friend, and a couple juniors, cheerleaders, and assorted shallow airheads had him hemmed in at a lunch table halfway across the cafeteria. "Don't they know how ridiculous they look?"

"New boy?" Esme asked, looking up from her AP world history textbook. She was luxuriating over feudal Japan. The toughest class in the school, and the most fun. Ton of homework, though. There had been some commotion earlier among the girls in a couple classes about a new boy from England, a junior. As if she were interested. She looked over her shoulder at the table. She could make out a boy in black with his back turned, and some clamor of girls laughing. "No thanks, I'll pass."

Esme scanned the cafeteria for Norm, usually easy to spot. They'd been talking on the phone and texting, consulting on homework. They'd Skyped occasionally, though that sort of ruined the fantasy for Esme. Norm was the perfect unofficial platonic boyfriend, as long as she could forget what he looked like. He was smart and funny—sometimes she reread the particularly clever texts over and over again. But Norm had been eating lunch off campus the past week or so. He had a car, and Wilson and his muscle-bound friend had been hanging out with the giant, working out in the weight room after school and going out for pizza and burgers to bulk up. Not that Norman needed any more bulk, but it was nice that he'd found some social acceptance.

Katy entered the cafeteria, searching the tables. Esme waved, but Katy walked right past them as if they weren't even there, and made straight for the table with the new boy. Esme watched in fascination as her kid sister strode right up behind him and hung her arm over his shoulder. He leaned back and draped his arm over her hip and gave her a very familiar hug, like they were the dearest of old friends. The boy gestured with his arm to the girl next to him, and she slid over on the bench, already fairly crowded, allowing Katy to take her place in the most coveted spot in the cafeteria, thigh to thigh, elbow to elbow with the object of their affections.

"Look, Ronnie," Esme said. "Katy has the inside track. Score one for the Silver sisters."

Veronica stood abruptly. She was crying. "How could she do this to me?" she blurted, running out of the cafeteria.

"Oh boy," Esme said, to nobody. She was alone at her table. Ronnie had left her lunch and her backpack. As if Esme didn't have enough stuff to carry already. Things were sure going to get ugly, soon. Katy, with her talent and personality, could pretty much have any boy she wanted, if she set her mind to it. But it would be a mistake to count out Veronica so easily. Sure, she was only fourteen, but she looked older, and Esme had learned never to underestimate Ronnie. Ultimately, the whole boys thing usually boiled down to a beauty contest, and there was no way Veronica was going to lose a beauty contest, not to Katy. Not to anyone.

Esme got a better look at the new boy in fifth period, AP world. There was no assigned seating, though Esme was always front and center. But today, Charlie Sexton was in her seat. Esme did a quick scan of the room, to figure out why. Charlie was in her seat because Lisa Vaughn was in Charlie's seat, which was next to the seat that the new boy had taken. Nobody was in their regular seats. The new boy had taken a seat in the middle of the room, and all the girls had taken seats around him, like carpels around the peduncle of a daisy, which had forced the boys to the periphery of the room like petals. Esme made her way to the rear of the room, where the last few unoccupied desks remained. She walked past the new boy, curious. Her sisters were already fighting over him. Okay, he was handsome, obviously, but what was all the fuss?

As she passed by him, he looked up at her and smiled, then did a double take, as if he'd just seen a ghost. Esme felt a jolt of inexplicable attraction. *What in the name of the Goddess was that?* She'd felt something, unmistakably. Pheromones, no doubt. That explained everything. Everyone emitted pheromones, but this boy, for whatever reason, was emitting a concentrated dose. The other poor dumb girls around him didn't have a clue what had hit them. Maybe she could talk some reason into her sisters after all.

Just as the bell rang, the boy grabbed his books and fled his seat. There was a moan of disappointment from the girls in the seats around the abandoned desk. He headed for the back of the room and took the desk next to Esme's, smiling at her again as he sat. And again, Esme felt that intoxicating sexual energy wafting from his pores.

"Zack," he said, by way of introduction, offering a hand. He was covered head to toe with clothing. He hadn't removed his hat or goggles or gloves.

"I'm Esme," she responded. Her palm was sweating, for some reason.

The teacher, Miss Edwards, was at her desk, examining an entry paper and entering Zack into the roll book. She looked up when she'd finished. "Zackery?" she asked. "Zackery Kallas?"

"Ma'am?" he responded.

"Zackery, we don't wear sunglasses in class, or hats," she admonished.

"Terribly sorry," he answered. He removed a file from his soft leather satchel, stood, and approached the teacher. She rose as well.

Esme watched Zack talking in hushed tones to Miss Edwards in the front of the classroom. He showed her the file, pointing to a few specifics on the pages inside. Esme couldn't hear any of it from the back of the room. Miss Edwards was into Zack's personal space in an inappropriate manner, to Esme's mind. It galled her. The teacher had a large bust, which brushed against Zack's arm as she leaned in to share the contents of the folder. She was even twirling her hair in a flirtatious manner. She wasn't bad-looking, but she was ancient, thirty at least. Esme wasn't the only girl in the class who was peeved.

$\sim$ ᖾ

"Mind if I look on with you?" the boy asked, scooching his desk over until it touched Esme's. Scientific objectivity notwithstanding, Esme was picking up on whatever it was about Zack that had already hooked her sisters. The unassuming confidence, the accent, the fact that he was the best-looking boy she'd ever seen . . . overkill. He didn't even need the pheromone thing: He was smoking hot. She slid her book over so the spine was on the crack between their desks, rereading a sentence for the fourth time.

"You know anything about the Edo period?" he asked, a second attempt to engage her.

No, not at the moment. "Yeah. Enough." Esme was resolved to resist his charms.

Centuries passed, before he spoke again. Edo came and went, then the Meiji dynasty. Esme read well into the Taisho period. Big earthquake and fire in Tokyo. Tens of thousands killed, cultural landmarks a millennia old destroyed.

"Listen, Esme," he said. "I'm in a bit of a mither here. Care to meet after school, and give me a few pointers? A brew at Starbucks all right? You can show me the town . . ."

His voice caused the blood in Esme's ears to pulse. Her palms were sweating. "Why me?"

Zack regarded her. The horn-rimmed glasses, the very ordinary brown hair, the unremarkable nose. She was just his size. Pretty at best, but not beautiful. "You remind me of someone," he said. "Anyway, I just need a friend right now."

Esme swallowed. "I have to drive my sisters home after school."

"Four o'clock, then?"

The bell rang. Esme swept up her books and held them to her chest with one hand. She scooped up her backpack, and Veronica's, and slung them over her shoulder. Her eyes were downturned, but she nodded an affirmation to Zack as she made her escape.

10

A MIDDLE-SIZED TOWN IN THE
MIDDLE OF NOWHERE

Ten minutes after four, and no sign of Zack. Esme nursed her latte. There was another coffee shop in town that she preferred, which the junior college crowd frequented. But this was where he said to meet her, on Fourth Street, in the middle of town. Zack struck Esme as a player, a charming, very good-looking boy who could and probably would have any girl he wanted. So why had she agreed to meet him? Curiosity? The fact that everyone else wanted him? Her sisters would be pissed, when they found out. And they would find out, because everyone in Middleton was always up in everyone else's business. Suddenly, he was there at her table, seating himself. She hadn't seen him come in.

"Sorry," he apologized. "A bit dodgy, getting here. A couple o' girls from school were shadowing me." He sat with his back to the window, facing her.

Esme had chosen the seat in the front window so he'd be able to find her easily, and so she could keep a watch out. Or possibly so she could be seen with him, although she didn't like admitting that to herself. "I thought you *liked* girls."

He grinned. Goddess, he was handsome. "It's kind of a drag, after a bit, eh? I don't know what gets into them."

Esme had a clue or two. "Are you having coffee?"

"Oh, right, I'll queue up and place my order."

Esme watched peripherally as Zack purchased a plain coffee. The counter girl was flirting shamelessly with him. Esme disapproved of her: covered in tattoos, half her head shaven, and enough hardware in her face to pick up radio transmissions. The barista also flirted with him when he received his coffee. Esme disapproved of her as well, though she didn't know why exactly. Something huge passed between Esme and the window, blotting out the light from the street, displacing all the air in the room.

"Hey, Esme, I saw you in the window," Norman said. "I thought you liked the other place."

She shrugged, sipping. "It's all right." There was no way she'd be able to get rid of Norman before Zack saw her talking to him. For some reason that was important. Past Norman, through the window, Esme spied Wilson and Nick hanging out on the street. Zack would think she hung out with the freakiest reprobates in the school.

"Hey, did you want to come by later and study for the biology test? My dad's in town, I remember you said you wanted to meet him . . ."

"Maybe another time," she said neutrally.

"Norman, innit?"

It was Zack's voice, disembodied. It came from somewhere behind Norman, who turned around with some delicacy.

"Zack," he acknowledged.

"You two know each other?"

"Hard to miss this bloke," Zack answered. "Bloody impressive, he is."

"Computer programming class," Norm explained. "Not that we spoke or anything."

There was something in Norm's tone of voice, in his expression. Esme almost didn't catch it. It recalled to her that one time, out by the Dumpsters, when Logan had pushed him too far. Norm was angry, aggressively so. For some reason, he hated Zack. It was so unlike him.

"Zack's in my AP world history class. He missed the first six units; we were just meeting to see if I can catch him up," Esme explained.

Norm was so menacing-looking, the way he loomed up like a mountain, with the scowl on his face, an expression of anger, and something else. Jealousy? "Does he know Katy's your sister? I saw him in the hallway today with his arm around her. And a few other girls."

"Katy?" Zack asked. As if it didn't even register. "Goth chick? Nice kid, that one. Is that what's got your knickers in a twist? Because we're all just friends an' all."

"Does she know that?" Esme asked.

"I suppose." Zack shrugged. "But if she got the wrong idea, we'll get her sorted, all right?"

"Good. Because if there was anything between you and my sister . . ." If there was anything between Zack and her sister, what? What was the implied ultimatum?

Zack edged past Norm and into the seat opposite Esme with his back to the giant. "It's nice, you looking after your sister an' all."

"Katy's the best," Esme testified. "We have our disagreements like any sisters, but we're very close. I'd kill for her. Or Ronnie."

"Ronnie? You have a brother?"

"Veronica. You can't have missed her. She's the most beautiful girl in town. Too young to date, of course."

Norm wasn't used to being ignored. It was impossible to ignore him. "On the record," he mentioned, "I'd also kill anyone that messed with your sisters. Or you." He clenched and unclenched a fist the size of a Volkswagen menacingly.

"Norm, we were having a conversation, so . . . uh . . . check you later?"

"Like sisters to me," Norm mentioned ominously, as he slowly walked out the door.

"That was so unlike him," Esme said. "He's usually so mild-mannered."

"I get the sense he didn't much care for me."

"I think he has a thing for me. But you know . . . not my type." Esme had a sudden inspiration about what her type might be.

"I'm not sure he's anyone's type," Zack said.

~ ᴐ ᴄ~

After coffee, the two took a stroll on the promenade along the river. The weather was comfortable in early November, with a breeze that rippled the Susquahilla. The leaves on the trees were yellow and red, in full fall color.

"Beautiful, this bit of country," Zack mentioned. "All the space is so open and wild. In Europe, everything is so manicured, you never feel like you're out in nature."

"You grew up in England? Whereabouts?"

"Oh, here and there," he demurred.

"Do you miss it much? England?"

"It's all right," he said.

But she could tell he did miss it by the wistful way he said it. "Ah. British understatement."

He smiled at that. "I can do Irish hyperbole, if you prefer: England is the greatest place in the world. Everyplace else is hell, in comparison."

He was so beautiful when he smiled. Esme couldn't help but steal glances as they walked, basking in him. "So . . . What was that, with Miss Edwards today? About the hat and gloves and glasses. You never take them off. What was in that note, that got her off your back? Or am I being too nosy?" She *was* being too nosy, but Zack made her feel at ease. He wasn't at all the flirt she'd expected; just an attractive, funny guy with a very sexy accent.

"Oh, that. I guess everyone will find out eventually. It's called solar urticaria. A rare form of photosensitivity. It's genetic. Dad has it, too."

"So you're sensitive to sunlight? How bad is it?" It hadn't hurt his looks, anyway.

"Oh, a bit worse than an albino I guess. I can't let direct sunlight touch my skin, or I burn horribly. Eyes are extremely sensitive, too. So I have to keep my skin completely covered in the daylight, and wear this industrial-strength sunblock. But at night, I can take off the glasses. I suppose I'd never come out in the day at all if I didn't have to go to school. But Dad, he wants me to have a normal life. Because *he* never could, you see."

"Wow, I'm so sorry. Now I feel like a rat for asking. But I'm glad you told me." She reached out and took his gloved hand in her hand and gave it a squeeze. He felt so natural, so right. She'd had objections to him before, but for the life of her, she couldn't remember them. He was a really nice guy. No wonder girls all liked him. They walked on, holding hands. Esme pointed out the pier and a few historical landmarks while they strolled.

"So," he asked. "Esme. You don't hear that name a lot. With love and squalor?"

So perfect, that he knew that. Everyone knew J. D. Salinger, because of *Catcher in the Rye*, but nobody knew his other stuff. Her copy of *Nine Stories* was dog-eared and ratty with the pages falling out of the binding, she'd read it so many times. "Not Salinger. Think Victor Hugo."

"Ah," he offered, "short for Esmeralda. That doesn't bode well for your giant friend, I'm afraid. But I do have a thing for gypsies."

That was when Esme pulled Zack toward her and kissed him on the cheek. Because he was perfect in every way. And he'd read *The Hunchback of Notre Dame*. And probably . . . oh, everything. Maybe she loved him. She'd never loved anyone else before, but she couldn't think of any other explanation for what she was feeling.

11

PARENT/TEACHER CONFERENCE

"Do come in, Miss Edwards. I'm afraid we weren't expecting you, but perhaps we could scare up a pot of tea." The Ancient held the door open wider to let Zack's history teacher into the entry hall.

"I'm sorry to impose, Mr. Kallas—"

"Please," he said, all charm, taking her hand. "Call me Drake. And you are . . . ?"

"Oh," she replied, feeling a bit light-headed. "Cecilia."

He led her by the arm into the living room, which was rather grandiose, though the furnishings were sparse. The real estate community had been abuzz for weeks about the rich European who'd bought the old Hampstead estate in a cash deal and brought a team of architects from Italy to renovate the place top to bottom in a whirlwind of activity that had employed half the contractors in the county. Laughton Hampstead had been one of the founding fathers of Middleton, and though the family fortune had fallen on hard times, there were still several hundred acres of prime farm and grazing land, now fallow, surrounding the estate.

"Please, have a seat," he insisted, steering her to the sofa. There was an enormous coffee table before it, comfortable armchairs opposite. "Zackery!" he called, though not very loudly, considering the size of the mansion. Zack had impeccable hearing, practically sonar. Like a bat.

Drake took the seat next to Cecilia on the sofa. There was very little space between them, but she didn't mind. She judged Zack's father to be in his late forties, and rousingly attractive. He wasn't wearing a wedding band, which she found intriguing.

"Is your wife at home?" she asked.

"I'm afraid she's departed," he confessed.

She found the information horribly tragic, and exciting.

Zack entered the room from the library. "What is it, Father?" He sized up the situation. The Master had not fed for several days. Zack was also feeling a bit peckish. "Oh, hullo Miss Edwards. In trouble already, am I?"

"Oh, no, Zack," she muttered, blushing. "I was concerned about your condition. I went right home after school and looked up solar urticaria, so I wanted to come by and talk to your father to see if there wasn't something I could do . . . uh . . . that is, we usually have an IEP . . ."

It was dark out, after 8:00, so Zack and Drake were not covered head-to-toe in clothing. The Master wore a smoking jacket and slacks. Zack wore sweats and a red Manchester United soccer jersey with the legend WAZZA across the back and an emblem of a red devil wielding a pitchfork on the front. "Zack, would you get our guest some tea?" the Master said.

"No thank you, I'm fine," Cecilia replied. Though in fact, she was feeling a bit dizzy.

"Does anyone know you've come to see us? Do you have a boyfriend, or someone you live with?" Drake's question, though rather personal, did not seem out of place.

"No, I'm just an old spinster," she demurred, smiling. Twirling hair.

Drake leaned toward the teacher. "Pardon me if I'm being forward, but you have something on your neck. Do you mind?"

Cecilia tilted her head. "Please." She was nothing if not cooperative. Drake licked the fingernail of his index finger, then reached out and scraped a bit of skin near her jugular, as if to remove a smudge. A trick he'd taught Zack very early on. Their saliva was a hundred times as powerful as the pheromones.

"Ooh, that feels nice," she cooed, eyes glazing, neck tilting, her tongue moistening her lips.

Zack liked Miss Edwards. He hoped the replacement teacher would be as nice.

HORMONES

The sisters spent Monday evening pursuing and hiding from each other all over the house. Katy was deliriously happy about the new boy, and wanted input from her sisters on what to wear to school and whether she should kiss him aggressively just to let him know she was into that kind of stuff. She pestered Esme from room to room, fluctuating between giddy joy and anxiety: She'd seen Zack walking the halls with a few other girls during the course of the day. She'd really felt a connection with him, and she was the intuitive one, so she figured she'd know if it wasn't the real thing. "Don't you think? Esme? Right? Don't you think so?"

All this, entirely clueless to the fact that Veronica was in her room, crying rivers into her pillow. When Ronnie stomped through the kitchen to fish a celery stalk out of the refrigerator for dinner, Katy was oblivious. "Did you see him, Ronnie?" she asked, giving Veronica a hug and attempting to dance her around the kitchen. "Isn't he the hottest boy ever?"

Veronica wriggled out of Katy's hug and stiff-armed her, fleeing the kitchen wordlessly.

"Well, what's gotten into her?" Katy asked. She shrugged. "Sometimes I think we've spoiled Ronnie, what do you think?

Esme? Esme! Anyway, like I was saying, he's from England, you should hear how cute he is when he talks . . ."

Esme had to run and hide in her room. She couldn't deal with the guilt. Poor Ronnie, already devastated, and Katy so sure her love was being returned. How utterly destroyed they would be when they found out their big sister was the one Zack really loved. She felt outright horrible about the entire thing. But not horrible enough to give him up.

Veronica knew precisely where Zack got out of his car, so she picked the perfect spot to wait for him before school on Tuesday. She wore her shortest, sexiest skirt and her suede wedge booties, which accentuated her perfect ballerina legs, and her little wire-framed push-up bra, with the—might as well admit it— padding. Boys liked that kind of thing, and anyway, it made her look older. She topped the outfit off with a little bolero jacket with faux fur collar and cuffs that dramatically accentuated her tiny waist. Her blond hair was straight and silky and very long. Her silver pentangle earrings accented her graceful neck. She figured he liked mascara, since he wore enough of it, so she did her vivid blue eyes up in the butterfly effect, perfect for her cartoonishly long lashes. With a precision liner, four shades of mascara and a lash volumizer brush, Veronica could give Modigliani a run for his money. Of course, she had a better canvas to work with.

While applying makeup and preening in the mirror, Ronnie always chanted allure spells under her breath. Nothing that would cause the heavens to split open and hordes of cherubim to emerge with little love arrows; simply a bit of willful influence put out into the cosmos that her grandma Sophie had taught her as a preschooler while brushing her hair and fussing over what a beauty she was. It had served Veronica well, over the years.

Unfortunately, by the time Veronica got to school, her so-called friends Carly and Michaela and Karina had already staked out the spot on the sidewalk that Zack would have to walk past, trying to act cool and failing miserably. She didn't want to be associated with any of that, so she waited on the stairs in front of Hampstead Hall, where she knew Zack had first period.

Veronica had one move for attracting boys: feigned disinterest. Girls at school were already throwing themselves at Zack and he'd only been there for a day, so she planned to stand out as the one girl who wasn't interested. Zack would realize, she reasoned, that she had higher standards, as was her due, being a great beauty and all. She put her earbuds in her ears and fiddled with her iPhone, watching for Zack out of the corner of her eye. She could hear some girls chattering as he approached. She had her back turned, but she could see him in the mirrored surface of her phone cover. Just as he was nearing, Katy ran down the stairs right past her as if she didn't exist. Katy gave Zack a familiar hug, and it was reciprocated. Veronica gritted her teeth stoically. *I couldn't care less, I couldn't care less, I couldn't care less* was her mantra.

Katy took Zack's arm. She'd doubled down on the Gothic Lolita thing today, a bit sexier than Monday's outfit. Zack wore his same boots, with jeans and a motorcycle jacket that went perfectly with his silver-lensed goggles and Ed Hardy skull-and-bones scarf. A different hat today: a derby. They proceeded together, a few girls tagging along but unable to keep up with Katy's energy and quick banter. They mounted the stairs, Katy so oblivious that she didn't even notice her own sister on the first step. But Zack halted as if he'd applied anti-lock brakes while Katy kept ascending stairs, her hand losing its grip on the boy's arm.

"You must be Veronica Silver," he said.

Slowly, Ronnie looked up from her device and hit Zack hard, with the eyes. She tapped the screen a few times, closing apps, and nonchalantly removed the buds from her ears. "Pardon?"

"Aren't you Esme's sister?" he asked.

Veronica shrugged. Pointed to Katy with her chin. "Hers, too." She returned her attention to her phone, as if Zack were boring her already. As if she didn't want to take him in her arms and smooch him mercilessly.

Katy tried to recapture Zack's arm. "This is my baby sister, Ronnie," she said.

Zack didn't even seem to notice Katy was there. "Esme didn't do you justice, when she said you were beautiful. You're a fitty, aren't you? I'm smitten. But you're so horribly *young*."

"Wait," Katy asked. "Where do you know Esme from?"

"We met up for coffee yesterday," Zack replied, pinpointed on Veronica. Around them, a small posse of girls was at the same time pleased to see Katy derailed and dismayed by the new competition.

"Juliet was only thirteen, when she hooked up with Romeo," Veronica said. "And I'll be fifteen soon."

"Yeah, well, Juliet . . . that didn't end well, did it?"

"Oh, don't worry about me," she returned. "I'm more the homicidal type than the suicidal."

"A girl after me own heart," Zack teased.

Veronica checked the time on her phone, replacing the buds in her ears as if Zack didn't even register. "Yeah," she said, scrolling through her playlist, the sarcasm in her tone uninflected. "Like you have a heart." And then she walked away from him.

⌒⊃ ⊂⌒

"Who the hell does he think he is?" Logan Rehnquist asked in a rabble-rousing voice of the other guys in the weight room after school. He'd spied Sandy Hardesty at lunch walking toward the student parking lot arm-in-arm with Zack.

"We should definitely kick his skinny ass all the way back to England," Jackson Gartner agreed, standing in front of the mirror-covered wall, curling 75-pound free weights. "Danny almost cold-cocked him in the hall today; he was talking to Diane."

"I wanna be there to see that," Logan said. "Danny Long could take his damned head off."

Danny was absent from the weight room because the varsity football team had practice five days a week after school. Wilson and Nick were not on varsity, so they had weight training on Tuesdays. They were spotting Norman, who'd earned himself a kind of grudging respect from Logan, Jackson, and Danny by virtue of his mind-boggling feats of strength and his bygones-be-bygones attitude.

"Let's put another coupla dimes on there and go for the record," Wilson told Norman. "I wanna see you bench a thousand."

Norman pumped the weights like a slow, rhythmic machine, a perfect set of ten. With his long arms, the weights had quite a distance to travel, touching his chest on every rep and fully extending. Coach had ordered a special Olympic competition 84-inch bar, and Norm was benching twenty 45-pound steel plates plus a few 10-pound discs. Jackson stopped admiring his biceps in the mirror long enough to watch the giant do his last set.

"Damn, Frankenstein, that's gotta be a world record," Jackson said, no disrespect intended. It was generally agreed in the weight room that "Frankenstein" was an apt nickname.

Norman replaced the bar and sat up, wiping his face with a towel. "Record's like twelve hundred pounds. But they only need to do one rep."

"Norm could beat it," Wilson attested.

"I can't believe I fought you and lived," Jackson joked. "I must have been crazy." He looked over his shoulder to see if he'd upset Logan. The topic was still a sore point.

"You know," Norm told Logan, "there's something not right about that Zack guy. He creeps me out. Like he's a sociopath, or a sexual predator, some kind of . . . I don't know what. Monster. He's bad news. I feel it in my gut."

"I know, right?" Logan concurred. "He's trouble, big trouble, there's really something wrong about him, something . . . I don't know, dangerous. Like, a threat to us all."

"You said the same thing about Norman," Nick reminded him.

"No, Norm's all right," Logan admitted, a huge concession. "I was wrong about you, okay? And I apologized. We're cool now, right? But this Zack guy . . ." Logan shook his head, like shaking off a punch. "Something's not right about him."

"You know, Logan, I totally agree with you," Norm said. "We need to keep an eye on him."

13

RESEARCH

Katy confronted her sisters that very evening, and the rest of the week was spent in accusations, threats, pleas, arguments, and tears. Esme admitted she'd had coffee with Zack and that she found him attractive, and not just physically, and that they'd had a great conversation:

"I mean, I mentioned Victor Hugo, and he knew exactly what I was talking about."

"Victor Who-go?"

"You know, *The Hunchback of Notre Dame?*" Esme clarified. "Quasimodo?"

"Rings a bell," Katy said. "Anyway, it doesn't matter. He's my boyfriend. End of story."

"You might be reading too much into his innocent flirtations."

"Well I saw him first," Veronica said. "So you can both back off. Or else."

"Bring it!" Katy challenged. She turned her back in contempt and stormed off to her room.

"Like she has a chance," Veronica said, walking down the hallway toward her own room.

Esme watched Ronnie go. Apparently, her sisters didn't

consider her much of a threat. She had to admit, between Katy's talent and personality and Veronica's beauty and charm, Esme's brains were not going to give her much of an advantage.

～つ ⌒〇

In her room that weekend, Esme attacked the problem like a complicated research paper. She'd seen Zack around campus with a few girls, notably Sandy Hardesty and Katy, but didn't think much of any other girls at school as competition. Zack liked her. Nobody could fake that. They were comfortable together, genuine. He sat with her in the back of history class every day, and he was so attentive, so engrossed in her take on everything, it was hard to imagine he could possibly be interested in anyone else. But it would be a mistake to discount Katy, with her intimidating talent for the craft. She could resort to jinxes and hexes and spells to get what she wanted. Esme didn't kid herself that she could compete there. Potions, now . . . she'd dabbled in a few, with some success in the past. Katy couldn't even cook a hard-boiled egg.

Veronica, on the other hand, had a ruthless streak that Katy didn't possess. Ronnie had always had a gift for charms, little sing-song spells. Things didn't come as easily to her as they did to Katy, who enjoyed the favor of the cosmos. Katy was so used to winning, she shrugged off the little losses with happy-go-lucky indifference. Ronnie had grown up watching things unfold in Katy's favor time and again. She'd learned to harness her tenacity, to win by refusing to accept defeat. The battle was never over until Ronnie had what she wanted. She had Katy and Esme and their dad wrapped around her fingers. She'd gotten a horse, from their cheapskate father, and dressage lessons, and more clothes than Esme and Katy combined. Veronica was far more intimidating than Katy. Goofy Katy, how could anyone ever take her seriously as a love interest? But Ronnie . . . Ronnie was irresistible. And she knew how to work it.

Esme used her superior brains to look for an advantage, a connection with Zack. First of all, she'd have to lose the glasses and go back to wearing her contacts if she was going to compete with Veronica. But she needed another edge. She researched British accents on the Internet, listening to examples from various regions, eliminating them as she went, using her ear. He was not from London or Liverpool. The vowel sounds were off for Cambridge, the consonants too pronounced for Birmingham. She noted some similarities of usage in Leeds, but Zack had a hard *G* in his *NG* combinations. She looked northeast, to Newcastle, and found the vowels flattening. Zack's vowels were over-enunciated. After three hours of painstaking research, Esme was fairly confident that Zack was from the Manchester area.

A furry body walked across the keyboard. "What are you up to?" Kasha asked. He sat down on her mouse and started licking himself. His whiskers were flecked with blood.

"I'm trying to figure out what soccer team this boy likes." She shoved the cat back.

He lay down on his side with complete indifference. "Why?"

"You wouldn't understand." She typed *Manchester soccer* into her browser.

"Norman likes soccer?" Kasha continued grooming himself. His breath had a carrion stench.

"Not that it's any of your business, but no." There were two major soccer teams in Manchester: City and United.

"You should date Norman," Kasha advised. "You'll never find another one that big."

"What's it to you?" she asked, focusing on stats. She'd need to know team members' names if she wanted to convince Zack she was a fan. She'd have to study the traditional rivalries.

"It looks like I may be your familiar for a while," he mentioned. "I don't want to deal with your boy troubles all the time. Your great-aunt Becky was pretty wild in her heyday; the melodrama was exhausting. Your mother had the right idea, pop out a few daughters, then abandon them for some poor sap to raise while she gallivants off with her lesbian friends."

"You horrible beast!" she said. "My mother did not abandon . . . and who says I want a familiar?"

"I have a contract with your family line, for three generations. Becky was the first, your mother was the second, and now it's either you or one of your sisters. And yes, you do want a familiar, so show some respect. I haven't made a decision yet. I might go with Veronica."

"Not Katy? I thought she was the talented one."

Kasha wrinkled his nose. "I refuse to lend my millennia of expertise to anyone without the sense to prefer cats to dogs. Even *I* think they stink, and I have a fondness for carrion."

Esme was of the same mind, but contrarian that she was, felt obligated to make a halfhearted effort in defense of the canines: "Cats are lazy, indifferent, sadistic little carnage machines capable of feigning affection when they want something."

"Just like people," Kasha argued.

"Dogs are loving and loyal and faithful," she insisted.

"Yeah, what's that all about? Sniveling, brown-nosing syco-phants. Their overall hygiene is deplorable, and their personal habits are disgusting. I've seen dogs eat feces and then lick people on the face, with no consideration of what was just in their mouths."

"Okay, you're right. But why not Veronica?"

"Fine," Kasha said, standing and stretching. "You've never tried casting spells or brewing potions with the help of a demon cat. I have sources of energy I can tap that would boggle your little mortal mind. But you obviously have no interest in witchcraft. I've been watching you for three months and you haven't even cracked that grimoire. All you care about are your stupid grades. I'll cast a little memory spell on my way out, and you'll forget all about the talking cat. Then you can spend the rest of your life watching Veronica get everything her heart desires: fame, money, boys, power, revenge . . . She's more ruthless than you, your little sister. More my type."

"Wait!" Esme said, in a panic. "Who said I didn't want you?" *Veronica, everything her heart desires? Boys?* "I'm a witch, aren't I? And I'm, like, totally a cat person, you know that."

Kasha climbed the cat structure. When he got to the landing by the door, he sat for a moment, grooming himself. Esme had no doubt that if Kasha went out that door, the next day Veronica would have a new pet. And everything she desired. *Everyone.*

"I suppose," he mentioned, "that Veronica would be willing to feed me whatever I wanted."

"I'll feed you whatever you want," Esme blurted immediately. *Demon cat? Did he actually say he was a demon? Was she crazy, making a pact with a demon?*

"I eat first," he negotiated. "Before the other cats. I sleep in your bed when it's cold, or whenever I want. No collars. No flea baths. No vets."

"Of course," Esme agreed.

"That's it," he said, jumping back down off the structure. "Anything else that comes up during our professional relationship, we'll negotiate case by case. I'll switch to Veronica if things don't pan out. The rest of the stuff is ironclad, under the original contract with Becky."

"Okay," Esme said. She noticed that her entire body was shaking with anxiety. Consciously, she made her shoulders relax. She breathed. She was a witch with a demon cat for a familiar. What had she gotten herself into? But Kasha had been her legendary great-aunt Becky's familiar, and her mother's. Both strong women who were nobody's fools. She could do a lot worse than to emulate those two. "Well, let's get to work," she told her familiar.

～౨ ౬～

"What I want to know is, how do I find out something that I don't know the answer for?"

"You've asked the right cat, mistress," Kasha replied. "Have you heard of Google?"

"Google doesn't have the answers I want," Esme explained.

"You'd be surprised." He poked at the keyboard. "How do you make this thing work?"

"Okay," she said, blocking the cat's flailing paw. "Just . . . stop that. The kind of information I want isn't online. I want to find out what Zack's favorite soccer team is, so I can make a connection with him. British boys are crazy for soccer, I know that much."

"So this boy's name is Zack? And both your sisters want him, too?"

"Everyone wants him," Esme explained. "But I think he really likes me."

"Well you're going about it all wrong," the cat admonished. "You're a witch. Don't you have a Ouija board?"

"That would be in Veronica's room. But we haven't played with it since we were kids."

Kasha looked around the room. "There," he said, indicating her bookcase. "You have a Magic 8 Ball."

"It's a toy," she said dismissively.

Kasha licked himself casually. "I'm a demon. You can trust me."

"Can I?"

The demon stared at her with unblinking golden cat's eyes. "Do I look like someone who'd corrupt you just to harvest your soul? Get out your tarot cards."

◦‿つ ⊂‿◦

Esme found the deck on the bookcase, buried behind a stack of YA fantasy. She'd never had much use for the cards, having had disappointing results in the past. Magic never worked for Esme the way it did for Katy. Magic came to Katy naturally, and Veronica was able to willfully focus her faith into spells or readings with the fervor of a snake cultist. Esme was always second-guessing magic. She had a rational, scientific mind and could not accept anything on faith. She needed to know how things worked, which was anathema to the practice of magic. Magic demanded conviction.

"I feel silly doing this." Esme sat cross-legged on the bed, shuffling the deck. It was a new deck, and the artwork was nothing special. Katy had inherited Aunt Becky's deck, which was centuries old with particularly beautiful and grotesque hand-painted artwork. Ronnie had Grandma Sophie's tarot cards, which had been in the family for half a dozen generations at least. "These cards are always cold, for me. I wish I could use Katy's deck."

"Don't worry," Kasha said, stretching out on the pillow. "You have a demon familiar now."

There were a million ways to deal tarot, but Esme preferred the way her mother had taught her. It was the old family method, passed down from witch to witch, through generations of Proctors, the maternal family line, and now Silvers. Four cards to the four directions, east for air, south for fire, west for water, and north for earth. Then she reshuffled the deck and placed it in the center, for spirit. She invoked the spirit for her answers, and flipped the card.

"Death," Kasha noted. "Does that answer your question?"

Esme stifled a yawn. "Uh, no. I was thinking about Zack, actually," she confessed sheepishly.

"And you drew the Death card," the cat noted. "Sounds like a great guy."

"I just forgot to ask the question. And anyway, Death isn't always bad. It could mean a transition." She mucked the deck, shuffled, and dealt the cards out again. She closed her eyes and invoked the spirit, one hand on the deck in the middle of the four cards. "Spirit, I want to know what Zack's favorite soccer team is," she intoned. Then she flipped the card.

"The Devil," Kasha observed.

Esme opened her eyes. She'd just drawn the two worst cards in the deck, one after the other. Talk about ominous. "Wait," she said, excited, hopping up from the bed. She ran to her computer and typed in a URL furiously. "Aha! Manchester United! The Red Devils!"

14

KID SISTER SKILL SET

"Can I catch a ride downtown with you?" Veronica asked, the next Sunday.

Esme started, caught off guard. She'd been sneaking out the cellar door to avoid running into her sisters, but Ronnie was a step ahead of her.

"I, uh . . . wasn't going downtown," Esme lied.

Veronica stood in front of her, hands on hips, glaring accusingly through her sunglasses. "Where were you headed?"

"The library," Esme improvised. It was in town, but not downtown.

"So drop me on Main, if you can't drive two blocks out of your way for your own sister."

On the way into town, Veronica slunk back into her seat, put her feet up on the dash, and fiddled with her smartphone. The car was a four-wheel-drive Subaru station wagon with more than 150,000 miles on it. It still ran well. Veronica was wearing strappy wedge sandals with four-inch heels that made her legs look a mile long. Her crop pants showed just enough calf. "Did you hear about Sandy Hardesty?"

"Yeah, she hasn't been in school. Disappeared off the face of the earth, I heard."

"The police are looking for her," Veronica said. "I heard they called Logan in for questioning. Her parents are really worried."

"Logan's a creep, but he wouldn't do anything bad to his girlfriend."

"Ex-girlfriend," Veronica reminded her. "And another girl disappeared, a barista at Starbucks."

"Miss Edwards? My history teacher? Just vanished, a few weeks ago. She didn't even call in, the school nurse was saying."

"Really," Veronica said. "I never heard about that. Can you drop me at the drug store? I need school supplies." She returned her attention to her phone, turning the ringer all the way down. She slipped the phone into the door pocket, behind some maps.

Esme crossed the bridge and caught the light at Main, cutting left. She wheeled into the parking lot of the drug store. "I don't know how long I'm going to be, you got a way home?"

Veronica opened the door and slid out. "I'll manage, but let me call you when I'm done, maybe you can give me a ride, if you're ready." She started to close the door.

"Ronnie!" Esme called out. Veronica turned. "If a weird-looking guy offers you candy and wants you to get in his car, you know what to do, right?"

"Get you a Snickers?"

"No, seriously. Be careful, okay?" Esme gave her sister a stern look before driving off.

15

DANCE: 10; LOOKS: 3

When you're a giant ugly freak, you wake up in the morning and go to the bathroom and brush your giant ugly teeth. Then you go to your closet and get out your giant ugly clothes that you bought at the big and morbidly obese store in the city because they're the only clothes that fit on your giant ugly body. And you're grateful. Because at least you're alive.

When you're a giant ugly freak, people stare at you and whisper to each other, and you pretend they're not talking about you and try to keep up a cheery disposition and be a good person and not let people piss you off. And when they ask you how the weather is up there, you don't tell them that it's cloudy with a chance of getting their lights punched out. And worse than the rude people are the ones who look at you with pity and say positive, affirming things. As if you had cancer or something.

Norm wished people would stop trying to cheer him up. He was fine. Though he did indulge in the occasional blue mood. *Cynical depression: a pervasive ennui affected by an inability to lie to oneself convincingly.* Esme had loved that line. She so got him.

Norman was happy to be cancer free, happy to have friends. Granted, they were not the kind of friends a boy with his IQ would normally hang out with. But when you're a giant ugly freak, you don't get many choices. You don't let yourself think about stuff you can't have, like nice clothes. Or friends you could have an intelligent conversation with. Or a girlfriend. You don't think about Esmeralda Silver, and the way her hair smells and how the bridge of her nose wrinkles up when you make her laugh. Or what it would be like . . . but you don't let yourself think of those things. You're grateful for what you have. And when your friend asks you to come to his house on a Sunday to help him get an engine out of the junker car he's restoring in the garage, you go and lend a hand. Because that's what friends are for.

"You ready, Norm?" Wilson asked from underneath the car.

"Yeah," Norm said. "Did you disconnect all the bolts?"

"Yeah, that was the last one," Wilson replied. "Engine and transmission mounts are all shot, that's another hundred bucks."

Wilson's dad had bought the car five years earlier, a rag-top '67 Mustang, to restore with his son. It was supposed to be a present for his sixteenth birthday, but that was before the divorce. Sixteen had come and gone, and Wilson was still riding his bicycle to school. Wilson's dad couldn't afford to buy parts. Alimony was expensive. Wilson was always complaining about the cost of all the parts he needed. So he skimped on some expenses. Like a shop crane.

"How much did you say this weighed?" Norman asked.

"Five hundred pounds," Nick replied.

"Plus the trannie," Wilson reminded him.

"Six fifty, tops," Nick said. "Just be glad he doesn't have the big block."

"We'll help," Wilson promised, scooching out from under the car.

"No, I got it. It's just a little awkward, is all."

It was tight, squeezing his thick arms around the engine, but Norm was able to get a grip and heave. He had to angle it out because of the transmission. He was carrying the engine across the garage to the engine stand when Jackson Gartner drove his large black pickup into the driveway. Danny Long and Logan Rehnquist jumped out.

"Damn, Frankenstein, my dad's got a half dozen shop cranes you could borrow," Danny said. He grabbed the front of the engine and helped Norman muscle it onto the stand. "Not like that, face it around the other way. Wilson, you idiot, why didn'tcha disconnect the trannie first?"

"Didn't have the tools," he mumbled.

"Come on, Danny," Logan demanded. "We don't have time for this." He addressed Norm, Nick, and Wilson: "You guys seen Zack anywhere?"

Norman wiped his face with a relatively clean shop rag. "Zack?" He shrugged.

"We don't hang out in the same circles," Wilson said.

"Well if you see him, we're looking for him."

"Sure, no prob," Wilson replied. "What're ya lookin' for him for?"

Jackson Gartner had a stack of flyers in his hand. He peeled off a page and handed it to Nick. "Town's organizing a search party for Sandy."

Norm read the flyer. "It's today. Shouldn't you guys be out looking?"

"I wanna ask Zack some questions," Logan said. "He's the last one to see her."

"They're meeting up at Miller's Field," Norman read. "An hour ago. Where's that?"

"Halfway to Mason's Crossing," Danny said. "That's where they found her car."

Norm looked at Nick, then at Wilson. "You guys want to go look?"

"Nah, it's too late," Wilson said. "You gotta be there on time."

"If you see him, call us," Logan reminded as the three returned to Jackson's truck.

There wasn't much to do on the Mustang except stand around and look at the engine and listen to Wilson reiterate how much all the parts were going to cost him and how long it would take to get the money. At about noon, Wilson's mom served the boys hot dogs and chips and iced tea in the backyard.

"Wow, too bad about Sandy," Nick said, taking a hot dog. He slathered on mustard and ketchup from the squeeze bottles. "Do you think Zack knows anything?"

"I don't know," Norm said, grabbing two hot dogs in one hand. "The guy creeps me out, but what would he have done with her? Kill her? I don't know if I'm ready to accuse him of that."

"I saw him all over school with Sandy," Wilson said.

"I see him all over school with a lot of girls," Nick reasoned. "All three of the Silver sisters. That's gotta piss you off, doesn't it, Norm?"

"You and Esme," Wilson added. "You like her, don't you?"

"She's okay."

"As long as you're fantasizing about girls you can't have, you might as well fantasize about Veronica," Nick suggested.

"Naw, she doesn't do it for me," Wilson said. "I like a girl with . . . you know, like Sandy."

" 'Orchestra and balcony,' " Nick said.

"Huh?" Wilson stared at his friend.

Nick sang: " 'What they want is whatcha see . . .' " He looked back and forth between the two blank expressions. "It's from *A Chorus Line*. Balcony, that's the breasts. And orchestra—"

"Yeah, I get it," Norm interrupted. Boy talk. Here he was in the thick of it. Objectifying girls for their physical attributes. It always made him a little uncomfortable.

"Well you can have all the Sandys," Nick allowed. "I'll take Veronica Silver any day. Every boy wants to be her, every girl wants to date her." Nick looked up from his glazed reverie a moment later to find Norm and Wilson staring at him with complete incomprehension. "Oh yeah," Nick said. "Reverse that."

16

TWO'S COMPANY

Veronica stood in the parking lot of the Rite Aid, watching Esme drive away. She removed Katy's phone from her handbag and entered the security code. Katy was easy to hack, with a little talent and an old Ouija board. She opened up the tracking app and set it to track her phone. Esme was headed south on Main Street. The library was north. Three blocks, five. Main Street came to a T at Hampstead. Esme turned right, toward the junior college. After five blocks, the car stopped, near the corner. Veronica waited a few more minutes. Esme was definitely parked, in front of the coffee shop. Ronnie slung her bag higher on her shoulder and headed for Main Street. It was a ten-minute walk, fifteen at most.

~ ᦕ ᦕ ~

Zack rose, smiling, when Esme arrived at the coffee shop. He kissed her on the cheek and gave her a hug, looking at her with his head tilted. "I can't decide if I liked you better with the glasses or now. Both, I guess." Then he held her chair out for her. "I'll get us some coffee, what'll ya have, luv?"

"Grande Guatemalan," she answered, and he went off to order. He'd called her "love." Just an expression, of course, but still . . .

She slipped her laptop out of the carrying case, opened it on the table, and powered it up. She'd taken care to recharge the battery before leaving the house, but she had the cord just in case. She looked around to see if there was an outlet handy.

Esme watched Zack from behind, which was almost as good as from in front. The coffee shop was nearly deserted. Football game at the college. Zack was wearing tight black jeans and his boots and a Red Devils sports jacket and a bowler hat.

"One Guatemalan, for the lady," Zack said on returning. "I got one for m'self as well. Figured you knew what you were on about."

"I like the coffee here better." She did, in fact, and the privacy. "It's shade grown, organic, and fair trade. I try to avoid exploitation in my cup of joe."

"I love your Yankee slang," he said. "And that you care about things like that. Fair trade, and all. And the Red Devils, of course."

She blushed. "Yeah, how crazy is that, we both like the same football team?"

"And I never mentioned that I was from Manchester area," he noted, puzzling over the coincidence. "How did you end up a fan of Manchester United?"

"Oh, you know," she demurred. "I played when I was a girl. Girls' soccer league. So I always liked it. But American soccer is, uh . . ."

"I know. Rubbish."

"Yeah, so I started watching European football on the Internet. You played, right?"

"I was a striker. Star of me school team," he declared with pride.

"I'll bet. Anyway, I couldn't understand the announcers, so eventually I just stuck with English games. I love the slang terms—you'll have to explain them to me I guess."

"My pleasure. So, what did you bring? I can't thank you enough for this, we don't have Internet at our house, Dad's so old-fashioned."

"Manchester versus Arsenal, last week," she said, as if it was nothing at all. Though it was huge, she knew. *Stick with me, baby, there's more where that came from.*

"I bloody love you, you're brill." He hugged her with shocking strength, and kissed her on the cheek. "I'm chuffed, have you watched it yet?"

"No," she said, tingling from the kiss. *Six times.* "I was waiting to see it with you." She'd memorized some of the Arsenal team's players by the numbers on their jerseys.

"You're the best. But I'll be totally gutted if they lose, I have to warn you. Bloody Islington. I hate them more than Chelsea."

"Me too," she agreed, caught up in his pleasure. Garcia, the new striker, would score the winning point just under the wire, but Zack was in for a rough time, it was a nail-biter. *Don't worry, Zack, I'll be there to comfort you.*

"Listen, you said you'd downloaded it, would you like to watch it at me house? No worries, Dad's there, if we need a chaperone."

"Uh, yeah, I guess." Esme tried not to appear too eager.

"Do you need to call somebody? You said you had to sneak out to meet me," he reminded her.

"It's really not anybody else's business where I go or who I meet," she asserted. "But you know . . . Katy. I guess she has a thing for you. You probably noticed."

"I wouldn't want to cause any problems between you and your sister," he said, "but Katy and I are just friends. She's a great kid, that one."

"What she doesn't know won't hurt her."

"Okay," he said. "Listen, let's take my car."

The two finished their coffees and started to pack up their gear, rising. The door opened and a girl walked in. Esme went into panic mode. Veronica. This was no coincidence.

"Hey, big sister," Veronica said, giving Esme a hug and a kiss on the cheek. "I thought you were going to the library. I wanted coffee and I remembered you telling me about this place."

Zack watched the two, beaming. "Hello, Veronica, lovely to see you again."

When Zack looked at Veronica, his face lit up. Even through his heavily tinted sunglasses, Esme noted the dilation of the eyes, the brows raised in focus. Zack was interested in Ronnie. With her hair, her makeup, her clothes, and the poise of her slim, graceful figure, Ronnie had never been more attractive. In her heels, the height advantage gave her an air of maturity. Zack had been totally into Esme not a moment before; suddenly she felt invisible next to her dazzling kid sister.

"Hey, Zack," Ronnie said, as if she didn't care. But she was sending him signals. There was an enigmatic smile there, pure flirtation at the highest level of execution.

"Esme and I were just headed to me house to watch a football game on her computer," he mentioned. "Do you like football? We can all watch together."

She wrinkled her nose in distaste. "American football? Those nasty sweaty guys with all the padding? I'll pass. I like soccer. Those men with their sexy legs get me hot."

"That's what I mean," he said, brimming with magnetism. "I'm from England, remember?"

She giggled and put her hand on his upper arm. "Oh, right. Well, in that case . . ."

"Shall we, then, ladies?" Zack said, facing the door and offering an arm to each sister.

Outside the coffee shop, the three stood beneath an old hawthorn tree, bare of leaves. It was mid-November, and the sun was weak, but there was no cloud cover. Esme considered Zack's condition. "We should get you out of the sun," she suggested, and he gave her a hug. It made her feel a little better. Zack was such a likeable fellow, you couldn't fault him for liking your sister. He had good taste, at least.

"Do your parents know you're going to be late?" he asked, looking at his watch. "It could be a long game."

"We're fine," Veronica assured.

"Let's take my car. I know where all the potholes are in our driveway."

"Gimme the keys, Esme," Veronica demanded. "I need to get something out of the Subaru."

Esme was sorting through her purse for the keychain when they heard a loud engine roar up, and a squeal of brakes. A shiny black Dodge Ram backed up noisily, engine revving. Mud was artfully splattered on the lower half, as if it had been washed and waxed and then taken off-road into a mud puddle just long enough to prove the driver was a rough-and-tumble sort.

"That's him!" yelled Logan Rehnquist, riding shotgun. The door flew open and Logan jumped out carrying a baseball bat.

A second later, Danny Long opened the back door on the passenger side and followed. Jackson Gartner backed the truck up over the curb at an angle and parked it halfway across the sidewalk.

Zack dropped his elbows and pushed the girls behind him protectively. It was surprising, how strong he was. Veronica and Esme were just moved back like children.

"Hello, gents," Zack said amiably. "Lovely day for a drive."

17

AN UNEQUAL AND OPPOSITE REACTION

"We've been looking for you all over," Logan growled menacingly.

"And now you've found me," Zack acknowledged.

"What did you do to Sandy?" Logan raged. "She was with you, and now she's gone."

Logan crowded Zack, chest to chest. Esme had seen Logan pick fights before, but this was different. This time he had a crazed look in his eyes. He had spittle in the corners of his mouth. Zack did not back down, though Logan had four inches and fifty pounds on him. He placed a hand on Logan's chest and pushed him back. Logan's body remained rigid, but his feet slid backward in the hard-packed dirt. Esme couldn't work the physics of that. No matter how much force was applied, the smaller body should be the one to move backward. People don't just go around breaking Newton's Laws of Motion.

"You were the one sent the police 'round me house, weren't you?" Zack accused. "The police were satisfied that I 'ad nothing to do with Sandy's disappearance."

"You did something, I know it," Logan hissed, struggling against Zack's palm. In his right hand Logan held the baseball bat, and he looked angry enough to use it.

"You better back off now, Logan, okay?" Veronica said. "I know, you're upset about Sandy. We all are. Everybody liked Sandy, okay? But Zack doesn't know anything about it. If he did, the police would have taken him in, don't you think?"

"I saw her get into her car and follow him," Logan accused.

"She did," Zack replied calmly. "I saw her in the rearview mirror, and I sent her home. I already explained all this to the police. They found her car, in Miller's Field."

"He's lying," Jackson said.

"We can make you tell us the truth," Danny snarled.

Esme tugged at Zack's elbow. "They're always starting fights, Zack. Let's just go, okay?" It was like trying to push a statue with a feather duster. Zack was rigid.

"I'm not intimidated by you oafs," Zack said calmly. "I don't have to explain myself. So I suggest you all sod off. Or else."

Boys. So pretty to look at, so impossible to reason with. "Zack, there are three of them."

"And they're much bigger," Veronica added. She pulled at Zack's other arm, to no effect.

Zack turned his back to the bullies. "You girls don't think I can beat them, do you?"

"Zack, that's not the point," Esme said.

"Come on," Veronica coaxed. "You don't have to prove anything."

Zack looked from Esme to Veronica and back. "Apparently, I do." He turned back around to face Logan. "Name the time and place."

"Right now," Logan said decisively. "At the cove."

"Do either of you know where this cove is?" Zack asked the girls.

Neither Veronica nor Esme would answer him. They tried to look away. It was tragic. He was so young, so beautiful. *What would his face look like, after?* Esme wondered.

"I'll follow you in my car," Zack suggested to Logan.

～ つ ｅ ～

Veronica and Esme didn't want to watch Zack get creamed, but they got in the car with him. There was nothing they could do to stop him. Esme tried to think of a spell or anything she could do. Veronica was working through playing the heroine, boldly stepping in at some point and putting herself physically between Logan and Zack, before things got out of hand. And then nursing her poor broken boy back to health with hugs and kisses.

The cove was on the east bank of the Susquahilla, about two miles north of town. The river bent in at the spot and a crescent-shaped beach of soft, dirty-blond sand provided a bathing spot in the summer. There was an ancient red oak tree bent out over the water with a rope swing for jumping off, and a clearing off the beach among the trees where people parked their cars away from the road. In the fall it was usually deserted in the daytime, though it was a frequent arrest spot in the evening, because police patrolled a service road on the opposite bank and watched for beach fires or the flash of blunts being lit. Stoners rarely thought these things through.

Logan still had his baseball bat in his hand as the three got out of Jackson's truck. Danny pulled off his warm-up jacket, tossed it aside, and rolled his shoulders back and forth, the muscles rippling under his tank top. Jackson held back a bit and circled behind Zack.

"All three at once," Zack commented. "I'd expect no more of a bunch of Yanks. Explains how we lost a war to you."

"I'm going to beat the crap out of you," Logan explained, "and then we'll keep beating you until you tell us what happened to Sandy."

"Lovely," Zack replied. "Is the baseball bat necessary? Because if you try to use that on me, I promise to take it away from you and ream you a new orifice."

Logan looked at the bat in his hand, then tossed it aside. "Maybe later, if my fists get tired."

Zack turned back to Esme and Veronica. "I wish you two hadn't insisted on coming. Please don't judge me too harshly for what I'm about to do to these chaps. I grew up in a rough neighborhood, I don't know how to play gentle."

"Let's do this," Danny said.

Logan was bouncing back and forth on the balls of his feet. He was too riled up to worry about proper martial arts form. And anyway, Zack was much smaller. Logan charged in, fist drawn back. Zack took a quick step forward at the last possible second and met Logan with force. With unnatural speed and agility, Zack dodged the descending fist and bashed Logan with an open palm squarely in the chest. Logan was lifted two feet off the ground and propelled backward at least three yards. There was a popping sound, like a string of small firecrackers going off in quick succession: all of Logan's ribs breaking like tumbling dominoes.

"Make sure he's still breathing," Zack instructed Esme, as he moved toward Danny Long.

Esme ran to Logan's side and checked to see if he still had a pulse. Danny was stumbling away, dazed by the sheer brutality of the strike. Zack pursued him. Danny changed direction and charged forward, head down, with the same force he used to barrel through offensive lines of very large high school athletes.

Veronica shut her eyes. Danny had a hundred-pound weight advantage. Zack swung an uppercut with precision at Danny's jaw. It was like a charging rhino meeting a swinging wrecking ball: The rhino's head snapped back. When she opened her eyes, Danny was lying on the ground, colder than a polar vortex, an assortment of teeth scattered around him and blood puddled from his distorted, shattered jaw. Her stomach churned in revulsion and she turned away. Why had Danny made Zack do that to him?

Jackson Gartner was no hero. He eyed the fallen bat on the ground but had enough sense not to pick it up. Danny's face was just a bloody, shattered mess, and Logan was lying at a very unnatural angle. And the most devastating, vicious fighter he'd ever seen was walking casually toward him. He held up his hands defensively. "Whoa, Zack . . ."

"Jackson," Zack said. "I want you to tell your friends, when they wake up"—he looked over his shoulder at Logan and Danny—"*if* they wake up, that is. Tell 'em I don't know what happened to Sandy, all right? I told her I wasn't interested in her as a girlfriend. She's a nice girl, but not really my type. She was crying; I hope you don't think I'm a cad, I had kissed her a few times, but I didn't want to lead her on. And after that, nobody ever saw her again. I feel a little guilty about what happened, but I didn't have anything to do with her disappearance. If you blokes had asked me nicely, I'd have told you that."

"I believe you, Zack," Jackson sputtered, still moving away defensively. He'd believe anything that left his teeth in his mouth.

"Do you want to help me get them into the truck? You can drive them to hospital."

After Logan and Danny were loaded into the bed of the truck, Zack spoke privately to Jackson and Logan. The Master had taught Zack the ancient technique to put the terror into a person. Zack spoke in an ominous voice, low pitched and deadly solemn. The voice caused such fear in Jackson that he lost control of his bladder. It was like worms crawling through his skull. Logan cringed in fright. The idea of defying Zack would never occur to either of them.

"You will tell nobody what happened here today," Zack intoned. "You three ran into some tough blokes in town for the football game, and you got into a fight with them. You don't know who they are, and you can't remember what they looked like, or what kind of car they had."

"Sure, Zack," Jackson agreed. His quick acquiescence did nothing to ease the fear.

"Because if you don't, I will hunt you all down," Zack portended. "And I won't take it easy on you, like I did this time." And then Zack punched Jackson, not hard enough to concuss, but hard enough to crack a cheekbone and loosen half his teeth and blacken his eye. "Sorry, I had to do that. Nobody would believe you were in a fight otherwise."

⁓ ⌣ ⁓

"I'm truly sorry you had to witness all that," Zack apologized as he drove the girls back to their car after the fight. "I simply cannot abide bullies. Sandy was a wonderful girl. I cared for her a lot, as a friend. I'd never harm her. It was a right awful thing to accuse me of." He spoke in a low hypnotic tone, repeating himself several times until he could extract, with confidence, promises from Esme and Veronica, who agreed not to discuss the fight with anyone. Zack seemed so remorseful that he'd allowed himself to be drawn into a fight, and horrified at how he'd lost his temper and injured the boys so severely. But both sisters, independently, had the same thought: There was something terribly dangerous, and at the same time devastatingly attractive, about a boy who could fight like that.

As they said their good-byes at the coffee shop, Veronica watched Esme move in for a hug. Esme promised Zack that they'd watch the soccer game another time. She kissed him on the cheek, and he kissed her the same way.

And then it was Veronica's turn. She gave Zack a hug, and then kissed him. On the lips. She put one hand on his neck, holding him there, and he kissed back, parting lips. Tongues came into play. It was hard for Veronica to remember later, because her mind was entirely blown. She knew unambiguously that it was love; she felt it in every fiber of her being. As if a big dish of quivering Jell-O could have fiber. He encircled her waist with his hands, hands that had felled Danny Long with a single blow. It was indescribable, the kiss. Time stopped. Her heart was pounding like a farrier's hammer on a white-hot horseshoe, sparks flying . . . She'd kissed at least a dozen boys, playing spin-the-bottle or seven minutes in heaven, but this was different. This was real. They might have been there for hours, for all she knew. All she could remember later, when they came up for air, was the expression on Esme's face.

18

ROCK, SCISSORS, HAND GRENADE

Veronica sat at her vanity that evening, gazing at her reflection dreamily. Her room was lacy and girly, all in pink: bubblegum walls and hot pink semigloss window trim and floorboards. The pink was offset by sharply contrasting black accents: stark, bold curtains and contemporary black furniture that cut into all the cute and made it edgy, despite the stuffed animals and dressage ribbons and trophies on all the shelves and stacked on her dresser.

She had a boyfriend. The one boy who every girl in school wanted, who her two big sisters wanted. Veronica fiddled with her bottles of nail polish, her lipsticks and eyeliners, tubes of moisturizer and bottles of toner. She'd chanted allure charms and glamour spells and placed hexes of enticement over every item on her vanity, and she always chanted more, sing-song, while applying makeup or brushing her hair. Grandma Sophie had taught her that repetition and redundancy added layer after layer of potency to magic. Ronnie had one particular bloodred Yves Saint Laurent lipstick that could practically go out and pick up boys on its own.

Veronica had feared Katy at first, and her talent. All the witches in the Wiccan community were always going on about Katy. But when she'd found out that Esme was actually going out on dates with Zack, she'd had to reevaluate the competition. Esme was intimidating in so many ways. Ronnie never could figure out what was going on in the chewy center of that Tootsie Pop head. But ultimately, they hadn't stood a chance. Katy was talented, sure, and Esme was smart. But Ronnie was the most beautiful, and in the game of love, beauty would always win.

～ ⌒〇

Everyone always expected Esme to just bow out gracefully, to be reasonable. Katy always got her way, and Esme was supposed to just shrug and give in, because the cosmos favored Katy, and who could argue with the cosmos? Or Veronica, who never quit until she got what she wanted. And Esme always let her get away with it, to keep the peace. But not this time. Esme knew she had something special with Zack. Veronica had to be using her little allure spells and beauty magic to steal him from her. There was no other explanation for what she'd seen when her sister had kissed him. Obviously, Zack was under Ronnie's spell.

Esme had gone to Katy's room and told her about the kiss, and how Ronnie had broken the Wiccan Rede and used spells to get Zack to like her. They could only use spells to defend a member of the coven, or a female in distress. Using spells to steal a boy from your own sister was strictly taboo. Esme confessed to Katy that she was still working through her feelings about Zack, but felt that Ronnie had crossed the line. Before she left Katy's room, she gave her sister a hug, and promised that whatever happened with Zack, she would abide by his decision. Then she returned to her room. She sat at her desk, riffling through the pages of the grimoire, looking for ideas. All the puppet master had to do now was sit back while Katy and Ronnie went at each other, and then use her superior brains to win Zack once and for all. She had to make sure her sisters never suspected, though. She was well aware of the dynamics of three sisters. As soon as two joined against one, it was all over.

Kasha tried to make himself useful. "Here's one that'll make Veronica's hair all fall out," the cat suggested, looking over Esme's arm at the grimoire.

Esme imagined, briefly, what Veronica would look like bald. Still pretty damned hot, she decided. "I'm not cursing my sister," she said, turning to the next page.

"Try to find one that will make someone's butt smell like carrion," Kasha suggested.

"For Ronnie, or Katy?"

"For me," said the cat. "The ladies likey."

"Your butt could already gag a maggot at fifty paces."

Kasha rubbed his neck against her face. "That's the nicest thing anyone's ever said to me."

Esme turned to the next page. It was the start of another potion, and it went on for four pages, with all kinds of notations from generations of great-great-aunts and great-great-great-grandmothers, scrawled in tiny script on scraps of paper. "Here's one. A love potion."

Kasha's eyes gleamed. "Perfect. I was hoping you'd turn dark. I haven't had any action for ages."

Esme was trying to translate the Latin names of the ingredients, which took up almost two pages. There were dozens upon dozens of steps to the potion. "Turn dark? What do you mean?"

"Dark, light . . . just two sides of the same coin," Kasha said dismissively.

Esme noticed the word *CAVEAT* in big script on the first

page, right below *Amatorium*. She flipped to the next page. She could get a lot of the botanicals from her mother's apothecary chest. "Why would you turn dark for making a love potion?" One of the mustiest-looking notes stuffed into the grimoire by an ancestor had warnings not to use the potion, on threat of *damnafion of thyne immourtal foul*.

"Making the potion isn't too bad. It's when you sneak it into someone's drink that you go over to the dark side. To defy another person's free will by corrupting his love? But it's a hoot to make, invoking iffy spirits, slathering on the blood of innocents . . . really fun stuff. Just ignore all those old rumors about how enslaving someone for your selfish desires is seven times worse than murder on the karmic scale." Kasha stood and stretched. "Of course, with a demon cat for a familiar, you can skip a few steps, but you still have to convert some of your shiny white creative energy into dark entropy to make the potion work. Let's get started!"

Esme looked up from the book. She had the creepiest sense of foreboding. Perhaps it was the shadows in the room, but Kasha was looking far more menacing than usual. "What do creative energy and entropy have to do with it?"

"Don't you find your mind-numbing ignorance embarrassing? Try to keep up: There's chaos, or entropy, and there's order, or creative energy. I'm a demon, so I'm on the side of chaos. The angels like to use the words 'good' and 'evil,' but that's just propaganda—"

"Wait. There are angels?"

"Don't ask stupid questions," he chastised. "There can't be creation without destruction. These forces we're playing in are the exact same energies and entropies that have been roiling around for billions of years. The tides shift back and forth a bit, kind of a cosmic tug-of-war, but everything falls apart eventually."

"That makes sense, thermodynamically," she agreed.

"Anyway, demons nurture entropy and harvest decaying energies and bring them to chaos, whereas the other side nurtures creative energies."

"So they're the good guys."

Kasha hissed. "You are so dense, it's amazing your head doesn't implode from the gravitational force of your own stupidity. There's no such thing as good or evil."

"Somehow, I think that's a one-sided argument."

"Well we do lie quite a bit," Kasha admitted. "Like a little white lie. Only huge, and black."

"I don't think I want to turn dark," Esme said.

"Before you condemn it, why don't you try it?" The cat cajoled. "I have a quota."

Normally, Esme would have picked apart every word out of Kasha's mouth, cross-examined him, deconstructed his reasoning, and dissected his lies. But she found her mind wandering, thinking about Zack, so she just shrugged it off. "Oh, look," she said, excited, flipping pages. "A beauty potion."

Katy's converted attic was very pleasant in the late fall, because the heat in the house always rose. Around the room were various instruments, including an electric keyboard, a classical guitar, and an accordion. Katy was competent in all of these, but she totally rocked the accordion, the dorkiest instrument of all time. She was a fool for zydeco.

There was an easel with a low stool and a half-finished

abstract-impressionist landscape in purples and greens. There was a drafting table in the corner with more art supplies, mostly art pastels, and *fude* brushes with ink stones for Japanese calligraphy. There were colorful Indonesian batik sheets hanging from the sloping ceiling, covering the aluminum joists and the rough, unfinished oak rafters, giving the attic a gypsy tent atmosphere.

Katy was in a foul mood. Her traitorous sister had swooped in and stolen her boyfriend. And the real crime of it was that Katy and Zack had something special. She was the only one who truly *got* him. He was wasted on Veronica, with her sneaky little allure spells and incantations. He was blinded by her, manipulated.

Nobody understood Zack the way Katy did. Zack loved to laugh, to banter. But under the cheery demeanor he had a dark, poetic soul. There was some terrible tragedy about him that nobody but Katy could see. She and Zack shared the artist's temperament. They could brood. They were complex, like icebergs, with ninety percent of their angst and pathos below the surface. Esme didn't truly understand him. And he was too good for a sneak like Veronica, creeping around, taking people's cell phones, spying, hacking, and manipulating with her little psychodrama flirtations.

Katy swung her legs off her bed. Six muzzles came off the floor. Dervish, the whirling pit bull, rose to meet her, head low, tail wagging. Dervish would rip out someone's throat for Katy. Kewpie, the bipolar golden retriever, would jump up on them with muddy paws. Socrates, the bearer of kisses, would nip at their hamstrings. Gordon, the lionhearted bulldog, would pee on them. Edna, the lap dog in the body of a Great Dane, would slobber all over them mercilessly. And Kilroy, the mischievous mutt, would knock them on their ass and sniff their crotch until they cried uncle. Katy Silver, leader of the pack, was not someone to be trifled with.

She stood in front of her full-length mirror. Compared to Veronica she was a troll. She wasn't fat, just curvy. But next to Veronica, she was a tub of lard. Ronnie had the game rigged, with her charms and spells. It made Katy mad. Ronnie should know better than to make Katy mad.

Katy focused her ire, her humiliation, her indignation. She let all the resentment stew and churn. A breeze blew up around her, like a miniature tornado. It blew around her hair, stirring it. Her eyes started to glow, like a dog's eyes in the headlights of a car at night. Static danced around her, buzzing. She raised her right arm, and the static pooled in her open hand, glowing like tiny lightning dancing over the landscape of her palm. The lights flickered in her electro-phantasmagoric aura. Katy suddenly squeezed her hand to a fist and brought her arm down at a sweeping angle, like a conductor stopping the entire orchestra at once. Everything was silent, the air still. But she still had a trace of the glow in her eyes.

"Come on, guys," Katy said to her pack, shaking the eerie eldritch energies off. "Time to go outside and poop."

19

BIO HAZARD

Second-period AP biology had become a slog for Esme. How had she ever enjoyed the thought of it? It was just something to get through, waiting for world history, and Zack. The material was nearly impossible to keep up with, these last two weeks. Information didn't go into Esme's brain the way it always had. Lisa Vaughn was in the same doldrums as everyone else, so Esme figured it was all just the fault of the convoluted, confusing material.

Norman confronted Esme on the way out the door, and followed her to her next class. "Esme, wait up!" Norm's leg brace had been off for weeks now, he had just had his bolts removed from his neck, and he was barely limping anymore. His long legs were more than a match for Esme's.

"I've gotta go, Norm," Esme insisted. The last thing she needed was to be seen with the freakiest guy in school, in case she ran across Zack. She couldn't be tagged ugly by association, not with Veronica looking more spectacular every day.

"Esme, I saw your test score in biology," he said, steering her with one hand toward a bank of lockers on the wall. "A sixty-five? You've never gotten anything less than an A in your life. What's wrong with you? You've been acting like a fool. Why are you avoiding me?"

Esme tried to look around him, to see if anyone had noticed them, but looking around Norman Stein was no easy task. "Leave me alone, Norm. I screwed up, okay? The test is graded on a curve, and I know for a fact Lisa Vaughn got a sixty-one. It was a very hard test; I'll bet top grade was like seventy or something."

Norman pulled a piece of paper out of his shirt pocket and unfolded it in front of her—his bio test, with a score of one hundred on it. "I had the top score, Esme. Stephan Reese got a ninety-eight, and Brandon had a ninety-six. It was a piece of cake. Your sixty-five is a D. Have you ever gotten a D before?"

Esme had never even gotten a B before. "So I had a bad test. Look, I need to get to class."

"I'm really worried about you," he said. "I think you might have walking pneumonia or something. You look delirious. Why don't you come over to my house after school and meet my dad? He has an office with a research lab there; he can give you a diagnosis in ten minutes. And I know you wanted to meet him."

"I'm fine, Norman." She had to get away. Zack always walked past Main Hall between second and third. She could still bump into him, if she hurried. Otherwise, she'd have to wait until fourth period. "Just back off, okay?"

She scrambled away from the giant, avoiding the hurt look in his mismatched eyes. She walked as quickly as she could without running, striding with determination out the side door. She clipped the corner of the quad on a well-worn path through the grass, rounding the stairs to the landing in front. She noticed Zack, his back to the quad, talking to somebody by a section of wall at the side of the building, obscured by a tall hedge.

The girl with Zack was short and wore jeans and a Middleton Timberwolves hoodie with a silhouette of a gray wolf baying at a gray moon on a background of twilight purple. She had fine reddish hair draped over her face. Her hand was on Zack's upper arm. Esme slowly backed away. Lisa Vaughn, again. The girl had been a thorn in her side since sixth grade, and here she was, trying to horn in on Zack.

Esme was furious the rest of the day, though when she sat with Zack in history class, she didn't say anything. The beauty potion could take several weeks, depending on the availability of the ingredients. Kasha had called it the "Irresistible Beauty Potion." It would do the trick.

∼‿∽

That night, Esme tossed and turned over the Lisa thing. It was always Lisa, dogging her, nipping at her heels. She considered a few choice hexes, just to amuse herself. She didn't know that Lisa would not return to school the next day. Lisa would just disappear.

20

QUALITY TIME

Detective Robert Sharp's second visit to the old Hampstead Manor to interview Drake Kallas and his son, Zackery, came two weeks after the first. For backup, he brought a uniformed officer, First Sergeant Manuel Hernandez, a nine-year veteran. They arrived in a squad car at dusk, because they knew about the rare skin condition the father and son shared, and Sharp preferred not to interview suspects wearing sunglasses. The eyes were the best tell.

"Do you mind if we come in, Mr. Kallas?" the detective asked at the door. "I want to ask your son a few more questions about those disappearances we'd discussed."

"Certainly, come in, gentlemen," Drake allowed.

Zack was on the living room floor in front of the coffee table, his world history homework spread before him.

"Zack, Officer Sharp had a few more questions for you. Of course, he had nothing to do with the disappearances," Drake insisted in an easy, rhythmic voice. He stared into Officer Martinez's eyes as he said it, nodding. Martinez was nodding his head in imitation.

"Nothing to do with it?" Martinez repeated, slowly.

"We haven't charged you with anything," Sharp noted,

blinking his eyes rapidly as if he'd just caught himself nodding off. "As I mentioned last time, an eyewitness saw Sandy Hardesty get out of Zack's car in the parking lot of the Ace hardware store on the night she disappeared."

"Zack had nothing to do with the girl's disappearance," the Master intoned hypnotically.

Martinez seemed to be on the same page. He nodded his head along with the Master, a slightly glazed look in his eyes. "Nothing to do with it," he agreed.

"You've already said that," Sharp pointed out. "That's what I'm here to find out. Martinez!"

The sergeant's head snapped forward, as if he'd awakened with a start. "Sir?"

"Zack," Sharp said, returning his attention to the boy. "The eyewitness says you kissed Sandy in that parking lot, on the lips. Is that true?"

"More on the cheek," Zack said. "But yes. I had nothing to do with her disappearance."

Martinez agreed, nodding back. "You weren't even there," he said.

"Sergeant Martinez, would you please stay out of this!" Sharp said angrily.

"Sorry, sir," Martinez replied, giggling.

"Zackery, according to the witness, Miss Hardesty got into her car and followed you out of the parking lot. The witness said that where Miss Hardesty should have turned left on Main Street to get home, she turned right and followed your vehicle. The witness is certain she turned left on Hampstead, following your car." Detective Sharp was reading from a small spiral notepad, which he was flipping from page to page for effect.

"Who was the witness?" Drake asked. "Where is he now?"

"Logan Rehnquist," Martinez volunteered. He looked like he'd had a few drinks. "He's inna hospital. On se-day-shun."

"Martinez, that information was classified," Sharp said angrily. "Go wait in the car."

"Hokay," Martinez volunteered, and headed out on his own. He almost bumped into the doorjamb on his way out of the living room.

"Sandy did follow me," Zack admitted. "I pulled over to the side of the road when I saw her lights in my rearview mirror."

"You didn't mention this in our previous interview." Sharp flipped back through his notes.

"I didn't?" Zack scratched his head. "Well, I might have been in shock, it was the first I'd heard she was missing. She thought I liked her. And I did, like her, I do. But I told her I wanted to be just friends. Do you think she might have run away from home because I jilted her?"

"Zack had nothing to do with the girl's disappearance," the Master reiterated.

"I have that in my notes already, thank you, you can stop saying that!" Sharp snapped. "Now, I'd like to talk to you for a minute about Miss Edwards . . ."

Detective Sharp spent fifteen minutes on Miss Edwards, looking for contradictions while reviewing his notes from their previous interview. They'd admitted she had been by the house, regarding Zack's special needs. Zack had been the last person to see both Cecilia Edwards and Sandy Hardesty alive, which was too much of a coincidence to ignore. It was suspicious, Sharp mentioned, tapping his teeth with his pen and flipping back and forth through his notes while he examined Drake and Zack for reactions. This technique usually unnerved people. Both father and son were either entirely without guilt or stone-cold liars.

"You know," Sharp mentioned, "I've always wanted to get a look around this mansion. I'm a bit of an architecture buff, and the Hampstead place is one of the oldest structures in the county."

"I'm afraid it's getting rather late," Drake mentioned, looking at his wristwatch.

"I'd heard that you did quite a bit of renovation here," Detective Sharp continued. "I heard you did some excavation in the cellar. Would you mind if I had a look around down there?"

"I had a wine cellar built," Drake said, his words slow and rhythmic. "You don't need to see anything down there."

"I don't need to see anything down there?" Sharp repeated, his eyes narrowing to slits.

"No, you don't," Drake repeated, soothingly. "We know nothing about those girls."

Sharp shook his head like a wet dog shaking off water. "Just the same, could we go down and have a look around?"

"I'm afraid I can't allow that," Drake said, his speech measured.

"I could get a warrant," Sharp supposed. "Bring a blood-hound, let 'im sniff around a bit."

"We had nothing to do with those disappearances," the Master repeated.

"Yeah," Sharp replied. "You keep saying that. Kinda suspicious, if you ask me."

Zack and the Master watched the running lights of the patrol car fade down the long gravel driveway. Zack was puzzled. "What was that, Master? It's like he's got us sussed."

The Master backhanded Zack across the face with supernatural power, tumbling him back over the sofa halfway across the room. "Idiot! You were careless when you acquired the blond."

"I'm sorry, Master," Zack cowered. "I can make it right, give me a chance!"

"You *will* make it right, you fool!" The Master strode to where Zack cringed on the floor and kicked him in the ribs, which sent him crashing to the wall across the room. "Do you know what your carelessness has wrought? You've killed her."

"No, Master, please," he begged.

Drake grabbed him by the ankle and dragged him across the living room, through the hallway to the cellar door in the kitchen. He removed a ring of keys from his pocket and unlatched the heavy door. He threw Zack down the stairs forcibly and pursued him to the foot of the stairs, where he opened a second door and shoved Zack into the wine cellar with his foot.

"Open it," the Master commanded.

Zack rose and removed a jeroboam of 1961 Margaux from its place on the large-format bottle rack on the middle shelf, and placed it in an empty berth on the shelf below, which set a counter-weighted latch at the back of the rack to release. Zack then pushed the entire rack to the side. The rack weighed over a ton, but it was resting on sliders that slid in undetectable grooves on the floor. Beneath the wine rack, flush with the floor, was a large granite tile. Using his nails, he pried up the trap door. It led to an unlit vertical passageway down, with iron railings on the side, like a ladder. Local contractors had excavated the wine cellar, but Drake's own workers from Italy had dug the catacombs beneath and finished the lodgings.

On either side of the hallway on the landing below were the rooms, six in all. Presently there were only six brides. Zack had picked up Michelle after work at Starbucks one night. Chang Lee, in the same room with Michelle, was a masseuse the Master had obtained at a sleazy massage parlor in the city. Danielle was a student from the junior college. The police were looking for her upstate. Lisa had met Zack at the cove after school. Her parents didn't even know she was missing yet.

Sandy Hardesty was very glad to see them. "Good evening, Zack, good evening, Father," she said when they entered. Sandy approached Zack, whom she loved beyond all measure and reason, tucking her hair behind her left ear in anticipation of a kiss. Perhaps Father would also give her a kiss tonight? It was all fine, they were a very close family.

"Finish her," the Master commanded.

Sandy unbuttoned the top button of her nightie in anticipation. She wanted to be finished. She smiled at Zack, with her glazed, love-struck grin. Zack removed his straight razor from his pocket and approached her from behind. This confused her a little, but in her current state, she was not the least bit frightened. Zack was dry-heaving tears, grieving for her. "But, Father," he pleaded. "It's such a waste."

"Not with the blade," the Master instructed his protégé. "With your hands. Slowly."

THE CURSE OF THE MIDDLE SISTER

Veronica let out a scream so piercing, so fraught with anguish, that it roused both her father from his upstairs bedroom and Esme from all the way down in the basement.

"Sweetie, what's the matter?" her father shouted through the bathroom door, pounding on the wood. His face was half covered in shaving cream. "Unlock the door, honey, I'm coming in!"

"Go away, Daddy!" she yelled.

"What is it?" Esme asked Barry when she arrived, panting, to the hallway outside the bathroom. "Is she okay?"

"Esme, get in here, I need your help!" This cry of desperation came through the door muffled, under Veronica's sobs of torment.

"Looks like I got this," Esme told her dad. "Carry on."

Barry made his way back to his bathroom to finish his shave. It was just another one of those girl things. Best not to get involved, for the sake of his sanity.

"Is he gone?" Veronica asked, unlatching the door. Esme slipped inside. She'd been roused from a sound sleep, and her bed head qualified for FEMA funding as a tri-state disaster area.

Veronica was sobbing desolately, to the point of hiccupping violently between sobs. Esme came in and put her arm around her for comfort. Though it soon became apparent that her big sister did not regard the disaster on Veronica's face with quite the gravity the situation called for. In fact, Esme was positively smirking at the sight of Ronnie's zit.

"Are you laughing at me?" Ronnie accused.

"Oh, sweetie," Esme reassured her. "You know I'll always be there for you, because I love you, and nothing can ever change that. And you also know I'll always make fun of you, because I'm your sister."

To say that Veronica Silver had good skin was an understatement on the scale of saying that Christina Aguilera had a good voice, or that Stephen Hawking was a clever chap. Veronica had skin like one of those freakish, unfreckled redheads the mascara companies were always scouting, a creamy epidermis as taut as the skin of a Celtic drum with pores the size of sub-atomic particles, offset by natural blond hair and cerulean blue eyes. The honking crimson zit in the middle of her alabaster forehead looked like the red rising sun on the white Japanese flag.

"Oh, honey," Esme said. "It's not so bad. We all go through it. It's part of growing up."

Ronnie sniffled, inconsolable. She looked closer, and the tears started to well up again. "What am I going to do?" she wailed.

"Consider it part of your spiritual path. You'll be a better person for it," Esme cajoled.

Ronnie sniffled again. "Do you think?"

"Oh, absolutely," Esme reassured her. "You're due for a spiritual awakening. Just as soon as that third eye growing in the middle of your forehead opens up."

～っ c～っ

There was no time for breakfast, what with Veronica's grandiose insistence that everybody stop whatever they were doing and deal with her problem. In the kitchen, Esme swallowed a handful of supplements with a glass of water, checking her watch, and offered some to Katy. "Neuro-enhancers? Katy? I have a new stack I researched. You should take them every day, they'll improve your cognitive function."

Katy turned up her nose at the fistful of vitamins and nutraceuticals. "No thanks, I'm done with those. The last time you gave me gingko, it improved my memory so much I can still recall how much I hated it."

On the way to school, Katy mentioned wistfully that she wished she'd at least had time for coffee before they'd hit the road, and Ronnie chimed in that she could certainly use a cup to settle her nerves after her ordeal. Esme suddenly had a perseverative image in her mind of sipping a comforting latte, and then all Ronnie and Esme had to do was convince Katy that there was plenty of time to stop for some.

They parked in the student parking lot and Veronica practically leapt out of the car, book bag swinging, still blowing on her coffee and testing it with tentative sips, walking with bold ballerina strides in her stiletto heels. She wore a head scarf to cover her zit. Veronica had taken to hanging out at the base of the steps in the mornings before school, at the very spot where she'd first talked to Zack. Girls all over the school had similar spots staked out. Ronnie was hurrying, as she only had a few minutes to get there.

"Come on, Esme," Katy said, picking up the pace to follow.

Esme and Katy followed their sister along the sidewalk. It curved up and around, and they noticed Ronnie slowing as she approached the stairs, trying not to look too eager. Zack was approaching from the opposite direction, a few girls in tow.

"Hey," they heard him say. Esme couldn't figure it, after the kiss she'd seen. Certainly Ronnie had earned something more intimate than "hey." She was ten feet away and closing, her arm positioning itself for the hug, coffee in one hand, cell phone in the other, bag at her hip.

"A klutz, a klutz," Katy intoned under her breath. Then she held her hands before her and made a motion, bringing her two fists together and snapping the wrists, as if she were holding a pencil in her hands and breaking it in half.

Esme heard the sound of something snapping. Veronica's stiletto heel broke and her ankle twisted. Veronica's coffee went flying out of her hand and the cup exploded against Zack, soaking his leather jacket, which was open in front, and his white button-down shirt underneath. Ronnie went down, catching herself on one knee, which she scraped on the sidewalk.

Katy caught her kid sister before she could face-plant on the concrete, yanking Ronnie to her feet with one hand as she swung her pack off her back. With the other hand, she reached into her open backpack and removed a small first aid kit, which she handed off to Esme. She reached back into her pack and removed a pair of sneakers, which she also handed to her older sister.

"Take Ronnie to the school nurse and bandage her knee," Katy instructed. "Are you okay Ronnie? You can wear my new gym shoes; I have my old pair in my locker." She handed Veronica off to Esme and turned to Zack, startled and soaked in steaming hot coffee.

"Come with me," Katy insisted, reaching into her magician's hat of a backpack and removing a bottle of club soda and a clean dry hand towel. "I have a shirt in here you can borrow."

Esme stared, mouth agape, as Katy grabbed Zack's arm and led him, unresisting, off to the boys' bathroom, where she would have the pleasure of patting him down and drying him off and touching up his clothes with club soda. She would take off his shirt and rinse off his chest and lean in too close while she buttoned up the replacement that she "happened" to have in her backpack. Katy would get Zack fixed up, too late for first period, so they probably would decide to ditch, and they'd take off and he would want to kiss her, because people always did what Katy wanted them to do. Because Katy had the universe in her pocket and people were just kidding themselves to think she wouldn't win. They'd fall in love and get married and that would be the last Esme would ever hear from Katy or Zack, until they needed a babysitter for their three perfect children. Or so Esme imagined, as she helped her limping, wobbly baby sister off to the school nurse. She'd never in her life seen such perfect planning and execution of magic and acting. Katy was unbeatable. And incredibly devious.

22

THE DEADLY AND THE DEAD

Ever since Detective Sharp's visit, the Master had been prone to fits of mercurial rage. After Zack had buried the remains of poor Sandy Hardesty deep in a fallow field off a country road, he'd returned to find another fresh corpse in the cellar. Chang Lee had been nearly drained and her neck broken like a twig. She'd displeased the Master somehow. The Master had been hard on all the brides. Miss Edwards was bruised from head to toe, and Lisa, the newest, was wearing bandages on her neck to cover a wound that was slow to heal, where the Master had bitten her far too carelessly.

Drake explained that there were certain people who were not susceptible to mesmerism. These rare types were always intelligent, analytical, skeptical men, difficult to fool in general. There were a lot of them in law enforcement, where they tended to rise to the upper echelons. Drake had been to the police station previously for purposes of mesmerizing the entire staff, but Detective Sharp represented a threat that they could not ignore.

"Master, I know it isn't my place, but I think we're making a mistake," Zack said gravely.

"Explain yourself." The Master had his feet up on the coffee table in the living room.

Zack paced, relieved at the reprieve. The Master had threatened, just the day before, to end him. "Master, it's barmy to attack the police in their station. They have security cameras all over the place. Even if we were to get in and out and kill everyone without taking too many bullets, the FBI would just come in the next day and find out about us."

"I've dealt with security cameras before," Drake argued. "We have only to go to the room where they keep the tapes, and destroy all the evidence before we depart."

"Master, they haven't used tapes for decades." Zack was treading on thin ice. The Master could be off the sofa faster than a wink, and Zack's head would be watching his body on the floor from the vantage of the Master's hand, hanging by his hair. "Everything's digital now, and it probably backs up to the cloud. So we can't destroy the evidence."

"The cloud," Drake repeated ominously, weighing the truth of the word on his lips. Kill Zack, believe Zack: a flip of the coin. "Yes, I've heard of this cloud." He stood abruptly. "Very well. We shall do the other thing, then."

⌒ᵔᵔᵔ ᵔᵔᵔ⌒

At 2:09 a.m. on Thanksgiving morning, the Sharps' German shepherd, Roscoe, started barking. Roscoe slept in the living room but had a doggie door to a fenced dog run along the side of the house. The barks were aggressive, with snarls. "Stupid dog," Detective Sharp muttered, rolling out of bed and hunting with his feet in the dark for his slippers. His wife, Janet, rolled over and went back to sleep. Roscoe barked at all sorts of things at night, usually raccoons or possums.

As Sharp opened the bedroom door, he heard Roscoe make a

whimpering sound. He couldn't imagine what would intimidate a police-trained German shepherd. He went back into the bedroom and slipped into the master closet. He had a 9mm Glock hidden in a pile of winter clothes on a shelf in the back.

"Wha' honey?" Janet asked, still half-asleep. "What is it?"

"Probably nothing," Robert reasoned. "Go back to sleep."

In the hallway outside the master bedroom, he paused to listen. The dog wasn't making any noise at all. He turned on the hall light and headed down the stairs. "Roscoe?" he whispered. At the foot of the stairs he flipped on the living room lights. The room was empty. His brain subconsciously processed a hundred little signals that his conscious mind couldn't put a finger on. Everything was entirely still. He raised the Glock in front of him, edging into the living room. There was no element of surprise, with the lights on.

In a blur, something all in black jumped out from behind the curtains and crossed the room on the opposite side so fast he couldn't draw a bead on it with the gun. And then something came from behind and tore the Glock away from him, breaking his wrist in the process, and clamped a steely hand across his mouth.

"I suppose I might as well confess now," a soft, hypnotic voice whispered in his ear in an amorphous accent. "We *did* actually kidnap those girls." But Detective Robert Sharp was dead with a broken neck before he could make any sense out of the whole thing.

"Upstairs," the Master whispered to Zack, motioning with the gun in his hand. He turned off the living room lights. "Go through those rooms and kill everyone."

Zack got the end with the master bedroom. He killed Janet Sharp quietly, in her sleep. He did not like killing people, but it was Drake's command, and he could not defy the Master. She would die anyway, at his hand or Drake's.

At the opposite end of the hall, Drake opened the first door. On a twin bed, a boy of about middle-school age lay sleeping with his mouth open, snoring softly, covers kicked this way and that. There was a cluttered desk in the corner of the room and model vintage American muscle cars on shelves. Drake tore out the boy's throat with his teeth. He did not usually drink the blood of males, but had few qualms with children of either sex.

The next door in the hall opened into a room with bunk beds. Drake killed the boy in the upper bunk first, with his talons. Blood leaked into the mattress and over the edge of it, and it spilled hotly onto the hand of little Billy below. Billy was a floppy sleeper. The boy's eyes opened, startled from a shallow dream about pumpkin pies and whipped cream and the Macy's parade, which they always watched. Billy's eyes adjusted quickly to the dim light of the nightlight. There, above him, was a stranger with blood on his hands. Billy let out a little scream then, but it didn't matter at that point. Nobody would wake up. Nobody would come to help. Everyone else in the house was dead already.

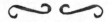

The fire they set on their way out was attended by nearly every police vehicle, fire truck and ambulance in the county, but there was really nothing left to save. The bodies were burnt beyond all recognition.

23

TURKEY DAY

"Ronnie, is this a good time?" Esme asked, peeking her head into the doorway on Thursday morning. Veronica was at her vanity, chanting over a tube of benzoyl peroxide.

"I think it's getting worse," Veronica said, on the verge of tears. On her cheek was a red, slightly raised bump.

"Oh, Ronnie." Esme hated to see her sister in such pain, even if she totally deserved it.

"Maybe the one on my forehead is going down a little."

"Listen," Esme said quietly. "I have something for you." She was carrying something large against her chest, wrapped in a bath towel. She laid the package down on the vanity, sliding bottles and tubes aside. She opened the towel to reveal the huge, ancient book.

"The grimoire? Why are you giving me the grimoire?"

"Because you need it more than I do. Somebody has been cursing you." Esme did not speak a name. Rather, she rolled her eyes up toward the ceiling. She made the motion three times, so Ronnie would get the gist.

"Katy?" Ronnie whispered. "No way." Then she thought about it. "How come she had all that stuff in her backpack? Katy's never drunk club soda in her life. She made me scrape my knee!"

"Yeah, you need to protect yourself."

Ronnie pulled up the leg of her sweatpants. "Look at that!" she seethed. "I could get a scar! I might be a model someday, did she think of that?" She shoved the pant leg back down forcefully and stalked around the room. She wheeled on Esme. "How come you know so much?"

"Ronnie, settle down." *Save some for Katy.* "Look, honey . . . I feel just awful about this whole thing. It could be partly my fault. I . . . told her about you kissing Zack. I mean, she really likes him, you know about that, right?"

"So you got her to curse me?" Veronica accused. "You like him, too, don't you? Admit it!"

Ronnie's mood had strayed into something a little more dangerous than Esme had anticipated. The girl really had it bad. She was bordering on hysteria and paranoia. "Ronnie, calm down already. Yes, I do like him. He's a great guy, anyone would like him. But I wouldn't resort to hexing my own sister. That's why I came to tell you. Katy crossed the line."

Veronica went back to pacing. "Yeah. Yeah, you're right. You wouldn't give me the grimoire otherwise. You wouldn't tell me." She turned to Esme again suddenly. "Are you still trying to get him? After you saw how he kissed me you don't actually think *you . . . ?*"

"Aw, honey," Esme cajoled. "I like him, but no boy is worth coming between me and my baby sister." *I don't actually think I what? Can get him?*

Veronica unwrapped the grimoire and started leafing through the pages. She could barely make out the writing, it was all old script. It was mostly Latin and other arcane languages she couldn't make head or tail of. She closed the book and sighed. "I don't understand a word of it," she complained. "Katy's going to destroy me."

"There are some simpler spells, here in the front," Esme mentioned, leaning over her sister's shoulder and flipping through pages. "Here's a charm—you're good at charms, aren't you?—for protection against the evil eye. And an incantation to protect you from curses and hexes. Just look up the Latin online." There were also a few very nice spells, in that general vicinity of the book, for retaliation. Esme was confident Veronica would find them.

~~~~~~~~~

At two in the afternoon, Barry got a call from Nancy Armond, one of his clients. Nancy was Robert Sharp's sister-in-law, mother to Wilson. "Barry, did you hear about the fire?" she asked, openly crying into the phone. "It was my sister Janet. And Robert, and the boys. Barry, they can't get into the house yet, the roof collapsed, but they think everyone's dead."

"Oh my god, Nancy, I'm so sorry. I hadn't heard."

"Barry, we're all outside the house. The whole family, and dozens of neighbors, and reporters. And there's a film crew from channel five. The police have taped off the whole area. Do you think you can come down? I know you handled all Robert's legal affairs."

"I'll be there in ten minutes, Nancy. Oh my god, I'm so sorry."

"They're trying to interview us, can you make them leave us alone? They're like vultures."

Barry went to his bedroom and put on a jacket and tie. Before leaving, he told Esme to watch the turkey. "You know how to use the meat thermometer, don't you?"

Esme's thumbs flew over her smartphone. "Here's a link . . .

with pictures. Fattest part of the thigh, one hundred sixty-five degrees . . . I've got it. Just . . . go. Give Wilson a hug for me. I'm so sorry."

He mussed her hair, daddy style. "Sorry about Thanksgiving. Maybe next year, huh?"

"Don't worry about it, Dad. Katy would just complain she couldn't eat anything anyway. And Ronnie wouldn't go near a carbohydrate in a hazmat suit. Go. Take care."

Esme walked through her parents' master bedroom, checking her iPhone for the list of ingredients she needed, past the large bookcase with Melinda's collection of ethnic ceremonial figures displayed on shelves. A large, rustic Lega fertility fetish was the centerpiece of a long, low mahogany cabinet against the far wall, displayed on an old Kuba mat. In the little office off the master bedroom was Melinda's humongous old Chinese apothecary chest and a roll-top desk full of other requirements of the craft.

Esme's mom, Melinda, had moved out. She and Barry were not divorced or even separated; Melinda had basically just stopped commuting back from her apothecary store in the city. They owned a duplex there, and aside from rare visits home, that's where she lived.

Melinda had imparted some basic knowledge about the craft, but had been cagey with details. It was almost as if she didn't want her daughters messing with it at all, for some mysterious reason, but Esme had deduced certain things. There were sources of power in nearly everything in the world, especially in nature. The pagans called it divine vitality. Certain things, some animal, some mineral, and some vegetable, had specific properties. Pharmaceutical companies were very good at exploiting these properties. Physicists were better, hence the atom bomb. Alchemy, up to a point, was just an enlightened approach to pharmacology and physics. The art of it all was knowing how to coax these properties out, how to combine them to finesse or magnify their powers, how to extract them, how to distill them. The oldest families of witches, families that predated modern Wicca by centuries, had multi-generational lore that was passed down, improved upon, and kept in the family grimoire. Esme had just spent the last two weeks scanning the entire book and all the notes and uploading it onto her computer, in a system of files that had utilized her particular genius for organization.

After a brief rifling through the drawers of the apothecary chest, Esme came up empty-handed on every herb on her list. There was enough sage for a purification ritual, that was about it. Katy had apparently gotten there first. Even the vials and special candles and little cook pots for boiling down herbs, the mortars and pestles, the ritually purified vinegars and alcohols for certain types of distillations . . . Katy had cleaned her mother's stash out.

Esme closed the roll-top desk and replaced all the drawers in the apothecary chest. She would have to start from scratch. Looked like a road trip was in order.

FRIDAY NOIR

"Hey, Esme, it's me," Norman said into the phone. He was in the dining room waiting while his dad worked his magic in the kitchen.

"Hi, Norman," Esme said.

He thought she sounded sleepy, like he'd woken her up or something. He checked his wristwatch again. It was almost ten a.m. Half the people in the country got up in the middle of the night on Black Friday and rushed to the big-box stores so they could kill each other to get a bargain on a flat-screen TV, but Esme slept in, apparently. It just made him like her even more, if that was possible. "So . . ." Just a month before, Norman had felt comfortable talking to Esme. They'd talked on the phone all the time, even Skyped doing bio homework together. But all that had changed since Zack had come on the scene. "Uh, what are you up to today?"

"Whattaya mean?"

"I thought maybe uh . . . you know, my dad and me are going to the movies today. You told me like a hundred times you wanted to meet him, he's here for the four-day weekend." Why did she make him feel so nervous now? It was like their entire friendship had gone back to square one.

"Thanks, Norman," she said, with zero enthusiasm. "But I've got plans."

"Esme, are you all right?" he asked abruptly. She was trying to get off the phone, so he needed to speak his piece quickly. "You've been acting so weird, about Zack. Like you're obsessed with him. It just doesn't seem like you, you're usually so sensible. I'm really worried about you, I think you should talk to my dad—"

"I'm fine, Norm. Listen, I have to go," she said, and hung up.

Dr. Stein entered the dining room with a carton of eggs in his hand. "Eight eggs, or ten?"

Norm looked at his dad. For a guy who was supposed to be up for a Nobel Prize, the man sure looked silly in his frilly pink apron. "Eight, I guess," he muttered with little enthusiasm.

"What did she say?"

"She's not coming," Norm said with resignation. "She's changed. It's so odd. She's so suspicious when I try to talk to her. Like I'm trying to harvest her organs and sell them on the black market or something."

"That's ridiculous," Dr. Stein replied. "Though you'd be surprised what they're getting for a healthy tissue-typed kidney these days."

KASHA'S STORY

Kasha accompanied Esme into the city on Saturday. It was a long drive, over three hours each way. There usually wasn't much traffic on Saturdays, but it was Thanksgiving weekend and the shoppers were out in force. Kasha rode in the front seat, his head just above the level of the window, and kids in passing cars waved and made faces. It wasn't every day they saw a cat riding in a car, sitting up on the front seat like a dog.

"Does my mom know you're with me now?" Esme asked. It was a question she hadn't raised before, but one that tugged at the parts of her mind that weren't occupied by all things Zack.

"Yeah, about that," he said. "Melinda probably doesn't remember me."

"Why not?"

"I don't like loose ends."

The hairs on Esme's forearms stood up, like a low voltage was running through her system. "How come I don't remember you, growing up? I must have seen you around, if you were with my mother all those years."

"I slept with you every night, when you were little. I liked your milk breath. Melinda never did trust me, so I snuck in."

"I almost remember," she said, scratching her head. He'd made her forget him! Had there been some reason?

"When you got a little older, you used to steal food for me and feed me at night in your bed. I used to talk to you, until you were about four."

"Why'd you stop then?"

"People over four are boring."

They were driving through Tuppelow, where there was an outlet mall. Traffic was crawling. "So how did you end up a witch's familiar?" Esme asked.

"I'll tell you," he said. "But if you ever tell anyone, I'll have to rip out your intestines."

Kasha was always saying things like that, and she never put much thought into it, because it seemed like something a cat would say. But when she considered the demon angle, it was a bit disconcerting. "I'm all ears."

Kasha examined her skeptically. "Get over yourself, those ears are pathetic." He twitched his beautiful tufted ears a bit, showing off.

"Figure of speech," she explained.

"Joke," he countered. "You're a little slow, aren't you? Sometimes I wish I could just harvest your soul and start over with Veronica."

The creepiest sense of foreboding made the hair at the nape of Esme's neck prickle. Still, it was hard to be properly terrified of a creature that so loved getting his belly rubbed. "Just tell me the story."

"It's a great story," Kasha said, "but you need some background for perspective. For billions of years, creation and entropy were just two forces that roiled and pulled at each other purposelessly in a cosmic give and take. Try to follow this concept, it's important: The universe manifested matter, then planets and stars, then ecosystems and life, and finally Homo sapiens, the first life that became self-aware through complex reasoning. Until then, the universe had no way of knowing itself. There wasn't even a way to ask a question. The energies that morphed into demons and angels always had form, but never self-awareness, until humans invented it. I formed out of the primordial muck about eighty thousand years ago. I'm not saying I was a genius or anything, because if I had been, I'd have gone with the opposable thumbs or at least a prehensile tail. But I had to have form, so I manifested as a cat."

"Good call."

"Right," he said. "So as you know, form is function, function is form, and my innate form has been a cat ever since. Anyway, I spent tens of thousands of years as a saber tooth tiger, *Smilodon populator*, eating people and ingesting their souls—"

"You *ate* people?" Esme exclaimed, taking her eyes off the road for a second to stare at the cat in shock, then hitting the brakes to avoid rear-ending a sedan.

"We all did in those days," Kasha said, unruffled. "Everything has divine vitality, even rocks and vegetables, but it's pretty weak stuff except for people, who have free will and creativity, so we call the vitality of humans a soul. You invented intelligence and observation and curiosity about the nature of reality, and we stole it from you and made it ours. It was pretty evident to the elder demons long before I came onto the scene that humans were where all the action was. Creative buggers, humans. Destructive, too."

"It sounds like you're saying 'in the beginning, man created God,'" Esme said.

"No, God, the universe, was always here. Intelligence was a game changer, but if you ask me, it's just something that makes people taste better." Kasha sat like an oracle, staring at Esme with unblinking golden eyes, testing her interest like a spider testing a web. "Anyway, about three thousand years ago, before there was much human culture or organized religion, there was a directive from hell that all the demons had to return to the netherworld. By that time I'd been on earth as a giant cat for over seventy-five thousand years. It was all I knew. And I didn't like hell at all."

"Is it hot?"

"It can be," Kasha replied. "Catholic hell sure is. But mostly it's just disconcerting."

"So what did they want?" Esme asked. "Why did they call you down to hell?"

"All the demons got called down to be sorted, assigned, rated, and ranked, like a mockery of the hierarchy of angels. Up until then, I didn't even know I *was* a demon. It took some convincing. Order and chaos were squabbling over the dispensation of human souls, both sides threatening Armageddon. Souls had become the currency of the cosmos."

"Don't people have any say in the matter?"

"Not as much as you'd like to think," he said.

"No. Wait," Esme said, mind reeling. "Are you saying I'm going to hell when I die?"

"I sure hope so," Kasha said. "I'm batting zero for two with your family so far. Anyway, things settled down when the demon lords and the angels figured out how to regulate the soul trade, through a system of tithing. But eating people and harvesting their souls was no longer allowed, because they decided humans had self-determination. The whole Armageddon thing was just a lot of saber rattling. Nobody wanted a war with heaven, there's no profit in it. I was pretty demoralized, until I scored this sweet gig in Japan as a corpse-eating cat. I did that for about two thousand years. The soul stays with the corpse for a while, after death. I'd stalk funeral processions of evil people and jump out and grab the corpse and make off with it, then eat it, you know, in private, because I'm a fussy eater. Seriously, you can Google it: 'Kasha, corpse-eating demon cat.'"

Another image that didn't sit well with Esme.

"So I'm banking souls in medieval Japan, and just when I feel like I'm positioned to set myself up as an independent operator, I get called back to hell. Rules changed again. Now we couldn't eat corpses, either. They said the soul was still with the corpse, so it was the same thing as eating a live person. Total bureaucratic bullshit. You want my opinion? They were trying to cut us small-time operators out of the action altogether. I'm onto them. But since I wasn't allowed to eat corpses anymore, my boss summoned me back to hell to work in accounting."

Esme didn't know how much of Kasha's story was true, or how terrified she should be, but the idea of her cat sitting at a desk with a visor in a cubicle totaling infinite columns of numbers was too ridiculous to take seriously. "How was that?"

Kasha stared at her emotionlessly. "You know Catholic hell, like in Dante's *Inferno*? I used to dream about Catholic hell. I'd have vacationed there. Sisyphus would have run screaming back to his giant rock and kissed it all over, if he got to go back to that after three centuries keeping records in hell. I used to keep a little blade by my desk, and I'd drive it into my brain periodically, just so I could feel something—*anything*—after a century of mind-numbing boredom. To this day, I can't look at an abacus without needing to eviscerate something. But then, just as my existence was bleakest, I got transferred into contracting. I had to kiss major demon butt to get that transfer, mind you. And I don't mean a little peck on both cheeks. They expect you to really get in there and smooch it."

"There's a picture that will haunt my nightmares."

"I hope so," Kasha said, grooming himself. "In contracting, I plotted how to get back to this plane. After I learned the system, I wrote up an ironclad contract describing a position topside with a certain quota and tithe that was a no-brainer for my boss to rubber-stamp. I knew my boss wouldn't read the demonic small print. That's what he had *me* for. The stuff in my contract is incredibly convoluted and arcane—twenty-eight languages, some I made up myself—so he signed off on it. I ripped my leg with a claw, dipped my paw in my own blood, and slammed it down on the contract, on the signature line. 'I'm outta here!' I told him, throwing it in his face. And I haven't been back since. Though I do have to make my quota, so if you don't mind dabbling in a little black magic from time to time, you'd be doing me a solid."

"Something tells me I'm going to be behaving myself from now on," Esme said. *As soon as you help me with my beauty potion.* "Anyway, you must have been happy to get back up here."

"I was. And I had a pretty solid plan. At the time, late sixteenth century, all the rage down in hell was about how demons were making bank in the Faust-style contracting. Humans have free will, so they can trade in their own souls. We were like door-to-door salesmen, trying to get people to sign over their souls for a bit of prosperity or the hot miller's daughter. But by the time I got back here, people were getting clever. People were asking for immortality, how was I supposed to work with that? Or, say, you give them one wish, and they wish for three wishes. Plus, being a talking cat, people were suspicious of my motivations."

"How inconsiderate," Esme said.

"You got that right, baby. I was just able to eke out a living for the next century or so, always looking over my shoulder for the hellhounds waiting to drag me back for not hitting my quota. That's when I stumbled onto this witch's familiar gig.

"I happened upon a coven of rather bedraggled hedge witches, plying little unguents and potions and séances. There was this young witch, living off the scraps of the senior hags, sweeping and cleaning and hauling wood as an apprentice, hoping to learn enough craft to set herself up with some kind of future besides . . . the kind of trade young girls with no economic prospects would end up working in London in the early seventeen hundreds. So I offered myself to her as familiar, to serve until she died, in exchange for an option on her soul and certain spoils."

Esme slowed the car to let an aggressive driver cut in front. "How did you figure you'd do better as a witch's familiar?"

"Mainly what it provided was breathing space," Kasha confided. "If I contract with a witch to serve for her lifetime, I have to serve. I'm an agent of hell, and hell can't welsh on a contract. I have to get value for the contract to be valid, but then I have to serve as her familiar until she dies. Here, on Earth. Where I want to stay."

"Oh my Goddess, you're a genius!" Esme declared. *An evil genius.*

"This is what I've been telling you," he said.

"So did you ever figure out how to reach your quota?"

"Yeah, sure. Gretchen—that was my first witch—soon rose to the top of the coven with my help. Her spells worked, for one thing, which was a novelty. And after a while, she got a reputation for her potions. My angle was, when I helped Gretchen make a potion or cast a spell for a client, we would work a verbal contract that the love potion or hex for the enemies or luck for the business deal or ointment for hemorrhoids could only be used for good, never to bad purpose, on forfeit of their . . . yada yada. I did very well for myself. I mean, who uses a hex to righteous purpose? Or a love potion, for that matter?"

"Hemorrhoid ointment?"

"You'd be surprised. Anyway, it was still catch-as-catch-can. A verbal contract isn't as ironclad as a written one. I had to give value for it to be valid, but they paid for the potions with coin, so they had some consumer protections. But most souls are pretty much borderline, they can go either way. If a demon has any kind of claim, he can make a case. And if they used the potion or spell to break a commandment, or commit one of the seven deadly sins, I usually had them dead to rights. I did the familiar scam for about three hundred years, in Europe. I started making multi-generational contracts, trying to keep the terms ambiguous, because it gave me more options. And if a witch wasn't generating enough soul action, I could switch to her sister or daughter. That's why I left your mother for you: no action in the apothecary and lesbian books game. Maybe you can introduce me to some people you don't like? Seriously, I'm way behind. Every time I turn around, I can hear those stupid hounds of hell on my tail."

"I thought you had to serve out your contract."

"If my contract with hell becomes invalid, my contract to your family also falls. The familiar gig gives me some protection, but try to remember what we're dealing with: demon bureaucracy. It's all fun and games until someone rips your head off and throws it into a pit.

"Eventually I emigrated to the United States with a nasty red-haired Irish witch named Colleen. She was third generation of a contract I'd made with her grandmother. She never trusted me not to go to her sister. She locked me in an iron cage sealed with demonic containment runes so I couldn't escape. I'd never bothered to put a 'no cage or collar' clause into my contracts. You'd think being a demon would be disincentive enough, right? But she got careless. I got out of the cage and harvested her soul."

"You can do that?" Esme asked. There it was again, that creepy sense of foreboding.

"Colleen's case was special," he reassured. "She was irredeemably evil. She was going to hell anyway, I just took a few liberties with some ambiguous Peloponnesian tenses in an obscure clause in the contract. Afterward, I headed to New Orleans in human form, with my quota met for a few years."

"When was this?"

"Nineteen forties, just after the war. I did a stint as a jazz musician. Then I got myself a beret and some sunglasses and took up bongos, playing in coffee shops, bebopping around San Francisco as a beatnik. That's where I met your great-aunt Becky. She was a live one, Becky. The times we had, when I was in human form."

"Wait," Esme interrupted. "I thought you always had to be a cat."

"A technicality. Cool it, daddy-o, you're such a square. I was a hepcat. Anyway, since I hit it off with Becky, we did the deal for three generations. Good old Becks. I wonder what she's been up to lately?"

"Nothing. She's dead," Esme said, flipping on her turn signal. Their exit was coming up.

"So? Some of my best friends are dead."

BRAIN TRUST

Dr. Frederick Stein and his son, Franklin, lived in a converted free clinic that had been run by a small group of local doctors and nurses and funded by a local charitable trust. The clinic had originally been a large house deeded to the trust by the wealthy dowager who'd lived there. The Steins had moved in at the end of July. Dr. Stein intended to see outpatients pro bono, but the new clinic wasn't operable yet, and they were still in the process of converting the upstairs back into a house.

Dr. Stein worked at the state university in the city, where he'd accepted a very nice position teaching neurobiology based on his world-class reputation and his ability to pull lucrative research grants from Fortune 500 pharmaceutical companies. During the week he stayed in a comfortable off-campus faculty apartment. He traveled home every weekend to be with his son. At about one o'clock in the afternoon on Saturday, there was a knock on the front door. Norm and his dad were in the partially refurnished living room, playing a game of chess.

"Hey, Wilson," Norm said, opening the door. Next to Wilson on the porch, with an expression of anxiety and discomfort almost painful to witness, was Jackson Gartner. The side of his face was covered in gauze bandages.

"Dude, we need to talk to you," Wilson said. Norm stood aside to let the two into the house.

"Wilson," Norm said when they were all standing awkwardly around the living room. He rested an enormous hand on the boy's shoulder. "I'm so, so sorry about your family, man." He didn't know what else to say. Everything he could think of seemed so meaningless.

"Yeah, man, thanks," Wilson said, studying the floor. "It's real bad."

"Jackson, this is my father, Dr. Frederick Stein. Dad, you know Wilson, this is Jackson Gartner. He's in some of my classes at school."

Dr. Stein rose to greet the boys. He looked clownishly short next to his son, paunchy, with curly, graying hair, a prominent nose, and wire-rimmed bifocals. He extended a hand to Jackson. "Call me Fred."

Jackson shook, weakly. He was perspiring freely. He looked like he wanted to run and hide in a closet. Very odd behavior for a boy Norman knew best as an insensitive lout and a bully.

"Can we go talk someplace?" Wilson implored, eyes darting to Norm's dad.

"Is this about Jackson's apparent case of malaria?" Norm asked, not moving. "Because he looks like he needs medical attention."

Jackson took one quick step backward, as if he wanted to bolt for the door and run for his life. Norm put a hand on his back to steady him. Dr. Stein moved decisively. He was a foremost expert on idiopathic neuropathy. "Jackson, would you please step into the clinic for a moment? Whatever you're nervous about, I'm a doctor, so you'll be in very good hands." He gestured toward the door to the lab. "Unless you bite, and then all bets are off."

Jackson looked around the room for an escape, eyes full of panic, but with Norman's hand on his shoulder, he allowed himself to be coaxed into an examining room.

"He's not sick," Wilson said. Dr. Stein and Norman waited patiently for elucidation. "But there's something wrong with him, I didn't know what else to do, and you're the smartest guy I know. He's just fine, unless you try to ask him questions about the fight. I saw Logan in the hospital, and he's the same. If you ask him any questions about the guys that beat them up, he's too terrified to say anything. He's got IV needles in both arms, and that thing that beeps, with the wavy lines? I tried to get a description of the pickup those guys were driving, and Logan tried to pull all the needles out of his arm. You know Logan, he's reckless, not nervous. What could have put the scare into them like that?"

"Let's find out," Dr. Stein said.

While Dr. Stein checked Jackson's vitals, Wilson and Norm waited on chairs in the hallway. "Why'd you want a description of the truck?" Norm asked, though he could guess the answer.

"Okay, me and some of the guys from the football team and the weight room were going to go to Davidsonville and try to find those guys. Because it's not right, what they did to Danny and Logan and Jackson. Danny . . . you should see him. He's so messed up. He's never going to be the same; he has massive head trauma. He coulda been all-state."

After the examination, they all returned to the living room to sit around the coffee table. "Let's give Jackson a few minutes to get acclimated to the meds I gave him," Dr. Stein said. Jackson's pallor and appearance seemed improved, though he looked a little lethargic. He certainly wasn't in the state of panic he'd been in on his arrival. "I've given him a sedative, and some serotonin re-uptake inhibitors. He's had an injection of anabolic steroids, some mood stabilizers I had handy, and some neurohormones. How are you feeling, Jackson?"

"Better," Jackson replied.

Norman decided that Jackson looked a bit giddy, like a stoner kid he knew at school who always reeked of pot after lunch. "A little heavy-handed on the sedatives, don't you think?"

"Well it was touch and go for a while there," Dr. Stein explained. "I had to give him a little post-hypnotic suggestion, and I told him he'd feel wonderful when he came out."

"So what do you think, Dad?" Norman asked.

"A very interesting case," Dr. Stein said. "Jackson is experiencing severe anxiety, panic attacks bordering on sheer terror. At first I assumed he was having extreme post-traumatic stress related to injuries he'd sustained in his recent conflict. But that didn't explain his mood swings. When I mentioned his friends or the fight, he had the panic reaction, but when I changed the subject, his blood pressure immediately dropped to normal range, and he calmed down. I drew blood and tested it three times, once for a base, two times during the panic attacks. I checked peptides, adrenaline, endorphins, serotonin, everything. In a normal panic attack or in a pathological case, the neurohormones drive the reaction. But in Jackson's case, the mention of the fight caused his endocrine system to spontaneously produce unprecedented quantities of glucocorticoids and catecholamine, the neurohormones associated with fear."

"So what do you think is the problem?" Norm asked.

"I'll need to do some research. But I think that Jackson here has been given a very intense post-hypnotic suggestion that stimulates his endocrine system to go haywire when he tries to recall the details of the fight. And it's not a normal pathology, either: Someone did this to him deliberately. Jackson, do you think you can talk about the incident now?" Dr. Stein asked. "Can you tell us who beat up you and your friends?"

Jackson still looked a bit anxious, darting his eyes back and forth. "Okay," he said at last. "But you can nev'r ev'r tell anyone I told you. And no police." He paused for a long time, gathering his nerve. "It was Zack."

"And this Zack fellow," Dr. Stein asked. "Is he um . . . as big as Norman here?"

"Pi'squeak," Jackson declared, shaking his head once with conviction.

"Don't worry," Dr. Stein assured. "We aren't going to tell anyone. I have to look into this."

"Are you crazy?" Norm asked. "We have to tell the police. I knew there was something wrong with that guy the minute I laid eyes on him. He's a danger to everyone. Somebody could have been killed! And he knows how to hypnotize people? We have to warn everyone!"

But Wilson had a look of deep consternation on his acne-riddled brow. "No, dude. We can't tell the police. We can't tell anyone."

"You too, Wilson? Don't you understand how dangerous he is?"

"Yeah," Wilson replied, worrying his lower lip between thumb and forefinger. "But I just thought of something that scares the hell out of me. Logan already *did* talk to the police. Remember, Norm? He said he saw Sandy following Zack's car on the night she disappeared, and that was the last anyone saw of her. And now he's in the ICU."

"But he was just talking smack, right?" Norman asked. "Did he really go to the police?"

"Was Sandy one of those girls who disappeared?" Dr. Stein asked.

"Yeah," Wilson replied, thinking deep, an odd expression for a guy who never rubbed two brain cells together to create a synapse unless he was deciding between a Big Mac and a Quarter Pounder with cheese. "Sandy was, like, the second one. After Miss Edwards. Who was Zack's teacher. Logan did talk to the police. My uncle Rob asked me did I know Logan and Zack. He asked me if Logan was the type of person to start trouble. He wanted to know what I thought of Zack. I told him, Zack gets all the girls, but we all think there's something wrong about him. Like you said, Norman, a sociopath or something."

"Yeah, but . . . you aren't saying . . ."

"My uncle was murdered. The whole family. They found the dog outside in the dog run, with a broken neck."

"You know," Dr. Stein said, "I really don't think it's a good idea to go to the police at this juncture. Because I just thought of something else it could be. And if this is that, we're going to have to think long and hard about what we intend to do about it."

27

BIRD IN A GUILTED CAGE

It was early afternoon when Esme and Kasha arrived at her mother's store. The front of the store was fairly busy, the result of Melinda's pseudo-magic crystal business and a few lines she'd recently added to pay the bills, including *tabi* socks, yoga pants, and aromatherapy candles. Melinda had originally intended for her store to serve the Wiccan community when she'd named it *The Old Town Herbalist*, but the Earth Mother–wannabe trade paid the bills.

Melinda only sold crystals because her customers wanted to buy them. She told them that crystals promoted domestic harmony and came in handy for spell casting. She didn't mention that crystals only promoted domestic harmony when you threatened to hit your man in the head with one if he didn't come to his senses, and were only useful in spell casting if you were working from an old scroll and needed something to weight down the edges.

Kitaro's meditative new age music wafted through the store, creating a spiritual mood, and sandalwood incense scented the air. The little bells above the door jingled when Esme entered, followed by her sleek, striped familiar.

"Excuse me, miss, is that your cat?" asked the salesgirl, a neopagan Goth with pink highlights and enough hardware in her face to back up an airport security checkpoint for a half hour. "Wait a minute." A look of consternation replaced her normally vacuous expression. "I know that cat."

"Is my mom in, Vanessa?" Esme asked. Vanessa had been working at the Herbalist for over three years, and she had a pathological inability to recognize people or put names to faces. So naturally, she'd pursued a career in sales.

"I go by Venus now," Vanessa corrected. "Uh . . . hi. Uh . . . yeah. You. Long time no see. She's in the back doing a tarot reading."

"I'll be in the apothecary getting supplies," Esme said. "When you see Mom, tell her I'm here, will you?"

The Old Town Herbalist was on the border of the warehouse district, over two thousand square feet zoned for retail, subdivided from a huge old feed store. The area was undergoing urban development and was in danger of becoming trendy. Coffee shops and secondhand clothing stores were sprouting like weeds. The apothecary section was in a back room with lofty ceilings of rough-hewn red oak beams. There was no direct light on the herbs, because exposure to light could change their properties. The room had originally been used for grain storage, so it was dry and dark and a little cooler than the rest of the store.

Esme used a wicker basket to gather packets of botanicals and minerals and dried animal products. She picked up some amber and sage and wolfsbane for the purification rituals the beauty potion required. She needed bachelor buttons and dragon's blood and poppy—both seed and flower—mugwort and mullein and powdered orrisroot, also known in voodoo as "love drawing powder." In her basket she put echinacea and citronella and skull-cap, which she needed to channel Kasha's eldritch energies for potency.

"Don't forget to pick up some catnip," Kasha reminded her. "Always useful to have around."

Esme decided to forego the little lidded teapots for steeping, the hot plates for slowly leaching herbs to maximize the potency of ointments, and the copper-lined pots for evenly boiling down extracts. She had already picked up a supply of Bunsen burners and test tubes and beakers from a laboratory supply website. Esme was not an old-school type of girl. As a scientist, she demanded clinical perfection.

∽◡◠

When Melinda entered the herb room after her session, she strode briskly to Esme, arms open for an embrace. And suddenly she halted, stunned, like a bird that had flown into a glass door. "Kasha," she muttered. "It's . . . wait . . . give me a second." Melinda bumbled around for a moment, punch drunk. "It's you, you've . . . I forgot all about you. I've been walking around here like a zombie for the last five months, looking everywhere for something I'd lost without knowing what it was. And now you're back."

Kasha was nonchalant. Nobody does nonchalant better than a cat, except maybe a demon cat. "Melinda," he acknowledged. "You look like hell. And I know what hell looks like."

Kasha had a point, Esme thought. Her mother was in her mid-forties but had always looked much younger. People didn't exactly confuse them for siblings, but in public it didn't usually occur to strangers that Melinda was Esme's mom. But she looked old enough now.

"I thought you'd dropped off the face of the earth," Melinda told Kasha.

"Stupid woman. The earth is a sphere. You can't drop off the face of it. It's all face."

"I'm glad you're back," she said, getting on one knee to scratch him behind the ears. "I need you. Don't ever disappear like that again."

"Too bad, I'm with Esme now." Kasha stretched out on the floor and began licking himself.

Melinda stood, slowly, like she was weighted down. She crossed her arms and regarded Kasha, then her daughter, back and forth a few times, before settling on Esme. "No you're not," she declared. "I won't allow it." She took a step toward Esme. "What are you doing here, what's all this stuff for?" she accused. She began pulling herbs and powdered animal parts out of Esme's basket. "What's this for? Orrisroot powder? Do you know what this does? And Osha root, Solomon's root, agrimony? Is somebody cursing you?" As she pulled the packets out of Esme's basket, she threw them on the floor.

"Those are for Ronnie, if you must know," Esme returned with bitter self-righteousness.

"Who said you could make potions? Who said you could have a familiar? I'm still your mother," Melinda reminded her.

But all she reminded Esme of was how demanding she could be. Esme had been locking horns with Melinda since her horns had first grown in. "You left us to fend for ourselves, *Mother*," she returned. "So I'm fending."

"I'm still your mother," Melinda volleyed. "I have a right to know what you're doing."

"Oh, you want to be my mother again, *Melinda*?" Esme

returned. Her horns were bigger now. She was a sixteen-point buck. "Are you planning to move back home? So *you* can make Ronnie keep her panties covered in school, because I'm tired of fighting with her every day about her microscopic skirts. And so you can cook us a meal, *Mom*? And do the shopping and vacuum and take Katy's dogs to their vet appointments and Ronnie to her ballet classes. And sleep with Dad, before somebody else gets the idea. And help Katy with her homework. If it weren't for me, she'd be in remedial math. Since you're coming *home*, you can deal with it. Because *I'm* not the mother, *you're* the mother."

Melinda took a step, arm drawn back, hand flattened for a slap. Esme stood her ground, defiant. She even jutted out her cheek a little, presenting a target. But after a second, Melinda only touched Esme's cheek with her hand tenderly. "I only want what's best for you, honey. I never want to stop being your mother. Not when you're ninety-nine years old, and I'm a hundred and fifteen."

"She probably shouldn't help Katy with her math," Kasha quipped.

Esme hadn't meant to launch like that, but all the putrid little frustrations and resentment had suddenly surfaced like a fart in a bathtub. "I want you to always be my mom," she said. "But you abandoned us! Can't you come home? We need you." *She* needed Melinda, to straighten out the boy thing. Ronnie was too young to date and Katy didn't have a responsible bone in her body, not even a sesamoid, which was only an ossified node.

"I promise, I'll try to get home more. But I have to go to Amesbury in two weeks for a council meeting on the solstice, and I won't be back until after the vernal equinox."

"Stonehenge? For four months? You can't go. Not now!"

Melinda hugged her. "It's a major pagan event. I committed

to this over a year ago. I told you all about it. There are solar, lunar, and stellar alignments that won't reoccur in our lifetime. I'm a keynote speaker."

"But you're never home. Can't you get out of it?" Esme pleaded.

"Honey. I wish I could. I'll help you with your potion, or whatever you're working on. But Kasha? Do you know what he is? Do you know what you're getting yourself into? I don't want you getting mixed up in this stuff. You need to get a little more experience under your belt."

"Unfortunately, it isn't up to you, Melinda," Kasha said.

"How could you just leave me like that?" she reproached the cat. "Damn you!"

"Redundant, that," he reminded her.

"I'll get you a Siamese kitten. Blue point. From a breeder. I'll let you pick her out."

"Tempting. Esme, I hope you're taking notes. I *do* have a fondness for Asian chicks. But no, I'm going to give Esme a whirl."

"But why?" Melinda pleaded.

"I told you I didn't want to move to the city," he said. "I have no intention of wasting another minute of this eternity as a house pet to a shopkeeper. You knew I had a quota. I haven't had a score in years, with your lily-white magic. Do you have any idea what's going to happen, when the hounds of hell come for me? There's no action here, not even any gophers."

"That reminds me," Melinda said. "There's a giant rat in the botanical garden."

"Rat, did you say?" Kasha asked, sitting up with interest. "How big?"

"Biggest one I've ever seen," she claimed. "I doubt you can take him."

Kasha was already bounding through the store, his mind on his prey.

"We don't have much time," Melinda whispered, "and he has unbelievable hearing." She grasped her oldest daughter by the shoulders with both hands. "You can never, ever trust Kasha. He's a demon. Did he tell you that?"

"Well yeah, Mom. He told me everything, pretty much."

"Did he also tell you there's no such thing as good and evil, only order and chaos, and they were flip sides of the same coin?"

"Uh . . . yeah?"

"It's a lie," Melinda said. "There's definitely good and evil, and Kasha is evil. So you must be *very* careful with your immortal soul, do you hear me? He can harvest your soul under his contract if you commit an unforgivably evil act. You must never, ever do anything to harm anyone. You must be better than good. The reason I moved out of the house was to keep him away from you girls, until you're old enough to know better. But I'm glad he went to you, anyway. At least he went to my one daughter who has a little common sense. If there was anything I could do to keep him away from you I would, but it's out of my hands now, so promise me, Esme, swear an oath, that you'll be very careful. And if you're ever tempted to do a spell that seems a little shady, just . . . just don't do it, is all I can say."

So Esme swore a sacred oath to her mother, knowing that such oaths are not broken in the Wiccan faith, especially between mother and daughter. It was an easy oath to make. Esme was a very cautious individual. If her irresponsible mother and wild great-aunt Becky could handle Kasha, Esme was quite confident that *she* could.

"Good, honey," Melinda said, hugging her daughter when they had finished. "Now let's get that tourist crap out of your basket and we'll get you set up with some botanicals from my private stash. And I've got some Peruvian pink amber that's the bomb."

Before they departed for the ride back to Middleton, Kasha consented to help Melinda mix up a quick batch of "Miracle Elixir Cream of Youthe for Face and Neck," an old recipe from the family grimoire. "If you insist on going around hairless, the least you can do is smooth out those hideous wrinkles," he said, making a few passes of the paw over the bubbling cauldron, and intoning several rather shocking Latin phrases in a surprisingly resonant voice.

Esme also obtained a jar of zit cream from Melinda's special stock in the closet behind the tarot room for Veronica. It was the premium stuff, with Kasha's juju all over it, the quality that Melinda sold to only the most discriminating customers for two hundred bucks a jar.

"Remember, when you give it to her, tell Ronnie her mom loves her," Melinda said. "And give Katy a big smooch for me. And tell Dad I'll be home at the end of March."

28

CURSES FOILED AGAIN

On Monday morning Katy awoke to the smell of singed ecto-plasm. Her head felt weird, like it was humongous and light as a feather, yet somehow so dense she couldn't lift it off the pillow. She tried to brush her mop of hair back from her face with her hand and rose abruptly, startled, displacing Socrates, who'd slept on her pillow. She swept the blankets off. At the full-length mir-ror on her wall by the wardrobe, she checked to see what the damage was.

Pretty brutal. One side of her head, including her eyebrow, was bald as a Magic 8 Ball. She still had hair on the other side, and on the top. She looked back at Socrates on the bed. He was half bald as well. She reconstructed the sleep positions in her mind and decided that some kind of magical depilatory dust had settled on her in the night, like a fine blanket of snow, and removed her hair down to the skin. The only thing that had saved her from a much worse outcome was the little miniature pinscher, who had protected the top of her head like a blanket.

Veronica's work, obviously. If Esme had done this she'd be completely bald and probably purple. Katy surveyed the damage from every angle. She had wigs, but they were all rather theatrical. She posed, angling every way she could think of. Then she ran her fingers through her hair, willing the colors. She chanted a few entreaties to the Goddess, until she felt the eerie static between her fingers. She insinuated black into her hair, at the roots, teal in the middle, and fuchsia at the ends. She made an impromptu part on the left side, a sort of zigzag, with hair over and under the part. She trimmed her bangs with a scissors and teased them stiff. Then she draped the bulk of her hair, Veronica Lake–style, over her right eye, half tucked behind the ear, the other half back, over the shoulder.

It was perfect. Ronnie would die a little, when she saw it. Katy shook her head vigorously once, as a test. It still had natural movement, but it held. Now what to wear? Daddy's borrowed white button-down shirt, open in front to either side of the leather bustier, knotted underneath. Hoop earring on one side. Leggings and army boots. The look was Tank-Girl-meets-Madonna-and-beats-up-Jessica-Rabbit-with-a-billiard-cue. Needed punk makeup, though . . .

Katy joined her sisters in the kitchen. "Ooh, raisin bread!" she exclaimed, fishing two slices out of the bag. She put them into the toaster and opened the refrigerator.

"New look?" Esme asked. Esme was no longer shocked by anything Katy wore to school.

"Thought I'd try it," Katy said. "Whattaya think, Ronnie?" she solicited, with a mirth and cheerfulness entirely out of place on someone who'd just been cursed.

Ronnie wouldn't give her the satisfaction. "That's so tacky, it went past tacky and looped into cool, then kept going back around the wheel to tacky again, and stopped in the worst place."

Liar, liar, Katy thought. Which gave her a brilliant idea for retaliation.

~~♦~~

The Internet, like the universe, is infinite and full of nonsense, Katy had observed. But there was also plenty of truth out there, if you knew where to look. There was a consensus among practitioners of the craft that there was no actual magic on any search engine in the first fifty pages of any search for potions or spells. A layman could spend an eternity on the Internet and never find anything useful at all. But Katy had found a number of great blogs and websites over the years that had yielded a trove of spells and potions and charms. Katy had her mentor's help, and uncanny kismet. She could throw jelly beans at her computer keyboard from across the room blindfolded and hit exactly the URL she needed at any given moment.

Katy decided to use good old-fashioned voodoo. She had an affinity for it, she practically had Haitian drumbeats in her pulse. She made a totem of her younger sister, mostly from modeling clay and art supplies, retrieving hair from Ronnie's brush in the bathroom and toenail clippings from the wastebasket that had to be hers, they were so dainty and perfect. The voodoo doll was a very good likeness. Katy was an artist, after all. She snuck into Ronnie's room and painted the doll's face with her makeup, which was where her sister kept her powers.

Tonight's spell was a powerful one. She needed either a small animal sacrifice or her own blood, according to two different websites. Katy frequently improvised, mixing and matching bits of Latin here, English there, Hindustani when the mood struck her, voodoo with Tibetan mysticism with Chinese medicine with Quaker prayer. It almost always worked out, somehow. She was just that good. So she opted for blood and pricked her finger resolutely. She dripped the blood on the throat of Ronnie's totem, chanting. Tomorrow was going to be a blast.

Veronica awoke on Tuesday morning with a sore throat and thought nothing of it. She'd been up late the night before with the grimoire, trying to finesse the pièce de résistance, a curse so vile she couldn't help giggling every time she imagined how funny it would be if she could pull it off. But in a spontaneous panic, she'd dropped everything to put up a protective spell from the grimoire, with some herbs and powders Esme had obtained for her. The ritual had turned out to be far more complex than she'd imagined. She ran through it six times and it never felt right. Her mind was too distracted worrying about what Katy would do to her. She'd crossed the line with the curse of misty baldness, and Katy scared the piss out of her.

Ronnie entered the kitchen entirely blemish free, thanks to her mom's miracle zit cream, guaranteed against curses, hexes, and French fries. She had her mojo back. Something in the protection spell must have kicked in. She felt bulletproof.

Katy was sitting at the breakfast table in the far seat with a very smug expression. Hair was growing back out on Katy's bald side at a ridiculous rate. She had almost a half inch of growth already. A shiver ran up Ronnie's spine ominously. She was insane, going head-to-head with a beast like her sister.

"Did you sleep well, beautiful?" Katy asked, in excellent cheer.

"Yeah, fine," Ronnie replied.

"Are you hungry?"

Of course not, she meant to reply. She was never hungry, as far as anyone was concerned. Appetite of a bird. She would never admit to being hungry, because then someone would ask her why she didn't eat something. "Starving," she admitted, and Katy laughed.

"So why don't you eat something?" Katy asked, absolutely gleeful.

Ronnie clutched at her throat. She'd been about to say she wasn't hungry, then she'd gotten a tickle in her throat and the other thing came out. She was always hungry, any idiot should know that. She starved herself, to keep those hip bones angular, to keep every muscle in her abdomen in perfect tone, to keep her waist small enough that Zack could encircle it entirely with both hands. "What did you do to me?" she gasped, aghast.

"I made an honest girl out of you," Katy replied. "So, why don't you eat something?"

Ronnie was mortified. She'd been cursed to tell the truth! What a nightmare! "Because I don't want to be a fat pig like you," she answered, wiping the smirk off her sister's face.

Then again, Ronnie thought, *there might be a way to work this honesty thing.*

❧ ❧

At school, the sisters hardly trusted each other out of sight anymore. Nobody wanted to give anybody else a chance to sneak off with Zack. They were like the three Graeae, the gray witch sisters of myth who shared one eye and one tooth, each guarding jealously for fear that one of the others might steal away with the cherished items. Each sister had places staked out where they knew Zack would pass, so among the three of them they'd reconstructed his entire schedule. They all caught up with him at lunch, as he was headed to his car.

"Wow, déjà vu," he joked as he paused for a brief chat. "It seems I'm running into you three all over today. Must be destiny."

The sisters all laughed, each in her own way. "That's odd," Katy mentioned. "We were just talking about you, Zack. Your ears must have been burning."

"All lies, I'm sure," he teased.

Esme hated how easily Katy could joke with Zack, how natural they seemed together, how his eyes sparkled with mirth behind the dark glasses when he looked at her.

"Lies don't do you justice," Katy said, taking his hand and swinging it in time to the banter. "Ronnie was just telling us how she feels about you. Go ahead, Ronnie, tell Zack how you feel."

Veronica paled, and her stomach churned. This is what Katy had planned all along, with her truth spells. Katy wanted to take away her entire game of hard to get, to drag her down to the level of girl-with-puppy-love-crush. But she could do nothing about it. It was like watching herself from a distance, saying words she'd never intended to say out loud:

"I love him," she confessed. "I love you, Zack. I don't think anybody else is good enough for you. Especially not Katy, she's a pig half the time, she makes noises when she eats." And then Veronica found herself concluding the entire spectacle by kissing Zack earnestly on the lips.

"Wow," Zack said. "I had no idea. I was just heading off campus for a coffee; care to join me? We'll have to hurry if we want to be back for fourth period."

Ronnie didn't hesitate. She dropped her hand from his shoulder down to his waist, and hooked a finger into his belt loop in back. Then she steered him toward the parking lot and they were off, before Katy and Esme even had a chance to pick their jaws up off the ground.

Watching them walk off arm-in-arm, Esme turned to Katy. There was nothing but resignation in her voice. "Nice going, genius."

29

ROLLING THUNDER

On Wednesday morning Katy woke up with farts so loud they could call a ship back to port through pea-soup fog. They were coming out of her like waves rolling up on the shore, one after another: As soon as one was out, she could feel the next one building. They were so stinky Edna the Great Dane tried to worm her way under the bed. Even Kilroy was offended by the stench, a dog that loved nothing more than to roll in horse poop.

Katy tried pulling the covers up over her head. Bad idea. She found herself in a Dutch oven that practically burned her flesh off. So she got out of bed and opened the window all the way. She couldn't go to school like this. And Katy needed to go to school today, because Ronnie had taken a solid lead in the Zack derby and was headed for the post eight lengths ahead.

What she really needed to do was stick her butt out the window for these, she decided, wincing at the stink.

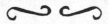

Esme awoke in a cold sweat to the sound of thunder, from a nightmare about being Cinderella's ugly stepsister in an ugly dress, fighting to steal a peek through a throng of enraptured fans mobbing the two most beautiful people in the world, Zack and Veronica, as they ran laughingly down an aisle strewn with rose petals, pursued by paparazzi and Hollywood directors waving contracts at them. Fourteen was too young to date. Ronnie was like one of those underage gymnasts with mad skills and muscles of coiled carbon steel and zero gravitational mass who China was constantly sneaking into the Olympics because they could kick the crap out of anyone over fifteen. It was unfair to have to compete against fourteen-year-olds. There was a good reason they were banned.

The thunder rolled over the house again, and Esme shot out of bed with a start. It was the first day of December and she'd left a vital element of her beauty potion to infuse overnight in the light of the full moon, but it couldn't get wet. She ran out the basement door in her pajamas and slippers into the chill morning air, slipping on the frost in the grass. But there wasn't a cloud in the sky. She heard another peal of thunder. Sonic boom? In the attic, Katy's butt was hanging out the window, mooning her. How horribly rude! Odd, but rude.

Upstairs for breakfast, Esme found Veronica on the floor by the sink and rushed to her aid. "Ronnie, are you okay?" The girl appeared to be having some kind of seizure, her face buried in her hands, writhing on the floor in apparent agony. With calming fingers, Esme brushed back her sister's hair, and felt her forehead with the back of her hand. She managed to get Veronica to stop quivering and catch her breath. Then the sound of thunder rolled over the house again, and Ronnie had a relapse. That's when Esme noticed that Ronnie was actually rolling on the floor laughing her ass off.

"Ka-Katy isn't c-c-coming to school today," Veronica managed, wheezing for breath.

"My Goddess," Esme said. "Do you smell that? What is it? It's like a sewer line exploded."

This observation only served to cause another relapse. "Help me up, Esme," Ronnie begged, gasping. "We have to get out of here."

∽ ∾

At school that day, Esme was confident in her red-and-white Manchester United Red Devils authorized winger's sports jacket, which had finally arrived. She couldn't wait for Zack to see it. But wherever she stalked Zack, she kept running into Norman. She didn't want to talk to Norman. She'd gotten a C on her calculus test and hadn't turned in two weeks of homework.

"Esme, I have to talk to you," Norm said with some urgency as they left first period.

"Not now, Norm," she replied. She cut left at the door and lost him, but she never caught up with Ronnie. And Zack wasn't on his normal route between classes.

Norman was already at his desk in biology, writing in his notebook. Esme slipped into a chair in the second row so she wouldn't have to look at him. She could feel his eyes boring into the back of her head. He caught up with her in the hallway after class.

"Esme, if you won't talk to me, at least read this note," he said, pressing a folded piece of paper into her hand. She grabbed the paper, glaring angrily.

"If I read it, will you stop stalking me?"

"Read it," he insisted. "I'll see you in the cafeteria."

Esme still had the note in her hand when she walked into computer lab. She'd been in the quad, waiting for Zack. He'd never showed up. She got out her workbook. She'd see Zack at lunch, or in world history. She dropped Norm's note and smoothed it out on her desk.

Norm's handwriting was a kind of tiny, jagged but even script. Crumbling the note had been a mistake. It was a wonder Norman could write so small. A pen looked like a toothpick in his gigantic hands. *Your life is in grave danger*, the note began.

She scanned the rest of the note quickly. It was about Zack. She had very little patience for Norm's opinion on the subject. He was jealous, obviously. The note mentioned how Zack had put Danny Long and Logan Rehnquist in the hospital. Well duh, she'd been there. And stuff about how Norm's dad had heard of certain types of people who were very dangerous, shadowy characters, and they all shared this odd characteristic illness, urticaria, a kind of photosensitivity. Zack had already told her about that. Then there was more nonsense, about how he was worried about her and cared about her and would she please come with him after school and talk to his dad? Norm had written about fifteen hundred words on the front and back of one page, all jumbled up tight. It was enough to give her eyestrain.

Esme gave up on the note. She flipped it back and forth, front to back to front a few times, to see if anything else caught her eye, but it was hard to focus on. Norman's letter was some pathetic attempt to get her attention. But there was P.S. on the back of the letter, and her heart felt like it had just crashed into a wall and flattened out and splattered inside her chest:

P.S. Wilson said he saw your sister Veronica ditching first period today with Zack and getting into his car.

174

By three thirty that afternoon, there were only two cars left in the student parking lot: Esme's Subaru and Norman's Denali. Norman drove the huge SUV out of necessity, for the size, though he was aware that the thing killed about a polar bear a mile from all the carbon emissions. His father had hired an auto-body shop to move the driver's seat back an extra eight inches. Norman had come to Esme's car and rapped on the window when the last straggling students had left the parking lot, but she would not acknowledge him. She kept fiddling with her phone, messaging Veronica, emailing her, calling her, texting her. Somewhere in Middleton, Ronnie's phone was beeping and buzzing and pinging and tumbling, but she never picked up.

It was after four when the Mercedes sedan pulled into the parking lot. Norman was there beside it before it had rolled to a stop, trying to yank the passenger side door open. It was locked. He gave the handle a tug that showed he meant business. It rocked the entire car. It was a wonder the door didn't come off the hinges.

Esme was beside Norman. There was an audible click as the door unlocked, and the giant yanked it open instantly. Norm had no business meddling whatsoever, but Esme was glad he was there. Ronnie was going to catch an earful from her big sister, and then Barry would be brought into it and Melinda, and Veronica would be grounded for the rest of eternity.

Esme was just about to give Ronnie a piece of her mind, trying to figure out how to sound mature and responsible in front of Zack without appearing a nag. Norm looked like he might erupt at any minute. "I need to talk to you, Zack," he said forcefully. "Alone."

"You two go ahead," Esme improvised. She'd give Ronnie hell in private, and Zack would never be the wiser. "I need to talk to Ronnie."

Zack casually unfolded himself from the driver's seat and stood. Next to Norman, he was tiny, but he held his poise perfectly. The two crossed the parking lot, away from the girls, toward the bleachers. The field was deserted. The Timberwolves' season was over. There would be no regionals, for the last-place team in the division.

Esme turned her attention to her deliriously giddy sister. "Ronnie, have you been drinking?"

Veronica spun around, arms extended, like Julie Andrews in the Alps. The parking lot was alive with the sound of music. "Not drinking, silly," she reported, giggling. "Kissing."

Apparently, Ronnie was not racked with remorse about missing school. "Do you know what Dad is going to say when I tell him you ditched school to ride around with a boy?"

"I don't care," Ronnie said petulantly, if it's possible to be petulant and blissed out of one's skull at the same time. She spun around a few more times, then teetered into her older sister, who caught her before she fell dizzily to the asphalt. "Oh, Esme, I had the most amazing time of my life. You are happy for me, aren't you?"

Before Esme could respond, which might easily have involved hair pulling and the clawing out of eyes, she was distracted by an altercation. Norm's voice was carrying over the parking lot, and he sounded angry. "C'mon, Ronnie," she yelled over her shoulder.

"I know what you're up to!" Norm yelled.

"You're barmy, mate," Zack said calmly.

"I'm only going to tell you this once," Norman said, looming. "You leave Veronica alone. You don't touch her, you hear me? Or Katy, or Esme. They're my friends. Think of them as my sisters. And I'm their overly protective, psychotic older brother."

"Really not your business, mate," Zack replied amiably. "Anyway, we were just snogging."

"I don't care what you were doing, cut it out," the giant warned, taking another step forward. Esme had seen this dance before. Zack hadn't given ground last time, but this time he did, a little. Norman was that intimidating. "If I hear about you going near any of them again, you're going to have to answer to me."

"Now wait just a minute," Esme objected. "Who the hell do you think you are, Norman? Do you have any idea how insulting that is, you coming on with your macho crap and trying to protect me? I'm an independent woman, and I can take care of myself. And my own baby sister, too, who's too young to date, by the way, Zack. So just butt out, Frank N. Stein."

"You tell 'em, sister!" Veronica chimed in. "But not the dating thing. I'm old enough," she reassured Zack with a wink that involved both eyes. She couldn't coordinate just the one.

"Esme. You're not thinking right at the moment. And I'm not going to let this . . . this *monster* . . ." Norm practically spat. "If he comes near you, I swear, I'm going to take him out. I don't need your permission. This is between me and Zack."

"Get stuffed," Zack returned. "I don't care how big you are, I'm not intimidated by you. Back off!" Then Zack did something that looked entirely stupid: He shoved Norman, who was nearly three times his size, with both hands.

Norman bent over a little at the shove, and had to take two quick steps back to keep his balance. Zack's shove had been lightning fast, and his strength was uncanny. In response, Norm backhanded the smaller boy with a hand like a steam shovel. Zack tried to duck away, but the hand sent him sprawling.

Zack came back at Norman with fists in a blur. There was

no way to defend against it, so Norman took body blow after body blow, and every strike was bone-shaking. Norm scrambled to get a punch in or defend himself or grab Zack, to no avail. And all the while, Esme was screaming "Norm! Stop it, don't hurt him!"

Me? Hurt him? Norman thought, as Zack continued to pound away at him with sledgehammer blows and near impunity. He took punch after punch, until he recognized a pattern and caught one of Zack's fists in his left hand in a grip like a bear trap. If Zack wanted his arm back, he'd have to chew off the hand at the wrist. Zack continued to punch with his right hand and kicked at Norman's shins. Norman felt those kicks. They were agony. Norm was trying to reel Zack in, but the smaller boy was elusive. Zack jumped up, gaining leverage, and pounded Norm hard with a downward strike to the temple that would have felled a bull elephant. Esme had seen a punch like that once. It had put Danny Long in a coma.

Norman reeled. His eyes rolled up in his head, but he held on to Zack's hand, and now he brought his own right hand in to slap at Zack's neck, except he held on and wrapped his huge fingers around the smaller boy's throat, squeezing. Esme was screaming in Norm's ears, pulling at him, and Veronica was pounding on his back, but it was like two flies buzzing around. Norm squeezed harder still. It would have been the end of almost anyone. But not Zack.

Zack used his free hand to pry Norm's thumb off his windpipe. Norman felt the thumb bend back. If there was one thing Norman was confident of, it was that he had the strongest grip on Earth. A hydraulic jack shouldn't have been able to move his thumb from Zack's throat. But Zack pulled it back with enough strength to break the bone. Something had to give, and soon.

Norm threw Zack to the ground. Zack was back on his feet in a flash, coming back for more, tapping at his neck and looking at his hand. "You bloody tosser," Zack snarled. "You cut me!"

"Oh, sorry," Norman replied. His anger of a few minutes before was dissipating. Norman looked into his palm and fiddled with something. "My ring, it has a sharp edge inside. Here, I'll take it off." The ring was a huge affair of braided copper and brass bands. Norman worked it off his finger and put it into his jacket pocket.

But as he did, Zack attacked again, enraged. He'd gone entirely feral. He moved like a mongoose striking a cobra. In one move, he had a straight razor in his hand. He wove into Norman's space, around the left arm on the outside, leaping and spinning, and slashed down at the giant's neck with the blade. His movement was so fast, Esme and Veronica never saw the knife. Zack slit Norman's neck, deep. Blood poured out, soaking Norm's collar. He slapped his right hand over the wound, trying to hold the blood in.

"Norman, stop!" Esme shouted.

Norm staggered back, holding his neck. In that moment, Esme and Veronica were in front of the giant, facing him, arms extended.

"Norman, get out of here," Ronnie screamed. "Leave Zack alone!"

Norm looked imploringly from Esme to Veronica. How could they side with Zack? The sisters were looking at him like he was some kind of monster, with their arms out to protect the actual monster from *him*. The wound to his throat was nothing compared to the betrayal he felt. Behind the girls, Zack was pacing with a feral glint to his eyes. He wanted more! Yet there was still the intelligence there. He wasn't going to attack, because he knew he'd won. In the battle for Esme and Veronica, Zack had won.

Norman wheeled his SUV into the parking lot of the clinic recklessly, steering with one hand, the other clutched to his throat, dizzy from loss of blood. His shirt and jacket were soaked with the stuff. He staggered into the living room. "Dad," he yelled, slamming through the swinging double doors into the clinic proper.

His father came running out of the lab in hospital scrubs. "Exam room one, stat!" he bellowed, grabbing an emergency kit from the nurses' station.

The wound was deep, but very clean. After stopping the blood with pressure, Dr. Stein sutured his son's neck. "I never meant for you to take risks like this," he chastised, trembling. He had to stop and pull himself together to continue stitching. "This could have been a fatal wound. Don't ever do anything like that again."

"Yeah, I think he was going for the jugular," Norm acknowledged. "Bet he didn't expect to run into titanium rebar. Man, he is fast. And strong! Superhuman, no question."

"I spent the morning at the police station," Dr. Stein said. "We'll get no help there. Everyone I talk to gets this glazed-over expression if I mention Drake Kallas or his son. Post-hypnotic, almost a drugged effect. All the cops can say is what great citizens they are, and how they had nothing to do with the disappearance of those girls."

"So if they mesmerized the police to believe they had nothing to do with the disappearances, we can conclude that they're responsible for the disappearances," Norm inferred.

"Almost certainly," said his father. "Norman, I don't want you confronting Zack anymore. I talked to the coroner; there's nothing left of the Sharp family to examine, but he confirmed what your friend Wilson mentioned, that the dog was found with a broken neck in the dog run outside. There was an open dog door leading into the house. The dog was a retired police canine; it would have warned the family of the fire, if it hadn't been a murder."

"Yeah. We should probably sleep with one eye open."

"The clinic is relatively secure. Remember, there used to be a pharmacy here, so there's a very high-tech security system." Dr. Stein finished suturing his son's neck and leaned back to inspect his handiwork. "You'll have a scar," he advised. He laughed at the absurdity of the statement. It was like telling Lydia the tattooed lady she'd have a smudge. "Anyway, I hope it was all worth it."

Norman reached into his jacket pocket and removed the very large copper-and-bronze ring he'd constructed out of twisted wire. On the inside of the ring was a small surgical lance, with a one-quarter-inch blade. Attached to the inside of the ring beneath the lance in a wire basket of copper was a small vial with a rubber stopper in it. In the vial was about a half ounce of Zack's blood. "Totally worth it, I think," Norm said.

30

TOIL AND TROUBLE

Esme's bedroom was starting to look like a sci-fi lab from a B movie. She still had the old door and sawhorses in her room, from the dinner party that now seemed like years ago. On top of this large workspace she'd set up her lab equipment, and now things were bubbling and distilling and infusing and smoking. A little theremin music to set the mood was all she needed.

Esme had test tubes and beakers from an old chemistry set her parents had bought for her eleventh birthday, but she'd supplemented this equipment with some sophisticated glassware from a lab supplies website. There were several Bunsen burners feeding off the propane canister from her father's grill. There were bell jars over smoke infusions of aromatics, and burettes with pinchcocks slow-dripping extracts of botanicals onto mounds of powdered minerals and dried animal parts in crystalizing dishes. There were mortars and pestles for pulverizing herbs and making poultices to be processed into infusions and extracts. There was distillation apparatus slow-cooking concoctions that had taken Esme days to prepare. There was a round-bottom borosilicate distillation flask feeding into a copper coil that dripped a greenish ooze into a glass separatory funnel with a stopcock.

Kasha walked up and down the length of the table, sniffing at everything. "Becky used to brew up a love potion in ten days flat in a couple copper pots and a big cast-iron cauldron."

"I intend to make a science out of this," Esme replied. "I'm going to study biochemistry and molecular neurology at Stanford, and bring alchemy out of the dark ages."

"Yeah, like you could get into Stanford now, with your grades."

"I have a demon cat for a familiar, it shouldn't be too hard to finagle something," she countered unconvincingly, gnawing her lip. She was wearing goggles and pouring the contents of two test tubes into an Erlenmeyer flask, watching for the color of the liquids to change as they reacted. "Hey, is this supposed to turn black?"

Kasha examined the flask, sniffing. "It's supposed to be brown, but darker is better."

The potion was taking forever because of Esme's obsessive inability to simply follow the instructions in the grimoire on faith. She insisted on knowing precisely what each herb was for, what the properties of all the ingredients were, and how they were used in other potions. The cross-referencing and research took forever. Kasha argued that Esme was too skeptical to ever be a good witch, that she had to throw caution to the winds and just go for it. Katy never thought twice about her magic, she just did it, he explained, and that was why magic worked for her. Esme overthought everything. She researched every incantation to the Latin roots of every word. She insisted on knowing what spirits she was invoking and how the eldritch forces affected the results in every step. Her argument was that once she knew the properties of every ingredient and the way the material and spirit worlds interacted, she'd have the building blocks to create her own potions and spells, and improve on the ones in the grimoire. Esme was giving herself an education not only in the practice of magic but also in the underlying fundamentals. Kasha could not sway her with his demonic mumbo-jumbo.

Esme went to the computer to research whether a specific Roma phrase, which she'd tracked to a Hindustani root, was invoking an elemental, a nature force she felt she could trust, or a spirit that might have malignant intent. She was disturbed by a soft but persistent rapping at the door. She went and opened it a crack. Veronica, looking exceedingly anxious. She'd driven her sister home after the fight at school, and Ronnie had been insufferably blissful about all the smooching she'd done with Zack that day. Esme hadn't ratted the girl out to her father, though, on the theory that Katy's retaliation was likely to be punishment enough.

"Esme, did you take the grimoire back?" Veronica asked nervously.

"Not I. Must be Katy. She was home all day with cosmic farts, for some reason. Didn't you set wards in your room?"

"No. What are wards?" Veronica craned her neck to get a look into Esme's room. "What are you doing in here with all the lab equipment?"

"Science homework," Esme lied.

∽ ᧁ ∽

When they'd gotten home that afternoon, Esme had reconstructed the fight blow by blow for the benefit of poor Katy, who again had missed out on all the violence. Katy had been on the toilet all day with the grimoire, searching for counter-charms, and had finally come up with an antidote in the early afternoon.

"Oh, it's not over," Katy had promised Esme with cold,

calculated intent. "Veronica Silver has crossed the line this time. I'm going to teach her a lesson she's never going to forget. She's going to beg me to lift this curse. And my price will be that she never speak to Zackery Kallas again." Esme had to take a step back from Katy. The girl was clearly crackling with static electricity. Her eyes were glowing.

"This isn't like you, Katy," Esme had pled, scared for Ronnie. "Maybe I could talk to her? And you two could stop this hexing and cursing."

"Sure, sweetie," Katy said, walking past. She touched Esme on the cheek. Esme nearly jumped out of her skin at the shock. "But after. Trust me, it'll all be over in a couple of days."

❦

Outside Esme's bedroom door, Ronnie was shivering. "Esme, I'm scared. Do you have any idea what Katy's planning?"

Esme stepped out of her bedroom to the strip of hallway at the bottom of the stairs, closing the door behind herself, then took Ronnie in her arms and hugged her, brushing her hair back from her face. "I have no idea, honey, but be prepared for the worst."

"I don't know what came over me. You know I love Katy, don't you? It's just . . . I can't explain how desperately I need to have Zack. She's never even kissed him. And she's trying to take him from me. It's so awful, why would she do that to me?"

"Honey, maybe she wants him just as much as you do, did you think of that?" *Do you ever think of anything except yourself? Do you even care that your oldest sister loves the same boy?*

"I just want it to be over," Ronnie said, sobbing. "Can't you do anything?"

"Maybe this would be a good time to reflect," Esme said.

"Like, maybe you should think of the consequences before you go around cursing the most talented witch this side of the Mississippi with thunder farts." She stroked Ronnie's hair, dabbing at a tear with the cuff of her sleeve. "I talked to Katy earlier. Maybe if you apologized, and begged her to forgive you, and promised her your allowance for a few years . . ."

Veronica sniffled. "I could do that," she agreed.

"And you'd have to give up Zack," Esme added.

Veronica's expression went from contrite to defiant in the blink of an eye. She dropped her sister's embrace as if Esme were a crumbling bag of wriggling, infectious worms. She turned on her heel and headed back toward the stairs.

"Tell Katy to bring it," she said over her shoulder.

"Hey, Ronnie?" Esme said.

"Yeah?" the girl replied. She'd halted but hadn't turned around.

"I'll still love you when you're a smoldering glob of boneless protoplasm."

HIS MASTER'S VOICE

Zack did not know, from one moment to the next, how the Ancient would react to anything he said or did. Sometimes they could carry on perfectly normal conversations for extended periods of time, but every word, every phrase, was fraught with underlying hazard. The Master could fly into a rage at the most innocuous things.

Zack hadn't felt any sense of danger during his fight with Norman. He was nearly indestructible. His bones could break or his flesh could be torn, but he was a fast healer, and he was fairly impervious to pain. Norman was unbelievably strong. When he'd punched the giant in the head as hard as he could, any decent sort of a bloke should have observed protocols and lost consciousness. Norman had earned his grudging respect.

Norman didn't frighten Zack, but the Master most certainly did. Over the centuries Drake had acquired speed, power, cruelty, and an encyclopedic knowledge of ways to inflict pain. Even with Zack's high tolerance, the beatings were excruciating. Sometimes, the Master would beat him for hours. Inflicting pain was one of Drake's greatest pleasures, and Zack was the only one who could survive more than a few minutes of punishment.

Tonight's torment had started with Drake's cat-and-mouse interrogation, after Zack had returned in the late afternoon with marks on him. At the Master's insistence, he'd told all about his fight with the giant. He could not lie or resist answering any question, if asked directly. He was little more than a cringing underling, insignificant in the shining magnificence of the Ancient. Their association had commenced under the guise of mentor and acolyte, had progressed to commander and soldier, and had now become that of master and slave.

The Master finished his interrogation calmly. Changing the subject, he informed Zack that they were in dire need of new wives, as if he were reviewing minutes from a board meeting. Miss Edwards was out of commission with a broken collarbone and extreme hematoma about the face and shoulders. That left only Michelle, Danielle, and Lisa. Lisa was rather petite, and Danielle was getting a distinct redness to the eyes and would most likely need to be destroyed in a few weeks. There was certainly not enough blood to sustain the two of them. If they went to the well too often, the well would run dry. Or bite back.

The Master had then asked Zack what he'd been working on, in terms of acquisitions. Zack made the mistake of trying to be vague. "There are a number of likely girls," he admitted hesitantly. "I know you have exacting standards."

The Master said nothing. That was not a good sign.

"There's a lovely redheaded girl who works at the organic food store in town. She smells exquisite," Zack offered. A pathetic attempt at diversion.

"Ah," returned the Master, studying Zack's eyes with interest. "Is that so?"

There were, in fact, three sisters, but he couldn't stand the thought of Drake getting them in his clutches. Zack wondered if he was getting sentimental all of a sudden, if he actually had feelings for them. They claimed to be Wiccans, but Zack had never believed in that Satanic stuff. Though they did have something about them, something almost magical. The youngest, Veronica, was the type of girl who'd make all your mates green with envy, strikingly gorgeous. She was far too young, of course, but in a different life, in different circumstances . . . if only he wasn't a bloodsucking monster. She reminded Zack of Helena, the Ukrainian girl he'd murdered. Helena had been so beautiful when first he'd seen her, willowy and lithe. She'd wasted away to nothing over the months. Not that it mattered; the Master would have made him kill her anyway. All the brides had to die, eventually. Veronica would have to die as well, if Drake caught her in his snare.

The middle sister, Katy, was the type of girl you just wanted to hang out with, to joke with and have a good time. She was quite goofy sometimes, and sometimes she said things that you wouldn't think anyone could ever come up with. Any lad would be very lucky to get a girl like that. And she could be quite alluring, when the mood struck her. With a girl like Katy, there would never be a dull moment. If he weren't a predator. If she weren't his prey.

And then there was Esmeralda, a girl with a good head on her shoulders. You couldn't go wrong with a girl like her. Esme was the girl you brought home to meet your parents, the one you'd marry if you had any sense. She'd go to football games with you and cheer for the Red Devils. You'd sit at home with Esme on a rainy day and read books and drink tea. Esme *also* reminded Zack of someone; she had from the moment he'd met her: Madeleine. And with his last shred of humanity, Zack had loved Madeleine.

Zack had thought about the three sisters, often and deeply. If he could get a do-over, if he could go back to just being a boy again instead of the horrible thing he'd become, he'd be lucky to get any of them for a girlfriend. But choosing any of the three sisters was a death sentence. Only a few weeks before, he'd thought to bring them back to the lair, to please the Master. But that was before he'd had to kill Sandy, before his regard for the sisters had grown to the point where he simply couldn't bear the thought of Drake destroying them. He wished he could keep them away. Worse yet, as much as he yearned for their company, he also yearned for their blood. It was getting hard to keep those two impulses separate. While snogging with Veronica, hadn't he also imagined guzzling her blood? Could he even trust himself with her? Could he kill Veronica with his bare hands, the way he had Sandy? If the Master commanded it, he would have no choice.

~~~

"Redheaded, did you say?" asked the Master, feigning interest.

That was when the beating started. The Master used his hands and his feet on Zack, and then a baseball bat until the bat was just a stub, and then the crow bar, avoiding only the face.

Zack told the Master all. He did so within the first twenty minutes of the torture session.

The additional three hours of abuse were just for Drake's amusement.

AN ACE UP THE SLEEVE

Veronica hadn't slept at all, or fitfully at best. She half expected to nod off and wake up with a pig's snout, she was so worried about what Katy was going to do. Without the grimoire, she was defenseless. But there was no sense trying to get it back from that attic with all those dogs. Katy had trained them to protect her stuff.

When her alarm went off at six a.m., she swept the covers off, kicking them as if they were tentacles grabbing at her legs. Which they weren't, thank the Goddess. She did a quick inventory check with her hands: hair, limbs, face . . . all seemed to be in order. If she could just lie there chanting and invoking the Goddess all day, maybe nothing bad would happen to her.

In the bathroom, nothing worked right. Her foundation clumped. She tried to apply eyeliner, but she couldn't draw a straight line. Her lipstick went on perfectly, if she'd only been going for the sad-clown-face look. A drunk toddler could have done a better job. Hair was even worse, entirely unmanageable, full of frizz and cowlicks and split ends. The more she brushed it, the worse it got, as if the brush were full of static electricity. She was in tears at the frustration. She scrubbed her face of makeup, getting soap in her eyes in the process. Stumbling around in the bathroom, feeling for a towel, she tripped and fell into the bathtub, and scrambling to get up, activated the shower, soaking her pajamas. Suddenly, she was a slapstick prodigy.

Ronnie dressed cautiously, managing to ruin a pair of nylons and pop all the buttons off a cotton blouse. She settled on jeans. Her hair was useless so she tied a neutral scarf around it. She finished the look with a trench coat. Most likely, she was going to end up in a trench at some point, the way her day was going. Big sunglasses finished the look: Holly Golightly in the rain. She scrutinized herself critically in the mirror. Still gorgeous.

Katy was waiting for her in the kitchen. "Be ready in fifteen, Esme's staying home sick today, Dad's driving us," she advised. Katy was drinking grapefruit juice with club soda, her newest fetish, and eating Nutella with bananas on multigrain bread.

Ronnie grabbed an apple and a glass of skim milk. She sat at the little table in the breakfast nook, and Katy edged away from her like she had Ebola or something. "Okay, Katy, I know you're dying to tell me. What did you do?"

"Classic jinx," she said proudly. "I gave you a triple whammy, so keep your distance. I don't know how far from ground zero is safe. Word to the wise: When something bad happens, it'll be followed by something worse, and something worse again. They'll come in threes. Devilishly tricky to cast, but . . . hey. I'm Katy. People shouldn't mess with me."

"Tell me how to get rid of it," Veronica begged, crying. Crying almost always worked.

"Oh, sweetie. It lasts forever, or until I remove it."

"How can you do this to your own sister?" Ronnie pleaded. Tears were flowing freely. The trench coat was coming in handy already.

"What was that?" Katy countered. "You'll have to speak up. I have a little ringing in my ears from all the farting yesterday. That was hilarious, by the way."

"I thought you loved me," Ronnie tried.

"I do love you, honey," Katy promised. "Look, I've prepared a bag for you to carry around, with all the stuff you'll need." On the kitchen counter was a small green gym bag. Katy unzipped it and started pulling out supplies. "I packed you plenty of safety pins, for when your buttons all fall off. Or your seams all tear open, whatever. I was going to pack you a needle and thread, but you'd probably bleed out before you could fix anything. Here's a pack of wet wipes. And here's a pencil sharpener; I guess you'll be breaking a lot of points."

"I could use a pen, I guess," Ronnie suggested.

Katy weighed the idea for a moment. "I wouldn't risk it, in your nice ecru trench coat." She reached back into the bag and pulled out a first aid kit. "There are bandages, for paper cuts or if your hand gets mangled in machinery, and some hydrocortisone, for burns and scrapes and poison ivy. And here's an umbrella. I doubt it will protect you if a meteorite falls on your head, but it's better than nothing. Oh yeah, here's a roll of duct tape! A thousand and one uses . . ."

But Veronica wasn't really paying attention. She was silently sobbing into her hands.

With the house to herself all day, Esme worked on her beauty potion. She boiled and distilled and combined liquids and powders and emulsions, her computer open to Google translate, making sure her Greek, Latin, Esperanza, Romany, and Yiddish incantations were correct. It was painstaking work, especially with all the compulsive cross-referencing.

"The language isn't really important, you know," Kasha advised, pacing up and down on the lab table. "It's the witch's intention that drives the results. However much commitment you put into it, that's how good a potion you'll get."

Esme scrutinized the text she'd uploaded to her computer screen. She enlarged the picture and scrolled. Then she retrieved her phone and went through her photo roll, expanding the picture with her fingers to see if the image was any sharper. "Damn," she exclaimed.

"Don't mind if I do," Kasha quipped.

Esme studied her phone screen intently. She magnified the text with the screen zoom tool, but the image lost resolution. "The text in the grimoire was on lambskin, and it's a palimpsest. There's something underneath scratched out. I think this word is '*omorphia*' but this letter could be a phi or rho or even an English 'P.' I need to examine the original text."

"It's in Katy's room," Kasha said hesitantly. "She's sure to have set wards."

"She doesn't need wards," Esme reminded him. "She has dogs."

They went upstairs and approached Katy's door with trepidation. From inside they heard growls of warning. Esme tried the door. "It's locked."

"Okay, so we tried," Kasha said. "Let's go get something to eat."

"A demon cat, afraid of some little dogs," Esme derided, waving a hand over the doorknob. "*Aperio,*" she intoned, eyes intently closed, envisioning the tumblers in her mind. Nothing.

"Try '*recludo,*'" Kasha suggested.

She didn't have to. She could hear the door unlock as the

demon spoke the word. She turned the knob and entered the room, to cacophonous barking and growls. Dervish the pit bull was crouched low, ready to pounce, bloodlust in his eyes.

"Woof!" exclaimed Kasha, entering the room in a slinky, cat-like manner. "Arf, arf! Uh . . . bowwow?" The dogs were momentarily shocked by the unlikeliness of this new threat, but the barking soon resumed, even louder and more aggressive than before. "These guys are jerks," he reported, backing out of the room between Esme's legs.

"What are they saying?" she asked, edging back out the door.

"I don't know, dogs are too stupid to make sense. Something about a squirrel, I think. Wait, let me try something else." Kasha reentered, puffing himself up. His fur stood out straight, so he appeared much larger and more intimidating. He arched his back, tail erect, hissing as he stalked into the room. The dogs picked up on the eerie vibe and started whining, but Dervish, with the jaws of a T. rex, stood his ground.

Kasha seemed much larger by the time he was nose-to-nose with the pit bull. His grin widened, and his feral teeth glistened like razors. Dervish took a step back. Kasha planted his feet, threw back his head, and roared. It was incredibly loud, something between a lion and an elephant, with a little Messerschmitt thrown in. The pit bull broke rank and ran behind the bed. The other dogs were quick to follow.

Esme was still shaking as they entered the room. "What the hell was that?"

"Godzilla, from the original 1954 Toho soundtrack," Kasha explained. "Look at the size of this one," he mentioned as they passed the Great Dane, quivering with her head and one foreleg under the bed. "I could feast for a month on all that."

On Katy's drafting table were all the supplies from Melinda's apothecary chest. There were powders of herbs and minerals in mortars, and residues of dried animal parts in shallow dishes. There were small covered enamel pots and a large copper one, cooking away on racks above all-day candles. An iron cauldron was ready for use. Esme couldn't touch anything on the table without raising sparks. She tapped at a glass vial and got an electric shock for her trouble. Wards.

"Looks like she's trying to make that love potion," Kasha noted.

Esme felt a thump of panic in her chest. She found the grimoire with a location charm her mother had taught her when she was five and kept misplacing her mittens. It was crammed into the stuffing of a large teddy bear. There was a bookmark between the pages of the love potion. "You're right, Kasha. What am I going to do? Once she gets Zack to drink this, it's all over."

"Yup. On the other hand, she's going to hell," Kasha reminded. "So you'll get the last laugh."

"I can't let Katy do that," Esme wailed. "It's not just about Zack; she doesn't understand the repercussions. Can I sabotage it somehow?"

"Don't worry. A love potion is the most difficult, advanced magic in the biz. There's no way Katy can pull it off, potions aren't her forte. Your great-aunt Becky was the most talented witch I've known in all my centuries, and it took her years to produce anything that would even make a guy *like* her a little, and then only if she wore fishnet stockings and a miniskirt. And Becks had *me* for a familiar. By the time she nailed it, she was too old for it to do her any good."

"Are you sure it's no good? I never underestimate Katy."

"She'd have a better chance of winning the lottery and getting hit by lightning at the same time," the cat insisted. "Now check your Greek letters in the grimoire and let's get out of here. The smell of dog is making me wanna hack up a gopher."

Midnight, the witching hour. Katy had noticed that Esme had been in her room and tripped her wards. The dogs were still upset about something. But it didn't matter. Esme couldn't get near the potion. She probably didn't even have a clue what it was.

In another two weeks Katy would have her potion, and Zack. She thought about him all the time. She'd kissed him on the lips today, and it was mind-boggling, though he'd seemed a bit reticent. She'd had his full attention all day, as Ronnie was having problems with pipes bursting on her and tree limbs falling on her and tripping over specks of dust, practically. Ronnie had been a lightning rod for cosmic doom. While crossing the quad, she'd been beaned in the nose by an errant Frisbee, conked in the noggin by a football, and had stepped in a big pile of dog poo. Three different people in the cafeteria accidently spilled their entire lunch trays onto her. Katy had never seen anyone endure such misery and pure dumb bad luck. The meteor threat didn't even seem that far-fetched anymore. Veronica would fold very soon. Or snap. No way she could take another day like today.

In the bottom of Katy's wardrobe, wrapped in African indigo, were special black beeswax candles and a bundle of dried sage and juniper for smudging. She lit the smudge and went about the room widdershins in a basic purification ritual, then lit the candles. She sat on the floor in full lotus and chanted: "I invoke the spirits of my ancestors." After all the years she'd been doing this, the connection was so strong it was easier than calling Esme on the cell phone.

Katy's gift for necromancy was her most closely guarded secret. Her natural talent for speaking to the dead had manifested at a very early age. She was five before she'd realized people were being condescending when they pretended to believe in her "imaginary" friends, and she'd been secretive about them ever since. Katy cherished the dead. They had so many interesting and quirky observations, and such indifference for the things that the living clung to. It gave Katy her unique perspective, having an ancestor for a mentor.

"Are you there, hon?" Katy asked again, peeking out with one eye.

"Of course I am, dear," came the answer. The smoke from the smudge, which was still thick and aromatic in the room, gathered and concentrated. It took on the appearance of substance, all in gray but vivid enough to carry on a conversation.

"Thanks for coming," Katy said. "I love spending time with my favorite great-aunt."

"And I love spending time with you, dearie," Aunt Becky replied. "How's the potion going?"

33

TRACHEOTOMY FOR DUMMIES

Katy had predicted that Veronica would either fold or snap after a day of triple whammies. Veronica, it turned out, was not the type of girl to fold. She was a pureblood snapper. Friday at breakfast, Veronica was in a disheveled state, baggy of eye and haggard, with hair that did not qualify as a rat's nest. Rats have standards.

"Did you sleep well, sweetie?" Katy asked in an overly glib fashion.

"I wouldn't goad her, if I were you," Esme advised.

Esme had spent hours with Ronnie in her room the night before, giving big-sisterly comfort in an effort to assuage her guilt. Her clinical impression was that Ronnie was in a state of induced psychosis affected by sleep deprivation, love obsession, hysteria, malnutrition, and a pervasive jinx. She'd made Ronnie some chamomile tea and tucked her in bed and sung her a lullaby. Ronnie could not afford to lose another night's sleep.

Friday morning, it seemed obvious that Ronnie had, indeed, lost another night's sleep. Her delicate, waifish beauty had turned sharp and angular. Esme felt the loss as a pang.

Katy was prattling on: "You really missed it, Esme. The way she got nailed by three lunch trays in a row makes you just marvel at the magnificence of the cosmos." Katy was sitting at the table in the breakfast nook, holding court. Esme was fishing cold cuts out of the fridge. Veronica was behind the counter, peeling a large Fuji apple with a paring knife.

"I don't want to hear about it, Katy," Esme said. This was all her fault. She noticed Ronnie had finished peeling the apple and kept on peeling, like she was going to take it to the core. Cue the music from *Psycho*.

"Lunch trays everywhere!" Katy continued, taking her dishes to the sink. "Spaghetti flying from three tables over like a guided missile—"

What happened next was a blur: Veronica spun with ballerina grace and closed the distance between herself and Katy in a heartbeat. With brutal strength, she grabbed her sister by the hair and tugged her neck sideways, swinging the right arm over her chest and pressing the paring knife into Katy's throat. The blade indented the skin over Katy's jugular.

"Remove this jinx, right now," Veronica instructed. The scary part was, her voice wasn't hysterical or nervous at all. It was icy cool, like a 911 operator instructing a little girl how to perform a tracheotomy over the phone.

Katy struggled for about a tenth of a second, thinking she could get a hand on Ronnie's wrist and push the blade away, but Veronica dug the blade into her neck a fraction of an inch, drawing blood. "Esme, do something!" Katy pleaded, her eyes wide with terror.

For the briefest moment, Esme allowed herself to imagine the clear path to Zack, with one sister dead, the other in jail. Did that make her a bad person? Esme was smart and Katy had talent, but Ronnie would always win in the end. A fight with Ronnie was like the number pi: irrational, never ending, and no way to figure any percentage to it. Esme noticed that Veronica was made up for her part, with a raccoon-eyed smudge of mascara and bobby pins holding her hair up in the bag lady motif. If Ronnie had had the foresight to dress the part of a psychotic sister killer, she'd probably also worked the angle that if she *did* kill Katy, the jinx would never be lifted.

"If I were you, I'd do what she says," Esme advised Katy as she opened a packet of sliced turkey on the counter. Veronica almost certainly wouldn't kill Katy, but was it really worth testing the girl's state of mind? Was it possible to fake a maniacal expression like that? She knew her baby sister well enough not to call her bluffs.

"*Expello btfsplk,*" Katy intoned, making a Bronx cheer noise of it.

Ronnie shoved her sister away, shivering from toe to crown with the heebie-jeebies. Katy's counter-jinx had sent a shock of static electricity through her.

"Okay, girls, I'm going to lay down the law," Esme said with such authority she got no argument. "You two, hug. Now!"

Her sisters embraced tepidly.

"There's to be no more cursing, hexing, jinxing, or spells of any kind, or so help me Goddess, I'm going to call Mom and tell her you've both violated the Wiccan Rede a dozen times each. And she is going to be royally pissed that she has to cancel her trip to Stonehenge to punish you. Am I understood?" Over Katy's shoulder, Esme noticed her father retreating from the doorway. A remarkably sensible man.

"Yeah," Katy agreed, rubbing her neck. There were beads of blood, but no serious damage.

"Okay," Ronnie said, clearly relieved.

"And, Katy, after school today, you go out in the yard and clean up all the dog poop, like you promised. The flies are thick as locusts out there." As long as Esme was in full-blown bossy mode, she figured she might as well restore some order.

"Okay," Katy agreed, humble. "Sorry."

"And, Ronnie, you eat something, or I'm telling Dad you're bulimic. He'll send you to puke camp, and they'll force-feed you cheesecake and duct-tape boxing gloves on you so you can't shove your fingers down your throat. And yes, it's a real thing; I saw it on the Internet."

"I'm not bulimic," Ronnie challenged, indignant. "Has anyone ever seen me binge? And I don't purge. I'd never ruin my teeth like that. I'm a ballerina."

"Okay, anorexic, then. You're five-seven and you weigh ninety-five pounds. Dad will believe me. I'm the responsible one, and you're a notorious liar. Now go back to the bathroom and fix yourself up, and I'll make you a fried egg sandwich with cheese, and we're not leaving for school until you eat every bite. And I'm packing you a sandwich for lunch, too, and I want to see you eat it. And drink a glass of orange juice, you're dehydrated."

"Yes, ma'am," Ronnie agreed. She was half psychotic from sleep deprivation, but not crazy enough to call Esme's threat.

34

BARRY GETS A NEW CLIENT

For a week, Norm had been desperate to talk to Esme, but she wouldn't give him the time of day. His entreaties were getting more pathetic and frantic daily. She and her sisters were in deadly danger, but there was no way of getting them to understand it. He'd gotten his throat slashed out of genuine concern for her, and she'd sided with the monster! And now she was so skeptical of his motives, she didn't trust him at all. Okay, he got that she thought he was jealous, but she refused to see the bigger picture of the danger he was trying to protect her from, out of his honest feelings of loyalty to her. Loyalty, friendship . . . or whatever.

Norm also tried his luck with Veronica and Katy, but they'd been forewarned against his pleas, which had turned into a kind of feverish proselytizing about the monster in their midst. They. Didn't. Want. To. Hear. It. Nobody did. At lunch, Norman sat with Wilson, Nick, and Jackson, watching the sisters, watching Zack.

∽ ∾

On Wednesday, Norman confronted Esme in the hall outside the cafeteria and wouldn't let her past him. With his bulk, he herded her against a bank of lockers. "Esme, you have to believe me," he pleaded. "My father can confirm all this, just stop by after school. He's so concerned, he's staying in town and having his grad students teach the rest of the semester."

"Your father?" she mentioned scathingly. "The mad scientist?"

"Zack has a kind of disease," Norm insisted. "It caused his skin condition. He can't eat solid food, because part of his intestinal tract is atrophied. Have you ever seen him bite into something solid? And his immune system is all messed up, so he needs to . . . Esme," he whispered, lowering himself to her ear and taking her upper arm in an inescapable grip. "His white cells need to be replenished every few days, or his system will—"

"Let go of me!" Esme yelled. She'd spied Vice Principal Shattuck with his Donald Trump comb-over and his hot pink bow tie. She'd heard enough nonsense. She wouldn't listen to any more of Norm's lies about her sweet Zack! Shattuck was making right for them. "Get your hands off me!" she yelled, for the vice principal's benefit. "And stop stalking me! Leave me alone!"

Vice Principal Shattuck approached them. People were watching, now. "Mr. Stein, would you please take your hand off of Miss Silver?" he requested reasonably. The vice principal's voice was naturally high-pitched, with a softness that made him sound gentle, though Esme knew him to be a rigid pedant with a sadistic streak.

Norman did as instructed, dropping his hands to his sides passively. "Sir, I was just—"

"Tut-tut, Mr. Stein," the vice principal interjected. "Let me hear Miss Silver's side of the story first." He turned and asked unctuously, "Was this young man accosting you, Miss Silver?"

Okay, she was the one who brought Shattuck into it. But

Norman had to learn. Esme cast her eyes at the ground modestly and nodded, once, twice.

"And did Mr. Stein have your permission to lay his hands on your person?"

This was the killer. There was an online package that you had to sign off on to register every year, with twelve pages of rules, and Esme was one of the few people who'd read them all instead of just scrolling down and clicking. Shattuck was talking about an automatic suspension. But the truth was, she hadn't given Norm permission to touch her. She was a feminist, wasn't she? He needed to learn about boundaries. She shook her head slowly. "No. He didn't."

"That will be all, Miss Silver," Shattuck said. "Would you like to go visit the school nurse?"

Esme told the vice principal that it wouldn't be necessary. As she headed into the cafeteria, she heard Mr. Shattuck instruct Norm to accompany him to his office. She had to avert her eyes, to avoid the look of devastation and betrayal on Norm's face.

$\sim\!\!\circ\;\circ\!\!\sim$

That evening, Barry informed the girls that he was meeting a new client and would appreciate if they'd refrain from thunderous farting noises and keep their dogs quiet. He addressed all three, but Katy took it personally, as she was the only one who'd ever had dogs or made thunderous farting noises. Barry asked Esme to vacuum the living room. He always asked Esme, never Ronnie, because he knew Veronica would complain about being persecuted and storm off to her room. Esme got all the chores because she was the only one who didn't complain. She considered this arrangement entirely unfair, a travesty of justice that rewarded the evil and punished the good, but she didn't like to complain, so she vacuumed the living room.

At eight o'clock the doorbell rang and Barry called down the hall for Veronica to answer it. Veronica grumbled at the injustice of having to get up from studying her pores in the mirror just to let her father's clients in. It was a conspiracy. They should hire somebody to answer the door, this wasn't the middle ages. Clients shouldn't visit lawyers at eight o'clock at night. They were probably criminals, why else would they need the lawyer?

Veronica opened the front door. It was Zack. She had to be dreaming. She blinked. He was still there. "Oh. It's you."

Next to Zack, now that she had a chance to notice him, was an older gentleman who must have been his father. He was a little shorter than Zack, and the resemblance was nonexistent, but he had an air about him, an irresistible magnetism. Definitely Zack's father. Ronnie rarely thought older men were attractive, but Zack's dad was something else altogether.

"How do you do, sir," she said, "I'm Veronica Silver. I assume you're here for the appointment with my father? Won't you come in, please?" She couldn't imagine where all the manners had come from. Zack's dad was so classy, he just brought it out of her.

They entered. "How very lovely," the father said in the entry hall. He offered a hand as if to shake, but when Veronica offered her own in return, he took her hand in both of his, intimately, and brought it to his lips. Veronica felt a tingle creep up her arm like a large, hairy spider.

"Oh, Zackery," the father said, "she's far more charming than you described." He was still in possession of Veronica's hand. "Darling child, would you be so kind as to summon your two elder sisters? I'd like to meet the entire family."

"Of course, sir," Ronnie returned, blushing. "But I can't leave you here in the foyer. Please, let me take your hat and coat." *Take your hat and coat?* Where did she get this stuff? And where she'd put the hat and coat she hadn't a clue. She wasn't even certain the entry hall *was* a foyer. In fact, she couldn't remember ever having used the word before.

In the living room, Drake Kallas made a fuss over each of the sisters, kissing their hands and complimenting them on their beauty and charm. They found themselves blushing, craving the compliments. Mr. Kallas was also lavish with his praise for Barry, as the progenitor of the three. Even Zack was congratulated, for having such lovely schoolmates. "I'd like to meet their mother as well," Drake mentioned. "I imagine she must be a great beauty."

"She's away in Europe for a few months," Barry apologized. "But we'd certainly love to have you and your son over for dinner sometime, when she returns."

Esme thought Zack's father was the most charming, sophisticated man she'd ever met. She imagined what it would be like to be accepted into such a cultured family. They'd lived all over Europe and traveled to exotic lands. Mr. Kallas vaguely explained that he was involved in "commodities," which he described as items of great value to those who appreciated their significance.

"Antiquities?" Esme asked.

This elicited an enthusiastic response from Zack's father. "What a clever, intelligent question, my dear. But no, let's just call them 'artworks,' since they are items of exceptional beauty." He used the opportunity to take Esme's hand again. She wished he'd never let it go.

The six of them chatted for a while, then Barry and Mr. Kallas excused themselves to discuss business in the den. The three sisters invited Zack to the kitchen for tea and a slice of banana bread Esme had made. They'd never seen him at night before, without his goggles and gloves. They were not disappointed.

"The tea, please," Zack requested. "But I'll have to give a pass on the banana bread. I have so many food allergies I never eat anything unless Dad or I prepare it."

"I'm so sorry," Katy consoled, taking Zack's arm and rubbing his hand possessively. "What are you allergic to? I'm a vegetarian, I'll bet I can scrounge up something you can eat."

"Ta," he replied. "But don't bother. I'd rather not talk about it, you all must think me a git, with me skin problems and me dodgy immune system. Just the tea please, I'm madferit."

"I've come to hire your services," Drake Kallas told Barry when they were alone in the den. "I've asked around. Your name came up several times, and my son mentioned he knew your daughters and that they were wonderful girls who'd made him feel welcome in a new school. A man who could raise such girls must have the qualities I require in my legal representative."

Barry was pleased. "That's quite a compliment, Mr. Kallas—"

"Do call me Drake," the Master insisted.

"I specialize in family law," Barry said. "Mostly divorce work, but I do estate planning and of course criminal law, not that there's much call for it in these parts."

"It's a wonderful community," Drake agreed. "People have been very kind to us."

"I hope you aren't put off by the recent spate of missing persons, or that terrible fire a few weeks ago," Barry said. "I've lived here for almost twenty years, and nothing like this has ever happened before."

"That's precisely what I've come to talk to you about." They were sitting opposite each other across Barry's desk, before a wall of law books. Drake leaned forward and put his hand on top of Barry's hand. Barry thought nothing of the intimacy. European customs were odd. They were always kissing one another on the cheeks. "Some allegations have come to my attention. It seems my son knew all three of the girls—one was a young woman, in fact—who disappeared."

"I'm not surprised," Barry replied. "They were all in the same school. My daughter Esme knew all three of them herself, and nobody is making allegations about *her*."

"Ah, but your daughter isn't new in town. I'm glad we see eye to eye on this, Barry," Drake said, squeezing his hand. Drake was very direct with the eye contact as well. "We had nothing to do with the disappearance of those girls."

"Oh, absolutely," Barry agreed, nodding his head. "You had nothing to do with it."

"I'd had an interview with Detective Sharp. A jealous ex-boyfriend had seen my son with his girl, Sandy, and he was trying to incite trouble for Zack, we assume. Zack was exonerated, but then that terrible tragedy happened to the poor detective's family."

"The Sharps were clients of mine," Barry said. "Such a tragedy. And the boys . . . so young."

"Truly, a tragedy," the Ancient agreed. He paused for some moments, out of respect for the Sharp family. "You know, Barry,

I feel that you are precisely the type of man I've been looking for since I arrived here in the United States. Do you have any familiarity with American tax law and international financial matters?"

"Well, I do estate planning, and I work with a CPA and a tax attorney."

"That's excellent," Drake returned. "I have some assets in Europe that need to be liquidated and transferred here, and I'd like to send a representative, someone with stature, to sign documents as proxy and to assure that all the tax implications are compliant with American code. Rather large sums of money, in fact. I simply cannot go myself; there were some dissolutions of partnerships, and my presence would only exacerbate hard feelings. I need someone whom I can trust. I will see to it that you are very well compensated for your time."

"I'd be pleased to do it, Drake," Barry granted. "I have a hearing on the eighteenth, but after that I suppose I can clear my schedule."

Drake Kallas again took Barry's hand in his and looked him square in the eyes. "It has to be next week, Barry. This is far more important than your other business."

Barry's eyes went out of focus for a moment, and his head bobbed in agreement. "Yeah, this business is far more urgent than whatever that other thing was. I'll get a postponement."

"That's excellent," Drake approved, much to Barry's pleasure. "How shall we proceed?"

"An itinerary would help. And I'll draft a power of attorney. It will have to be notarized, but I have people. Do you have a signature stamp? We can have one made . . ."

"I have one," Drake assured. "And in the meantime, if any

more of these insinuations should prompt the police to enquire about missing persons?"

"Just refer them to me," Barry assured. "You had nothing to do with the disappearances of any young women." In the truth of that statement, Barry was quite confident.

In the car, on the way back to their mansion, Drake praised Zack. "You've done well, minion. I have a sense for these things, and those three are exquisite."

"I learned from the best," Zack returned, hating himself for craving the Master's praise.

The Ancient was not immune to flattery. "The youngest will be like a nuanced white Burgundy, and the oldest, a first growth Bordeaux in an excellent vintage. But the middle sister, that's the treat. Young vintage port, unless I miss my guess."

"So . . ." Zack concluded. "It's to be Katy, then?"

"Why choose?" The Master asked rhetorically. "The hat trick, I should think. I've just sent their father off to Europe."

On leaving, Zack had kissed each of the sisters in turn. The kiss had been very chaste, just on the lips, but it was the first time Esme's lips had touched his, and the sensation lingered. She'd felt the spark. People either had chemistry or they didn't, and she was certain, from the kiss and the little squeeze he gave her, that the chemistry was obvious to both parties.

Still, Esme needed to check her potion, cross-referencing all the components against her organizational list. Friday night she'd channel the eldritch energies while she combined all the ingredients in a six-quart Le Creuset stockpot. She had only to boil the extraction down, with periodic chanting, to complete the potion. And then she was going to steal Zack's heart.

Kasha jumped up onto the worktable. He sniffed a distillation in a beaker. "So I saw you kissing that boy, through the kitchen window."

"Zack? Isn't he dreamy?"

"I can certainly understand what all the fuss is about," the cat agreed. "You know he's a vampire, right? And the older one, too."

"Oh my Goddess," Esme exclaimed. "You're worse than Norman. Zack has photosensitivity. Just because he's pale doesn't make him a horror movie monster."

"No, but being undead and drinking people's blood is a pretty good indication."

"Well I don't happen to believe in vampires," she argued.

"Said the witch to the demon."

"Just . . . lay off, okay?" she commanded, exasperated. "I really want this, and you're not going to talk me out of it, so why don't you go outside and kill something?"

Kasha jumped down from the lab table and headed back toward the cat door. "Talk you out of it? *Moi?*" He jumped up, level by level, to the top of the cat contraption, before he turned for the last word. "At least, not until I figure out how to play this to my best advantage."

35

A CONSULTATION

Monday night at last. Becoming an irresistible beauty was a thing that Esme would do just once in her life, and she intended to watch her transformation in the mirror. The potion had been the most difficult, time-consuming project she'd ever undertaken, but she expected stellar results. She'd strained the solids off the potion with an unbleached coffee filter and distilled the remaining liquid a final time while chanting ancient rhymes that sounded like gibberish. The end product was about an ounce of liquid and brownish, per spec. It was in a small brown glass vial with a cork stopper. Kasha had sniffed at it and pronounced it good.

Esme positioned herself in a chair in front of her closet door, which had a full-length mirror on it, and pulled the stopper out of the vial. Kasha had chased all the other cats out of the room so they wouldn't misdirect any of her mojo. She'd smudged the room with sage and mugwort. "Here goes nothing," she proclaimed, holding the vial up. She was jittery with nerves. She was really going to do it. In a moment. Okay, in another moment.

"I did explain to you about the price for invoking this magic, didn't I?" Kasha mentioned.

Esme moved the vial away from her lips. "No. You didn't.

It's too late, I'm going through with it. You should have said something before I spent three weeks working on it."

"Sorry," said the cat. "I'm sure it's nothing. Carry on."

Esme stood and paced. The price of magic. Precisely the thing her mother had always warned her about. "So tell me already," she demanded. The stupid demon was tormenting her.

"Think nothing of it."

Esme scanned the surface of the lab table for something to hit him with, something heavy enough to dent his thick skull. "Are all demons this exasperating?" she asked.

"Demons? No, it's a cat thing."

"You've gained weight. I think you should go on dry food for a while."

"I really have no idea what the price will be," Kasha gave. "You might turn evil. Or it may be nothing at all. On the other hand, he's a vampire who's going to drink your blood and ultimately kill you, so whatever the side effects are, it's a fairly moot point."

"I don't believe anything bad you say about Zack," she said. Though the hairs on her neck were standing on end. *Turn evil?* Her mother had warned her not to do that.

"Of course not. He's mesmerized you. Anyway, it will probably just lower your IQ by thirty points—"

"Lower my IQ by thirty points?" she yelled. "And you almost didn't tell me?"

"I really don't know. But the universe usually doesn't allow people to be as smart as you and as beautiful as you're going to be. There's a trade-off. I suppose we could consult someone . . ."

"Who? My mom?"

"I know a guy," Kasha said. "But we'll need to summon him."

It took most of Tuesday afternoon for Esme to assemble the pentacle to the specs in the family grimoire on her hard drive. "Does the size matter?" she'd asked Kasha for guidance.

"Microcosm, macrocosm, it's all the same to a demon. Just make sure the lines are perfect. And we're doing the containment runes in Hebrew, they have to be perfect, too."

Kasha was extremely impressed with the finished product when he returned later that night. "That's genius, Esme. What do you call that?"

"A portable pentacle," she explained. "I've gotten the top grade on every project in school for ten years, not to mention blue ribbon in every science fair. This is nothing; you should have seen my diorama of Lincoln and Booth at Ford's Theatre."

"It's so shiny. How'd you get the Hebrew letters to sparkle like that?"

"Glitter. I used one of my mom's old hatboxes, because it was round, then I printed out the runes from the computer and glued them around the inside. Then I traced them all in Elmer's glue and sifted glitter over it until it dried."

"The angles have to be perfect." Kasha walked around the open hatbox, inspecting it.

"I used a compass," she explained. "I cut out a perfect circle from plywood with a jigsaw to fit the inside the box. Then I traced a concentric magic circle inside, used a protractor to make the pentagram, and hammered nails through from the bottom at the points of the star. I traced the lines of the star with a ruler, put down more glue, and sifted ocean sand on top. When the glue dried, I had a perfect pentangle made of sand, and we don't have to worry about the lines being broken, because they're permanent. The ceremonial candles are centered on the nails."

"Genius. Now listen, Esme. You have to do the ceremony, but don't worry about all the Talmudic mumbo-jumbo, you can do it in English. This is the twenty-first century, we're all pretty cosmopolitan now. And none of that 'I command you to appear in the name of Mephistopheles' stuff. In fact, don't ever mention *any* of the demon lords by name, especially with an open pentacle." Kasha swished his tail nervously. "I need that like a tumor on my ass. Just be polite, introduce yourself, mention my name, ask for Shikker, and say you'd like a courtesy consultation."

Esme smudged the room, this time with sage and lavender. She lit the candles of the pentacle and made obeisance to the north, south, east, and west. With a demon cat to channel her intent, Esme felt herself making contact immediately.

"Uh . . . hello?" she asked the pentacle. "Is anyone there?"

The candles flickered. Esme felt a sensation like maggots crawling under her decomposing flesh. There was a palpable absence of sound, like shadows screaming in a billion silent voices, and the wafting scent of brimstone. Kasha nudged her with a paw to proceed.

"My name is Esmeralda Silver, I'm here with Kasha. Uh . . . please don't be offended if I'm doing this wrong, it's my first time. We'd like to have a courtesy consultation with Shikker."

There was a puff of smoke from the middle of the pentacle, and a toy-sized imp appeared. He had row upon row of nasty sharp teeth like a shark's in an enlarged mouth, and twisty horns that appeared to have no coherent direction. He was clad only in a loincloth. He was rust red all over and had wrinkly, leathery skin, like an elephant's hide. Eerie blue flames danced over him, especially around the horn region of his head.

"*Oy,*" said the imp, looking up from his tiny perspective within the hatbox. "Kasha, you *schnorrer*, first time I'm up here in fifty years and you've called me for a *farshtinkener* pro bono?"

"Shikker, it's not like that," the cat cajoled. "I think I'm onto something big here."

The imp was looking around the hatbox at the Hebrew runes. "Hey, sparkly! Nice touch. You got anything to drink around here?"

"Esme, this is my lawyer, Shikker. Give him the offering." Esme retrieved a test tube full of amber fluid, sealed with a rubber stopper. "Just hand it straight down."

"It's nice to meet you," Esme said, doing as instructed. Shikker grabbed the test tube out of her hand as she lowered it. He ripped the stopper out without decorum and stuck his prodigious nose into the test tube. "Scotch," he mentioned with approval. "My favorite." He took a huge swig. With his diminutive size, drinking from the test tube was equivalent to Esme drinking out of a ten-gallon aquarium. "Chivas Regal," he noted, smacking his lips.

"The guy knows his Scotch," Kasha said. "Don't ever go on a binge with Shikker here, he's nuts. Remember Frisco, '64?"

"They hate when you call it Frisco," Shikker reminded him, swigging Scotch.

"That's why I do it," Kasha confided.

"I'm not surprised to hear from you," Shikker said. "I hear you're behind on your quota. Rumor has it your old boss has half the accounting department auditing your account, waiting for the exact second when he can unleash the hounds of hell to drag your sorry ass back to the nastiest pits of Tartarus."

"I'm working on it, okay?" Kasha hissed. His tail flailed in agitation, ears pivoting back and forth as if desperately straining for the sounds of baying hounds.

"Nu," Shikker said amiably, with the satisfaction of torment delivered. *"Fregen der kashes."*

"This is regarding my present contract, under the name Becky Proctor. You did the paperwork."

"Too bad they don't trust you to do your own anymore," the imp chortled.

"The contract was for three generations of service. Esme is the last generation. My question is, if Esme here becomes a vampire and lives to be a thousand years old, the contract is still good, isn't it? I can stay topside for a thousand more years, right?"

"What in the hell are you talking about?" Esme protested. "Who said anything about me becoming a vampire?"

"She's in denial," the cat explained.

"I *schlep* all the way here from the other realm for this *pilpul*?" Shikker waved the Scotch about imploringly at Esme, for sympathy. "Two hundred years this *nudnik* spent in contracting, and he forgets the first rule of making a pact between a human and a demon."

"I didn't forget it," the cat denied, miffed. "The human party has to put his soul on the line in the contract. Which Becky did, for three generations. What, are you telling me a vampire doesn't have a soul?"

"A vampire has got *bubkes* for a soul," Shikker said, drinking from his test tube. "If your *tsatske* here becomes a vampire, your contract is *kaput*."

"Really? No soul? How do they stay animated?"

"By ingesting the life forces of their victims," the red demon explained. Impossibly, he'd already managed to drink almost a fourth of the Scotch. "Yeah, I've had some experience with vampires. They hang on to their souls for a few years while they absorb the souls of their victims by ingesting their lifeblood. They become a kind of receptacle for all the souls they've stolen, and their original soul sort of fades away into the crowd. The stolen life forces are the source of their powers. The more souls they absorb, the more powerful they become. The souls stay there inside the vampire until somebody kills it, then they go where they would have gone in the first place, to heaven or hell. The vampire's soul sort of un-comingles itself, and everything gets sorted out. We always drag the vampire's re-amalgamated soul to hell, that's a no-brainer. But most of the stolen souls go the other way. Vampires tend to prey on the innocent."

"So the contract would become invalid if Esme became a vampire," Kasha said.

"Yeah. It's a shame." Shikker shook his head gravely. "If some genius could figure out how to harvest a vampire, it would be quite a haul. All those unclaimed souls, even if you lost ninety percent of them to the heavenly host, you'd still make a pretty *shekel*."

"Yeah," Kasha mused. "Somebody should work an angle on all those unclaimed souls."

"Well, I should be getting back. I'll just take the rest of this Scotch to go."

"Hey," Esme said. "I thought we'd called you in for a consultation about my beauty potion."

Shikker shrugged. "Not my area of expertise."

"But I worked really hard on it, and I want to know what will happen to me if I take it."

"You're a bit of a *yutz*, aren't you?" Shikker asked. "Listen, *bubee*, it all depends on your intention. If you give a beauty potion to some poor *schmo* who needs it, out of the goodness of your heart, there's no fault in that. But if you're asking a demon lawyer are there any loopholes, because your intention is *malum in se*, uh . . . you *capiche*?"

Between her magic and law studies, Esme understood the Latin. "Wrong in itself?"

"Smart girl. I think you have your answer. You'll get what you deserve. And then some." And with that, the candles extinguished themselves and Shikker was gone.

"Your friends are the coolest," Esme told Kasha as the sulfurous smoke the imp left behind billowed up in a tiny mushroom cloud. Already, all the talk of vampires was fading from her memory. "I'd like to have him back, just to hang out. Do you think he'd visit again, if I got a really good bottle of Scotch?"

"He likes the 18-year-old Macallan," the cat advised. "But don't be fooled, if you let him out of the pentangle, he'll eat your face."

"Yeah, I guess so," she sighed. She was exhausted. "Because he's a demon, right?"

"No, that's a lawyer thing."

36

MEANWHILE

"What do you think, Aunt Becky?" Katy asked, holding up the little brown vial.

Aunt Becky's wispy, ephemeral form hovered over the love potion. "Looks like a winner to me, child," she replied in her eerie, raspy voice. "I hope this boy is worth the immortal soul you're damning to hell for eternity."

"Don't worry about me, Aunt Becky. This is true love, the most redeeming force in the universe. He just doesn't realize it yet, is all. He needs a push. And then I'll love him forever, a perfect love. What could be wrong about that?"

"How do I know? I've been dead for decades. And I have no moral authority to lecture you. I had a lot of talents in my day, but good judgment wasn't one of them."

"I know you'll approve, when you meet him."

"When are you giving it to him?" asked the apparition, gathering her ectoplasm about her.

"It's almost Wednesday. There are three more school days until winter break. I've made a date to meet him in private on Sunday, which is the solstice."

"An auspicious day," Aunt Becky's spirit agreed. "Mix the

potion with some juice or tea. He has to be next to you when he drinks it, because whoever he's with, that's who he'll love. He'll imprint on your scent, and his hormones will ramp up whenever you're around. And he'll obsess about you when you're *not* around. We should get started on the antidote right away. He'll get so annoying, you'll want to be rid of him pretty soon."

Katy laughed. "Trust me, I could never get annoyed with Zack."

"You can always kill him, if it comes to that," the spirit advocated. "I'd do it in a heartbeat. If I had a heartbeat."

"Aunt Becky!" Katy admonished. "You know I could never bring myself to do such a horrible thing, not even to a fly."

"A shame, ain't it?" Becky quipped. "The spirit is willing, but the flesh is weak."

At three o'clock on Wednesday morning Veronica filled the electric Crock-Pot up with water in the kitchen sink by the light of her iPhone. She really didn't have a clue what she was doing, just a dead certainty. Her grandma Sophie had imparted certain inalienable wisdoms to her as a very small child, and it had influenced her style of magic from that time on.

Veronica, like Sophie, was a slow-magic witch. She was not flashy like her sister Katy, or ingenious like her sister Esme, but she bulled her way through her spells and charms through sheer force of intention and tireless ritual repetition. She was successful because she committed fully to every charm and spell.

She knew a little spell. It was probably the oldest magic in the book. In fact, it predated the proverbial book altogether. For four days, Veronica had done almost nothing but pluck the petals off of flowers, sitting in the swivel chair in front of her vanity, chanting, "He loves me, he loves me not" over and over again. The petals plucked to accompany the half of the chant "he loves me not" she fed tirelessly into a flaming charcoal brazier. She wanted to destroy those petals: They had bad juju. Those love-me-not petals could not be permitted to survive and spread their toxic influence into the universe. Conversely, the petals that she'd plucked to accompany the "he loves me" part of the charm she saved in the Crock-Pot. These petals had the right intention, so she nurtured them, running her hands through the pile lovingly.

She'd plucked an armload of roses and daisies she'd bought for half off from the florist, but most of the flowers were late-blooming perennials that had survived the frost and that she'd gathered from their garden: Michaelmas daisies and turtlehead and Helenium, and chrysanthemums, which took forever to pick apart, and perennial sunflowers. In the four days she'd worked at it, she'd filled the Crock-Pot up to the rim.

As the final step, Ronnie set it to slowly simmer in her room. She could continue to chant her intentions while it steeped, to draw the cosmic forces of "he loves me" entirely into the brew. She still wasn't entirely sure if she was going to drink the concoction as a tea or let it boil down until it thickened and use the residue to make a perfume to spritz behind the ears. Perhaps she'd mix it into her conditioner.

Veronica put the lid back on the Crock-Pot, open just a tiny sliver to allow the brew to cook down. Tomorrow, she'd chant over the petals as they slow-cooked, and probably drink a cup of the tea. It smelled wonderful.

37

DOUBT

Barry gave his three daughters hugs and stern instructions before they left for school Wednesday. He had a three o'clock flight for Amsterdam and wouldn't be back stateside for two weeks. Whatever emergencies came up, the girls would have to rely on their own resources. They'd all been fighting for months it seemed, but they'd been getting along recently, so he hoped it was all over. He took Esme aside and spoke to her in private. He handed his oldest daughter, the dependable one, an envelope full of cash.

"Esme, I'm sorry I have to leave you in charge again," he said. "It seems like you're the one I always have to rely on to take up the parenting responsibilities."

Esme shrugged. "I'm used to it," she said. "I'll watch them."

"While I'm gone, you're in charge, sweetie."

"I was in charge when you were here," she reminded him.

He laughed. "I'm serious. You're officially their mom while I'm gone. *In loco parentis.* Try to make Ronnie eat something. And don't let her wear those cutoff denim pants without tights; I've seen bikini bottoms with more fabric. And if Katy gets gas again like last time, take her to a hospital or something. That wasn't normal."

Esme gave her dad a kiss on the cheek. "Go and have a good trip. Don't worry about us."

"If your sisters give you a hard time, tell them they'll have me to deal with when I get back."

"That should leave them quaking in their shoes."

"Okay, tell them their mom will deal with them."

"That will work," she agreed.

Zack wasn't in school on Wednesday. Esme missed him with an emptiness beyond reason. She couldn't focus on the biology test she hadn't studied for, and she felt awful whenever she saw Norm. His suspension had been only one day, but it went on his permanent record. Universities checked that stuff. After all the precautions Norm and his dad had taken to avoid trouble, it was Esme, his so-called friend, who'd gotten him suspended. Norm was avoiding her, waiting at his desk until she left after every class. She wished she knew how to apologize. When she tried to make eye contact, he looked through her, as if she were invisible. She'd tried to approach him in the parking lot, but he'd shunned her like she had leprosy or something. Between her lack of prep for the biology test and the tell-tale heart pounding in her chest when she looked at Norm, her final in her most important class was a complete disaster.

Wednesday night in her room was a repeat of Monday. Esme sat in front of her mirror, holding the potion that would get her the boy she loved. But there would be a price to pay. And her demon cat might be waiting to collect. Would it be worth it, for Zack? In her gut, Esme knew no price was too high. But in her brain, she wasn't so sure.

"So, are you going to drink it, or what?" Kasha asked her.

"Yeah. I'm going to. Zack is too important to me." But she made no move to drink the potion.

"Maybe I'll come back next year," the cat said. "I spent three hundred years as an accountant in hell and every minute was an eternal agony, but that was nothing compared to watching you with that potion. Veronica would have drunk it Monday, not that she needs a beauty potion."

"If only I knew what was going to happen," she explained for the thousandth time.

"Just drink it," Kasha prompted. "Nothing bad is gonna happen to you. You can trust me. I wouldn't steer you wrong just to harvest your soul and drag it to hell."

"Trust you?" she asked incredulously. "Trust a demon? I don't think so. My mother warned me never to trust you. She said you're evil."

"Who are ya gonna believe?" the cat argued. "Me, or your lying mother?"

Later that evening, Esme studied the family grimoire for some solution to her dilemma. There were caveats all through the book about this spell or that potion, but there was never anything specific about the worst-case scenarios for their misuse. Damnation seemed to be the most common threat. Her reverie was broken by a sudden ruckus up in the attic among Katy's dogs. Kasha launched off the armchair, tore around the room, and skidded under the bed.

"What is it?" Esme asked, startled.

Kasha peeked a whisker out. "That mutt Kilroy sounds just like a hellhound," he complained, coming out from under the bed with as much dignity as he could muster. "You have a visitor."

Esme's door opened to a concrete landing with stairs up to ground level. She flipped on the outside light. Norman loomed on the landing. She opened the door to confront him: "Norman, do you have any idea what time it is?" she scolded halfheartedly. It was an ungodly hour for a visitor, but she was relieved to see him. The guilt was only half of it.

"Don't you have a clock?" he returned, checking his wristwatch. "It's a little after ten."

"What in the world are you doing here at this time of night?"

"I need to talk to you," he insisted. "I'm worried about you. I can't sleep, I can't focus. I need to say my piece and get it out there. Then you can take it or leave it, but at least I'll know I've done everything I could."

If Esme hadn't been so happy that he was even speaking to her, she'd have slammed the door in his face. But this was Norman. He used to be someone she could talk to, and she needed someone to talk to. She couldn't sleep or think, either. "Ten minutes," she allowed, opening the door all the way and stepping back. When he entered, she turned on him with a finger raised in warning: "Not one word about Zack."

Norman tried to raise an objection, but restrained himself. "Esme," he struggled. She'd effectively shut down his argument at the onset. "I'm worried about you. And I'm not giving up on you, no matter what. Maybe you don't think of me as a friend anymore, but I still have . . . I can't stand to see you like this."

"I'm fine," she promised. "Don't worry about me, I can take care of myself."

Norman started to pace, thinking. He needed to get through to her. Her mind was shut down, she was resistant to reason, opposed to rationality, blinded to reality. He needed to jump-start her brain. "I believe you've changed," he offered. "Your brain isn't processing information the way it did a few months ago. Do you agree with this diagnosis?"

"No, I don't agree," she asserted. "What's this based on?"

Norman counted off on his fingers: "One, your grades have gone to hell. You've gotten straight As your whole life, and now you're flunking tests and not turning in your homework. This alone should be enough to indicate that your brain isn't functioning the same."

"Conjecture," she argued. "The one might imply the other, but your inference is precipitate."

"Can you provide a better explanation?" he asked.

"Sure," she replied. "Maybe I've continued to process information the same as always, but concluded that there were more important things in life than just getting good grades."

"Well played," he conceded. He counted out on a second finger: "You told me once that you didn't wear makeup because the beauty industry exploited women and tested products on animals. But you've taken to wearing lipstick and eye shadow."

"I'm entitled to change my opinion," she argued. "In fact, it's the mark of an evolved brain to be constantly formulating new opinions and re-evaluating old ones. The brains that are resistant to change are the ones that can be said to be inflexible." She missed arguing with Norman. He was the only one who could really challenge her. "Also, I use cruelty-free makeup."

"If a brain changes away from personal integrity and toward conformity, would you still argue that the brain is demonstrating flexibility? I'd argue that an exceptional brain that gave in to societal pressure was not challenging itself."

"A spurious argument. Perhaps it's challenging itself in different ways." Esme waved a hand toward the lab equipment on the makeshift workbench. The beakers and test tubes and Bunsen burners were all cleaned and organized, but the sheer inventory of equipment was impressive.

"Working on a cure for cancer?"

"No, an antidote for stupidity. I need test subjects for the clinical trials, so stay in touch."

He laughed. "Okay. None of my business. Still on point two, your appearance: You told me you wore those thick glasses instead of contacts because you didn't have time for people who judged you based on your looks instead of your brains. So what's with the contacts?"

"I don't have to justify anything to you," she replied, fidgeting.

"That's not an answer," he challenged.

"You have five minutes left, Norm," she said, glancing at her watch.

Norm counted out on his third finger. "That thing in the hallway, with Shattuck. I propose that the reason you got me suspended, which was definitely uncool and not like you, by the way, was because I was challenging something that had become a fundamental tenet of your worldview. Your brain shut me down right away. Two months ago, you'd have been able to at least listen to what I had to say and process the information in a rational manner, taking into consideration that I'm a scientist and your friend and a rational person."

"Yeah, well I'm sorry that happened, Norm," she said, an apology of sorts. "But you need to know when to back off. And you can be intimidating, you know."

"Do you agree that your brain shut me out?" he asked. "Stop trying to sidestep the issue."

"You could be biased," she argued. "You could have been telling me that stuff because of your feelings for me. I think you're jealous of Zack."

Norm smiled. "I'm glad it was you who brought Zack into the discussion. Now I get to use him in my rebuttal. I admit that I'd considered that my feelings for you might be influencing my analysis of the situation. But my father happens to agree with me on this. In fact, the whole hypothesis about the cause is his. And he's never met you. Ball is in your court."

Esme searched her head for a counterargument to this, and found only fuzz. There was this area in her head that she couldn't get into regarding Zack. She trusted Zack. She loved him. She couldn't accept that he was anything except a great guy whom she couldn't live without. She stared into Norman's face blankly for a moment, then glanced at her watch. "Time to go, Norman," she said.

Norman checked his own watch. "I still have two and a half minutes," he said. He counted out on his fourth finger: "Next point, your sisters. I've seen Katy and Veronica both hanging on Zack—"

"Where?" she asked frantically. "When?"

"Does it matter?" he asked. "You seem agitated, is everything all right?"

"I'm fine," she replied, calming herself. "What's your point?"

"My point is, it's weird. You love your sisters, and the guy's dating all three of you. Does that seem right? You're making fools of yourselves. If you were thinking straight, you three would have figured out which one of you would date him. But it looks like— this is my observation, anyway—it seems like you're all trying to undermine one another. Is he really worth it, to ruin your relationship with your sisters? Why would you even want a guy who flirts with half the girls in school? If your heads were on straight, you'd all see that. Two of you would back down. Or all three, if you had any sense."

"You seem to have this all figured out," Esme stated flatly. *He's right! He's absolutely right! Every word of it!* "So how long have you been stalking us, Frank N. Stein?"

"Please," he replied evenly. "These *ad* homonym attacks are beneath you."

"Time to go," she said unequivocally. "I mean it this time."

Norman stared down at her, looking for cracks in her armor, looking for any indication that he'd gotten through to her. He shrugged. "I tried. And I'm not giving up on you. I hope you'll call me, if you ever need to talk about it."

Esme showed Norman to the door. He looked dejected. She held the door as she watched the giant trudge up the eleven steps to ground level. "Norm!" she called after him.

He turned at the top of the stairs. "Yes?"

"Not that I agree with you, but what's your hypothesis? Why do you think I've changed?"

"Oh, that's an easy one," he answered. "You're thinking clear as a bell, as long as we don't discuss Zack Kallas. But when we do, your mind shuts down, and you can't process any information objectively. I think you've been mesmerized by a guy who exudes extremely strong pheromones that have addled your neurohormones, leaving you highly susceptible to post-hypnotic suggestion."

"Yeah. Just as I suspected. You're nuts," Esme said, closing the door. She returned to the bed, where Kasha had lain through the entire discussion, grooming himself. She flopped down backward onto the mattress.

"He's right, you know," Kasha mentioned. "Zack's a vampire. It's what they do."

"Oh, shut up," she sniped, tossing a pillow at him. In response, Kasha laughed, an unpleasant sound coming from a demon cat. "What's so funny?"

"'*Ad* homonym attacks,'" he chortled. "Get it? 'Homonym' as a homonym for '*hominem*.'"

Norman was always coming up with clever stuff like that. She missed it. Zack's jokes were pretty lame in comparison. She kicked off her shoes and rolled over on her side. It didn't really matter, did it? You don't get to pick who you love, it just happens.

38

CLARITY

Esme's sleep was unsettled that night. She had only two more school days before Christmas break, and Thursday night would be the last chance to take her potion if she wanted to regain the edge for Zack's affections. At school, she and her sisters had achieved a kind of détente, because they could monitor one another. But there was no way she could police her sisters for two weeks over the break.

She couldn't bring herself to drink the potion. Her head was fuzzy, but she knew the risks were too high. It was like what Norm had been talking about. He made a lot of sense, except for the stuff about Zack. Which she couldn't remember very well. There was a cloudy area in her brain, whenever she thought about Zack. She could see his smile clearly in her mind. His accent sure was cute. She hugged herself a little, imagining she was holding him. She loved him, that was for sure. So, that was good, wasn't it? She decided that it was. She couldn't remember what the original point had been. She focused, and sat up in bed abruptly. Norm was right! There was definitely something wrong with her mind.

In the light of morning, Esme knew what she had to do. She couldn't get Norm's words out of her thoughts. Her decision meant abandoning Zack to the mercies of her sisters, but she needed to take a day off school and get her head straight. Otherwise, Thursday night would just be a repeat of Monday and Wednesday.

Esme dropped her sisters at the drop-off spot and promised to pick them up after school.

"Aren't you coming?" Katy asked, scandalized. Esme almost never missed school; she practically had a phobia about it.

"I'm exhausted," Esme explained. "I finished all my finals yesterday, and I was up all night, and now I just . . . I need to take a day, okay? For myself."

Katy and Veronica exchanged glances. "Stay out of my room," Katy warned. "Some of my wards are, uh . . . dangerous."

"I'll take a day off, too," Veronica said, thinking of her Crock-Pot of flower petal extract. Too easy for Esme to sabotage.

"Pinkie swear," Esme promised, proffering the digit. "I won't go anywhere near your rooms."

The oath was sufficient for Katy and Veronica. Over the years, they'd imbued the pinkie swear with so many curses and hexes, to defy it was worse than death. Especially some of the weirdness Katy had added, like being turned to cheese and nibbled by rats, eyes eaten by spiders, bones turned to Jell-O, and itches all over so horrible you'd claw your own skin off.

Esme returned home and wandered about the house. It was so quiet. In her room she pulled all her books and notebooks and assignments from all her classes out of her backpack and organized them into piles. There were crumpled tests in the bottom of the knapsack. She'd always made a habit of keeping her paperwork neat—she hated creases in her papers or dog-ears or especially torn binder holes. But she'd been shoving all her lousy tests into her backpack as if the act of crumpling them negated the points that were leaching out of her GPA. Good-bye 4.5. Good-bye Stanford—she'd never get in now. She sat on her bed and examined the history test she'd just received back the day before. There was a big red D on it.

"Well that's D-grading," she told the test.

Then she got to work.

Esme *wasn't* thinking clearly, but she was not entirely without resources. She was different from her sisters. She had the ability to distance herself from her emotions. She'd always been an intellectual creature, until she'd met Zack. He was so wonderful, he'd blindsided her, like a Mack truck running a red light and T-boning a little tinny econo car. But when she was alone, she could manage, with effort, to focus.

Like many high school nerds carrying five AP classes with dreams of Stanford, Esme had spent long hours working on her "stack," the combinations of vitamins and supplements she took every day to enhance her cognitive function. She was something of an expert on the subject of nootropics, holistic neuroenhancers that optimize brain function. Every Silicon Valley bio-hacker knew about Bacopa, peptides, caffeine, green tea extract, B-complex, and the racetam family. But where Esme left those pharma nerds in the dust was in her knowledge of arcane eldritch alchemy, the lore about divine vitality and the techniques for coaxing the maximum efficacy out of every herb and botanical.

There were recipes in the grimoire for teas and infusions that would calm the mind and relieve anxiety, but she needed something more powerful. It would take the form of a tea, she decided, and there would be hybrid magic involved. Fortunately, she'd exhaustively studied all the botanicals while she'd been making her beauty potion, so she had a comprehensive, cross-referenced knowledge of all their characteristics and uses. She had some ideas about the state of mind she wished to achieve: clarity, mindfulness, tranquility, insight, and transcendence.

Esme decided to pulverize the herbs into a powder like matcha and whisk it in a Japanese tea bowl with the bamboo *chasen* she'd seen in her mother's room. The efficacy of the herbs was in the leaf and flower, so powdering them and drinking the plant matter as well as the brew would intensify the results. She'd studied Japanese tea ceremony while reading the biography of Rikyu, the tea master. Not enough to perform a ceremony, which took a lifetime to master, but hopefully enough to whisk the tea with ceremonial panache. Rikyu had refined the tea ceremony into a focused meditation, and through it achieved a kind of transcendence and clarity which enabled contemplation and a unique perspective. Also, Japanese tea ceremony had evolved from Zen and Taoism, which brought a lot of powerful invocation into the ritual. She decided to use some actual matcha in her brew, for the caffeine, L-Theanine, flavonoids, and polyphenols.

Esme worked through the day on her tea, while thinking about the other elements of the ceremony. She would incorporate some Tibetan meditation with candle staring. Meditation was useful in achieving transcendence of thought and mindfulness. She'd preface the session with a Wiccan ritual and invoke the Goddess for guidance.

Esme took a break at three o'clock to go pick up her sisters at school, and was relieved to find them waiting for her. Both sisters were tight-lipped about their day. At the front door of the house, each went their separate ways, into their own bedrooms and secret projects.

By nine thirty that evening, Esme was ready. Instead of a smudge, for a purification ritual she lit sandalwood incense and held it between her palms. To each of the four corners, she held her hands together as if in prayer and bowed, like a Thai *wai* greeting. Esme first offered to the south, fire, energy, the masculine principal, and forgiveness. To the north, then, she offered up her thoughts to Earth, mother, Goddess, body. She transitioned then to west, water, and offered a prayer for healing and purification. She saved east for last. Air. Esme's element was always air. To east, she offered up thoughts to breath, light, and mindfulness.

When the room was purified and Esme's mind calm from the ritual, she stood the incense in a bowl of salt. She then went around and lit white ceremonial candles, for truth and purity, in each of the four directions. Her spirit candle, in the middle of the circle, was sky blue, for tranquility. She would use this focus for staring in her meditation.

Esme retrieved an iron teapot from a Bunsen burner on her workbench and carried it to the center of the circle, where she sat on a yoga mat and crossed her legs in half lotus. She focused on her breath. She dipped her bamboo *chashaku* into her large container of powdered herbs, and measured it into her mother's *chawan*, a very old and valuable tea bowl Melinda had received as a gift. Then, channeling the spirit of Sen no Rikyu, she whisked the brew into a froth with the *chasen*, as she'd seen in an online video. She held the tea bowl in both hands and drank, clearing her mind.

Then she put the bowl on the floor, stared at the candle, and began to meditate.

The tea calmed Esme's mind right away. She breathed, releasing each thought. Esme's last bit of internal dialogue before she entered her trance was that the tea was certainly some good stuff. Then she released the thought with her breath and entered into a state of mindlessness and transcendence. She lost all sense of time or place, like falling into the cosmos.

She had no idea how long she spent in that state, before her vision began. In the vision, she was in a field of wildflowers, meditating, in a state of contentment. She opened her eyes and watched a beautiful woman of indeterminate age approach through the fecund meadow, wildflowers woven in her hair. She wore a flowing sundress, a little hippie-dippy, but it worked with her long, strong legs and cowboy boots. Her eyes were rainbows, and her hair was sunshine, and her skin was fresh and rosy. Definitely the Goddess. Or a composite of Goddesses, because she had all the elements of Earth Mother, seer, healer, and spirit guide.

Esme never invoked any Goddess in particular, because she was more a pantheist than a polytheist, and she was skeptical of the ones from Egyptian and Norse and Greek mythology. What did they even have to do with witchcraft or paganism? Esme was a nature spirit kind of girl. "The Goddess" was an abstraction. But who was this here now?

"Shush your mind, you," the Goddess chastised in Esme's vision, reading her thoughts. "I'm all the Goddesses, and any and none of them. And the Gods, too, do you want to see?" The Goddess grasped the hem of her skirts, laughing, as if she were going to prove it.

"Goddess, I—"

But the Goddess pulled Esme to her feet, and placed a finger over her lips. "Let it go, child," she said soothingly. "Always thinking, never being. Release the thought, open your mind."

Esme was five foot nine but the Goddess was way taller. Esme had no sense anymore that this was either a vision or a dream. It just was, as it was supposed to be. The Goddess embraced Esme, and she felt whole and serene and wise. And then, the Goddess placed a hand over Esme's heart, and her heart opened up, and she felt infinite love and compassion, and a terrible sadness, which is part of acceptance. "Just a taste, my child, of what you could have, if you dedicate your life to serenity. It's for this place here and now, but try to take some back with you, okay, hon?"

And Esme nodded her acceptance, because compassion was a gift that she hadn't earned, and she knew she was unworthy to keep such beauty inside herself, but she was determined to remember whatever she could, and take it back with her into the world.

Then the Goddess bent and kissed Esme on the forehead, where her third eye would be if she had a third eye, and Esme had clarity. And she knew her feelings, truly knew them, for Zack, and for her sisters, and her mother and father and everyone. "Is this what you came for?" the Goddess asked, laughing.

"Thank you, Goddess," was all Esme could say.

"Mindfulness is such a beautiful state," the Goddess said, her eyes full of wisdom and sorrow. "But there's one more thing. We've skipped a chakra." And the Goddess punched Esme in the solar plexus so hard she doubled over. And that's when she came out of her trance.

She spent the rest of the night in a fetal position on the floor, crying her eyes out.

39

REMORSE

At five o'clock in the morning Esme gave up on the idea that she was ever going to get to sleep. She was entirely cried out, literally dehydrated from the nonstop flow of tears she'd shed. She'd been curled up like an embryo on the floor all night, a little sad fetus, wracked by remorse, heaving and blubbering, but finally reborn with some retention of clarity.

Esme had wrung herself through the wringer of guilt and emerged, humbled by the beauty of what could have been, by the ugliness she'd made of it, and the determination to make it right. She knew one thing: She did not love Zack and never had. What she'd felt had been a kind of madness. She saw him for what he was, a user and a cheat and a flirt and a cad. She didn't know why she'd had those feelings for him, but she knew they were false, some hormonal thing, some compulsive insanity that had possessed her. So Esme had grieved for the innocence she'd wasted on the wrong thing and the knowledge that love was not some blissful jolt of giddy infatuation. She didn't know what to call that, but it was not love.

And then had come the guilt and remorse for her behavior. Because she did have love in her life, a very fine love, her love for her sisters, and what had she made of that gift? The backstabbing, the lies, the manipulations she'd pulled on the two very dearest people in her life, and for what? To cheat them out of a boy she'd never truly loved.

After Esme had finished mentally flagellating herself about her sisters, she'd replayed all the nasty things she'd done in her life, the people she'd betrayed, the mean things she'd said to poor Lisa Vaughn, probably kidnapped and murdered by now. How she'd fought with her own mother, who loved her as only a mother can. How she'd been snarky and mean-spirited to her father, treating him like some kind of clueless jerk when he was the best man she knew, generous with his time and his heart, until she'd worn him down with unwarranted contempt. And a hundred other people she'd mistreated over the years.

When she'd finally stopped crying and quaking in her own sweat and tears and begun to calm herself, to promise herself that she'd be a better person, would give her father hugs and cherish her sisters and allow her mother the gift of loving her . . . that's when she remembered Norman Stein, whose only offense had been to be a good friend. What she'd done to Norm . . . it was really too much, she couldn't stand it, and she bawled again, like a baby.

∞ ∞

When Veronica, and then Katy, finally came to the kitchen that morning, Esme had been waiting for over an hour. She was so relieved to see them she started blubbering again. She couldn't tell if it was psychosis from sleep deprivation, but as the sunrise filtered through the blinds, everything took on a rainbow effect, as if seen in the light of a prism, noticeable only at the very edges of things, where shadow hit light. She caught glimpses of it at the edge of Ronnie's beautiful cheek as it curved into shade, or in Katy's eyes. There was something of the Goddess's rainbow eyes to Katy, Esme realized in an epiphany, because Katy was the Goddess, and Veronica was the Goddess, and everything in the universe was the Goddess, and if she could only hold on to that clarity, everything would turn out okay.

"I'm so sorry," Esme promised Katy, taking her in her arms and hugging her for all she was worth. "I love you, Katy, I love you forever, and that's final." And Katy hugged her back.

"I love you, too, honey," Katy swore, because that's what middle sisters do, in a perfect world.

Veronica tried to run, but Esme nailed her in the hallway before she could escape into her room. Esme tackled Ronnie and sat on her and planted kisses all over her face and told her she loved her until Ronnie gave up struggling and kissed her back and promised she loved Esme just as much. Because that's what baby sisters do, too, in a perfect world. If you can catch them.

While Veronica was in her room fixing the mascara Esme had smeared with her kisses, and Katy was in the yard watching the dogs do their doggie business, Esme prepared a breakfast for her baby sister of grapefruit juice and a half a banana and toast with fruit spread, and a glob of yogurt in a bowl for a protein. Veronica looked at all the food and tried to object, but Esme started to cry again. Esme swore it would break her heart if Ronnie didn't take care of her health, and Veronica finally acquiesced, on condition that Esme didn't start kissing her again, because she'd had to redo her makeup from scratch.

In the car on the way to school, Esme told her sisters that she was done with Zack for good. "Honestly, I don't know what came over me, but it's gone now. And I hope you two can look within your hearts, and see if what you think you're feeling for him is real or not. But if either of you ever want to talk I promise not to judge." And then she proceeded to enumerate all her new insights about him being a user and a cheat.

"What are you trying to tell us, Esme?" Katy asked. "Zack is not a user. If he'd wanted me, he could have had me a dozen times by now. If anything, *I'm* the user."

"You're just pretending you don't want him anymore," Ronnie accused. "I knew it was a trick, with all that huggy-kissy stuff this morning."

"Yeah," Katy said. "She's just bad-mouthing him to chase us off."

Esme silently prayed for restraint. Choking the life out of her sisters just a few hours after gaining insight into how much she loved them didn't seem like a grateful response for the Goddess's gift. Veronica and Katy were acting to her as she had acted toward Norman, when he'd tried to get through to her on the very same subject. Esme had a new perspective about just how entirely creepy and obsessive her feelings for Zack had been.

"I swear to the Goddess, I do not want Zack," Esme declared. "I swear I love you, Katy and Veronica, and that I would never betray you."

Katy raised an eyebrow. Ronnie shrugged. "Just lay off the trash talk about Zack," Katy said.

"Yeah, we don't want to hear it," Ronnie agreed.

"Okay, okay. I promise." Esme slowed the car for the bridge traffic. "But will you two have tea with me this afternoon? I want to share this really great recipe I came up with. In my room. Four o'clock."

"I gotta take the dogs for a walk," Katy said. "And clean the poop in the backyard."

"Yeah, I'm busy, too," Ronnie added.

"Tonight, then," Esme said. "After dinner, eight o'clock?"

Katy was suspicious. "Since when do we all have tea together? Is this a thing now?"

"Yeah, what are you putting in the tea?" asked Ronnie. "I know you're making potions in your room."

"No, it's just . . . I made this great tea, it gives you clarity. I'll make it up fresh, right on the spot, so you can be there for the whole process."

"Yeah, right," Ronnie said. "Like we trust you."

"You two can make the tea," Esme pled in desperation. "Just . . . please. Do this for me. If you ever loved me. And I'll never ask you to do anything else ever again."

"Not tonight, I'm busy," Ronnie said.

"Me too," Katy added.

"If you don't do this for me, I'll never do one more favor for either of you as long as you live, and don't even *think* of testing me."

"Okay, okay," Katy conceded. Her dogs had vet appointments the next week, and Esme was the only one who could drive.

Veronica, as the number one recipient of Esme's favors, was also quick to acquiesce.

40

YOU SAY YOU WANT A REVELATION

True mindfulness, Esme knew, was not a state of consciousness that could be achieved in just one night. Her consciousness, her very soul, was stained and polluted and flawed, and it would take a lot of laundering before it was truly clean. Already her clarity wasn't as sharp as it had been during her vision, or even in the early hours. But what she had held on to, what she focused her mind on, was a kind of penetration through the preconceptions and reality biases that had always kept her in a kind of fog. She could see through the deceit that masked the world, the lies people shrouded themselves in, which she herself created around other people. And more important, she could see through the lies she'd always told herself.

The school campus that Friday morning was like a new world to Esme. Clarity was intense, when she used it to observe people. Katy had to practically drag her along toward the school from the student parking lot, because Esme was staring at everyone, picking up clues with her penetrating insight, stuff that had always been right there but she'd never put together. Facial expressions juxtaposed to snippets of recollection; observations and associations she'd made over the years about a million little things all revealing in-depth details about people's emotional states and desires and true characters. The harder she focused, the more was revealed. Merely by strolling through the parking lot and casting rapid glances, the clarity yielded quick if superficial little synopses of people's most defining characteristics.

Esme had never imagined, for example, that Stephan Reese lived and breathed musicality, but was too shy to perform in public or even talk about it, so nobody knew that there was a potential rock star on campus. She picked up on it as soon as she saw him in the parking lot, recalling that a music teacher in nursery school had mentioned he was a prodigy, before she'd known what the word meant. He was sensitive to sounds and always drumming in a nervous tick, and a thousand other observations all came together to reveal his secret.

She also noticed that Brandon North had mild Asperger's syndrome. She just knew. It was rude, but Esme couldn't help staring, as people's deepest qualities were revealed to her. The information was overwhelming. She saw a ninth grader who cut her wrists— she always wore long-sleeve shirts with holes cut in the cuffs to poke her thumbs through. Ronnie's ex-friend Michaela was bulimic; Esme could tell from her skin and teeth and emaciation. Nick was gay. In his heart, he knew it, but didn't want to admit it to himself, because his family was religious and he feared he'd lose their approval, or worse, their love.

Esme observed that the defining characteristics of girl after girl she cast her sight upon were vanity, obsession with popularity, or self-loathing. The defining characteristics of many of the boys were overall horniness, macho posturing, or denying their own vulnerabilities, which were often their most redeeming qualities. She'd often suspected, but now she knew.

The sisters approached the stairs in front of Hampstead Hall. Katy had to keep tugging Esme along as if leading a stubborn dog that was sniffing every telephone pole. Images were coming to Esme in quick flashes now, in the thick of the school with dozens of students around. A tall blond sophomore she'd seen around campus was obsessed with money. A dark-skinned freshman boy with beautiful dimples had a massive inferiority complex. Debra Weller, a girl Esme had known since grade school, was a devout religious fundamentalist who didn't believe in science. A sophomore boy she'd seen hanging out with guys from the football team was a racist. A few girls were flirting with Zack: Karina, social climber; Nancy Getty, a hormonal nutcase; and Dawn, surprisingly conformist for a Goth. And Zack, of course.

Vampire.

Zack had *DANGER!* written all over him in a very large font with exclamation points. Pale skin, elongated canine teeth, a predatory stance, all were plain to Esme now. He never ate solid food, he only drank liquids. He was a mesmerist and he exuded neurohormones to attract prey. Esme could kick herself for having been so clueless for so long. *Of course* Zackery Kallas was a vampire. It was obvious.

Esme's clarity kept her from exclaiming something awkward, like "Oh my Goddess, Zack is a vampire!" She couldn't let Zack know she knew. That would be very dangerous. She had to get her sisters away from him immediately. Zack must have been responsible for Miss Edwards's disappearance, and Sandy's, and Lisa's. Katy and Ronnie were next. And Esme was all alone, with nobody to turn to. Was Zack's dad a vampire as well? Esme focused her insight on Zack's facade, to reveal . . . conflict? Tragedy? It was hard to get a good read. But yes, Drake Kallas was a vampire, by far the more dangerous of the two.

"Katy, Ronnie, we have to go," Esme said cautiously.

"Whattaya mean?" Katy asked.

Calm, calm. "We have to go back home and take care of that thing. That we promised?" She looked pleadingly from sister to sister, begging them to play along.

"What in the world are you talking about?" Veronica chastised. "You're out of your mind. You've been acting strange since yesterday."

Sick! She should have said she was sick and needed them to take her home. Now Zack was looking at her oddly, his piercing intuition penetrating her act. He had some sixth sense, some instinct. It was too late to say she was sick. He'd never buy it. Did he know she knew?

She had to get away from Zack. She was showing all her cards in a game of poker with the direst stakes imaginable. "I remember, I did it the other day. Hey, I have to get to class."

Esme stopped outside her first-period calculus class and scrambled in her backpack for a piece of note paper. She tore off a corner and hastily scribbled a note:

URGENT! I NEED YOUR HELP! SEE ME AFTER CLASS! DESTROY THIS PAPER!

On the way to her seat, Esme walked past Norman's desk and, concealing the note with her body, dropped the paper, folded twice, onto the desktop, making sure he saw it. Then she sat down to wait out the class. The teacher spent the whole period reviewing the semester and giving them reading for winter break. Over her shoulder, Esme watched Norm shred her little note into tiny strips, and cross-shred it into confetti.

After class, Esme made sure she was the first out of the room, so she could catch Norman whether he was willing to talk to her or not. She didn't know what else she could do. There was nobody else to turn to. Nobody else would believe her.

Norm exited the classroom and nodded, tilting his head toward the east exit of the hall, which nobody used because it opened opposite the quad. They pushed up the hallway against the tidal wave of students, Esme moving in the giant's wake like a jet skier behind an aircraft carrier. Outside, she found him, back against the building to the right of the doorway. His huge presence was very reassuring. She felt safe with Norman. Feeling the need for a protector was a female weakness she'd always disparaged— who needed a man, for anything?—but her nerves had been on edge since her revelation about Zack.

Norm looked down at her expectantly. "So, what's the emergency?"

Esme couldn't shut off her clarity. She could see Norm, for the first time, as he truly was. He was humongous, was what he was. But not just physically. Everything about him was huge and powerful: his intellect, and his empathy, and his sense of humor, and his integrity. The tragedy of his life was huge, the loss of his mother, his illness, and the monstrosity he'd become. His remorse, his regret about what he was and what he could have been, was overwhelming. He was so wounded, and yet he accepted it all with dignity. Esme's heart chakra pulsed with compassion. Yes, he was physically unattractive, but with her insight she saw his spirit, which shone like a beautiful, blazing star. No boy she'd ever met was his equal.

But Norman's most defining characteristic, which he could not hide from her, caused Esme to turn away from him, ashamed that she'd read the truth in his heart: Norm loved her, deeply and with unrequited, tragic futility. Loved her the way a boy should love a girl, for what she was, all of her, the good and the bad, and for no other reason.

But he was waiting for her to say something, so she cleared her throat and spoke up:

"Zack is a vampire," she said.

"So?" he replied. "What else is new?"

41

THE GOOD GUYS

"Okay, I need you to send a text," Norman instructed, glancing at his watch. "Wilson has second and sixth periods with Zack, Nick has third period, you have fourth period. Nick and I have fifth period. We've been monitoring him for weeks, so we've worked out the surveillance."

"Why don't you text Wilson yourself?" Esme asked.

Norman held up his hands. His fingers were as thick as bratwurst, his thumbs like pepperonis. "I can't text, except with a stylus, and it takes forever. You're much faster."

Esme opened the app. "He's trying to get Ronnie or Katy," she said.

"We'll track him," Norman promised. "If they get within fifty feet of his car, we'll all converge and get them out of there."

"We have to call the police! Zack's father is a vampire, too! We have to do something!"

"No police!" he insisted. "It's too dangerous. You need to come to my house after school. My dad's there, he can explain everything. You have to trust me on this."

At the end of the school day, Esme herded her sisters to the car. There was a jovial mood among the students, despite the bleak weather. They assembled in small groups in the student parking lot, comparing vacation plans. Some girls had on their pointy red Santa hats with white fur lining. Boys were already sporting ugly Christmas sweaters. Winter break had begun.

Esme could see Nick by the exit to the parking lot, and Norman by his huge SUV. Wilson was near Zack's Mercedes, pretending to hold a conversation with someone on his cell phone while he paced back and forth. Zack was talking to Melody, Karina, and Dawn. Esme had the distinct sense that Zack was watching her out of the side of his heavily tinted goggles.

Esme dropped Katy and Ronnie off at the house, at their insistence. Esme tried every trick in her repertoire to cajole and threaten her sisters into coming with her, but they would have none of it. But they agreed to have the tea ceremony when she got back home. It looked to be a long meeting, so Norm had suggested dinner. Esme and Norm had discussed the advisability of leaving her sisters alone in the house with bloodsucking predators on the loose. Norm arranged for Wilson and Nick to keep the house under surveillance in two-hour shifts until Esme got back home. If they saw any vampires, they'd call in the fire department and Norman, and everyone would converge.

Esme was surprised when she met Dr. Stein. If not for the acromegaly, Norman probably would have been as short as his father. The doctor was in the kitchen when they arrived, fussing over pots and pans. Esme was taken instantly with Dr. Stein's intellect. Channeling her clarity, she'd honed in on the man's brain. He was defined by it.

"We'll let the brisket cook until it's dry enough to choke a shark," Dr. Stein said, rinsing his hands in the sink, scrubbing under the fingernails with a bristly brush as if prepping for surgery. He dried his hands on a kitchen towel, then offered one to shake. "Please, call me Fred."

"It's an honor to meet you, sir." She'd been worried about this moment, having betrayed Norman to the vice principal.

"Did you hear that, Franklin?" he asked his son. "I *told* you it was an honor to meet me." He turned and confided to Esme, "He thinks I'm an embarrassment."

"The man wears Bermuda shorts, black socks, and Birkenstocks," Norman returned affectionately. "I rest my case."

"Einstein said, 'Once you can accept the universe as matter expanding into nothing that is something, wearing stripes with plaid comes easy,'" the doctor retorted.

"Well, yeah," Esme said. "Stripes and plaids, fine, but Bermuda shorts with black socks? I don't think so."

Dr. Stein's eyes lit up with a spark of mirth. He pinched Esme's cheek. "You'll do, kiddo."

꩜

In the living room, Norm's dad launched into a very long narrative about his time in Europe while Norman was frozen in a state of suspended life, raising funds for research and bouncing theories off the brightest minds in medicine regarding his son's case. He met with pharmaceutical companies and medical researchers, mostly people in fields related to cryopreservation, neurosurgery and stem cells. In the evenings, he met with unsavory characters who traded in human body parts. No lead was too obscure, no back alley too seedy, no character too ghoulish for him to ferret out, in search of what he needed: tissue-typed limbs and organs of extreme size. There was a black market for such things.

Dr. Stein would meet with a few colleagues periodically, people more interested in advancing medical science than in ethics and legalities. He found his way into the society of the most brilliant and secretive scientists in Europe. He picked up the nickname "Dr. Frankenstein," as his son's state of cryogenic suspension and rumors of his search for large body parts became known. An elderly Nobel Prize laureate whose name Stein promised never to reveal was introduced to him in a secretive men's club in East Berlin. The laureate in turn referred him to a man who lived in a castle in the Austrian Alps who had a rather exotic private library of esoteric medical texts dating back many centuries . . .

"Perhaps we should skip over some of this," Dr. Stein proposed. "I went to Austria, and stayed with the duke at his castle for a month. I came upon a very old tome that referred to an unsanctified graveyard in a tiny hamlet in Estonia where was kept, in a long-forgotten crypt, a decapitated corpse that had not decomposed at all in four hundred years. Which was of particular interest to a doctor worrying about the cellular degeneration of his son in a cryogenic freezer.

"I wouldn't have thought anything of it, except I judged the book to be at least three centuries old, and full of the most uncanny medical information you can imagine. I soon departed Austria for Estonia. It was a rustic village, bleak and nearly deserted. I contacted an unpleasant man to whom I'd been referred by one of my grave-robbing acquaintances. We located the vault and stole into the crypt in the dead of night. We found the sarcophagus in an alcove on the lowest level, behind a rusted iron gate, undisturbed for centuries. We broke open the padlock with a pickax and entered the alcove. It was far creepier than I could possibly describe. We worked the stone cover of the sarcophagus until we discovered the trick to it, and then slid it back. And do you know what we found, in that forgotten sarcophagus?"

"A body?" Esme ventured, on the edge of her seat.

"The brisket," Dr. Stein said.

"There was a brisket in the sarcophagus?" she asked skeptically.

"No, in the oven. I just remembered. It's probably done by now."

Nick arrived in time for dinner, having been spelled by Wilson from the stakeout of Esme's house. Esme set the table and filled water glasses. They dined on a full beef brisket and a mound of asparagus in butter and lemon, a coarsely cut rye bread, and crisp, hot potato latkes, which Norman advised Esme to slather in sour cream and eat quickly while they were still hot. The latkes were amazing.

Dr. Stein continued his story over dinner. In the sarcophagus, he and his colleague discovered a perfectly preserved body, sans head. The body had been subject to numerous autopsies. In the bottom of the sarcophagus, they found the skull. It had a complete set of dentals, and the fangs at maxillary 6 and 11 were prominent. The skull had been burned of flesh in a fire. There were scrolls in a tube of hollowed wood, which Dr. Stein removed carefully and photographed extensively, before returning them. He also harvested miraculously well-preserved tissue samples from every major organ. Then they returned the cover to the sarcophagus and closed the iron gate, leaving the body in the crypt where it had lain for more than seven centuries.

"I returned to my labs in London with my tissue samples and my photographs and my notes," Dr. Stein lectured. "I had the photos of the scrolls translated. There were medical notes from researchers who'd come to examine the body in centuries past, with their observations. The fourth scroll retold the story of the corpse:

"He was described as a man of indiscriminate age, killed by locals of the village in the year 1306. He had settled there two years prior, and his arrival had marked the beginning of unusual goings-on. Maidens of the village had started walking around in mesmerized states, smiling a lot as if in love. Bite marks had been found on their necks and wrists. The maidens all had very high fevers, but seemed in good spirits. Few in the village would speak against the stranger. He had a charm that people found irresistible. When some of these lovelorn maidens started to turn up dead, a magistrate—an elderly man who'd never succumbed to the lothario's charms—started to decry him about the village. The father of one of the girls who'd died became suspicious also, when a younger daughter caught ill with the fever. He waited up at night, saw the stranger enter his daughter's room through a window, and witnessed him drinking her blood. But he didn't intervene, because he knew the man then for what he was. A few like-minded individuals of the village got together and sent for a specialist, a self-proclaimed vampire killer, who managed to stir up support in the village to ambush the predator. Five villagers lost their lives in the struggle, as the villain was inhumanly strong, fast, wily, and brutal.

"As part of his payment, the vampire hunter bade the villagers keep the corpse in the crypt, for proof, and for others to come and examine at will. By burning all the flesh from the skull, they killed it beyond regeneration and resurrection, which the slayer informed them tended to be a problem with vampires."

"Well that's an amazing story, Dr. Stein," Esme said. "You actually knew about vampires, having studied one. When did you make the connection with Zack?"

"I first became suspicious when I examined young Jackson, and heard reports of Zack's superhuman strength and his ability to inflict post-hypnotic terror. That plus the reports of missing young women, and Norman's musings about so many girls in his school walking around mesmerized as if in love. When Norman obtained the blood sample, I was able to confirm my suspicions. Zack and the body in the sarcophagus have the same pathology. The genetic markers are unmistakable. By the way, I heard you were at the scene of Jackson's fight?"

"Yeah," she admitted. "I was there."

"You never thought to tell anyone?"

"Uh . . . Zack asked me not to. Until last night, I guess I thought I was in love with him."

"What made you come to your senses?" Norman asked.

Esme hedged. "I guess . . . meditation and prayer? And I had some very strong herbal tea."

42

SATURDAY

Esme got home after midnight, Norm following in his SUV, and they found Nick, on his second surveillance shift, in his car across the street. The temperature was in the twenties. Nick was in high spirits. He said nothing eventful had happened, and Esme thanked him again and again for his help. Norm insisted on staying overnight on the couch, just in case, but Esme assured him that there was no reason to expect Zack and Drake that particular evening. Katy's dogs would certainly wake the house if anyone approached. She promised to keep Norm's number handy and her phone with her at all times. In truth, Esme would have felt safer with him staying, but she couldn't allow it. The debt of gratitude she felt to Norm, his father and the guys was already overwhelming.

When Esme entered the house, all the lights were out. She rapped lightly on Veronica's door, but there was no response. The door to Katy's attic was locked, as always. Esme was quiet, so as not to rouse the dogs. She was exhausted. She'd had almost no sleep for two nights. Her clarity was almost entirely gone: Apparently, it needed to be renewed daily. She'd work Katy and Ronnie through the tea ceremony in the morning, and by the afternoon she'd have her talented sisters by her side when she met back up with Norm and his dad to deal with the vampire problem.

~° ͡ c͜°

Esme awoke in the morning to the sound of howling dogs. She checked her clock: only six a.m.! And on the first day of vacation. She rolled over and tried to get back to sleep.

A cat jumped onto the bed, displacing Charlie, Kali and Mandela. Why wouldn't they let her sleep? She pulled her blankets over her head. It was cold in the basement but warm under her down comforter. Murasaki, under the blankets with her, clawed herself over Esme's leg and fled.

Kasha nosed his way under the blanket, by Esme's face. She smelled his fetid carrion breath. "Hey, sleeping beauty," he taunted. "Are you going to stay in bed all day?"

"It's Saturday," she complained. "Let me sleep."

"Oh, sorry," he said, pulling his head back out. Then he snaked his way back under the quilt to mention, as an afterthought, "I just thought you'd be interested to know that while you were out last night, the vampires came and took your sisters away."

Esme jumped out of bed so fast, all the cats in the room scampered for the cat door. "What?! Why didn't you tell me last night?!" she screamed.

Kasha didn't startle easily. "I wasn't here. I followed them. I thought you'd want to know where the vampires' lair is."

"I *know* where their lair is!" she yelled. "*Everybody* knows where their lair is. It's the old Hampstead mansion. It's on the national register of historic homes!"

259

"Well you could have said something before I spent all night tracking them. But at least it wasn't a complete waste of time."

"You know how to get them out?" she asked desperately.

"No, but I found a field on the other side of town that's full of gophers. Big suckers, too."

Esme frantically pulled out drawers and scrambled into clothes. "We have to get Norman and his dad. We'll get the police and the FBI and the National Guard if we have to, but we're getting them back. Today. Right now!"

"Esme, calm down," Kasha advised. "You don't want to do anything that's going to get your sisters killed, do you?"

"I don't have time to argue with you!" she yelled. Keys in hand, she slammed through the basement door and ran up the stairs. Esme got into her car, fumbling with the keys, and started the engine. She put it in gear. Then she put it in park. Then she turned off the engine. She had no idea what she was going to do. Of course she couldn't just go get her sisters out. She couldn't even call the police. Norm and his dad had been very insistent on that point. The windows fogged with her breath, and the mucus ran freely down her face as she sobbed onto the steering wheel.

The opposite door opened, and Kasha jumped into the passenger seat. "Were you planning to take on those vampires by yourself?" he asked casually.

"You," she blubbered. "You're a demon. You could help me. Couldn't you?"

"What good is a little cat against two big vampires?"

"So you can't help me?" The cat stared at her, unblinking. He licked a foreleg and ran it back over his head, slicking down fur. "You can, but you won't?" she tried.

"I got my own problems," he replied. "I haven't had a soul in years. I'm way behind on my quota. The hounds of hell are breathing down my neck here. I need some action. Now."

"You . . . horrible . . ." she accused, sobbing. "My mother was right about you. You're evil. What was all that, with Shikker, about me becoming a vampire so you could extend your contract another thousand years? You were actually going to let me become a vampire?"

"You must have dreamed that," he replied, grooming. "It never happened."

"I had an epiphany of clarity the other night. I remember every word."

"Oh. Well that changes things. Yeah, the vampire stuff. You'll recall, I'd tried to warn you off Zack, but you wouldn't listen to me. I needed a contingency plan."

"So the lesson here is, you aren't trustworthy at all."

"Oh, I'm entirely trustworthy," Kasha argued. "You can always rely on me to act in my own self-interest. You learn to work with that, you'll come out just fine."

"Getting my sisters out *is* in your own self-interest!" she yelled. "If we all get killed, you won't have a contract anymore!"

"A fairly moot point, with the hellhounds nipping at my heels."

"What should I *do*?" she pleaded, shaking the steering wheel violently.

"I suggest you get your head straight and come up with something that doesn't involve getting yourself or your sisters killed," he suggested, jumping down out of the car. "There's nothing in my contract about any vampires."

Back in her room, Esme tried to empty her mind of images of ripping Zack and Drake Kallas limb from limb and pleas to the Goddess for lightning bolts to shoot out of her fingertips. She needed to assemble her resources and formulate an intelligent course of action. With lightning bolts coming out of her fingertips. Why wasn't there a spell for that? Stupid grimoire was practically useless.

Esme searched Veronica's room. There was no sign of a struggle anywhere, no forced entry, no resistance. Ronnie had left the house with little more than the clothes on her back. Her cell phone was on her dresser, and all her makeup was still all over her vanity. Esme closed Veronica's door behind her and approached the doorway to the attic. Kasha joined her there.

The dogs started barking furiously when they sensed Esme outside the attic door. Kasha jumped up onto the *tansu* chest in the hallway, out of reach. *"Recludo,"* Esme intoned, eyes closed. The tumblers clicked. A stampede of dogs tore out of the attic, jumping and barking.

"Something's not right," Kasha said, when they were inside the room.

"You think?" Esme snarled. "My sisters were kidnapped by vampires. How did they get past Nick?"

"Kid in the car? The older vampire walked right up to him and knocked on the window. They talked for a few minutes, then the vampires walked up your sidewalk and knocked on the door. They left with your sisters about ten minutes later. They were expecting you to be here, too. They came downstairs looking for you."

"And you did nothing!" she yelled. "Big fierce demon."

"As a matter of fact, I hissed at them," Kasha said. "They

didn't seem too intimidated." The cat was sniffing around the room at the air. "Is that sage and juniper I smell?"

Esme sniffed. "I don't smell anything except the dog poo in the corner over there."

"Okay, this is going to sound weird, but nobody smudges with sage and juniper. Except . . ." The cat paced, nose in the air. His tail twitched violently. "Use your locator spell and see if you can find a set of black candles," he commanded.

Esme closed her eyes for a moment and cleared her head, echoing the words in her mind. She walked over to the wardrobe and opened it. "Here," she said, removing a bundle wrapped in African indigo. She was so confident in her vision, she knew what the candles looked like before she unrolled the bundle. There was also a small vial of green fluid.

"Your great-aunt Becky always used sage and juniper together," the cat explained. "It was her thing. Did you know Katy was a necromancer?"

"No way," Esme complained. "That's so not fair. On top of all her other gifts?"

"Open the vial and let me smell that potion." Esme uncorked the vial and held it low, beneath his nose. "Yeah, that's the good stuff. Becks helped Katy brew up a dose of her famous love potion."

Esme put the vial into her pocket. There was no way she'd ever let Katy use a love potion. Especially with a jumpy demon cat around desperate for a soul fix.

"Stein residence." Norman's voice came over the phone, sleepy but so, so reassuring.

"Norm, they took Katy and Veronica." Esme tried to be strong, but she started crying into the phone. She'd been okay up until the very moment she'd had to tell someone, and then it all came pouring out.

"I'm on my way," he said, steady as a rock. "Don't move. Don't answer the door or do anything until I get there. They could be anywhere."

Ten minutes later there was a knocking on the front door. It had to be Norman, the way the pounding reverberated through the whole house. Esme had been waiting in the kitchen. She parted the curtains, just to be sure. Norm's SUV was in the driveway.

"Oh, Norman," she cried, falling into his arms. She barely came up to his chest. She couldn't get her arms all the way around him. His size was so reassuring. She felt safe. Norm was exactly what she needed.

Norman waited with Esme while she gathered her stuff. He was very insistent that she move into the clinic with him and his dad. It took two trips to Norm's SUV to get everything she felt she'd need, including her laptop and all the botanicals and witchcraft supplies and the large tin of her special powdered tea. She also brought the hatbox pentacle, as Kasha had suggested, as well as her mother's black ceremonial wooden knife, from her shelf of African fetishes. The cat had warned her that it probably wouldn't kill a vampire, but it might slow one down.

43

A DELICATE OPERATION

Dr. Stein and Wilson were waiting for them at the kitchen table with fruit and coffee and bagels when they arrived at the clinic. "So what happened last night?" Norm asked Wilson.

"How can you people be so calm?" Esme yelled. "They took Katy and Ronnie! We have to get them back!" She looked around the kitchen table from face to face. Nobody was moving! "Wilson, your family has guns! Let's go! Now! Call the police and the FBI and the fire department! Let's move, people!"

"That's a very stupid idea, Esme," Dr. Stein said bluntly. "Even if we don't all get ourselves killed, we would most certainly get your sisters killed. Please. Calm down. We need to talk."

There was a knock at the door. Norman got up and returned a minute later with Jackson. He seemed a shadow of his former self. He'd lost about twenty pounds since the fight. His face was still bruised where Zack had hit him.

Esme cut to the chase. "What's the plan?" she asked Dr. Stein.

"The plan is, we don't do anything that Zack or his father would regard as suspicious."

Esme's fists were tight in her lap. "If we all went to the police, they'd have to believe us."

"If we went to the police, your sisters would be dead in minutes, plus whoever else is there," Norm said.

"The police would have to get a court order before they can enter," Dr. Stein explained. "Vampires are always plugged into the judicial system. Get the wrong clerk, or the wrong judge, they'll be gone before the paperwork is signed, and your sisters will be nothing more than ashes."

"You can't know Zack and Drake would do that," she argued.

"Do you want to take a chance?" Jackson asked, his voice cracking.

"So, how about like . . . the FBI? Or Homeland Security? We could say they're terrorists . . ."

"If we call the FBI, they'll contact our local law enforcement, even if we tell them not to," Dr. Stein explained. "Vampires always have informants. They operate beyond the law, in the world of human trafficking. They have ties to organized crime all over the world. The Tong, the Yakuza, the Cosa Nostra, and the Russian mob fear them. There's a secret unit within Interpol that tracks them. Interpol gets its funding from a hundred and ninety member nations, and they do not go around discussing vampires in public. In fact, only four or five people at Interpol even know about them. My friend the duke arranged a teleconference for me last week with an agent at headquarters in Lyon."

"So . . . ? What? How do we kill them?" Esme asked.

"We need to be very cautious," Dr. Stein said. "Whenever Interpol has been on the verge of catching one, they end up at an abandoned lair with the bodies of multiple victims on-site. Vampires are tremendously wealthy and powerful, and their network for intel is vast."

"I have to get my sisters out of there," Esme pled. "You can't tell me if we went up there with automatic weapons we couldn't shoot our way in, kill the vampires, and rescue my sisters. If you pumped enough bullets into them, you'd have to do some damage."

Dr. Stein shook his head. "Interpol coordinated an ambush in Turkey a few years ago. Highly trained team all in Kevlar, heavily armed, with advanced intelligence and communication. They lost five agents and the suspect escaped. His lair in Istanbul was burned to the ground. There were thirteen girls burned beyond recognition in the rubble. Vampires are incredibly fast and ruthless. They're fearless and unbelievably strong and impervious to pain. They can sustain tremendous injuries, damage that would be fatal to a normal person, and recover quickly. You have to sever their heads to stop them."

"So we're just going to do nothing?" Esme yelled, banging both hands on the table.

"Esme, sit down," Norman pleaded. "We *have* a plan, we've been working on it for weeks."

Esme glared at them, but took her seat. "What is it?"

"Jackson? You want to give your report?" Norman prompted.

"Yeah, okay." Jackson leaned forward with his arms on the table, eyes downcast. "So, like, I've been watching the old Hampstead place, whenever I can. It's not like I sleep much anymore, anyway . . . So, uh . . . you know, there's just the county road, Hampstead Drive, that goes out there, right? It runs up the hill past the Hampstead estate, and backs onto Darner Woods. A lot of the land used to be part of the estate. I don't know who owns it now. There's signs posted to keep out, but lots of people hunt those woods for deer in season." Jackson scooted up to the table and wedged his elbows in, giving his head a little leverage. "Yeah. Anyway, I've checked out the manor, there's no way in or out except the driveway, and there's a gate there, and almost a half mile of gravel through rough territory until you hit the old orchards. Then there's some field, and the house. You cross a little wooden bridge over a stream, maybe four hundred yards from the house, but they'll see you coming a long time before that. And you won't get through that gate in a car without dynamite anyway. Forget about off-roading it. It's too rough. The whole property is fenced in wrought iron, with security cameras and motion detectors all over. We can't sneak up on them."

Wilson added an opinion: "If you go over the fence and across country with heavy weapons, figure on them having ten minutes to torch the place before you get there, and more time to escape out back across country while you try to get into the house. So, everyone inside will die if we just attack. That's assuming they don't decide to fight us."

"So your plan is: It's hopeless," Esme said.

"Not at all," the doctor reassured her. "We're planning to wait until the older one is out of the house and coordinate a quarantine with Interpol and the Centers for Disease Control. The CDC doesn't need a warrant, and they don't have to inform local law enforcement. I'm meeting tomorrow at my lab at the university with an old colleague. I'll show her my tissue samples and we'll confer with my contacts at Interpol. She's an epidemiologist with the CDC. She coordinated the response to that Ebola outbreak last year. The CDC response team is a group of hard-core operators. They know how to control a quarantine site. "

"I've been watching the only road out for weeks now," Jackson reported. "The older one leaves for up to eight hours at a time, two or three times a week. There are three cars, but he's the only one who drives the Bentley."

"All we have to do is wait until the old one goes out, then move in while Zack's alone. I can take care of him," Norman promised.

"But you almost lost, when you fought him," Esme reminded him.

"I never fought Zack," Norm said. "That whole fight I staged, that you saw? That was just a lab procedure with a difficult patient."

"But we're going in tomorrow, right?" Esme asked.

"No, I'll need at least an extra day to bring the CDC on board," Dr. Stein said. "Once we have them, we'll contact Interpol."

"And we'll have to wait until the older one goes out. Two or three days, tops. Don't worry," Norm added, noticing the homicidal expression on Esme's face. "Your sisters will be fine."

"Yeah, as long as they have blood," Wilson said.

Esme noticed Norm's expression, his reaction to her own anger, and she forced herself into composure. Every muscle in her body was tense with fury, but she pulled her elbows off the table, clasped her hands calmly, and put them on her lap. She couldn't display any indication of what she was thinking, of what she intended. Because two or three days was not going to fly. Not with her sisters' lives at risk. If Norm and his dad and friends were not going to help her, she'd find someone who would, or go in alone if she had to. But they couldn't know. They would try to stop her.

There was a shave-and-a-haircut rap at the door and Nick let himself in.

"Hey, folks," Nick said, entering. "Mom said you wanted to meet here? Cool, bagels."

"Nick. How are you?" asked Norman. His voice was even, but Esme heard the concern.

"Never felt better in my life." He grabbed an empty plate off the counter and started walking around the dining table, loading up on bagels and fruit.

"Did you sleep well?" Dr. Stein asked.

"Like a baby."

Esme asked, "Did you notice anything unusual last night, on your stakeout?"

"Stakeout?" he replied, slathering cream cheese on a bagel. "What stakeout?"

"You were in front of my house, watching out for vampires," she reminded him.

"Vampires? That's a good one. Hey, is there any coffee left?"

Everyone traded looks. Norm edged closer to Nick at the table, and Wilson rose to flank him. "Wait," Esme said. "I've got this."

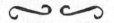

Esme took Nick into an exam room and poured them both a steaming cup of her mindfulness tea and took him through an abbreviated ceremony.

"Hey," Esme said when Nick opened his eyes.

"Hey," he replied.

"How are you feeling?"

He was looking at his hands, as if he'd never seen them before. "I know what happened last night, with the old vampire. I remember everything. And so many other things, suddenly I see it all. I've been lying to myself."

"Do you want to talk about it?" she asked.

"I guess I can tell you," Nick said. "You were sort of my spirit guide. Turns out, I'm gay."

"Yeah, I know," Esme said. "How do you feel about that?"

Nick turned his hands over and examined the backs. "Fabulous," he admitted.

"Oh. Uh, that's good. Listen, let's go outside, and you can tell the others about last night."

"Yeah, sure," Nick agreed, standing. He was a little wobbly. "But, Esme?"

"What is it, Nick?"

"Honey, you're not going to wear those shoes, are you?"

44

STUPID IN LOVE

"It's the Yule tomorrow, you know," Katy mentioned.

"Really?" Veronica said. "I'd lost track. Are you sure?"

There were no clocks in the room, and no windows, so it was impossible to tell how long they'd been there. They'd slept twice, though, plus long, luxurious catnaps in between. "I feel it, in my bones," Katy proclaimed.

"Esme said she was going to get a Yule log and cast a circle."

"I miss Esme," Katy said. They were in Ronnie's bed together. They'd awoken entwined.

"I'm so happy. Did I tell you that?" Ronnie mentioned.

"Nonstop," Katy said, and the two giggled like little girls. Veronica snuggled in closer. She was so warm. "I wish Zack would come."

There were comfortable chairs in the room, and a dresser and a vanity. They had toiletries and a little bathroom with a shower stall and a toilet and a sink. There was a bookshelf full of YA romance, which Katy suddenly had a hankering for. She'd always liked anything about werewolves, or urban fantasy with a feisty female protagonist battling ruthless overlords across futuristic wastelands, but post-apocalyptic dystopia was now a thing of the past.

"I wish Zack would come, too," Ronnie said. "And Drake, of course."

"Of course," Katy agreed. "I miss his kisses. His kisses are the best."

"I like Drake's kisses, too."

"Yeah, they're the best. I could use a few right now."

"And Zack's. Don't forget about Zack's."

Veronica's voice was raspy and thin, and she was very pale, Katy thought, and frail and indescribably beautiful. "Oh boy, really, and Zack's," Katy said.

The thing about the kisses wasn't creepy at all. It was just affection. But Katy loved them so, so much. She supposed, somewhere in the back of her mind, that being smooched on the neck from her boyfriend's *dad*, who was old enough to be, like, her *dad*, practically, was uh . . . whatever. Or something. One day, Zack would be like his dad, so mysterious and sophisticated. She loved her sister, why shouldn't she share the boy she loved more than anything with her sister, whom she loved more than anything? It was all family. And Drake, too. He was affectionate, to his son's girlfriends.

There was a noise at the door then, of locks being unlocked. They had to be locked in, Drake had explained, because they had bubonic plague, and were highly contagious and probably delirious, though Zack and his dad were immune. It made perfect sense. Veronica rose up in bed and swung her feet off over the side delicately, just as the door opened. Her eyes lit up as Zack entered with a tray of food.

Katy's heart felt as if it would jump out of her chest like the monster from *Alien* and attack Zack all over the face and neck and everywhere. Love nips, not like tearing out his throat or anything. They *lived* to see Zack. When he was there, it was the best, but when he wasn't, there was the delicious anticipation of when he'd return. Veronica stood, unsteadily. Katy ended up just taking the tray out of Zack's hands and setting it down on top of the dresser.

"'Ello there, me lovelies," Zack said, beaming. And then he had a couple of arms full of Katy, and she was pushing into him, backing him up across the room, until his knees came up against Ronnie's bed and he tipped over backward. "Miss me, then, did you?"

Ronnie sat on the bed as Katy straddled Zack, leaning over him, hair hanging on both sides of her head, tenting her face above his face. She kissed him several times, sloppy kisses on his eyes and forehead and cheeks and nose, and on the lips. Always, her kisses returned to his lips. "Ronnie, get in here for some of this," she invited.

Veronica lay back on the bed, on one elbow. She pulled her hair to one side and let it hang behind. She presented her neck for a kiss. She liked kissing Zack just fine, but it was his kisses she craved, the way he nibbled at her neck and gave her hickeys. Zack acquiesced, and stretched out his neck and lips, as far as he could, as he was pinned down by Katy. His lips touched Ronnie's neck, and she shivered in pleasure.

"Veronica, you're burning up," he said, alarmed. He removed Katy from his chest as if she weighed nothing at all, and sat up. "You need to eat something to keep up your strength. Katy, bring your sister something." Zack touched the back of his hand to Veronica's forehead to test the fever; fairly pointless, as his hands were always cold.

Katy arose and perused the choices on the tray he'd brought. "Look, Ronnie, Zack brought us cheeseburgers! Oh, Zack, I haven't had meat in like forever! It smells so good! And French fries! And orange juice, and a salad!! It looks so delicious, thank you, Zack."

Zack rose abruptly and went to the door. "Katy, come here for a second."

Katy followed him. She'd follow him anywhere. "Hey," she said, snuggling up, backing him against the door. "You."

Zack held Katy at arm's length. His expression was deadly serious. "Katy, Veronica's too hot," he whispered. "She hasn't enough fat on her to fight through it, do you understand me?" He stared into her eyes, to see if anything was registering. Katy returned the gaze, goo-goo eyed. He gave her a little shake, for emphasis. "You have to make her eat something, understand? And keep her hydrated. I have to go talk to Drake."

"Sure," she replied, nodding. "No prob."

"I'll be back in a bit," he said, reaching for the doorknob.

Katy yanked his arm back roughly. "Oh no you don't," she cooed. "Not until I get my kiss."

Esme spent hours on Saturday listening to the guys make plans for their coordinated attack on the Hampstead mansion. The more she heard, the less she liked. They seemed to be too concerned about transportation contingencies with Interpol in case the Chicago airports got shut down for snow, and not concerned enough that there were killer vampires draining her sisters of life by the minute. She couldn't just sit by and let her sisters die a slow death. She needed to go right away: she felt it in her bones, with her last vestiges of clarity.

Alone in her guestroom, she made herself tea several times, but in her agitated state found mindfulness elusive. There was too much going on in her head: tumultuous, violent thoughts. She felt a desperate need for a consultation with the Goddess, despite an increasingly nagging suspicion that her vision and epiphany had been little more than a dream.

Frustrated, she studied the grimoire on her cell phone, looking for anything she could use in a confrontation with two vampires, memorizing spells and gestures in half-dead languages, practicing them in a whisper in front of a mirror. There were no spells to make lightning shoot out of her fingers, or anything more than a flash of light. There was nothing to give her superhuman strength, only an invocation for fortitude. There were no spells for invisibility or fireballs in the grimoire, though there were four good cures for warts. If Zack and Drake had been warts, she could obliterate them.

That evening, after Wilson and Jackson and Nick had all gone home, Esme waited until she could hear Norm in the bathroom on the second floor, preparing for bed, and crept quietly down the stairs. It was almost eleven o'clock. She avoided Dr. Stein, asleep in a reclining armchair in front of a TV tuned to The Weather Channel, and snuck out the back door through the kitchen.

The snow had been falling for hours, and there was a thick blanket over everything. She tromped through the backyard around toward the street, lugging her duffel bag full of supplies.

"I hope you aren't going to try something stupid," said a raspy voice behind her. She turned and saw Kasha, leaping through the snow in her boot-steps.

"Kasha. What are you doing here?"

"Protecting my interests."

"I'm going to get my sisters out of that vampires' lair," she announced with determination. "I'm going in alone. I have a plan."

"No, you're not," the cat said. "You can't get yourself killed. With your sisters about to die, I could never find another soul to harvest in time."

Esme kicked out at the cat, almost losing her balance in the slippery snow. "Do you ever think of anyone except yourself?"

"Frankly, no."

"I'm going to go in there alone and give myself up. I have a thermos full of tea, and everything I need here to take Katy and Ronnie through the ceremony. When my sisters have clarity, there's nothing in the world that can keep us in there." Esme stomped her boot in the snow defiantly.

Kasha laughed—the most evil demonic sound a cat could possibly make. "For a smart girl, you sure say some stupid things. The minute you walk in that door, those vampires are going to bite you and your system will be flooded with twenty thousand volts of pure love juice. If you walk in that door alone, you're never going to walk out. And neither will your sisters. And believe me. You. Will. Tell. Them. Everything. About your friends and all their plans. So you'll be killing Norman and his dad and those three goofy-looking boys you're palling around with, too."

Esme's face fell as she heard Kasha's words. Then she dropped the duffel bag and fell to her knees in the snow. The cat was right. Every word of it. How could she have been so stupid? One ineffective little witch against two vampires? When a team of trained professionals couldn't even take *one* down? "Kasha, can't you help me?" she begged, her tears hot on her face, mixing with the falling flakes of snow.

"Of course I can help you, Esme," he said. "But only if we do a new contract. My terms are your soul, for your sisters' lives. Just say yes, and we'll go right now. Your sisters will be safe and warm with your friends by the crack of dawn."

"But I don't want to go to hell for eternity," she cried. "I don't want to die."

"No, you probably do want to die. What kind of life would that be, without your soul?"

"You . . . evil . . ." she hissed, as loud as she could. "I hope those hounds of hell *do* come for you. I hope they drag you back to where you belong."

"Is that a 'no,' then?"

"I . . . don't . . ." She wrung her gloved hands in anguish. "I need to think . . . There's not enough time . . ."

There was a baying of dogs in the night, and Kasha dove for the cover of a dormant hedge. Esme looked around wildly in all directions. "Kasha?"

The demon poked an ear out, then rejoined her in the snow-covered yard. "The hounds are coming," he whispered, ears cocked in opposite directions. "I've never been this far behind." Esme reached for him, to take him in her arms, but he swiped at her with his claws. "I'm not your pet!" he hissed. "I'm a demon from hell!"

"Kasha, help me. We'll figure something out, for your quota."

"I've already figured something out. Are you in, or not?"

Esme put her face in her hands and fought the tears. "I just can't. Make a decision like that."

"Here we go," the cat said with contempt. "It's going to be the potion all over again, isn't it? You know what your problem is? You're too smart for your own good. You think too much." He took a single leap away and turned. "Shall I give you a few days to think about it? Do you want to have some tea? Make a decision, Esme. I'll try to make myself useful in the meantime."

And then he bounded away in the snow, and was lost in the flurries.

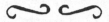

"Master, a word?" Zack requested.

It was after midnight, and Drake had only just returned from the city. He was reading, reclined on the sofa, in a very dim light. Outside the snow was falling relentlessly. "That was three already," replied the Master. He bookmarked the old tome and set it on the coffee table.

"It's Veronica, Master. The fever is very high. She doesn't look well."

"I was afraid of that," Drake replied. "One gets a sense for such things. I've seen such a reaction before, many times. A shame, she was quite exquisite."

Zack did not like the sound of that. Veronica had barely been in their clutches for a day, and already Drake was referring to her in the past tense. "Will she recover?"

"No, she won't," Drake stated. "Her body is fighting the illness but it will lose, when she's exhausted all her resources. Remember Helene?"

"But Helene lasted for months!"

"Veronica will be dead in a week. A shame, a terrible shame. Her blood was so effervescent."

"Couldn't we . . . abstain? Until her fever comes down? Katy could nurse her back to health."

"You know nothing," Drake said flatly. "The intelligent course of action is to end her now, while her blood is still fresh. She'll be useless soon. Would you have her die in vain?"

"Three days?" he pleaded. "I'll force-feed her, if necessary."

The Master rose, and paced, as if pondering judiciously. He stopped by the heavy drapes, on the south side bay window, and looked out into the cold, dead winter. "You can have tomorrow," he adjudicated. "Tomorrow I'm going into the city again. I've found us a lovely new bride, and I intend to retrieve her. When I return, unless Veronica recovers, which she won't, we shall have us a feast of her."

"Yes, Master, thank you, Master," Zack groveled. Only one day! But it was a concession, anyway, from a creature without mercy.

"And you'll bring Esme to me tomorrow, while I'm out. She must be wondering where her two sisters have gone. It's highly suspicious that she hasn't tried to contact the police. Do not fail me, or you'll be sorry. You respect my ability to make you sorry, don't you?"

"Yes, Master. Of course, Master," Zack fawned, bowing. Then he jerked his head around suddenly, toward the doorway. "Did you see that, Master? I'd swear I saw a cat run by."

45

THE DEAD OF WINTER

The flurries in the Susquahilla Valley continued through the wee hours, and with them the wind. It gusted against the house in buffets and rattled the windows with small, icy snowflakes. Esme fretted fitfully in bed. Every half hour or so she opened her eyes and wondered if she'd been awake or if she'd drifted off for a few moments.

At three a.m. there was a noise at the window, too rhythmic for random gusts of snow. Esme wondered what it could possibly be, on the third floor. Resigned to her insomnia, she got out of the bed to check and drew back the curtains. She opened the window for Kasha.

The cat leapt into the room, bringing weather on his heels. "It's colder than a witch's tit out there," he remarked. "No offense."

"I don't know what you think you're doing here," Esme said, slamming the window shut. The temperature in the room had dropped ten degrees in a matter of seconds. "I can't decide, okay? I know, I'm a completely useless wreck, and I can't stand it that my sisters got captured by vampires. But the guys think they can get Ronnie and Katy out of there, if we wait a few days . . ."

Kasha licked himself. "You need to go get your sisters out of that vampires' lair right away." Kasha said. "Veronica's dying, so they're planning to kill her tonight. Drake is heading into the city this morning. That's your window of opportunity."

Esme paled. "Veronica? Tonight? But Dr. Stein is meeting his epidemiology friend today, and we can't go in until at least Tuesday!

"Okay," the cat said. "Go in Tuesday, and rescue Katy. Forget about Ronnie. She'll be dead."

"I'm going today." Esme was stunned by the sudden finality of the decision, but oddly relieved. No more thinking about it, no more waiting around for other people to decide. She was going in. If Ronnie's life depended on it, nothing could keep her away.

Kasha jumped up onto the desk beneath the window and waited for her to open it. "Bring your portable pentacle; you'll need it."

Esme opened the window and Kasha leapt out. She watched him drop and land elegantly in the snow twenty-five feet below. She stood at the window until she couldn't see any sign of him anymore. Then she picked up her cell phone and sent a text to Jackson:

can u stake out the hampstead place this morning, early? have info drake going out

She paced. Should she tell Norm? He'd want to know where she got her information. He'd never believe her, especially if she told him the truth. He'd try to stop her. Forget about that. Her phone buzzed with a text. She grabbed the device off the nightstand:

I'm on it

Apparently, Jackson wasn't sleeping, either. Esme set the kettle on the hot plate to boil up some tea. She needed clarity here, as never before.

When Esme crept downstairs in the morning, Dr. Stein was already gone to the city to meet with the epidemiologist, at the university. She'd waited until she could hear Norm in the bathroom before making her move. Even tiptoeing about, Norman's footsteps caused the floorboards to creak and complain.

It was still early. Esme shrugged into her coat and wrapped her scarf around her neck. She sat on the footstool by the entry and buckled on her snow boots.

"Where are you going, Esme?" Norman asked from the hallway.

Esme rose and reached for the doorknob. Norman was barefoot. If she scurried out the door he'd never catch her. "I'm going to the house to feed the animals," she improvised. Anyway, she needed to retrieve her car. And she had to make preparations while she waited for Drake to leave.

"In this weather? It's twenty degrees out there! The roads are all covered in ice. Wait a minute, then, I'll drive you."

"Norman, no. You can't go with me."

"Why not?" he demanded.

"Because I have to go get Veronica and Katy. I can't tell you how I know, but you need to trust me. Drake is going into the city today, and if I don't go in and get my sisters, something terrible is going to happen."

"Is this something to do with Wicca? Because I don't believe in it. I can't let you go, it's too dangerous even if Drake isn't there. And how could you possibly know he's going out?"

"He won't be there," she promised. "And it isn't a Wicca thing, it's a witch thing. I'm a witch, Norman. And it isn't your decision to make. So, are you going to try to stop me?"

"No, not physically. But I'll use all my powers of persuasion to try to talk you out of it. My dad's on the way to the city right n—"

"It's too late." Esme cut him off. "By the time he returns, Drake will be back. If we wait until the next time Drake goes out, Ronnie will be dead. And everyone else. You heard your dad, vampires are too dangerous. There's no way to fight them."

"Look, Esme," he argued. "You can't walk all the way to the Hampstead Mansion with that big duffel bag. I'll drive you to Long's service station, and maybe on the way you can explain to me how you know it has to be today. How's that sound?"

"Okay," she said. Though she'd have to invent a reason. "My demon cat told me" wasn't going to fly with Norm. Psychic connection with Ronnie? Something more along those lines.

"Good," Norman said. "We'll get Jackson to stake the place out, and he can tell us if Drake leaves, or if your information is not as good as you think it is."

"Way ahead of you," she replied, showing Norman a text. "He's been there for hours. Listen, I have to send Wilson a text to go to my house and take care of the animals, like he did last night. They must be going nuts by now. He still has the keys."

Esme started to send a text, but her phone suddenly vibrated. It was a new message from Jackson. "Jackson says 'the Bentley is on the move.'"

"So. I guess your intel is good after all," Norm said. "Unless it's just a big coincidence. Shall we go?"

"Yeah," she agreed. "But before we go in, I want to make sure Drake is at least an hour away, in case Zack calls him."

46

CERTAIN DOOM

Zack sat on the edge of Veronica's bed with a bowl of cool water and a hand towel. Every few minutes, he dipped the towel into the water and wrung it out, then applied it to the girl's forehead. Veronica's breathing was shallow. Her face was pale as snow, her silky blond hair damp from perspiration. An hour before, he'd made Katy bathe her in ice-cold water, to no avail. Veronica was rapidly dehydrating. He'd been trying to force-feed her broth and noodles, but she'd been retching up every drop and more since early that morning.

"She's so beautiful, don't you think?" Katy asked. She was sitting beside Zack on the bed, holding his left arm, her head on his shoulder. "She's sleeping."

"She's dying," Zack countered angrily. Katy didn't grasp the gravity of the situation. She just wanted to make out. It infuriated him. If Veronica died, he would harden his heart until he could never feel anything again.

"Don't worry, Zack. She'll be okay. Nothing can kill my baby sister. She's too tough."

Zack stood abruptly, violently shaking himself loose from Katy's grasp. He marched to the door. "I'm going to get her some antibiotics." He had hours before the Master returned. He could mesmerize the pharmacist at the Rite Aid easily enough. The Master had said they wouldn't work at all, but he had to do something. Anything.

Norm's SUV pulled up into the parking lot of Long's Service Station on the corner of Hampstead Drive, where Main Street came to a T. The gas station was owned by Danny Long's father, Rick. For the past three weeks, Rick had allowed Jackson to sit in his waiting room every day, drinking coffee and watching Hampstead Drive. If anyone went in or out of Hampstead Manor, they'd have to go through that intersection. The trees were dusted with a heavy white cover, and every once in a while Jackson watched a large clump drop from this tree or that, as the snow loosened up in the morning sun. The snow plow had been down Main Street, but hadn't cleared Hampstead Drive. It was a dead end.

Norman and Esme entered the waiting room, decked out in boots, coats, scarves, and gloves. "Where's Rick?" Norman asked, tossing Jackson the keys to his car.

Jackson caught the keys in one hand. "In the bay doing a lube—oil filter. Zack just pulled out."

"So, do we go in now?" Norm asked.

Esme checked the time on her phone. "Drake's not as far away as I'd like. But maybe I can get in and out before Zack gets back. It's too good an opportunity to pass up. Listen, Norman: I'm not risking anyone else. I'm going in alone."

"The hell you are. I'm not letting you go in without me." Norm grabbed Esme's arm with an unbreakable grip.

Esme conceded with little resistance. "Okay, okay. You can come. I was hoping you would, I was just trying to be noble and brave."

"Sure had me fooled," Norm said.

Jackson was weighing something in his mind, and Esme guessed it was chivalry versus fear. "I guess . . . I'll go in with you?"

"We need you to drive us," Esme said. "Then come back out here and stand guard. If either of them return, text me. It might give us enough time to get out."

The look of relief on Jackson's face was obvious.

Norm received a text on his phone. "It's my dad," he said. "I told him what we're up to. He said he's going to tell his source at Interpol in Lyon. At least if we get arrested or something, Interpol might be able to pull some strings. He also says if I can't talk you out of going in, at least be careful and get out of there at the first sign of trouble."

"Not without my sisters," Esme said. "Now let's roll."

47

HAMPSTEAD MANOR

Esme, Norm, and the duffel bag went over the fence at the gateway as Jackson drove off, then the two hiked up the long driveway, careful to walk only in the tire tracks in the snow. At the front door, they met with a major obstacle. The wide, high double doors were made of heavy wood, with ornate, forged iron bracketing and a dead bolt that looked to be beyond Esme's magical prowess. "I can get us in," Norm said, "but I'd have to destroy the door."

"Let's go around the side and try a window," she suggested. Better not to destroy the door, and clue a returning vampire to their presence.

The windows on the ground floor all had heavy iron security bars bolted into the brick facade. They walked around the side, looking for other ways in, mindful of the tracks they left, and the time. Behind the house, they found a service door off the kitchen. It was also heavy wood, locked and double bolted, but Norman didn't think they'd find an easier entry. "Stand back," he instructed, and kicked the door in. The wood of the jamb shattered with just one kick, and the door flew open. "My first felony," he mentioned.

Jackson saw, through the window of the waiting room, the black Mercedes turning wide onto Hampstead drive, fishtailing in the snow. The car evened out and sped up the road. Jackson took out his cell phone and texted Esme. Then he called, but the phone went to voice mail. He was equally unsuccessful reaching Norm. Jackson had a strong desire to follow the car up the road. He'd brave almost anything to see a fight as epic as Norman Stein versus Zack Kallas.

"This place is huge." Esme looked around the main hallway. At the rear of the cavernous room were ornate curved staircases to a landing on the second level. There was a cut-crystal chandelier hanging from the thirty-foot ceiling. The room, for all its airiness, was dark and somehow gloomy. Heavy drapes covered every window.

According to Esme's research, there were two three-story wings to the house, each with hallways full of rooms. She knew her sisters would be hidden underground, but she didn't know where the stairs were. Behind a secret panel in the library? She reached out with her location spell, and wasn't surprised to get nothing but a vague sense that they were below her. The spell had never even worked through walls, let alone tons of rock and earth.

The library was open, but empty. There were floor-to-ceiling bookcases on two sides. There were crown moldings and recessed windows and wainscoting and a hundred other fine architectural details in every room, but the library was especially ornate, with a massive fireplace set into a carved marble mantle. As Esme and

Norman returned to the hall, they heard the front door open. Esme peeked out at the driveway through the drapes. "It's the Mercedes."

"Zack," Norman said. "You keep looking for your sisters. I'll take care of him."

~~⌒~⌒~~

Traffic was crawling in Tuppelow. Three days before Christmas, and the shoppers were out in force. Drake Kallas was not the type to be annoyed by such things. The days of his past stretched endlessly behind him, and the days of his future stretched endlessly ahead. The sound system of his Bentley was superb, and the machine was a pleasure to drive. Cars jockeyed for positions to edge into the second mall exit, but Drake was content to listen to Maria Callas in her dramatic interpretation of "Casta Diva." Drake had heard many coloraturas in his day, and tasted a few as well, so he considered himself a true connoisseur of opera. His cell phone rang and he answered, pausing the sound system. "Yes?"

The voice on the other end was raspy. "Drake Kallas?"

Drake didn't recognize the voice, but he took it for one of the elders. The accent was entirely ambiguous, a culmination of dozens of languages and countless centuries to sand the rough edges off. "Yes? Do I know you?"

"They're coming for your brides, Drake," the voice purred. Then the line went dead.

Drake didn't bother with the exit. He yanked the wheel to the left, cutting off a Toyota Camry, and went straight across the median strip. He gunned the engine when he regained the highway north, making his own lane with two wheels on the median, two on the road. He was doing ninety as he blew past traffic and left it all in his wake. The road was clear to Middleton. He judged he could be there in a little over an hour.

When he passed the last exit to Tuppelow, Drake phoned Zack at the house, and was annoyed when he didn't answer the landline. Doubtless, the youth was in the cellar with the dying girl, and didn't hear the phone upstairs. Zack's cell phone, of course, was useless at the manor. There was no cell reception.

"Now the fun begins," Kasha said, on the other end of the line.

Zack had barely closed the front doors behind himself when Norman Stein stepped into the grand hall. His heavy footsteps echoed thunderously. Zack handled it with aplomb. "Norman," he acknowledged with a nod. He removed his scarf and hung it on the coatrack by the door, then shrugged out of his overcoat. "If I'd known you were coming, I'd have picked up some watercress for sandwiches."

Norm stood in the doorway to the west wing, placing himself between Esme and the vampire. "Zack. I was hoping you'd show up. We have unfinished business." Norm tugged his down-filled jacket off his frame and dropped it, taking a step. His duck boots squeaked on the wooden floor.

"Why are you here?" Zack asked amiably, dropping a small white paper bag from the Rite Aid pharmacy on the bench.

"We came to get Veronica and Katy."

"What makes you think you'll find them here?"

Norm advanced, covering the doorway like a runner taking a lead off first base. "We checked with all the other vampires in town and couldn't find them, so we figured they had to be here."

"We?" Zack asked.

Stupid, Norm told himself. "All of us," Norm covered, throwing out a bit of confusion.

Zack sniffed the air. "Just you and Esme." He was close enough to strike, given his vast advantage of speed, but still angling for position.

Norm took a step back, covering his door. He crouched, spreading his arms out by his sides. With his massive wingspan, the vampire couldn't get past him. "How about you and I have a little rematch?" he suggested.

Zack laughed. " 'Fools rush in where angels dare to tread,' " he quoted. "Alexander Pope."

" 'And the angels are all in heaven, but few of the fools are dead,' " Norm countered. "James Thurber."

"I adore Thurber," Zack confessed, edging for a strike. He removed his straight razor from his hip pocket and flipped it open. The steel gleamed menacingly in the thin light. "Shall we?"

Esme moved quickly through the hallway, opening each door with her *recludo* spell and checking for stairways. She'd been over the rescue plan a hundred times in her mind, but since Jackson had told her about Zack being out of the house she was improvising, and making stupid mistakes. She was distracted by thoughts of Norman. In all the scenarios she'd plotted through the night, she hadn't considered that her friend could easily die. She wished she could help him, but she knew she'd be a liability: If Zack got around him somehow and grabbed her, Norm would do whatever the vampire said.

Kasha wasn't lying about Drake, she was certain. Even if she got her sisters out, there was no place to hide from him. At some point, somebody would have to face him. But she couldn't worry about that now.

Esme couldn't shake the terror, for her sisters and for Norman. She'd had almost no sleep for four nights, and even with three cups of tea coursing through her system, she had not managed to reenter her state of clarity. She sprinted through the rest of the west wing. She had to keep her wits about her. She entered a south-facing room, the last on the hall. There were no drapes, only old leaded-glass windows, distorted with age. The sunlight streamed through, and the room was lit with prismatic light. A million little rainbows on the walls.

She drew a breath. Could it be a sign? She decided to take it as one. She focused her mind, stilled her terror, and calmed herself. She exhaled. Whatever happened, she would deal with it.

48

VASTER THAN VAMPIRES AND MORE SLOW

Zack lunged with his blade, supernaturally fast. Norman barely had time to swing his arm defensively in front of himself. It was only respect for Norm's power that made Zack settle for a slash of the blade across the giant's hand. Zack danced in and out, watching Norm's two huge hands, slashing. The cuts he made on Norman's arms and hands were superficial, but Zack had patience. Better to bleed the giant out a bit, until he lost strength.

Norm edged back and forth, but he was pinned. He couldn't let Zack break for the door and Esme. When Zack moved in, Norm waved his hands about like a bear swatting at bees. Zack was everywhere and nowhere. The blade stung, but the pain wasn't much for someone who'd had every kind of cancer in the book. It was a good, clean pain. Lot of blood, though.

The scent of Norman's blood drove Zack into a frenzy, like a shark smelling blood in the water. It made him want to slash harder, deeper, more violently. He wanted to sink his teeth into Norm's neck. He'd never tasted the blood of a male before. The Master disdained it. He lunged in, spinning, leaping over the giant's shoulder, sweeping backhanded for the jugular with the blade. He almost got it, but Norman's huge hand came crashing into him and Zack was thrown into the wall with a resounding crash.

Norm was on Zack in two steps, but not fast enough. The impact hadn't hurt the vampire in the least. He was on his feet in a fraction of a second, never giving an inch of ground. It should have knocked the wind out of him at least, but maybe vampires didn't use wind. What would it take to beat someone like this, to mash him up enough so he couldn't get back up again, couldn't harm Esme? Norman slowed his movement down a little. He needed to get his hands on Zack, but he wasn't fast enough.

Zack danced about back and forth, showing some of the fancy footwork that had made him his high school team's first-string striker. He went in high: Norman swept after him with his right hand, grabbing at the arm with the razor, but the fingers closed on empty air. *Pathetic*, Zack thought, drawing blood from the far shoulder, then tossing the blade to his left hand and slashing up across Norm's chest. That one definitely did some damage. The giant was staggering. Time to finish him off.

Norm abandoned the doorway. Esme could be anyplace in the house by now. He edged around the hallway, toward the huge front doors. Zack was tireless. In addition to the blade, Zack punched and kicked him at will. His kicks, in particular, were brutal. Vampire soccer players, how does one prepare in life for such contingencies, with only a public school education? Norm was bleeding profusely from two dozen wounds. Most of them were superficial but too many were significant. He was losing blood, but he had more than most people.

～ᗒ ᗕ～

Zack saw opportunity after opportunity as the giant weakened. He kicked hard at the right knee, watched it nearly buckle, then feinted in high to the left with the blade, only to spin low to the right, fancy feet flying, slip under the right arm, and backswing the blade at the giant's left ankle. A quick hamstringing would end it fast, then he'd still have time to find Esme before the Master came home and beat him to a fine, bloody pulp. Norman managed to backhand him, not hard enough to do any damage, but enough to roll him end over end halfway across the room. The slash had cut into the back of the shoe, but Zack hadn't drawn blood.

"Dude!" Norm said. "Do you know how hard it is to find these boots in size twenty-four?"

"Sorry, mate," Zack replied, regaining his feet in a flash, grinning despite himself. "But you won't be needing them, soon enough."

Norm approached. He was moving very slowly now, and blood was pooling on the floor. Norm's right shoulder was oozing blood, and his right arm was drooping. Incredibly, the die-hard Yank was waving Zack in with his left. Norm's right arm struggled up a bit, then dropped uselessly to the side. Zack had to admire the spirit. Crouching, he moved in for the kill.

Norman tensed. Zack charged in, feinted to the left, as he'd done two dozen times at least, then came in for the death blow, switching his grip on the blade as it sailed past Norman's neck, and reversing. Norman dodged his head back with speed the vampire didn't know he had left, then followed with a walloping blow against Zack's head with the full power of his right arm. The arm Zack didn't know he could still lift. The hand crashed into the vampire's face like a windshield hitting a mosquito, smashing the dark goggles to smithereens at the impact, snapping Zack's head back, and sending him sailing across the room like a tape-measure home run, to crash against the wall at the other side of the immense hall.

Anybody else would have had jelly for vertebrae after a blow like that, but Zack staggered to his feet, ripping the shattered, useless goggles off his face. His blade had flown somewhere, but he was more concerned about the giant. Literally, he'd seen stars when he'd been hit that time. Supernovas, even. But Norman hadn't taken advantage by charging him. He was across the room, near the front door. Norman walked immediately to the two large bay windows at the front of the hall. They were heavily curtained, and he drew back the drapes of one, then the other. The room had a southern exposure and it was the dead of winter, barely noon, and it was a crystal-clear day. Sunlight poured into the room. Only then did Norman turn and advance.

Zack moved to the rear of the hallway into the shadows, but the sunlight was still too bright. Vampires can't tolerate much sunlight in their eyes, because of the unnatural dilation. He looked around the room frantically for his straight razor, but with his blurred, squinty vision, he had little hope of finding it. The skin on his face was burning. He backed toward the stairways. Zack saw the giant as a blur, but could track him well enough by the scent of blood. He edged back some more, watching the huge hulking form. Zack feinted left: Norman followed but shifted his weight to go right, where Zack actually went. Zack then feinted left and went left with lightning speed. He slipped under Norm's arm, but instead of escaping, he reversed and leapt on the giant's back, razor-sharp nails clawing for eyes, teeth sinking into a neck the size of a first-growth redwood. Teeth in the neck: that was the end of the game. Giant or no, Norman Stein would be in his power, once the venom took hold.

∽ ᴐ ᴖ

Norm felt light-headed with Zack chomping on his neck. Hormones coursed through him, the oxytocin, the endorphins and adrenaline and serotonin, causing elation. But the love chemicals flooding his system were all for Esme, and he wasn't going to let Zack get his hands on her. He reached back with his left arm and grabbed Zack by the neck. His hand went entirely around the vampire's throat, and the thumb touched the pinkie on the other side. Then he squeezed.

Zack's hands continued to scrabble at Norm's eyes, but Norm tucked his chin under. Zack's arms didn't have the length to go around. Norman squeezed harder. He could feel Zack's bones through the flesh, and they were making snapping noises. The heel of Norm's hand was against the back of Zack's head, as if Zack were a club and his neck was the handle and his head was a knob on the end that gave Norm a better grip. Zack went limp, and Norman swung him over his head and smashed him against the floor like an ax into a log. Zack was a rag doll, but Norman still didn't trust him, so he smashed him against the floor a few more times for good measure. "Stay down," he yelled, with his knee on the vampire's chest, punching him hard in the face. Bones were giving way. Lots of them. Zack's blood was dark and very thick. It spread like molasses, slowly out in a puddle. Norman released Zack and stood. Zack scrabbled to get up again. What would it take to stop him? Norm stomped on Zack's leg, breaking the femur. He knew the names of every bone in Zack's body, and he'd break them all if he had to. He stomped an arm when Zack tried to rise again. Then he took out the other leg.

"Esme!" he bellowed into the hall.

Esme stepped out from behind the door to the east wing. "Is it over?"

Norm stood above Zack, surveying the damage. His shirt was in tatters, and blood was dripping all over the floor from several places. But he didn't look anywhere near as bad as Zack. "I don't know how fast these vampires heal, but I don't think he can move anymore. I broke all his major bones, not to mention his neck."

Esme raced to him. "Norman, are you all right? I've never seen so much blood!" She was on her knees, digging through the duffel bag. Time was flying, but she had to be sure Norm wasn't going to bleed out. "I packed bandages, but I don't think I have enough. Off with your shirt."

"Esme, we don't have time, we should keep searching," Norm objected. But he took off his shirt. It was all in tatters and saturated with blood anyway.

"I know where my sisters are, and we're going to get them. But not if you bleed to death."

49

UNDER

Esme ran to the kitchen for towels and water, despite Norm's protestations that he was all right. Norm insisted on staying in the big hall to watch Zack, afraid that he'd miraculously recover and need to be pounded into pulp all over again. Esme returned quickly with water in a cooking pot and an armful of clean kitchen towels. She handed a damp towel to Norman for his face and neck and focused on his torso and arms. Now that she could see Norm without his shirt, she noticed that he was built like a comic book hero. He looked thick in the clothes he bought off the rack, which were designed for very tall, morbidly obese men, but his waist was compact, his shoulders and arms immense. It was the wrong time to look, but Esme couldn't help noticing that his abdominal muscles were incredible. Norm definitely had something going for him with his shirt off.

"Let's go," Norman said, as she finished taping him up. "The older one could come back any time." He retrieved his enormous overcoat and put it on over his bare skin, wincing. Esme helped him, suggesting he leave it unzipped, to air his wounds. *And show off those abs.*

"Esme," came a soft, creaking voice from the middle of the hall.

Esme had been avoiding Zack, not wanting to see him all broken. Sure, he was a bloodsucking monster who'd stolen her sisters and tried to kill her best friend, but nobody was perfect. She didn't exactly have the moral high ground, consorting with demons and all. "We have to run," she said, stepping toward the kitchen.

"Esme," Zack repeated, the effort draining the last reserve of his strength. "On the bench. Medicine. Veronica . . . sick." And then his head fell back and he was still.

Esme ran to the bench and scooped up the little white bag from Rite Aid. She hastened toward the kitchen, shucking the bag on the way. Amoxicillin. An antibiotic. Couldn't hurt.

∽ ⌒ ∽

The door to the cellar was locked. *"Recludo,"* Esme commanded, and the tumblers clicked. The door opened to a large passage with a staircase down.

"How'd you do that?" Norm asked.

Esme flipped on the lights. "Coincidence?" she suggested. If Norman didn't believe in magic, he was on his own to explain it. The stairwell went down to a small landing, then doubled back and went down again before ending in a short brick passage. Opposite was a heavy wooden door, bolted shut with a padlock. Esme again opened the padlock with her spell, and the door opened into another room. She fumbled for the light switch.

It was a wine cellar and it was very roomy, at least twelve by twenty feet. There were no doors in the room. They were at the end of the road, and no sisters to be found anywhere. "This can't be it. I was so sure . . ." She dug into the duffel bag for the flashlight. Vampires would have a secret passageway, in case someone got a search warrant. She closed her eyes and held out her hands.

They were drawn to the large wine rack on the far wall. Her sisters were below that floor. "We have to move this wine rack."

Norman gave the wine rack a shake. It was solidly attached to the wall behind it. "I might have to bring the whole thing down, but if there's a passage, we'll find it."

Esme shimmied under the rack on her back. She shone the flashlight up in the narrow crevice between the frame of the rack and the wall. "I think I see something." Then she heard a crack, like an aluminum baseball bat connecting solidly with a ball, and a thud like a ton of beef hitting the floor. Esme shone the flashlight back into the room. Norman was on the floor, on his face. His eyes were open, but his features slack.

"Norm! Are you okay?" Esme yelled. She scooched out on her elbows and butt until she got closer to the giant and shone the flashlight in his eyes. His irises had completely rolled up under the lids.

A monstrously strong hand grabbed her ankle in a bone-crushing grip and tugged Esme out from under the wine rack. She found herself on her back in the middle of the wine cellar, shining the flashlight up into Drake Kallas's face.

50

DAEMON EX MACHINA

"Good of you to drop by, Esme," Drake said. "I wish you'd called first, there's not a bite in the house to eat." He leaned over her, sniffing her like a connoisseur. "I stand corrected."

Drake yanked Esme to her feet. She shrunk away from him, backing as far into the corner as the wine cellar permitted. In the vampire's hand was a crowbar. Esme glanced back and forth, from the crowbar to the back of Norman's head. There was blood a lot of it. "Did . . . did you kill him?" she asked, her voice quivering.

"I certainly hope so," Drake replied. "He's probably ruined my minion." Drake used the hook end of the crowbar to flip Norm over on his back, as if he were no more than a piece of meat. "He's still breathing. Absolutely astonishing. What a specimen; that should have shattered his skull like a melon." Drake drew the crowbar back to strike the death blow.

"Wait!" Esme shouted desperately.

Drake stopped his arm at the apex, tilting his head. "I can't imagine why I should."

Esme tried to gain calm through her terror, but couldn't hold it. "Be-because . . ." she stuttered, stumbling over the word, "because . . . I'll do whatever you tell me?"

Drake laughed at that. "That's quite amusing, Esme. You'll do whatever I tell you anyway." He returned his attention to Norman, raising the crowbar decisively. Esme yanked her mother's ceremonial wooden knife out of her belt and waved it in front of her.

"What do you intend to do with that?" Drake asked, his voice soothing and melodic. The crowbar dropped to the concrete floor with a metallic ring, and he took a step closer.

Esme felt her defiance slipping away, as Drake's hypnotic voice echoed through her mind. It was so easy just to go along. There was something she was trying to remember with one part of her brain, but the rest was a blank. Entirely free, clear of those pesky thoughts, so clear . . . *Clarity!* Esme blinked. She made a gesture, shut her eyes, and shouted: *"Lŭmĭnăblĭs!"* It came from the pit of her chest, from the heart, and there was a brilliant flash of light, like a hundred flashbulbs all going off at once. The vampire staggered back, momentarily blinded, his hand shielding his eyes.

"Forterë!" Esme then yelled, her spell for strength and fortitude, and she plunged her wooden knife with conviction into the vampire's undead chest.

Drake stumbled back, clutching at the wooden blade. A viscous black ichor oozed from the wound. Esme scrambled for the crowbar on the floor and put herself between Norman and the villain, the giant iron candy cane in both hands before her. She had to pound the vampire with it and keep pounding until his head was mush. She leapt at Drake and swung the crowbar at his skull with everything she had.

Drake caught her arm in mid-stroke. He was three times as

fast as her, and ten times as strong. He dug his nails into her wrist until blood dripped out from deep wounds, giving her arm a violent shake until the weapon dropped from her fingers. Then he cuffed Esme across the face so hard her neck snapped back and she went careening across the cellar and into the rack behind her, crumpling to the floor.

The images before Esme's eyes were spinning. Drake withdrew the wooden knife from his chest and examined it with little more concern than a florist might give a thorn he'd just plucked from a finger. He tossed it away nonchalantly, grabbed her by the neck with one hand, and lifted her off the ground. With his thumb, he angled her neck back. His other hand was hooked in deadly talons. His fangs protruded.

"Tricky little witch. That was very ill considered, Esme," he snarled. "I consider myself a reasonable man, but you have tested my patience to the limit. So I will rip out your throat now, if you don't mind, and drink your blood. All of it."

"Ahem," said a voice from the doorway.

The "ahem" was not the clearing of a throat. It was the articulation of a word from a throat that usually cleared itself by hacking up a gopher. Drake turned. There was a large cat with vivid markings entering the wine cellar, tail erect. Drake set Esme down on her feet, though he didn't release the grip on her neck. Soon it wouldn't matter whether he ripped out her throat or not. She'd be brain-dead from lack of oxygen. "Did that cat just say something?" he asked her.

Esme's eyes were bulging in the sockets from the pressure, but she nodded in affirmation. "Ghaaakckkckckck," she said. She'd meant to say yes, but it came out like that.

The cat jumped up onto Norman's chest and sat erect. He

licked his forepaw and slicked back the fur on top of his head. "Have you given any more thought to my offer, Esme?" he asked.

Drake relaxed his grip on Esme's throat. "Did that cat actually speak?"

Esme could barely reply. "Yes," she managed to squeak out.

"Uncanny." Drake released Esme. "I've been alive for over two thousand years and I've had my share of witches, but I've never heard of a talking cat." The vampire knelt by Kasha and extended a finger. "Puss-puss," he warbled, scratching Kasha under the chin. "Kitty-kitty." The cat's claws raked out with demonic speed. Where they tore into flesh, it burned and crackled. Drake recoiled. "Don't be frightened, pretty kitty. Would you like to come and live with me? I'll get you a nice saucer of milk." The cat ignored him and continued his grooming. Drake turned to Esme: "You know this animal? It called you by name, you must know it."

"His name is Kasha." Her neck and shoulders were in agony.

"That's the most astonishing thing I've ever seen," Drake stated with glee. The bloodsucking horror of a moment before was now like a little boy, eyes shining in wonderment.

"You sure took your sweet time getting here," Esme accused. "Kill him!"

Drake roared with laughter. "Kill me, did you say? That *is* amusing."

"I can't go around killing people. Not even vampires. It's against the rules," Kasha said. "You know that."

"The two of you are hilarious," Drake said. "I believe I shall call you Mr. Whiskers. Have you ever had human flesh, Mr. Whiskers? I'm going to kill Esme now. I'll tear off a piece for you." He recaptured Esme's arm in an iron grip.

"Wait," she said, her mind stilling. She looked at Drake's hand on her arm, at the refraction of the dim light going into shadow where the fingers indented her skin. "He's already dead." *Corpse. Eating. Cat.* "He's a corpse. You *can* eat him."

Drake backhanded Esme across the face again, sending her crashing to the other side of the cellar. "Don't you dare call me a corpse!" he roared, all feral beast. Then he genteelly dusted off a sleeve, regaining composure. "I'm undead," he explained, for Kasha's benefit.

Kasha paced around the vampire, as if inspecting a rental car for scratches. "You know, Esme," he appraised, eyes bright with mischief. "I believe you're right. He *is* a corpse. It's a shame I'm not allowed to eat corpses anymore."

"I'm not a corpse!" Drake bellowed.

"That's exactly what every corpse I meet says. He's in denial," the cat explained. "I gigged in Japan for two thousand years as a corpse-eating cat. Nobody knows corpses better than me."

The vampire grabbed Kasha by the scruff of the neck and hoisted him to eye level, his rage simmering. "That's enough out of you, you horrid little beast," he admonished, shaking the cat violently. He pointed an accusatory finger at Esme. "And don't think I've forgotten about ripping out your throat." Kasha hung from the vampire's hand by the scruff of the neck, muscles rigid. "A few weeks in a cage should teach you some civility."

Kasha hissed, puffing himself up, extending his claws and baring his teeth as he started to take on his true form. He grew, slowly but unmistakably. His snout contracted, and his mouth widened, so it hinged very far back on the jaw. The golden eyes glowed redly.

"I should have mentioned," Esme said, wiping the blood off her mouth with a sleeve, "he's not a cat. He's a demon. And he *hates* cages."

By the time Kasha was the size of a bobcat, Drake had decided that there was something very strange going on. He threw the cat fiercely to the floor and took a few steps toward the open door. Kasha landed on all four feet solidly, poised to strike. He continued to grow, and the nubs of horns sprouted from his head, between the ears. He took a step toward the vampire.

Drake crouched defensively, looking more dangerous by the second. His eyes filled with ferocity, his hands curved into claw shapes, and his fangs grew in his mouth until they protruded wickedly. "Demon!" Drake warned. "Do not incur my wrath, I'm warning you!"

Kasha took another step forward, standing erect on his hind legs, his features becoming more anthropomorphic. "Isn't that cute, Esme, the corpse thinks those are fangs," he taunted. His teeth grew in his mouth and curved up and down like sabers, fully twelve inches long. By now he was the size of a mountain lion. "*These* are fangs!"

Drake retreated out the door as Kasha grew to the size of a tiger. The paws were immense, the claws were scythes. The horns were aflame with an eerie blue flicker. Drake suddenly slammed the door to the cellar shut, jammed the lock into the latch, and ran away as fast as he could.

"Wait for it," Kasha said, ears cocked, listening for something. Then he tore out of the cellar in a blur, leaving the heavy steel-reinforced wooden door in splinters.

Esme sank to her knees. She crawled over to Norman to check on him. She could feel his immense chest heaving, but there was so much blood! And she had to get to Veronica! There was a horrible screeching sound in the stairway, and muffled words which became clearer as the sound got louder: "Let me go, demon! Help! You're crushing my skull, beast!" A moment later, Kasha dragged the vampire back into the wine cellar, skull clamped between massive jaws, teeth like fence pickets puncturing the head as Drake's body scraped and bumped along behind, scrabbling and clawing at the demon to no avail. Kasha deposited the vampire onto the floor in a heap, pinning him with one foot. The demon was in all his glory now: nine feet tall and a half a ton at least, with hellish flames flickering all over and licking the ceiling.

"Kasha, help me with Norman!" Esme said. "I think he could die."

"He's fine. And Veronica will be okay, for now. First, we have business to attend to."

"Kasha, I can't thank you enough—"

"Save it," he cut in.

"Wait," she said. "Let me ask him something." She knelt by the struggling, hissing vampire on the floor. "Mr. Kallas, can you understand me?" she asked.

"Yes!" the vampire hissed, clawing at the concrete. "Let me go, I'll spare you," he pleaded. "I have money! A fortune! It's yours!"

"I'll put in a good word for you with my cat, if you cooperate. How do I get to my sisters?"

"If I tell you, will he let me go?" Drake bargained. There was a popping sound of cracking ribs, as Kasha pressed down on his rear paw, driving the vampire against the concrete floor.

"Why not?" Kasha replied amiably.

Drake explained how to work the locking mechanism on the rack to the rear of the cellar. He told her how to slide the rack, how to make the trap door spring, and about the ladder to the dungeons, where she'd find her sisters. "And that's all there is to it," the vampire said, with his remaining shred of dignity. "Now, if you don't mind, Kasha, good sir? Per our agreement?"

Kasha lifted his paw from the vampire's chest. "Toodles," said the demon.

Drake stood, as best he could. He brushed himself off, hobbling into the corridor, oozing thick, dark ichor like syrup from a dozen major wounds. At the stairs he began his painstaking ascent.

"Esme, we have very little time. I can't kill him, technically. There are too many rules. But I'd prefer if he doesn't kill you and your sisters. You're the last generation on my contract."

"Thanks for the sentiment."

"I'm a demon. I don't do the huggy-feely stuff. Okay, maybe I like the way you scratch me behind the ears. Here's the problem: If I let him go, he'll be back, and then you're dead. And your family and your friends. He won't let you live, with what you know. So you have to do a deal with me. If I don't get your soul, I can't help you. Therefore, your sisters die, and everyone else, including you. Bottom line, there's no way you can walk out of this cellar alive. But you have a chance to save your loved ones, at least." The demonic flames flickered over the demon's horns, burning with the horrors of damnation and endless agony. "It's nothing personal, Esme. I wish it didn't have to go down like this. But I need your soul. It's time to decide. Your sisters, or your soul. Now."

Staring into the blazing eyes of a nine-foot demon cat, Esme trembled with true terror for the first time. Eternal torment in the clutches of such creatures was infinitely worse than the simple threat of death she'd just faced at the hands of a vampire. "I-I-I don't think he's coming back," Esme stammered, stalling. "He's lucky enough to get away."

"In an hour, he'll forget he ever saw me," Kasha reminded her. "Remember your mother? And she's known me for decades. He'll be driving away in his fancy car, and soon enough he'll start wondering why he's bleeding all over his leather seats. All he'll remember is, he was about to rip your throat out. Then he'll come back and kill every living thing in the world that you love. There's a reason why humans think vampires are a myth: because they have rules about never allowing anyone who knows about them to survive. I have to run and fetch him now; he's almost at the front door."

"I thought you let him go."

"I did. I let him almost get away, and then I run and catch him at the last minute. It's a game. You should try it, it's fun." Kasha tore out of the room, leaving trails of eerie flame.

Esme crouched by Norman. She tore a strip from the bottom of her blouse and made a bandage, which she soaked in the last of the witch hazel before dabbing it gently to the bleeding lump on the back of his head, her mind churning frantically for ideas. She could hear something bumping down the stairs, snarling and cursing in a half dozen languages she was glad she didn't understand.

Kasha entered on all fours with Drake's thigh in his jaws, long fangs piercing the limb all the way through and sticking out the other side. The demon pawed the vampire off his fangs onto the concrete floor as if removing an hors d'oeuvre from a toothpick, then pinioned him with a rear leg grinding the chest.

"You had another concern, mistress?" Kasha asked Esme.

"Uh . . ." she improvised. With Drake a limp, oozing heap on the floor, it was clear that Kasha was the real danger. "I guess. Mr. Kallas, you're going to leave for good, right? I mean, we'll never see you again, will we? If we let you go? Do you agree to that?" She stared at Drake critically. Could she trust him? At least long enough to get her sisters out? But one glance at Kasha dashed her hopes. He was in charge. He'd played this game a thousand times. There was no hope to be had, from a merciless demon.

"Of course I intend to leave for good, Esme. Thanks for giving me the opportunity to clear that up. Middleton is a nice town, don't get me wrong, but I think I'd prefer to live somewhere without so many demon cats. No offense."

"None taken. I guess you can go. Unless Kasha wants to eat you?" she asked hopefully, checking with the demon.

Kasha removed the hind paw from the vampire's chest. Drake just lay there, studying the two of them. Kasha gave him a little nudge toward the remains of the door with his paw, to get the vampire moving. Drake could barely stand, as one leg was fairly chewed up. He half hopped, half dragged himself up the stairs for the second time.

"This is the best part," the cat said. "He suspects I'm playing cat and mouse with him. He'll probably putter around upstairs for a bit, to see if I come, then make a run for it. In the meantime, I'll be needing your decision."

"Why can't you just eat him?" Esme demanded.

"Because that would violate the sacrosanct treaty that keeps heaven and hell from uh . . . trust me, let's not go there. I shouldn't even be in this form on this plane, that's one of the worst no-nos. Any minute, the hounds of hell could come ripping up here and drag me down for an eternity in the lowest levels of the inferno. Guy just pissed me off, is all. Nobody calls me Mr. Whiskers."

"But you agreed he's a corpse," Esme argued. "Aren't you a corpse-eating cat?"

"I can't eat corpses anymore, either, since humans were granted self-determination and judicial due process even after death. I told you all this stuff already."

"But he doesn't have a soul!" Esme reasoned. "Shikker said so. That could be a loophole."

Kasha pondered. "No, I don't think it matters. They're sticklers for those little details."

"Obviously, the rules were designed to protect the soul, not the corpse," Esme argued desperately "A vampire is just a receptacle for stolen souls, remember what Shikker said?"

"How come you remember that?" Kasha accused. "You were supposed to forget it all."

"I have clarity now," Esme reminded him, tapping her head. "I remember everything. Listen, if Drake doesn't have a soul, we can make the argument that he doesn't own his own remains. You said it would be a big score if you could figure out how to harvest a vampire. Don't tell me you're willing to settle for my pathetic little soul when there's a big prize like an ancient vampire right under your claws. Explain how the vampire soul thing works." Esme started to pace, working herself into argument mode.

"If I ate the corpse, it would free up all the lost souls that are stuck in the vampire," Kasha considered. "Most of them would go over to the holy host as murder victims, so I think they'd give us a waiver on humanitarian grounds. The rest I'd harvest for myself and the hierarchy of my superiors. It could be a huge score. But I'm not allowed to eat corpses. It's not legally defensible. Also, I'm not allowed to do my own contracts anymore. Long story. Are you following so far?"

"Yeah, you aren't even trustworthy in hell. Okay, we treat the corpse like *bona vacantia*, abandoned goods," she improvised. "I'll claim it's mine, and I'll sell it to you, in exchange for another few generations of service to my family. I get my sisters, you get another century topside, everyone's happy."

"Have you done this before? Because you're a natural."

"My dad's a lawyer," Esme reminded him. "I've read up a bit."

Kasha rose to his full height, cocking an ear. "It's worth a shot. Did you pack the hatbox? You need to summon Shikker again. I don't know if we can pull this off, he's nobody's fool."

"Leave him to me," Esme said. "I've got this."

"I gotta go, the vampire is about to get into his car." And with that, the demon was gone at a speed that Esme was pretty sure defied laws of space-time.

51

HER IMMORTAL SOUL

Esme retrieved the hatbox from her duffel bag, forcing herself to master her terror. Kasha was still playing her, but she was onto his game. He must have alerted Drake somehow, to manipulate her into giving up her soul. She straightened the edges of the box, dumped the excess glitter on the floor, and inspected the runes on the inside. Then she sorted lavender and sage from the bundles of dried herbs and tied them together with hemp. Kasha padded quietly into the wine cellar, holding the vampire by the torso, fangs piercing the abdomen. Drake was not resisting anymore. He looked utterly demoralized.

"Let's do this," Kasha said.

Esme placed the hatbox in the center of the wine cellar. She lit her smudge, then proceeded with the ritual. She lit the candles of the pentacle and summoned the demon: "Shikker, it's me, Esme, again. I'm here with your client, Kasha. We need you to do a contract for us."

There was a puff of smoke within the pentacle and the little red imp appeared. "Hey, it's the little *shiksa*," he said. "Did you get the single malt this time?"

"No, I'm sorry," Esme apologized. "I didn't have time."

"You need an offering, Esme," Kasha said. "It's like a retainer. You summoned him."

"That's okay," Shikker said. "I can take a finger. Just stick it in the pentacle here. And not one of those pinkies, either. Like an index finger, or a thumb. I like thumbs."

Esme examined her hands. A finger? She looked around the cellar in desperation. "Uh . . . do you like wine?" A rich vampire had to have something the demon would find acceptable. "Lafitte," she read off a label. "Domaine Romanee Conti. Here's an 1863 port, Taylor Fladgate. Latour, 1900, do you think it's still good?" She looked into the hatbox to see if the red demon was interested.

"I think we can do some business, kid," he appraised, rubbing his hands together.

Against her better judgment, Esme agreed to release Shikker from the hatbox, on condition that he return to his pentacle immediately upon request. He was absolutely not permitted to eat anyone's face, nor leave the wine cellar. Shikker grew, stepping out of the hatbox. He quickly achieved his full height of five foot seven. Next to Kasha, he looked like a toy, albeit a foul, horrifying toy. His skin was like elephant hide, his horns twisted every which way, lethal from any direction. A demonic blue flame flickered over him. His sharklike mouth had an industrial look to it, like it was full of rusty iron saw blades at all angles designed to grind anything within range to a bloody pulp. His feet were gruesome, like eagle's talons; the hands human, but malevolent. A chill ran up Esme's spine. Shikker wore malice about him like a cloak of pure evil.

"Kasha, you're looking good, have you lost weight?" the red demon asked.

"It's the gophers," Kasha replied. "Organic free range."

"Yeah, yeah." Shikker had a jerky, nervous way of moving about that Esme could only regard as menacing. "Nice vampire. Don't you just love that part, where the guy that thinks he's the biggest badass around finally meets something like Kasha here? And would you look at the size of the *landsleit* in these parts," he mentioned, regarding Norman. The demon went immediately to the wine rack with the dustiest-looking bottles. "This'll do nicely. '45 Mouton Rothschild. I always wanted to try it."

There was a gurgling noise coming from the vampire. "Don't touch that!" he sputtered, struggling vainly, dark ichor splattering from his broken mouth onto the concrete.

Shikker bit the top off the bottle at the neck and chewed the glass, cork, and foil pensively. "It's good!" he pronounced, swallowing. "Sometimes these older bottles are corked." He guzzled half the bottle, pouring the priceless claret into his up-tilted maw.

"Don't you dare!" the vampire screeched, struggling to drag himself out from under a half-ton demon cat. "I spent centuries tracking down the greatest bottles in history for my collection!"

"Totally worth it," Shikker complimented, smashing the bottle to the concrete floor in the corner, where the remaining wine ran down a drain. "*Nu*. What else ya got?"

$\sim$ᘓ ᘓ$\sim$

"So, what do you think?" Kasha asked the red demon after explaining the situation. "Esme here has an extra corpse she wants to sell, and I'm interested. Can we make a deal?"

"You and your cockamamy ideas," Shikker declared. "How do you think you have a deal here? Since when is a vampire a corpse?"

"Since I say it is. You got an expert witness somewhere who knows corpses better than me?"

"Okay, don't get huffy."

"I'm not a corpse," Drake argued. "I'm undead."

Kasha sat his enormous bulk down on top of the vampire's head. "Corpse doesn't get a vote."

Shikker paced the cellar, swigging ancient port from a jagged broken bottle neck. "Okay, suppose the corpse angle holds up. And that idea that the law is to protect the soul, not the corpse. I don't see anyone giving you any arguments about that, if you spread enough graft around. If you do a contract with a witch, you can buy the corpse for a generation of service or so. It's a pretty valuable corpse."

"There's going to be a lot of goodwill for this caper, Shikker," Kasha cajoled. "I'm a licensed soul transporter. And this vampire here is pretty old. Imagine all the lifeblood he's ingested, all the souls he's sucked down, over the years. To harvest the souls of an ancient soul sucker! How many do you think are in there?"

The red demon smashed the bottle into the corner of the cellar and went back to the shelf for more. The room was starting to reek of wine and port. Shikker returned, biting the head off another bottle. He guzzled, then scrutinized the label. "Nice. Get off him for a second, Kasha, let me take another look at the *momser*."

Drake struggled into a sitting position. "Not the Latour!" he pleaded. "A taste, I beg you!"

"Nah, it's wasted on a corpse," Shikker said, guzzling.

The vampire hissed. "Demon! Do you know who I am? I'm the Ancient, the arbitrator of records. I'm over two thousand years old!"

"Wow, two thousand. Impressive," Shikker allowed. "How old are you, Kasha?"

"I'll be eighty thousand in a few centuries," the cat replied. "Big one, coming up. You?"

"I'm a hundred thirty-seven thousand years old," Shikker said.

"Really? You look great! What's your secret?"

"I always use toner, and moisturize with an SPF fifteen million."

"Well the weather in hell is pretty brutal," Kasha commiserated.

"Yeah, but it's a dry heat." The red demon examined the vampire more closely. "Gotta be twenty, thirty thousand souls in there. You sure you can handle that many?"

"Only one way to find out," Kasha supposed. "You still work on commission, right?"

"I'll kill you all," Drake sputtered, through his broken fangs.

Kasha sat on his head again.

"This would be so sweet, if we could pull it off," Shikker admitted. "Problem is, your witch doesn't have clear title to the corpse. The body should go to the next of kin."

"Next of kin died twenty centuries ago," the cat reminded him.

Shikker confronted Esme: "What's your claim to this corpse? And don't ask the cat; he can't coach you."

Esme thought fast. "His so-called son made me and my two sisters fall in love with him. He mesmerized us and corrupted our innocent hearts for his devious purposes."

"His 'so-called' son?"

"His agent. On his behalf. So, he owes me. He's liable for damages. I have a solid claim."

"Your pound of flesh, so to speak," Shikker said. "You've got *bubkes*. Nothing."

"Okay." Esme loved to argue. She had this. She paced the cellar. She took the bottle of Latour out of the demon's hand and took a swig, mindful of the jagged glass, before returning the bottle to him. "He drank my sisters' lifeblood. And I demand compensation."

"Lifeblood, that's a little stronger," Shikker admitted. "But your sisters? By what right do you make a claim on behalf of your sisters?"

"They're like my daughters," she argued. "And I'm the only one who has a driver's license. I've been raising them, practically, since my mother—" She snapped her fingers. "I can do better than that! My father is away in Europe, and he said that while he's away, direct quote, I am uh . . . 'You're officially their mom, while I'm gone.' *In loco parentis, mater familias.*"

"That's fine, for human law," Shikker disputed. "But not demonic law."

"*Lex loci* applies," Esme challenged. "The law of the land. *Ad coelium et ad infernos.*"

" 'Up to the heavens, and down to hell,' " Shikker mused. "Well, I guess if there's a Latin legal term for it, it must be all right. Though I think that phrase applies to property law."

"It's a *corpus delectable*," Kasha added. "Come on, Shikker, nobody has a stronger claim."

"Here's our case," Esme said. "I have a claim, so my familiar, who is my agent, took possession of the remains. Possession is nine-tenths of the law. *Beati possidentes.*"

"True in demonic law, too," Kasha agreed. "Unless the other side has a good exorcist."

"Still," Shikker hedged. "We should wait and see if anyone else steps forward with a claim."

"After two thousand years?" Kasha protested.

The debate stalled at that point. Shikker went back to the wine rack. Kasha adjusted his position on the vampire's head. Shikker returned, biting the top off another bottle.

"Was that long enough?" Esme asked.

Shikker chugged, then wiped his toothy mouth. "Let it be written: We waited a reasonable time for another claimant to step forward, but none was forthcoming, so we proceeded." He reached into the pentacle-in-a-hatbox and rooted around. His hand disappeared up to the elbow, as if he were a magician pulling a rabbit out of a hat. "Voilà," he said, producing a scroll with a flourish and handing it to Esme. "Just sign here. Kasha, when you harvest the girl's soul, can I decapitate her? I hardly ever get to decapitate anyone anymore."

Harvest! Decapitate? Esme's heart pounded in her chest. "What the hell, Kasha?" she accused. "You bastard! I thought we had a deal!" She was shaking wildly with terror. And even more than the terror, with the fury of a violent storm, at Kasha's betrayal.

Shikker laughed, a horrible, cackling, gurgling laugh full of pure demonic evil. "Did you see the expression on her face, Kasha?" he howled. "She thought we were gonna let her go!"

Esme threw the contract in Shikker's face. "The deal is off." She retrieved the crowbar from the floor. "Let the vampire up, Kasha, I'll finish him off myself."

"I will if you want, Esme, but if we're not doing a contract I won't be able to stop him from killing you," Kasha advised, "which he absolutely will. And your sisters and Norman here. I've only been able to do what I've done so far because we're not sticklers about retroactive causality and the space-time continuum thingy."

"What'sa matter?" Shikker complained. "Look how pretty I made the letters!"

Shikker was malevolent evil beyond anything Esme had ever imagined. But could she reason with Kasha? The cat was lying about something; she could tell by the way his tail swished. The crowbar shook in her hands as she positioned it between herself and the red demon. The deal on the table was, she would die, and her soul was forfeit, but her sisters and Norm would live. "M-my father raised me never to sign a contract until I read every word, and I can't read this," she improvised, stalling. "It's in about six dead languages, and the fine print is microscopic."

The red demon let out a furious stream of Yiddish invective that went on for two full minutes. "What are you making such a *tzimmes*?" he protested. But ultimately, he calmed down when he found she wouldn't budge, and he looked at her slyly. "Listen, what if I redo the contract in English? Something in a Times New Roman, twelve-point font?"

Esme spent five minutes going over the new contract with a red Sharpie. "Katy's firstborn son?" she complained, crossing out an entire paragraph. "You're out of your twisted demonic mind. And Kasha's terms of service, in exchange for the corpse: one generation? Don't be ridiculous, my family already has him for one generation. I want five."

"Five generations? You have some chutzpah. For one *farshtinkener* corpse? Two, maybe."

"Shikker, you're killing me here," she said. *Show no fear.* "But I like you, so let's just say four generations, not counting this one." Kasha had told her he'd act in his own best interest. So if she dangled that in front of him, would he help her?

"Three, final offer," the demon countered.

"Done," she agreed. "And take out all this stuff about my soul. Don't try to scam me, this vampire is going to bring in thousands of souls, you don't need mine."

Shikker went off again. His rage was terrifying. He screamed at Esme, and threatened her, and held his murderous hands by her neck as if he wanted to choke the life out of her. His eyes bulged out of his skull, but Esme held her calm. Veronica had been prone to violent temper tantrums from an early age, so she knew how to ignore people who screamed in her face.

"Actually, we do need your soul in the contract," Kasha clarified, when Shikker's fury had run its course. "It's the only unbreakable rule in the book."

"Then no deal," Esme said. She crossed her arms and waited.

Kasha and Shikker exchanged looks. Kasha shrugged, and stood up. Drake scrambled back, dragging his broken body to the side of the cellar. He had his hands over the worst of his wounds, as if trying to hold in the thick black stuff oozing from dozens of punctures, but Esme did not delude herself that he was no longer a deadly threat.

"She'll take the deal," Shikker contended.

"I don't think so," Kasha calculated. "Maybe we should cut her a deal."

"I don't cut deals!" Shikker screamed. "You think I don't see what's going on here? *I* do the contracts, not *you*! Do you take me for a *shmendrick*?"

Kasha shrugged, and opened his paws to Esme, as if to say he'd done his best.

Stalemate. And Veronica getting sicker by the minute! But what option did she have? She looked around the cellar in desperation for a better weapon against the vampire. She spied the hatbox, the candles in the pentacle still burning. *Open pentacle!* "I'm going to summon another demon and try to get a better deal," Esme announced.

"She's bluffing, she doesn't know any more demons," Shikker asserted.

"Don't sell your soul to a demon, pretty child," Drake implored. "You don't want to burn in hell for eternity. I can make you a vampire. You can live and be young forever, and Zack can be your eternal love. Like in those books—"

"You!" Esme shouted. "Just shut up, okay? I'm a witch. I make deals with demons, that's my thing." She whirled on Shikker. "And as a matter of fact, I know the names of hundreds of demons. I memorized them when I was researching on the Internet. Kasha here is pretty famous. But guess who there was no mention of anywhere? So, I have to ask myself, what kind of low-ranking demon am I dealing with? If you don't have the authority to write a contract I can sign, maybe I'll just summon up Asmodeus. Or Pazuzu—"

"Stop!" shouted Shikker and Kasha, at the same time.

"Maybe I'll just call up Moloch, and see what he's offering for a two-thousand-year-old—"

"No!" Shikker yelled, cringing. Kasha stepped out of the wine cellar, poised to run.

"I'll bet Beelzebub or Mephisto—"

But Esme couldn't finish the word, because a half ton of

demon cat had her on her back on the floor of the cellar with a paw the size of a sofa cushion stuffed over her mouth.

"Hey, genius!" Shikker was screaming at her. "Knock it off! Open pentacle here! You think *I'm* scary? Our boss is hard-core!"

Eventually, Kasha got off her and she stood again. Shikker was almost bouncing off the walls, howling invective and chugging wine and eating the bottles to calm himself. "Your little witch can't possibly be that crazy!" he accused Kasha.

"She's not," the cat assured. "But she might just be that stupid."

"Genug shoyn," the red demon conceded. "Enough already. You put your soul on the line in the contract, but we'll put in a clause that we only reap it if you're so bad in this life you're gonna go to hell anyway. And that's the best deal you're ever gonna get."

"It's the deal your great-aunt Becky got," Kasha said. "For all three generations."

"Just make sure all three generations are covered in my contract, too," Esme stipulated.

"Sheesh," Shikker complained, reaching back into the pentacle for a third contract. "I feel violated. I'll tell you something, kid, I hope you're good as gold in this life, because hell will be a much better place without you in it."

52

SOUL FOOD

Shikker couldn't leave fast enough once the contract was signed. "Come visit us again sometime," Esme told him as he shrunk down and vanished into the pentacle, sucking the flames of the candles along into the vortex. Next time, her life wouldn't be on the line. "I'll get you that Scotch you wanted!" she promised, shouting into the hatbox after him. But he was gone.

"Ya done good, kid," Kasha congratulated. "I got another century topside, and I'm about to make my quota for the next thousand years or so."

"Despite the fact that you tried to sell me out a dozen times. I'm going to keep my eye on you, and make sure my daughters and nieces know what a sleazebag you are."

"Yeah, I think we make a great team, too."

Drake was still leaning against the wall of the cellar. "Esme," he implored, his breath wheezing out through the holes of his perforated throat with every word. "Don't let the demon eat me. You'll never see me again, I promise. I'll go back to Europe. I have ten million dollars in the boot of my car. It's yours, you can have it all. Just . . . have mercy, I beg you."

Esme stood above the vampire. "Mr. Kallas, you should

appreciate the irony of this, as your business is human trafficking. I've just sold you to Kasha here, and he's going to eat you. Kind of like what you did to all those girls you bought and sold over the years."

"But . . ." he sputtered. "You can't sell me. You don't own me."

"Yeah," she said, turning her back on the vampire and kneeling by Norman, brushing his hair back from his face gently. "You didn't own those girls, either." Then to the cat she said, "I think Norman's regaining consciousness. Would you eat the vampire someplace else?"

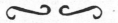

Norm started to come to, so Esme put her coat under his head for a pillow. Then she moved the wine bottle on the rack to the rear of the cellar, as Drake had instructed. She heard the levers click, and she felt the rack shift, but she didn't have the strength to move it by herself.

Norman groaned on the floor. "Did you get the license of that truck?" he asked.

"It was Drake," she explained. "I took care of him. Try not to move, you have a concussion."

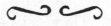

Esme went upstairs. She found Zack in the entry hall, his body broken into dozens of odd angles. "Mind if I use your phone?" she asked.

"It's in the library," he replied. "Did you get the medicine to Veronica?"

"Not yet. Drake told me about the latch, but the rack is too heavy for me to move."

"Wish I could help. Norman?"

"Alive, but barely conscious. I'm going to call Jackson to bring Wilson and Nick."

"Good thinking," Zack said. "Listen, Esme? Be careful, there's some kind of tiger or something running around. About the size of a rhinoceros. It's been dragging Drake back and forth through here for more than an hour now."

Esme knelt by Zack on the floor. "Yeah, he's with me. He's probably eating Drake by now. Listen, Zack, I'm trying to figure out whether or not to let you live."

Zack cringed, as a wave of pain washed over him. "I'm afraid I can't make much of a case for myself," he admitted, brow knit in concentration against the agony. "But luv? I know you'll do the right thing. I'm summat a monster, maybe it's fer the best, innit?"

But she'd already decided. "If I let you live, you have to promise never to mention my cat again. To anyone. Can you do that?"

Zack nodded, such as he could in his shattered state. "I'm the soul of discretion," he promised. "But when you see your whatever-it-was, tell it thanks, from me. For killing Drake."

Esme used the landline in the library to call Jackson on his cell. Then she called Dr. Stein and told him to set up the clinic for patients. He was still an hour away.

"Esme," Zack called. "There's a switch by the front door. It opens the gates to the driveway."

"Thanks, I didn't think of that." She went to the entry and pushed the button marked GATE.

"And could you shut the curtains, please?" Zack requested. "My eyes are burning."

While shutting the curtains, she saw Kasha in the driveway, crouched over a pool of black goo, chewing on something. She exited through the front door and joined him. A foot was hanging out of the demon's mouth, the last anyone would ever see of Drake Kallas.

"How was he?" Esme asked with aplomb. She'd never seen anything so revolting in her entire life, but she was going to have to toughen up in the future if she was going to keep the upper hand with a demon cat she could never trust.

Kasha crunched the last bones of the foot and swallowed. His face was covered in gore. He sat on his haunches, grooming himself. "It's an acquired taste. It's a lot of souls, but I think I can keep them all down if I purge the material remains. Listen, kid, I'm going to have to take off for a while. I know a guy, an angel who's not a complete jerk, so I'm going to pay him a visit about all these innocent souls in here. They're no use to us, might as well get them to the right place before I cash in my haul. Politics. I don't want to be the one to bring on an apocalyptic conflict between heaven and hell. You might want to turn your head for this, it won't be pretty."

Esme turned her head away as Kasha started to hack. He steeled his mighty body and heaved, and Drake Kallas's remains slid out in a wash of visceral fluids and black ichor, a jumble of body parts and splintered bones. Many parts were still recognizable, like a petrified heart, a mangled foot still in a shoe, a bifurcated skull, and a piece of forearm with a Rolex wristwatch still ticking away.

Kasha took off then, leaping through the snow and bounding toward the tree line, shedding demonic attributes as he went, until all Esme could still make of him, in the distance, was the shape of a rather large feral cat in the snow, tail flying jauntily.

Esme heard the sound of tires crunching over snow, and she

turned to watch Jackson and Nick, in Jackson's SUV, followed by Wilson in Norman's. Esme waved them down, and they pulled up next to her in a two-car caravan, by the disgusting pile of bones and steaming vampire guts on the driveway. The three surrounded her in a semicircle around the remains.

"Dude," Wilson asked, "is it . . . like . . . is that Zack?"

"No, it's the other one. Zack's inside. Norman messed him up pretty bad, but he doesn't look as bad as Drake here."

"What happened to this one?" Jackson asked.

"He hit Norman with a crowbar," Esme replied. "After that . . ." She considered, for a moment. Obviously, she couldn't tell them about Kasha. "I guess, after he hit Norman, I sort of lost my temper a little."

All three boys took a step back from Esme. And then another. "Girlfriend," Nick said, "if I ever do anything to piss you off, do me a favor and let me know."

"Come on, guys," Esme commanded, and led the three back into the house to get her sisters.

LOOSE ENDS

In April the hearts of young maidens stir with thoughts of romance, but not Esme's. She was ruled by her brain. She knew all she needed to know about love. All the madness with Zack had been so intense and now it was gone, leaving such a cynical hole in her heart. How could she love, ever again, knowing that what she felt would pale in comparison to what she'd had? And knowing that what she'd had was a lie.

Yet here she was, having dinner by candlelight alone with Norman in her room. She'd spent all day shopping and cooking. The food, at least, she was enjoying. And the company. Norm was funny and smart and sweet and loyal, and he was someone she knew she could always rely on if she ever had to fight her way into a vampire's lair and rescue her sisters again.

Ronnie had been in very bad shape when they'd carried her into the clinic, but Dr. Stein had treated her with a course of antibiotics and shots of an antibacterial and had set up an IV to rehydrate her. Katy had been fine. She kept asking about Zack, to the point where Nick had to restrain Esme from slapping her silly. Miss

Edwards had abrasions and lacerations, a broken collarbone, and anemia. Lisa Vaughn had a fever of 104 and severe bruising from bites all around the neck and wrists. Michelle was in pretty good condition but had mild amnesia. Danielle had developed light sensitivity and needed restraints until Dr. Stein could cure her of the worst ravages of the disease.

After contacting the authorities, Dr. Stein treated everyone at the clinic and then had them all admitted into quarantine at the university hospital under his care, in coordination with the epidemiologist from the Centers for Disease Control, who was instrumental in shutting off police access not only to the entire Hampstead estate but also to the victims, until they could all get their stories straight. Dr. Stein's contact at Interpol was called in, and he coordinated the investigation with the CIA. Elite Interpol agents led the inquiry into the affairs of one Drake Kallas, wanted on hundreds of counts of human trafficking and murder in Europe. The victims, according to Interpol and Dr. Stein, had been drugged and abused, though not sexually.

The way the story broke, it was determined that Drake Kallas, a known organized crime boss, human trafficker, and psychopath, had forced his son, Zack, to recruit girls for purposes of trafficking, having manipulated the boy into submission through years of psychological and physical intimidation and abuse. The story was supported by the victims, who recalled that Zack had always been kind to them, and with prompting, owned that he'd often intervened on their behalves when his father resorted to violence.

There was some grumbling in town about Zack's involvement in his father's affairs, but Zack, in a full body cast in quarantine under Dr. Stein's care, testified that his father had gone crazy and beaten him nearly to death for purchasing antibiotics for one of the victims. The testimony was corroborated by a pharmacist at Rite Aid and Esme Silver, hero of the day, and it swayed public opinion substantially.

Very high-ranking people at Interpol, coordinating with very high-ranking people at the CIA, commandeered Drake Kallas's mortal remains to whisk off to France under some kind of obscure extradition treaty. The official cause of death was "eaten by bears."

Drake Kallas's lawyer, Barry Silver, produced documentation that Zack was the sole heir. Hampstead Manor was owned free and clear, and Mr. Silver also produced banking information for sixty million dollars and change, which he'd recently, at the behest of the deceased, gone to Europe to have transferred to American banks. Interpol and the CIA were very interested in that money. Barry became executor and manager of a trust he arranged for Zack. Dr. Stein agreed to take Zack on as a foster, and as soon as was medically feasible, had his ward discharged from the university hospital and moved back to the Hampstead Manor, where he was locked in Veronica and Katy's old room, retrofitted with a steel door, because nobody was entirely confident that he was the least bit trustworthy.

Zack was entirely compliant to all restrictions placed upon him. In Drake's absence, his humanity was slowly returning. Wracked with guilt and remorse, he owned that he was deserving of any punishments that could possibly be meted out to him, and some of his own, which were practically medieval. His unique dietary requirements were met by his foster dad, Dr. Stein, who could easily obtain as much blood as his charge required.

Ronnie and Katy made full recoveries in a matter of months, with the help of weekly tea and meditation sessions in Esme's room, invoking the Goddess for clarity. The sisters were never closer. Katy's grades improved markedly. Veronica decided to give up on her modeling and ballet ambitions, switching to modern dance. "Maybe I'll be a swimsuit model," she said. By March she'd gained eight pounds. Impossibly, she was more beautiful than ever.

Veronica turned fifteen in January, and Katy turned sixteen in February, and Esme turned seventeen in March. Esme had to come up with explanations for all the insanity that had occurred. The bear alibi gained some traction among the locals. Jackson, Nick, and Wilson formed a mini cult of adoration—not to mention fear—for Esme. Well, what could she say? She was pretty awesome at that. And she found she needed Nick, for shoe shopping. Zack conveniently forgot all about Kasha, and puzzled over what might have rid the world of Drake Kallas, worst dad in history.

Esme told what she could of the story to her mother, leaving out specifics about Kasha's manipulations. Melinda, appalled by the details, blamed alternately herself and Kasha. "If I'd been a better mother, this never would have happened," she rued remorsefully. One thing Melinda couldn't deny was that Katy and Veronica had been kidnapped by vampires, and Esme and Norman and Kasha had gone in and gotten them out. She still didn't trust Kasha, but figured Esme could handle him. In penance, Melinda started returning home to Middleton on alternate weekends, which pleased Barry no end.

⌐◦ ◦⌐

Esme had found some organic peaches at the store that would do for pie, so that was what she served Norm in her room, after dinner by candlelight. She'd asked him to bring a bottle of wine from Drake's cellar, but straitlaced old Norm had refused. He was of a mind that people below the legal age should not drink the stuff, or otherwise engage in illegal activities, with the possible exception of breaking and entering vampires' lairs and killing bloodsucking predators, which the law seemed fairly ambivalent about. They chatted easily, about classes and books, and movies they'd like to see together, and the AP biology test that Esme had just set the bell curve on, beating Norman by two points.

"You really should try my tea and meditation, Norm," Esme recommended. "It's one hundred percent holistic, and it gives me such focus. I meditate for a bit before I study at night, and then before I take the test, and I have perfect recall."

"Well it worked wonders for Nick," he said. "But it probably allows some alien intelligence from outer space to take over your brain, because that's the only logical explanation for how you could possibly have beaten me on a bio test."

It was after ten o'clock, but it was a Friday. They moved over to the sofa at the side of the room, and Norman put his feet up on the steamer trunk that served as a low coffee table. Esme had found the trunk in the boot of Drake's Bentley and moved it to her room the same day she'd used the car to drive Katy and Ronnie to the clinic, after Kasha had eaten Drake.

❧ ❧

The trunk contained about two million dollars in crisp hundred-dollar bills, and another two million or so worth of large-denomination euros. There were some gold bars and unset gems, and a cache of very old gold coins that were probably valuable, but it wasn't anything like the ten million dollars Drake had claimed. There was also an extensive collection of records and Swiss bank account passbooks and property deeds and account numbers in the Caymans and a significant amount of damning information about criminal cartels run by vampires in Europe, including addresses and email accounts and names and photos.

Esme had no intention of keeping the money, or not much of it. She had an immortal soul to protect. She did enjoy driving the Bentley around, though. Nobody seemed to mind. She'd toyed with the idea of just handing the entire mess over to Interpol and washing her hands of it, but she didn't trust them with the information. Vampires were serious business, and the world needed to be rid of them. Human trafficking was an atrocity that galled her to the pit of her soul. Esme wanted time to decipher all the information she had, before acting. Interpol was well meaning, but she had a line on some folks who were better qualified to handle the vampire problem. But there were complex legal ramifications to be worked out. She'd need to consult an attorney. And first, she had to find someone who was willing to purchase some good Scotch for a retainer.

<hr />

Esme, beside Norm on the sofa, tucked her legs under. She leaned over on the couch, against Norman's chest. Norman stiffened, so she took his right arm and draped it over her shoulders. It weighed so much, she couldn't have achieved the task without Norm's cooperation. She'd spent hours going over all this. Norm was the right guy. Everybody saw it but her. In a perfect world, she'd kiss him, and then she'd know that she really had loved him all along. If it was right. If it was meant to be.

Esme rose up onto her knees on the couch, taking Norm's enormous head in both her hands. The light was dim, but his face was . . . well, she liked him, genuinely, enough that the word *repulsive* did not come to mind. But he was not attractive. And he was so *huge*. She leaned in and kissed him, on the mouth. Esme had never kissed a guy before, not in a romantic way. Their lips parted. Norman was gentle. Nothing wrong with his breath, anyway . . .

After a few minutes, Esme pulled away and sat back on the sofa beside Norman.

"That was nice, Esme," he said. "Thank you, for that."

But Esme knew. She knew the kiss had meant everything to Norman and not a whole lot to her. Zack had ruined her, with all his surging neurohormonal love chemistry and mesmerism. Whatever she felt for Norm, it would never be more than a shadow of those false feelings for Zack.

"Norman, do you trust me?" she asked.

"Of course," he said.

Esme rose, went to her desk, and opened a drawer. She removed two small brown vials. On the desk were two empty ceramic tea cups and a pot of her magic tea, now room temperature. There was also a petrified vampire heart, which she'd retrieved as a souvenir from a pile of goo in front of Hampstead Manor. She poured tea into each of the two cups, then opened the two vials. She poured the love potion into one cup, and the beauty potion into the other, then she stirred both. She handed Norm one before seating herself beside him again.

"Drink this," she insisted. "Drink it all."

Norman stared at the cup in his hand. It went against every impulse in his brain to drink something he'd just seen a professed witch pour into his tea from a little brown vial. It also went along with every feeling of regard he had for the girl he honestly loved to do exactly what she asked him, to trust her with no hesitation. "It tastes nasty," he said, placing his empty cup down on the trunk in front of him.

"I'll bet mine's worse," she countered, making a face and setting her empty cup down. She stared at Norm, not wanting to miss a thing.

According to Kasha, she was supposed to notice some changes almost immediately, though the full effects would take a week or so. It all happened very slowly. The first thing Esme observed was the improvement in Norm's color. Then his scars started subtly to fade, his skin to smooth. His one brown walleyed eye seemed more centered. His jaw seemed less severe. Esme was pretty pleased with the results already. "Damn, I'm good," she bragged. She could hardly wait to see what Norm would look like in a week. There would be no side effects like loss of IQ, she knew, since Norm was taking the potion with an innocent heart.

Katy's love potion was taking its sweet time, though. She couldn't tell if her improved attraction for Norm was from the love potion or the tea or his enhanced appearance, but she felt something. It wasn't anything at all like what she'd felt for Zack. So that was good news. Esme unbuttoned Norman's shirt a few buttons, recalling what he looked like without it. Okay, without the shirt, Norman was pretty hot. But that could wait.

She had to give Katy credit. Her feelings were subtle, but there was the ring of truth to them. She was certain, absolutely, that Norman was her guy, but nothing had changed. She was definitely more attracted to him. Though it was hard to be objective. But she was getting clear results. She could feel them, stirring. Kudos,

Katy: a love potion so good, it could even convince a girl nothing had changed.

But everything had changed. Maybe you *do* get to pick who you love after all.

"Let's give that kissing thing another try," she suggested to her boyfriend, snuggling up.

EPILOGUE

The witching hour on Midsummer's Night found Kasha creeping about the barn, doing pro bono work, ridding the world of the scourge of underground rodents. Veronica's horse was in a neighbor's field. The pasture was heavily scented with horse poop, but he picked up a whiff of something wonderful: feral feline. He tracked the scent, twisting his whiskers in the breeze, peeking out through the patches of dandelion and weeds and wildflowers. In the thin moonlight, he spied his prey: a smoky gray tabby, very young. And in heat.

Kasha stalked: She played hard to get. She fled, he pursued. Always, she was just out of reach, just out of sight. When he espied her, it was as a blur, as if in a mist. He chased her through the blackberry bramble, through the coyote brush, into the witches' herb garden, and back around to the barn. He finally cornered her behind the woodpile.

"Come out here, you little tease," he coaxed, sideling in toward the woodpile, tail erect, poised to pursue in either direction should she make a break. She poked out an ear, a whisker. Her tail curled up and around provocatively, toying with him. He liked that. The tabby darted out in a blur, but Kasha was on her, herding her. He pounced, claws extended to scoop her into his rough, sharp embrace, but the paws passed right through her. She was made of moonbeams and mist, and nothing more.

"Ha! You old fleabag," the voice of Aunt Becky rasped. "You're not my type."

The mist of the spectral feline reassembled itself in the summer air, and took the shape, vaguely, of Kasha's former mistress.

"You wrinkly old bag of farts," he said contemptuously. "I never liked tabbies anyway."

"You're nothing but a neutered old housecat," she charged.

"Talentless hedge-witch," he replied. "Satan's armpits, I've missed you, Becks. What brings you around these parts?"

"I always like to see family on the high holy days. But nobody's around."

"Ronnie and Katy are in the city with their mother for the weekend, and Esme's out with her boyfriend to a late-night movie."

"She's dating the giant now?" Becky asked. A thin breeze blew up, and she wavered in it, losing form, but it settled and she took shape again. "I always liked that boy. He smashed that vampire up pretty good, didn't he?"

"You should have seen the one I got *my* fangs into."

"Well I'm glad to hear she's with a decent type."

"You didn't know?" Kasha asked. "Esme wasn't really attracted to Norman, but she knew he was a good choice, so she drank the love potion that you helped Katy brew. Seems to be working pretty well, too. You haven't lost your touch."

At that, the specter laughed a raspy, ghostly laugh. "Ya durned fool," she chortled. "It isn't the love potion at all. It's a dud."

"You mean, a placebo? But it smelled good to me."

"We left out the blood of innocents," she said. "Do you think I'm daft enough to help my favorite grand-niece brew up a love potion and damn her immortal soul to the likes of you for a two-bit vampire?"

"Becks, you surprise me. You never showed such good judgment in life."

"Yeah, well," she cackled. "I may be dead, but I'm not stupid."

"So," the cat said. "Esme isn't under the influence of a magic potion that makes her love Norman? Their love is based on regular old common give-and-take, mutual respect, honest affection, and all the ups and downs and stupid fights and pitfalls of a normal relationship, no better than any other human ever had?"

"That's right," Becky replied. "Just a normal, plain old mundane love, with all the problems people have had to deal with since the beginning of time."

"Wow," Kasha said. "That sucks."

~~ACKNOWLEDGMENTS~~

GUSHING GRATITUDE

I'd like to thank Rachel Griffiths, without whom . . .

But no. There can be no Rachel Griffiths "without whom." Without whom, what? *Bubkes.* Nothing at all. Even now, with the whole thing done, I can't bear to consider a world without whom Rachel. Let me start again:

I'd like to thank Raymond Lesser, editor of *The Funny Times*, for publishing my stuff and opening up the door to this industry a crack wide enough for me to shove my foot into, and for giving me the best advice of all time: "Don't quit your day job." And I'd like to thank Mickey Novak—aka the Mickster, aka the New York Mickerbocker, aka Typhoid Mickey—my first agent, who opened up that same industry door and said, "What are you doing out there? Come in out of the rain and warm yourself by the fire!" And I'd like to thank Merrilee Heifetz, my forever agent, who blew that damned door off the hinges and took out a big chunk of wall in the process. And then clawed back our security deposit. I knew this metaphor would get silly eventually.

Kudos to readers of earlier drafts for their comments: Mary Lou Bloom (mother, and also thanks for the other stuff, I heard it was a long labor); Yasuko Bloom (wife, and thanks for marrying me when a lot of people didn't); Isabella Bloom (daughter and inspiration for all three sisters); and Mary Kate Flugum (also, for watching the dog while we were gone).

Thank you, Sherry Audette Morrow, for industry advice; Alisha Bloom, cousin and fellow writer, for editorial advice; my friend Kitaro, for inspiration; and a special thanks to David Lubar, a true mensch, for being so generous with your time and friendship.

Thanks to the various and sundry geniuses at Writers House: Julie Trelstad for all the Internet stuff; Alexandra Levick, Merrilee's assistant; and Albert Zuckerman, for making it all possible.

At Scholastic, thank you, Erin Black, for stepping in for editorial services above and beyond the call of duty; Nina Goffi, for the inspired book design; Jon Gray for the artwork; Kelly Ashton, for making it all run smoothly; David Levithan, the man behind the magic; Elizabeth Tiffany, the production editor; Jennifer Abbots (there's the meta: publicity for the publicist); copy editor William Franke, who does it all with a plum; Lauren Festa, the marketer; and Maya Marlette, the only one of her kind and not a mere device.

And last, but also first, did I mention Rachel Griffiths? She's awesome. Thank you, Rachel, for editing this mess. You're the only force in the galaxy powerful enough to have pushed this thing through such a wall of obstinacy. Though I hear in Andromeda they have editors who just give you a pill and you go to sleep, and when you wake up the whole manuscript is perfect. But really, what fun would that be?

ABOUT THE AUTHOR

Ira Bloom makes his literary debut with *Hearts & Other Body Parts*. Previously, Ira was a teacher of junior high English, ESL, and Japanese for the Los Angeles Unified School District. Ira and his wife currently operate a fashion and vintage kimono business, and he is something of an expert on Japanese textiles. Ira lives in Northern California with his family and an assortment of furry beasts. None have proven to be demons . . . yet.